PRAISE FOR
THE NOVELS OF KIMBERLY FISK

"[A] celebration of all the deepest things in life—family, friendship, and the healing power of love . . . An emotional roller coaster of a story."
— Susan Wiggs, #1 *New York Times* bestselling author

"*Lake Magic* is pure magic. This is a stellar debut from a writer who is destined to become a reader favorite."
— Debbie Macomber, #1 *New York Times* bestselling author

"[A] good old-fashioned romance, with family, hometown details, ball games, and beach cottages. It's a thoroughly satisfying treat."
— *RT Book Reviews*

Berkley Sensation titles by Kimberly Fisk

LAKE MAGIC
BOARDWALK SUMMER

Boardwalk Summer

KIMBERLY FISK

BERKLEY SENSATION
New York

BERKLEY SENSATION
Published by Berkley
An imprint of Penguin Random House LLC
375 Hudson Street, New York, New York 10014

Copyright © 2017 by Kimberly Fisk

ISBN: 9780425235157

Berkley Sensation mass-market edition / July 2017

Printed in the United States of America

1   3   5   7   9   10   8   6   4   2

Cover art by Anna Kmet
Cover design by Alana Colucci
Book design by Kelly Lipovich

For Rachael
Only because of you do I know the true meaning
of strength and courage

With deepest appreciation to Christina Hogrebe
who supported and championed me not only during
the bright days but especially through my darkest hours.

And to Katherine Pelz who helped me find my voice once more.

One

THE phone felt heavy in Hope Thompson's hand. She traced the buttons, unconsciously pausing at the numbers that would soon connect her to a voice she hadn't heard in nearly sixteen years.

She thought about shutting herself away in a closet. Maybe then, if she was hidden with only darkness surrounding her, this call wouldn't be so hard to make. But Hope knew darkness did not shut out memories—if anything, it enhanced them, becoming a large ebony canvas that allowed them to play over and over in her mind until sleep was impossible.

She reached for her cup of tea on the end table next to the sofa and took a sip. It was cold. She was halfway off the couch to reheat it before she stopped. Stalling. That was what she was doing. She sat back down, grabbed the phone, and dialed quickly before she lost her nerve.

"Hello?"

Hope's grip tightened. Sixteen years. It had been sixteen

years since she'd heard her mother's voice, but it felt as if it were yesterday. "Hello, Mo—Claire."

There was a long pause and then, "Charlotte, is that you?"

A pain settled in Hope's chest. Why had she believed her mother would recognize her? "No. It's me. Hope."

A faint crinkling drifted across the phone line, and Hope knew it was her mother shifting positions on the sofa's plastic protector. "Hope?"

"I know, Claire. It's been a long time."

After so many years, there should have been a thousand things they had to say to each other. A million tiny details that had filled their lives and the lives of the two grandchildren her mother had never wanted to meet. Instead, Hope didn't know where to begin—what to say. Should she start with: *Your grandchildren's names are Joshua and Susan, and they are bright and beautiful and make me so proud every day. Or: They will be sixteen in a few months, and they can't wait to get their drivers' licenses. Joshua loves football, music, and cars. He has his first steady girlfriend, and I don't know if that makes me happy or scared. And Susan. She's everything I wish I could be. She's confident and smart and funny. She was elected class president, and captain of her soccer team for the second year in a row.*

But Hope knew what she should tell her mom was the complete truth: *My whole life is about to fall apart for the second time and this time I need you. We need you. Please don't send us away again.*

She was thirty-two years old and still she hesitated, not wanting to face the rejection she knew she'd hear in her mother's voice. So instead, she heard herself asking, "How have you been?"

"Been good. Been real good except for my garden. With this terrible heat spell we've been going through, I should have mulched, that's what I should've done. Sue Ellen down at the Piggly Wiggly told me she was going to mulch but I thought for sure I wouldn't need to. I got an air conditioner last week. You got one?"

An air conditioner. After all these years, her mother wanted to know if she owned an air conditioner. "No, I don't."

"Well, don't suppose you'd have much use for one up there in the Pacific Northwest. Not with all that rain. Never could understand why anyone would choose to live in a place that rained nine months out of the year."

"I didn't choose."

Claire ignored Hope's comment, as she had with anything she found unpleasant. "Well now."

Why had she even bothered to hope that her mother had changed? That small crack in her heart—the old hurt that would never completely heal—wedged open a fraction more. "Aren't you going to ask about your grandchildren?"

There was a long pause. "My show just got over, Hope. I need to go. If I don't leave right after the third hymn, I'll be late to the committee meeting. I made my special pineapple rum cake, though I didn't add the rum because Pastor Gilbert may stop by. I don't believe he'd take kindly to us ladies consuming outside of the sacramental wine."

"Their names are Joshua and Susan."

"I have to go, Hope."

"Wait." Hope closed her eyes and took a deep breath. "Please, Mama, I need your help."

A soft whoosh of air filled the earpiece. "My help?" Another pause. "Well, Hope Marie, you're a big girl now. I don't see how I can be of any help. I thought you were doing just fine up there in Washington."

"We're not fine." Hope could feel her entire life crumbling away like a dry sand castle. "My son has leukemia and needs a bone marrow transplant. The doctors told us our best hope for a match is with a family member."

Silence filled the phone lines. "Leukemia? I always knew something like this would happen. Didn't I tell you?"

You keep that baby, Hope Marie, and something bad will happen. You just wait and see. Should have named you Hopeless because that's what you are—hopeless.

Hope wasn't seventeen anymore; this time she wasn't going to let her mother refuse to help.

"What about your other one?" her mother asked. "His sister? Being twins and all, wouldn't she do?"

Hope swallowed, praying the bitter taste in the back of her throat would go away. "Susan and I aren't a match." Did her mother really think Hope wouldn't have explored every other option before contacting her?

"Well, I just don't see how I can be of any help. I'm not much for doctors. I couldn't even go and see Pastor Gilbert's wife before she passed away, God rest her soul. All those smells and sick people. Really, Hope, you know how they affect me. Besides, don't they have radiation or something for this? When Hester Pritchett's second cousin down in Alabama got the cancer, they did something that fixed her right up. I do believe Hester said she lost all her hair but really, Hope, she didn't go asking her relatives for help. No, I don't see how I can be of any help."

Hope gripped the phone so tight she was surprised it didn't shatter. She kept her voice deadly calm, knowing it was the only way to deal with Claire Montgomery. "Joshua has had chemotherapy, Mother. It didn't work."

"Maybe you aren't taking that boy to the right doctors."

"My son's name is Joshua and I have taken him to the very best doctors."

"There's no need for that tone with me. All I was saying, maybe you should take him to one of those specialists."

"We've seen the specialists. And they agree that what my son needs is a bone marrow transplant."

Her mother could ignore Hope all she wanted. She could continue to pretend to her church friends that her only child hadn't gotten pregnant at seventeen but instead had graduated early and received a full scholarship to some college far, far away. She could go on living that lie, but if she thought for one moment Hope would let her refuse to help her grandson, she was mistaken.

"I still don't know why you're calling me when you should be calling that man."

"What man, Mom?"

An impatient grunt came across the line. "Their father, that's who. Call him."

Their father.

For just a moment Hope's heart ached. "I need *all* of Joshua's relatives to be tested. The initial test to see if you are a match is simple. All you have to do is go to your doctor and explain what you need done. I can call him, or I can have Joshua's doctor call and explain if that would be easier."

"This is not a problem that concerns Dr. Brown."

Hope sighed tiredly. "I thought you might feel that way. Joshua's doctor gave me the name and number of a colleague in St. Paul. Call him, please, and set up an appointment as soon as you can. I will arrange for a taxi to take you." Hope gave her mother the doctor's name and telephone number.

"How much will this cost?"

"Don't worry about the money. If your insurance doesn't cover it or even if you don't want to submit the claim, I'll pay for it. It won't cost you a cent to see if you can save your grandson."

Hope had no idea where she'd come up with the money, but she'd find it somehow.

"You know I live on a fixed income. My question isn't a bit out of line."

"I know, Mama. I know."

A heartbeat of silence filled the air. And then another. Enough time to say *I've missed you* or *I love you.*

When it became apparent her mother wasn't going to say anything else, Hope said, "Call the doctor—"

The other end of the phone disconnected before Hope could finish.

Wearily, she hung up and leaned back on the sofa. A familiar, queasy feeling settled in the pit of her stomach and she grabbed the afghan from the back of the couch and wrapped it around her as silence descended once again.

She hated this new reality. A too-quiet house that used to be a home full of teenagers—full of laughter and music and noise. Where the fridge and cupboards were frequently raided and either Susan or Joshua or one of their many friends were asking if she was making her famous enchiladas for dinner again tonight and were there more of those homemade ice cream sandwiches in the freezer?

Now, the house was silent and filled with a coldness that had nothing to do with the temperature and where too many days were filled with nothing but Hope's own thoughts.

Call their father.

Hope pulled the afghan tighter and stared at the phone in her lap. Even before she'd called Claire, she'd known she had one more phone call to make, but she also knew this call would be even harder than the first.

For her children, she could do anything. She reached for the well-worn magazine and pulled it into her lap. As if by habit, the slick pages slid open to the exact spot she'd been seeking.

A flashy racecar filled the center pages, its black body covered in bright decals. She skimmed the text, not having to read a word, already knowing everything it said. Her eyes continued down the page, across the lengthy column of awards the driver had won and the records he'd broken. It wasn't until she hit upon a picture of the driver that she stopped.

Nick Fortune.

Sometimes she could go weeks . . . months . . . without thinking of him, but then she'd see him on TV or on the cover of a magazine and her heart would remember what her mind refused to let her forget.

Before she could stop herself, her gaze drifted to the side

table where a tabloid magazine's headline read: *Fortune's Trophies*. In the center of the cover was a picture of Nick. Surrounding him were no less than ten beautiful, highly recognizable women. A somewhat smaller caption underneath summarized: *Fortune Conquers All*.

The magazine and its article were nothing new. Hope had seen such stories about Nick for years. A month or two couldn't go by before another story about him was plastered all over the Internet or the front pages of the tabloids by the checkout stand. She remembered the first article she'd ever seen about him. It had been just after the twins' fourth birthday. *NASCAR's' New Bad Boy*. Hope hadn't had to read very far to get the gist. Nick Fortune was playing fast and loose. And not just on the track.

Her gaze refocused on the article in her lap. In the side margin, written in black ink, was the number she'd researched and found online. She drew in a deep breath and quickly dialed.

After what seemed like an eternity, a woman's soft, elegant voice answered. "Fortune Enterprises."

Hope was surprised to hear an actual person on the other end. "Hello. I'm trying to reach Nick Fortune."

"I'm sorry, Mr. Fortune is unavailable. Would you care to leave a message?"

Before becoming a teacher, Hope had worked as a secretary to put herself through school. She could spot an automatic "the boss is unavailable" reply in an instant. "I understand you probably receive at least a dozen calls a day from people trying to speak directly with Nick."

The receptionist laughed softly. "Try fifty."

Hope shouldn't have been surprised, but she was. "I'm an old . . . friend." She stumbled, wondered what word would accurately describe their past. "It's urgent I speak to him. Could you put me on hold and check to see if he'll take my call?"

"I am sorry." The receptionist sounded sincere. "But

Mr. Fortune is out of the office until next week. If you want to leave a message, I'll make sure he gets it."

Hope sighed. "Could you please tell him that Hope Thompson—" She stopped, realizing he wouldn't recognize her by that last name. "Could you please tell him Hope Montgomery called and it's urgent I speak to him?" She gave the receptionist her home and cell number.

"I'll make sure Mr. Fortune gets your message when he returns."

"Thank you. And please. I can't stress enough how important it is that he return my call."

Long after she'd hung up the phone, Hope couldn't help wondering. What made her think this time would be any different? What made her think that now, after sixteen years, Nick would return her call, when he never had all those years ago?

ROCKINGHAM wasn't his favorite racetrack, but it was a hell of a thrill.

Nick Fortune's gloved hands tightened on the steering wheel as a fresh surge of adrenaline rushed through his body. His arms burned as he pulled the car down into the corner, laid his foot heavy on the gas, and kept her low on the bank of the turn. He didn't have to look behind him to know that over a dozen cars stuck to his spoiler, fighting him for the lead.

Right. Left. Right. Left. The steering wheel seesawed. He kept the accelerator floored and eased up only at the last minute—when nothing but pure instinct told him to. He hugged the corner low . . . lower . . . lower still until—*BAM!* He jumped back on the gas and flew down the straightaway.

"Five laps," his crew chief, Dale Penshaw, said over the headset.

Nick nodded automatically. He headed hard into turn two. Gravity and a set of tires that were wearing thin pulled him to the outside. He fought to keep the car close to the inside line.

Out of the corner of his eye, he caught a flash of blue and orange. Number twenty-four, Rick Jarrett, broke away from the pack and tucked in behind.

Nick smiled. The young kid was good—but not good enough. Nick eased down on the accelerator and started to pull away. Jarrett followed him.

They rounded turn four. Nick went high, then wove back down on the track to ward off Jarrett.

A hot wind whipped through the mesh-covered side windows. Grit coated his mouth. Sweat drenched the inside of his helmet and his throat was as dry as chalk.

"Four laps." Penshaw came across the headset again.

Nick squinted through his dirty visor into the bright rays of the sun. He came off the turn and looked down the backstretch. He knew the fans would be on their feet, their deafening cheers blending with the roar of eight-hundred-horsepower engines.

He kept one eye on the track and one eye on the mirror. The cars blared over the heat-warmed ribbon of gray.

Jarrett began to weave behind Nick. Nick grinned. The kid was looking for his spot. Nick knew he was going to try to use the draft to slingshot past.

They roared by the white flag. One lap left.

With movements so perfectly executed they seemed rehearsed, Nick and Jarrett sped around an oval of pavement. They headed into turn three. Gravity pulled Nick up. He fought to keep the car low and prayed like hell the tires would stick. When Jarrett made his move, he'd have to do it on the outside. The lower line was a fraction faster. There was no way Nick was going to hand over that advantage.

They headed down the final stretch. Jarrett faked to the right. Nick wondered if the young hotshot really thought he'd fall for that old trick. For just a second, he let Jarrett believe he'd fooled him. At the last second, he swerved back down to the inside line and hung on for all she was worth.

Ahead, the checkered flag snapped back and forth.

"Nick. Nick," Penshaw yelled into the headset. "Twenty-four! Twenty-four is making his move!"

Seconds. It all came down to seconds.

The home stretch was upon them. He shifted out of the turn, kept her low, and hit the gas. The car shot out.

"You got 'em," Penshaw yelled. "YOU GOT 'EM!" As Nick took the checkered flag.

Life didn't get any better than this.

Shouts of excitement from Penshaw and the rest of his pit crew filled his headset.

A few minutes later, he spun into the winner's circle, his tires smoking. A crowd surged forward, hands reaching through the window and clapping him on the back. A black baseball cap with his sponsor's logo landed in his lap. He took off his hot helmet and put it on.

He eased himself out of the car window to shouts of congratulations and a roar of approval from the stands. The minute his feet hit the ground, it rained champagne.

A loud, distinctively southern whoop of satisfaction rang out. Dale Penshaw fought his way to the front of the crowd, carrying another bottle of champagne. "You did it!" he yelled above the crowd.

Nick grinned as he grabbed his crew chief and slapped him on the back. "*You* all did it. The car ran like a champ."

"Thought Jarrett might get the better of you on that last lap."

"Not even close."

They laughed as the crowd kept pushing in.

"Number eight, here we come."

"Don't jinx us," Nick said good-naturedly, wiping champagne from his eyes.

"Jinx? Boy, haven't you heard—you've got the Midas touch. Nothing's gonna stop you. In just a few months, you're gonna make racin' history. The only man to win eight NASCAR championships. You'll be a legend. The best of the best."

As Nick made his way up the stairs to the winner's stand, his crew chief's words echoed in his mind.

The best of the best.

A legend.

As he stood there, surrounded by his friends and fans, he waited for that old feeling of exuberance to overtake him.

But it never came. Not even when they placed the trophy in his hands and the cheers from the crowd grew even more deafening. But it would. Nick was sure of that. Once he clinched the eighth championship he knew that feeling would never leave him again.

NICK looked up from the report he'd been reading to see his secretary, Evelyn Summerfelt, at his office door. Her short gray hair and conservative business suit were in stark contrast to the bright interior of Fortune Enterprises.

"Congratulations," she said. "Great race yesterday."

"Thanks."

Evelyn took off her coat and draped it over her arm. "I didn't think I'd see you in here today. Monday's supposed to be a day off for you drivers."

Nick grinned and tossed his pen onto the desk. "When have I ever done what I was supposed to?"

"Never." Her smile faded and was replaced with a look of genuine concern. "You really should take some time off. You can't keep up this pace."

"I'll have plenty of spare time in December."

She gave a soft huff of disbelief. "I've worked for you for eight years and not once have I seen you slow down during the off-season."

"You slack off, you lose." He leaned forward and grabbed a file from the edge of his desk, ending a discussion he didn't want to have. Racing was his life, his whole life. Take time off for what?

"I'm expecting a fax on the new restrictor plate requirements," Nick said after a moment's pause. "Let me know when it comes in, okay?"

"Restrictor plates? Is that Greek?"

Nick smiled. "After all these years of working for me, you've had to have learned something about cars by now."

"I've learned two things. If they don't start when I turn the key, it's time to trade them in, and you like your coffee black. It'll take me just a minute to brew some."

She was halfway out of the room when Nick's voice stopped her. "I already made a pot."

"You know, one of these days you're going to have to stop being so self-reliant and let me do what you pay me for."

"You do plenty," Nick said, and he meant it. "Besides, if I didn't have you, who'd answer that damn phone that never stops ringing?"

As if on cue, the phone rang. Evelyn laughed as she went to answer it. A few moments later she was back. "That was Dale. When he couldn't reach you at home, he knew you'd be here. He told me to tell you that since you're working today, he'll be here as soon as he can."

"Call him back and tell him to take the day off. God knows he works too hard and doesn't see his family enough."

Evelyn gave him a look that didn't take a mind reader to interpret.

"Just call him," Nick said.

"Fine. By the way, here are your messages." She handed him a thick pink stack.

Nick took the stack from her and quickly thumbed through them. "These are all mine? You'd think I'd been gone a year, not a couple of days."

Evelyn turned to leave, then stopped. "Oh, the message on top is from some woman. She called Friday afternoon and said it was urgent you call her back."

Nick tossed the pile into the corner of his desk. Both he and Evelyn knew what *urgent* meant. *Urgent* was some reporter wanting some interview for their next publication or broadcast. There had been hundreds of urgent messages before this one and there would be many more to follow. Ignoring the slips, Nick picked up the report he'd been studying and got back to work.

A half hour later, Evelyn returned. "Here's the fax you wanted." She set in on his desk.

"Thanks." Nick didn't bother to look up.

It wasn't until later, when he went to reach for the fax, that he noticed the phone message and the name on top.

Hope Montgomery.

His hand paused midreach.

He read the name again.

Disbelief flooded him. How many years had it been? Fourteen? Fifteen?

No. Sixteen.

It had been sixteen years since he'd last seen her.

He raked a hand through his hair and leaned back in his chair, propping his feet on the windowsill. *Hope.* The last time he'd seen her, she'd been standing at the bus depot waving good-bye to him as the bus pulled away from the curb. Her face had been swollen and wet with tears.

Once, she'd meant everything to him. He had thought she'd be the one person who'd never lose faith in him. But she had. Just like everyone else, she thought he'd never be more than the son of Jack Fortune, the town drunk. Now, with the distance of time and wisdom of years, he understood what he hadn't then. She'd been so young. And her mother strong enough to convince Hope she'd end up living in some dirtwater town, married to a bitter drunk with only dreams in his pocket—as Nick's father had been.

He looked at the note again. At the word *urgent.* For just a second he toyed with the idea of not returning her call. What was the point in revisiting a past that would never be more than that?

But even as his mind told him one thing, his hand grabbed the cell off the desk and punched in the first number. As he waited for the call to go through, he thought about hitting End, but before the thought could fully formulate, the phone rang.

And rang. And rang. And rang.

At the fifth ring, voice mail clicked on and a woman's voice came on the line.

Hi. You've got the machine, you know what to do.

Hope's voice? It sounded like her but then it didn't. It sounded younger, lighter, than he remembered. But then what did he know? Too many years had passed for him to remember clearly. Hadn't they?

Beeeeep.

He hit End without leaving a message, tossed the note aside, and got back to work. But no matter how hard he concentrated, his eyes and mind kept straying to his phone.

Shortly before noon, Evelyn walked in. "In case you're gone when I get back from lunch, here's your week's itinerary. There's a separate sheet detailing your endorsement shoot tomorrow." She put the folder on his desk. "Do you need anything before I head out?"

Nick ran a hand through his hair. "Yeah, there is something. This message." He held it up. "The one from the woman who called saying it was urgent. Did she happen to say anything else?"

"No. Only that she was an old friend of yours and it was urgent you contact her. Why? Problems?"

"No."

He stared down at the note in his hand.

HOPE sat back on the heels of her tennis shoes and pushed the damp hair off her forehead. The grit and dirt from her garden gloves felt rough against her skin. Once her garden had been her sanctuary, her place of solace, but not any longer.

Now there was no solace to be found. Not when her son was sick. Not when she constantly felt torn, needing to be in several places at once. At work, at home with Susan, and especially at the hospital with Joshua. But this morning, with a bright July sun gilding the yard in a golden glow, Joshua had asked Hope to *chill* and not rush into the hospital first thing, as was her norm. A group of his friends were going to visit and he wanted *space*. And with Susan having spent the night at her best friend's and not due back until later this afternoon, when she and Hope would head to the hospital together, Hope found herself in the unusual position of having time on her hands.

All morning she'd been on edge. She'd stared at her phone until her eyes had blurred, willing it to ring. Just as she'd been willing it to ring all weekend. When it had, the caller had not been one of the two people she was desperate to hear from. She'd tried cleaning to keep busy, but her house was already spotless from too many restless hours. Plus, the silence was unbearable. Even cranking up music hadn't helped. So she'd escaped to the garden. But as with everything she'd tried, it was an effort in futility.

Last night she'd lain awake, remembering a past she'd tried so hard to forget. Now, all these hours later, she still couldn't outrun the memories.

She stared at the rose bushes in front of her. A slight breeze brushed against their petals, which had begun to turn brown and curl from lack of water.

The last time she'd been home the roses had been in full bloom and she was seventeen, scared, and standing in her mother's yard.

You can't stay here, Hope Marie . . . what would people say . . . you have to go . . . you have to go. . . .

Hope felt an ache in her heart and wondered how after all these years her mother's rejection could still hurt. But that pain paled in comparison to the heartache caused by Nick's abandonment.

Hope shivered, suddenly cold. It was almost as if she were seventeen again and in her mother's living room, racing for the phone every time it rang, praying it would be Nick.

In three months, Hopeful, I'll be back. I promise. Three months to the date. Wait for me at the courthouse. I'll be the guy wearing the smile and holding the rings.

For a year after Joshua and Susan's birth, Hope hadn't been able to think about Nick without falling apart. But as the years passed, she understood it was easier to walk away from a small-town girl when you were someone like Nick—a man with big ambitions.

Men left. Her mother had told her that for years, only Hope hadn't wanted to believe it. But when Nick never returned her calls, she had to face two truths: Her mother had been right, and she was pregnant and on her own.

She'd learned from her parents you couldn't force someone to love you. She'd seen it in her own life and in Nick's. Their parents had let them down. She refused to make the same mistake her mother had made by coercing a man who didn't want her into marrying her.

So when her mother threw her out, Hope had boarded a bus and left Minnesota for Tranquility, Washington, a tiny speck on the map located in the Pacific Northwest and the home of an aunt she'd never met. Her scared seventeen-year-old mind had created one horrid scenario after another. She'd been convinced her mother's half sister would never welcome a pregnant teenager, especially one she didn't know.

But that was exactly what Margaret Watkins had done. She'd opened not only her arms but her home and her heart as well.

Not for the first time, Hope wished her aunt were still alive. Even when she was young and pregnant, she hadn't needed Aunt Peg as much as she needed her now.

A soft wind blew through the yard. Hope closed her eyes and took a deep breath. Fresh-cut grass and the scent of summer flowers filled her senses. She had learned to accept her mother's and Nick's betrayal, but she wasn't going to let them ignore Joshua. If she couldn't reach them by phone, she'd find the money somewhere and fly to see them. Locating her mother would be a piece of cake. Locating Nick would be easy; getting in to see him might be another story.

With renewed determination she reached for her shovel, but the sound of tires crunching on her gravel driveway drew her attention. She shielded her eyes, glancing toward the front of the house. The long hedge blocked her view. It was probably her best friend, Dana, who spent as much time at Hope's house as she did at her own.

Hope gathered her gardening supplies. A visit and a glass of iced tea sounded pretty close to heaven about now.

A shadow fell over her, bringing with it a cool relief from the sun and the faint smell of leather.

"Hello, Hopeful."

Two

HOPEFUL.

The familiar nickname wrapped itself around her like a long-forgotten caress. Briefly, she closed her eyes and took a deep breath. Then another. It couldn't be.

Very slowly, she tugged off her worn gardening gloves and stood. "Nick." His name came out on a whisper. She wasn't sure if she'd heard it or if it had just floated through her mind like it had so many other times.

He took a step forward, then stopped; the soft worn leather of his bomber jacket slid open, revealing a white T-shirt beneath. He removed the dark sunglasses that hid his eyes. Blue—deep, startling blue—just like she remembered. And yet . . . different.

Gone was the young boy who had held her hand under a canopy of stars and vowed, "I'm going to make it, Hopeful. One day I'm going to make it so big everyone will know my name." In front of her today stood the man she'd always known he'd become.

Nick ran his hand through his thick black hair. The gesture was as familiar to her as her own reflection.

"Oh God, it is you . . . it's really you," she said before she could stop herself.

Her Nick. The boy who had made her teenage years bearable; who'd taught her how to fish and drive; how to swim and then skinny-dip. Who had dried her tears time after time when living with Claire had become too hard.

He closed the small gap that still separated them and pulled her into his arms, and she was as powerless to stop herself now as she had been at sixteen.

It was as if the years of separation had never been. The anger she should have felt failed to materialize, and it was the most natural thing in the world to rest her cheek against his soft shirt. Her eyes drifted shut, and she felt herself melt into him. For weeks, months . . . *years*, she'd waited for this moment.

The rhythmic beating of his heart became the only sound she heard. For just a moment, she let herself ignore reality—ignore the fact that Nick was a man who had left her pregnant and alone.

Hope stiffened and backed out of his arms.

He wasn't her Nick any longer, and she didn't want him to be. There was only one thing she wanted from him now.

She wrapped her arms around her stomach, angry for falling back into his arms the moment she saw him again.

"How did you find me?" The question came out sharper than she'd intended.

Nick shoved his hand in the front pocket of his Levi's and sent her a quizzical glance. "Addresses aren't hard to come by with a landline."

"I'm surprised you didn't just call."

He studied her for a moment, his broad shoulders blocking the sun's rays. "Your message said *urgent*." He gave a slight shrug. "It's been a while."

Four words that encompassed so much. Images of Susan and Joshua flashed into Hope's mind, and she knew what she had to say. But standing out in her front yard, where anyone could walk by, wasn't exactly an ideal spot for this conversation. She dropped her hands to her sides. "Yes, it has been a while. And I'm glad you decided to . . . stop by." *Stop by* sounded so casual, like he was in the neighborhood. Like they were friends. People who had stayed in touch for all these years.

"There is something important I need to talk to you about, but why don't we go around back and sit on the porch," she suggested. "I could use a glass of iced tea. How about you?"

Nick continued to study her, and she felt herself grow even more self-conscious under his intent stare.

"Sure," he finally said.

Hope led him to an outdoor patio table and motioned for him to have a seat. "I'll be just a minute." She ducked into the kitchen, shut the French doors behind her, and took her first deep breath since he had arrived. Her mind whirled with a thousand different thoughts. But it all boiled down to one thing. Nick was *here*.

She set her gloves and garden tote on the counter and headed to the refrigerator, only to stop short when she caught a glimpse of herself in the mirror Susan had hung by the back door—a last-minute checkpoint before she headed out. Hope grimaced at her reflection.

The shirt that had once been blue was now a faded pale gray, dotted with yellow paint from when she and the twins had repainted the house two years ago. And her shorts were no better off. Stray blond curls had escaped her now-lopsided ponytail. With a shake of her head she walked over to the kitchen sink and turned on the water to wash her hands. How she looked was of no importance. Only one thing mattered today.

She squirted soap in her hands, lathered, and was just about to rinse when she looked out her window and caught sight of Nick.

He'd wandered over to the edge of her property, looking around as if drinking in every detail of her house. Her yard. She wondered what he was thinking. Was he noticing the vegetable garden that was never finished because during the tilling, Joshua had taken sick and everything else had failed to matter? Or did he see the small flower bed the kids had planted for her one Mother's Day where the blooms spelled out *MOM*?

While she stood there watching him, he turned and walked a little farther down the back, running his hand over the tops of the white pickets that defined her yard.

She'd thought when she spoke with him for the first time after all these years it would be over the phone, where she'd have distance to insulate her.

Quickly she rinsed her hands and shut off the water, anxious to move away from the window. Away from visions of Nick. Drawing in several deep breaths, she told herself she could do this. She could do anything where her children were concerned. But even with that truth fresh in her mind, her hands still shook as she poured iced tea into the tall tumblers.

Nick turned at the sound of her approach. When his gaze connected with hers, glass clinked against glass. He smiled as if to ease her discomfort but, if anything, it only made her more nervous.

He walked toward her and accepted the drink she handed him. "I wasn't sure I'd catch you at home," he said.

She took a seat and waited for Nick to take one across from her. Her mouth felt so dry. She lifted her glass to take a sip, then set it down on the table and shoved her hands in her lap. She couldn't stop their shaking. "I'm one of those lucky few who get the summer off. I work at the local high school." For a reason she didn't want to examine too closely, Hope chose not to mention her night job at the local family-owned grocery store. A job she had taken to help cover the overwhelming number of medical bills insurance didn't pay.

"So you did it. You became a teacher."

Hope thought she detected a note of pride in his voice but that couldn't be. Why would Nick care about her achieving her dreams?

It had taken Hope an extra year and a half to obtain her teaching degree. College had been a challenge with two little babies. There had never been enough time or money, but all the sacrifices had been worth it. "I teach ninth-grade English. The kids are great."

"Sounds like you enjoy it."

"I do." She tried to smile, but her cheeks felt frozen. A small gust of wind whipped around her. Loose hairs escaped her ponytail, blew in her face. She tucked them behind her ear as she gathered her thoughts. "Except for hearing myself referred to as Ms. Thompson all day. It makes me feel a hundred years old."

Nick rocked the bottom of his glass back and forth. After several silent moments, he said, "Yeah, I noticed the name on the mailbox. So, you're married."

His assumption surprised her, though it shouldn't have. It was a reasonable deduction. It was just that she had never come close to getting married. "No. Thompson was my mother's maiden name."

She wasn't going to offer any further explanation; her past, her last name, was so unimportant in the scheme of things. But Nick remained silent, looking at her expectantly, and she found herself saying, "Growing up I went by my father's last name even though Thompson is my legal name. My mother gave birth to me before she and my father were married. So the name on my birth certificate is Thompson, my mother's maiden name. But my mother didn't want anyone to know I was born before they were married, so I used Montgomery."

Nick leaned back in his chair. "Good old Claire." He gave her a wry smile that hinted at a shared past. "You never told me."

"I didn't tell anybody. When I moved to Washington, using my legal last name, Thompson, seemed appropriate." It had been a new start, a new life. And a new name fit the bill.

Nick didn't say anything for a moment. "I thought we knew everything about each other back then."

Back then . . .

"Not everything," she said quietly.

Images from her teenage years flashed through her mind. Her mother staring out the living room curtain whenever Nick would bring her home. The outside porch light flicking on as a signal for Hope to hurry in. And the time her mother had gone to the high school dance to check up on her and discovered she and Nick had left early. They'd gone down to the lake, where passion had overruled sense and the dress Hope had saved for all summer had become a mass of unheeded wrinkles on the pickup's bench seat.

But talking about Claire Montgomery and remembering a past better left forgotten was the last thing Hope wanted to do. She needed to tell him about the twins—about Joshua's illness.

"So, you've never been married?" Nick asked.

"No. Look, Nick"—she leaned forward, folding her hands on top of the table—"there's something I need to tell you."

The words were no sooner out of her mouth than the heavens opened up. Ignoring their glasses, they sprinted for the shelter of her house and spilled inside.

"Whew." Nick whisked the rain off his shoulders and closed the French doors behind them. "Does it do that often?"

Hope wiped the rain from her face. "Only about nine months out of the year."

"And people actually want to live here?"

She walked around the edge of the kitchen island and grabbed two clean, dry hand towels out of a drawer. "More every year. Here." She turned to hand him one of the towels and found he was right behind her.

Her kitchen was so small and he was so close. She could smell the fresh, outdoorsy scent of his aftershave, his breath tinged with spearmint, and see the droplets of rain that dotted his black hair. Moisture clung to his forehead and the angular planes of his cheeks. The towel hung forgotten in her hand as his gaze caught and held hers. A catch formed in her heart and she found it hard to breathe.

She had always heard the expression about time standing still, but now, it was as if time were moving backward.

The music she'd turned on earlier murmured in the background. Rain splattered outside and hit the roof. The rhythmic *pitter-patter* of the drops blended with the country song. Hope felt suspended by its melody, captivated by the nearness of the only man who had ever held her heart. The intensity in his blue eyes sent a spiral of . . . she didn't want to say it, didn't want to admit that it was desire. Warmth flooded her cheeks and she dropped her head forward to hide her embarrassment.

She watched his chest rise and fall, the way his upper body seemed to expand and then slowly release. Suddenly she felt a subtle shift in his position. A stiffening of his shoulders, a barely perceptible shortening of his breath.

Hope eased back and when she looked up at him, it was to discover that his eyes were fixated on a photo on the refrigerator.

She didn't need to look at the picture to know what one it was. It had been taken two summers back, when they had spent a week at Lake Chelan with Dana. After days of relentless badgering, Josh and Susan had managed to get her on a Jet-Ski. She'd been scared to death. With Josh and Susan standing on either side of her in the shallow water supporting her, Dana had yelled "smile" and snapped the picture.

It was a photograph of a time when they were still untouched by the horrors of cancer. When sitting on a Jet-Ski had been Hope's greatest fear.

"You've changed," Nick said. "You never would have gotten on one of those back in Minnesota."

"I have changed. More than you realize." Hope looked at the picture, at her two beautiful children, then back to Nick. "Those are my children, Joshua and Susan. They're twins. And you're their father."

Three

YOU'RE *their father.*

The words ricocheted through Nick's mind and pounded through his body. He stared at the picture, stared at the two children smiling back at him. He reached forward and pulled the photo off the refrigerator. Unconsciously his thumb moved over their faces. He drank in their features: the girl with her long blond hair and bright green eyes. A replica of her mother. And the boy, so much like Hope too with his wide smile and high cheekbones. But his bright blue eyes and black hair were all Nick.

He turned to Hope, his fury building. "How could you?"

"How could I what?"

"How could you hide this from me?"

Hope took a barely perceptible step backward and wrapped her arms around her stomach. "I didn't hide anything."

"Don't play games with me, Hope. You may be a lot of things—"

dishonest
devious

traitorous

"—but stupid isn't one of them. Why didn't you tell me about them? About Joshua and Susan?" Their names felt foreign on his tongue and that made him all the angrier.

"I tried to tell you."

"Don't lie to me. You should have told me."

"You should have called me back." Hope was all but shouting. "What was I supposed to do? Leave a message that said, 'Tell Nick I'm pregnant'?" She laughed bitterly. "That's not the type of message I'd leave with a stranger."

"Don't blame this on me." Fury consumed him and he didn't know if he'd be able to speak. She'd deceived him. Lied to him. Kept his children from him. But not any longer.

"I want to see them." *Meet them* would have been more accurate. Christ. *Meet* his teenage son and daughter.

"Look." Hope took a step forward and set her towel on the counter. "Why don't we go and sit in the living room. There's something I need to tell you."

"Do they know about me?"

She had the grace to flinch. "No."

If possible, he grew even angrier. She'd lied to all of them. "I want to see them," he said again.

"No."

"What do you mean *no*?"

"Th-they're not home." Hope unfolded her arms and took a deep breath, as if she were gathering strength for a battle ahead. "Nick, please, shouting will get us nowhere. We need to talk. There are things you don't know."

"All I need to know is when Joshua and Susan will be home." He knew he should calm down, get a handle on his emotions, but he couldn't do it.

"Susan will be home later, but—"

Nick couldn't stay here a moment longer. He had to get away. He had to think.

"I'll stay in town." He made the decision instantly, wondering even as he turned to leave if this small town had a motel.

"I will see them tomorrow." He stormed out of the kitchen. Out of the house.

She ran after him. "Nick, wait. Please. Listen to me. There's something I have to tell you."

He was done with listening to her. "I will see my children tomorrow."

His tires screeched as he left her driveway.

LATER that afternoon, Hope sat by Joshua's hospital bed and watched the uneven rise and fall of his chest. Ever since she'd arrived a little over an hour ago, he'd been sleeping, and from the update she'd gotten from his nurse, he'd been mostly resting since his friends had left. But even in sleep, it was easy for her to see that Josh wasn't at peace. How could he be? How could any of them ever be until he was once again healthy?

Careful not to wake him, she gently stroked his left hand, the one free of the IV. Her heart clutched and she bit her lower lip, afraid her sorrow would escape. She had to stay strong, strong for all of them.

It hadn't surprised Hope when Susan had once again begged off from coming to the hospital, pleading to spend one more night at her friend Chelsey's. Hope understood. The reality this sterile environment forced upon you could not be ignored—especially for a fifteen-year-old.

Not for the first time Hope worried about her daughter. Cancer was a greedy beast that wasn't satisfied until it had infected the whole family. Even then, it wanted more.

Hope worked hard to be there for both of her children but knew that even with her best efforts, she didn't always succeed. She worried constantly about their visible pains and heartaches, but she also spent countless hours worrying about the struggles they tried to hide. Joshua's illness had robbed him of so much, but it had stolen from Susan, too. All Hope could do was continue to be there for her children, trying to be the best mom she could.

I will see my children tomorrow.

Even now, hours later, Nick's parting words—spoken like a threat—heralded through her mind. It was ironic. His words wouldn't leave her, but she knew he would. Just like he'd done before. But this was one battle she could fight for her children. One pain she could spare them from.

She tried not to remember the heartache from those long-ago years. How she'd measured time from one phone call until the next. How, in the beginning, Nick had called as often as promised and the minute they heard each other's voice, they'd resumed their conversation as if it had never ended.

Life had been perfect. Exactly as they'd planned. They had talked for hours, about anything and everything but mostly about his plan to make it big in NASCAR. But as the days turned into weeks and then into a month and then into another, the calls had dwindled. Her calls to his cell went unanswered and unreturned. The few times they did connect, there was a stiltedness to their conversations that had never been present before. It was almost as if he didn't want to talk to her anymore. As if he'd lost interest in her, in the plans they'd made.

And why wouldn't he? She was nothing but a small-town girl with nothing to offer a man with dreams as big as the sky. So her life became a game of waiting and worrying. Waiting for the phone to ring. Worrying it never would. Waiting to hear his voice. Worrying he was never coming back for her.

Waiting for her period to start . . .

Then reality set in. She was pregnant.

The first thing she did after she found out was to call Nick's cell only to discover it was no longer in service. Desperate to get in touch with him, she called the only other number she had for him and left a frantic message with a stranger for Nick to call her as soon as possible.

But his call never came.

Not even when she left a second and a third message.

When she realized he was never going to call and he'd undoubtedly turned off his phone to sever all ties with her, she still couldn't let him go. She still couldn't stop loving him, waiting for him. She'd packed her bag, ready to flee and find him. Only she didn't know where he was. And if by some miracle she had found him, what then? Tell him about the baby and force him to stay with her? She'd seen how that had played out in her own parents' marriage; she wasn't about to force a child of hers to endure that pain.

But she was a pregnant seventeen-year-old still in high school. What was she to do?

Her mother hadn't been as indecisive. The minute she learned of the pregnancy, Claire gave her daughter two options—get rid of it or get out.

Not for one second had Hope entertained the thought of not having their baby. So she left and fled to her only other relative, her Aunt Peg.

As Hope's tummy blossomed and she felt her baby (then babies when she learned she was having twins) move inside her, her jumbled feelings for Nick faded and a new emotion took hold. One more powerful and protective than any she'd ever before felt. She was no longer the young girl madly in love; she was Susan and Joshua's mother. She would do anything for her children. Even if that meant protecting them from a father whose abandonment would crush them just as it had crushed her.

But now Nick was back in her life, insisting on seeing her children. She wasn't exactly sure how she would continue to protect them, but she would. She would find a way just like she had since they'd been born.

Joshua let out a soft snore and rolled onto his side, pulling his covers down as he turned. She leaned forward and re-adjusted them.

A gust of wind rattled the hospital window and splattered rain against the glass. Through the darkness small rectangles of light from the windows of neighboring high-rises punctured the Seattle skyline. It was nearing five o'clock. Hundreds of people would soon be getting off work in those buildings, hurrying home for the evening, rushing to get dinner on the table, to throw a load of clothes in the wash, to spend time with their healthy children.

How she envied the normalcy of their days. Where schedules didn't revolve around hospital stays or medical procedures but around school projects and sport activities. How she wanted that for her own child.

She turned back to her son. Even in sleep he looked drawn and pale. Half-moon bruises smudged the undersides of his eyes. She brushed the hair off his forehead and felt an almost unbearable agony when strands fell out and tangled in her fingers. A sob caught in the back of her throat. This should not be happening to her son. To anyone's child.

She felt the start of tears and willed them away. She turned to gather her strength and saw Dana coming down the hall. When Dana caught Hope's gaze, a gentle smile graced her lips and she gave a wave. For the first time that day, Hope felt her spirits lift. What would she do without her best friend?

They had met on Joshua and Susan's first day of kindergarten; Dana had been their teacher. On that long-ago September morning, the twins had let go of Hope's hand and, grasping their shiny new backpacks and each other, had bravely walked into that new world. It had been a bittersweet moment, having to let go. They'd looked so young, too little to be starting school. Dana must have seen the lost look on her face because she'd walked over and said, "I can always use an extra pair of hands in the classroom."

Hope had become a familiar face in the classroom when her school and work schedule allowed. As the days lengthened and the months went by, Hope and Dana developed a wonderful friendship.

It had been Dana who stood beside her as she made funeral arrangements for her aunt. When Dana achieved her master's degree in education, Hope and the twins had cheered and clapped from aluminum chairs at her graduation ceremony. When Hope had been hired at Tranquility High School, Dana had insisted on taking the four of them out to celebrate.

And when they'd first learned of Joshua's leukemia, it was only Dana whom Hope let see the endless black hole of despair that filled her.

"How's our boy today?" Dana asked as she slipped through the door and walked over to where Hope was sitting. She gave Hope a bolstering hug and, as always, held her for a fraction longer than was necessary.

Hope hugged her in return, so thankful for Dana's constant support. "He's slept most of the day."

"Poor baby. But sleep isn't a bad thing," Dana said quietly as she looked pointedly at Hope. "His mother would do well to follow his example."

"I sleep."

"Yeah, and I'm a size six." Dana patted her size-twelve thighs.

Hope tried to smile.

"Not only do you look exhausted but you look like you've lost another five pounds." Quietly, Dana pulled up a chair and sat next to Hope. "Have you eaten anything today?"

"Yes."

"You're lying," Dana said with a sympathetic smile. "I work with five-year-olds, remember? I can spot a fib from twenty yards." She dug around in the worn leather backpack she used as a purse, pulled out a granola bar and handed it to Hope. "I would have brought something a little more substantial but I thought you had a dinner date with Ben. That's why I'm here, to stay with Josh while you went out. We had it all arranged."

Hope took the food but didn't bother to open it. "I cancelled. And how do you do that? Remember everything, even my schedule?"

Dana set her backpack on the floor. "It's easy when you're not juggling ten things at once."

"I'm sorry you made the trip for nothing. I tried to call but your cell went straight to voice mail."

"You called?"

"Twice. You can remember my schedule but not to charge your phone."

"Give me some credit. I told you. I've turned over a new leaf." Dana fished through her purse once more and produced her cell phone. "See—" Her sentence broke off when they both saw her battery was dead yet again. "Shoot. I really thought I'd remembered this time."

A small smile found its way to Hope. Dana was legendary for forgetting, losing, or just plain not charging her cell phone.

"Was Ben upset when you cancelled on him again?" Dana dropped her phone back into her purse and set it on the floor.

"He was as understanding as always. You should get to know him better, he's a wonderful man. Kind and loyal and a wonderful listener."

"You just described my mom's poodle."

"Not funny."

"While it's true I'm not Ben's biggest fan, you should have gone out with him. A night away might do you a world of good."

"This is a surprise. You've never thought my dating Ben was a good idea before. Besides, as I've told the both of you on many separate occasions, getting Joshua well is my priority. Right now, dating doesn't even register on my radar. Ben understands and knows not to push."

Hope knew Dana believed Ben lacked excitement, spontaneity, that sweep-you-off-your-feet type of personality. But those were all the reasons Hope found Ben Allen so attractive. She didn't want to be swept off her feet—that had happened to her once already with Nick, and while there was nothing else in the world that felt as wonderful, the sad truth was you had to come back down to earth sometime. And it was a *long, hard* fall, one Hope never wanted to repeat.

"So why did you cancel?" Dana asked.

"I just told you—"

"The real reason."

Nothing got past her best friend.

Dana sat up. "Wait. Did you hear back from your mother?"

"No." Hope set the unopened granola bar on the small table next to Joshua's bed.

"She'll get tested. I know she will."

Hope wasn't nearly as optimistic as Dana, but it didn't matter because whether Claire Montgomery knew it or not, she was going to get tested. Hope would make damn sure of it.

"I'm so sorry," Dana said.

Hope looked at her. "For what?"

Sorrow darkened Dana's features. "For not being a match."

"Oh, Dana." Hope leaned against her friend, took her hand in hers. The moment they'd learned Joshua would need the transplant, Dana had been by Hope's side, insisting on getting tested at the same time Hope and Susan had. "You have nothing to be sorry for."

After a moment, Dana drew back and looked at Hope. "Now are you ready to tell me what's really going on?"

With one last look at Joshua to make sure he was still sleeping, Hope motioned for Dana to follow her. This was one conversation she didn't want Joshua to overhear. They made their way down the hallway and into the small family waiting room near a bank of elevators. Except for the two of them, the room was empty.

The bright, overhead light had been dimmed for the evening and while a cartoon played out on the TV in the corner, the sound had been muted. Even knowing this was a children's hospital, sometimes the harsh reality—like cartoons on television—hit Hope hard.

"Now I know it's serious," Dana said the moment the door closed softly behind them.

Hope sat down on one of the upholstered chairs that lined the perimeter only to pop back up. She began to pace and twist her hands into knots as everything—*everyone*—that had happened today rushed back at her.

She stopped and faced Dana. "Nick showed up at my house today."

"Nick? As in Susan and Joshua's father, Nick? As in 'NAS-CAR's Fortune,' Nick?" Dana sank down onto the chair Hope had vacated as she repeated the phrase that had graced more magazine covers than Hope cared to think about.

"Yes, that Nick."

"I guess now I know why you cancelled your date. What did Ben say when you told him about Nick?"

"I didn't tell him."

"You're going to have to at some point."

It was an argument she and Dana had had before. Naturally, Ben knew of Hope's plan to contact the twins' father. He even knew Nick's name. His *first* name. But Hope saw no reason to go into the full explanation of who exactly Nick was. Why should she? The chance of the two men ever meeting was slim to none. And *none* had a huge head start.

The intercom system clicked on, summoning a doctor, and then clicked back off only to come immediately back on with another scratchy summons.

"So," Dana began, and Hope tensed, knowing what question was coming next. "When are you going to tell the kids?"

It was the question that had troubled her from the moment Nick stormed out of her house. "I'm not going to."

Dana shot her a look. "They're going to have to find out sometime."

"No, they're not. They know I got pregnant when I was a teenager and the boy had other plans. Nothing like a teenage pregnancy to open up a frank dialogue with your kids about using protection." Hope sighed. "They know everything they need to know about Nick."

Dana's brown eyes were full of compassion. "Everything but his name."

Hope sat down next to Dana, her shoulders weighted. "His name isn't important. Nick has nothing do to with our life."

"He is their father, Hope."

"No, he's not." Hope drew in a breath. "He might have helped bring them into this world, and for that I'll always be grateful, but that's all he did. A father is so much more. He's someone who comes home from work every night and helps you with your homework. A father tosses a ball out back with you. He's there for your baseball practices and soccer tournaments, ballet recitals, and school plays." Hope turned to Dana. "Nick could never be a father to Joshua and Susan."

Dana didn't say anything for several moments. "Maybe he's changed."

Hope shook her head. "Nick is just like my father, and my father never did. He and my mother were forced to get married when she became pregnant with me. He hung around for a few years, but he never wanted to be there. Then, one morning, he went to work and never came home. For years I blamed myself. If only I could have been a better little girl; if only I could have made him love me, then maybe he wouldn't have left. But you can't make someone love you. I learned that too late. I'm not going to put my children through that same misery. Nick Fortune could never be the father my children deserve. Remember that Internet article you showed me a few months ago? The 'Day in a Life' piece? The reporter said Nick wasn't even home long enough to change his shoes. The man hasn't changed. He knew what he wanted all those years ago, and it is the same thing he still wants. Fame and fortune—" Hope paused and then gave a short, humorless laugh when she realized what she'd said. "Even his name proves it."

Dana gave Hope's hand a squeeze. "I'm sorry, honey."

"Don't be. Aunt Peg was my mother in every sense. Through her example I learned having one loving parent is all a child needs."

"And your children have that in spades."

Hope smiled tiredly. "If I told Joshua and Susan who their father is, he would end up breaking their hearts."

Dana's eyes were full of understanding when she said, "Like he broke yours?"

For several heartbeats Hope didn't answer. Couldn't answer. "I won't let him hurt them. There's only one thing I want from Nick and that is for him to get tested to see if he can save my son."

"So how did he react to the news?"

Hope briefly closed her eyes. "He didn't give me a chance to tell him. When he learned about Joshua and Susan he became so angry he stormed out of the house and was gone before I could stop him. I jumped in my car and tried to find him, but he was already gone."

"He didn't say anything?"

"He said"—God, she didn't want to remember what he'd said—"he said he'd be back tomorrow to see the kids."

"What are you going to do when he shows up tomorrow?"

"I'm not waiting until then."

"What exactly do you have planned?"

Hope looked at her best friend. "I have no idea, but I'm going to do something. I'm done waiting for Nick Fortune."

Four

NICK lifted the long-necked bottle and took a healthy swallow. In the nearly deserted lounge, a country song rasped from the scratchy sound system. Less than a dozen people were scattered throughout the dimly-lit room. Above them the air hung heavy with stale smoke and stale dreams.

The bartender made his way down the counter, pausing across from Nick. A soggy towel lay bunched under his hand. He lifted his chin in a nod toward Nick's beer. "Need another?"

Nick tipped the bottle and studied the nearly empty contents. For the first time in nearly ten years he was tempted to tell the bartender to keep them coming. But if Nick had learned anything from his old man it was that answers couldn't be found at the bottom of a drink.

Nick shook his head. "No thanks."

"Let me know if you change your mind."

The bartender moved on and left Nick with only his thoughts and a warming beer. Neither of which he cared for.

What, after all these years, had made Nick think of Jack

Fortune? His father had been one mean son of a bitch who cared more about his next drink than his only child. And after Nick's mom died, the drinking only got worse—impossible as that seemed. But even though his father had been a miserable excuse for a human being, at least a person knew where they stood with him. A whipping so hard it left your back scarred was a hell of a lot better than being told lies and being deceived.

Anger pulsed hard and fast through Nick.

Goddamn Hope for lying to him. For keeping his children from him.

He reached into his jacket pocket and carefully removed the photo he'd taken from her house. For a brief moment, he stared at her image. His anger returned, pounded through him. He tore his gaze away from her and, instead, focused all of his attention on the only other people in the snapshot.

Not people. Kids. His kids.

He was a father.

No matter how many times he said it or thought it, Nick could hardly make himself believe it.

A kid (let alone kids) had never been a part of Nick's plan. Fatherhood was one club he flat out refused to join. He'd been dealt a crap hand in the gene pool department and refused to pass along that burden to anyone. Let alone a child. He'd always been damn careful when it came to protection. He wore a condom as religiously as the pope wore his ring.

Except with Hope. When passion and need and a sense of belonging had overridden all other thoughts and he'd been young enough and dumb enough to believe where you came from didn't matter.

Nick rubbed his thumb across the image of his son, down the slope of his daughter's cheek. He stared at their faces, committing them to memory, but really there was no need. He'd memorized them hours ago.

As he continued to stare at the picture, worry continued to weave its way through him. What if he turned out to be like his old man? The Fortune blood ran just as hot through Nick's veins. There was no doubt in his mind he would screw up their lives just like his father had screwed up his.

Unable to stop, he found his gaze sliding over and focusing on Hope's image once more. In the picture, she was smiling, laughing, like she didn't have a care in the world. There must have been a gentle breeze because her blond hair all but floated in the air.

His anger returned full force. How could she look so carefree when she'd been lying nearly her whole life?

"Hi," a seductive, feminine voice purred on his right, catapulting his thoughts back to the present. "I don't mean to pry, but aren't you . . . aren't you Nick Fortune? The racecar driver?"

"No, ma'am," Nick replied, lying easily. He appreciated the people who loved racing as much as he did and always made time for the fans—except for tonight. Tonight he was in a foul mood and unfit for conversation. Polite or otherwise.

"Oh." The well-built blonde studied him for a moment. "It's just that you look so much like him. I mean, I've seen your—*his*—picture in over a dozen magazines and watched him race. . . ."

Nick gave her a polite but dismissive smile. "Sorry, wrong guy."

"I was so certain—"

"Mr. Fortune?" A hotel employee approached.

Nick inwardly groaned.

"Mr. Nick Fortune." The young kid's pimpled complexion turned redder and redder the closer he came. "Ex-excuse m-me, Mr. F-Fortune. The hotel manager sent me to f-find you. You have a telephone call. A Mr. Sterling. He says it's urgent."

The last person Nick felt like talking to at the moment was his business manager. Sterling had already left a half dozen messages on Nick's cell. If Nick didn't know him so well, he'd wonder just how in the hell Sterling had managed to find out where Nick was and where he was staying. "Tell him I'll call him later," Nick said to the kid.

"Uh, o . . . okay." The teenager fumbled with his tight collar before turning to leave.

"Wait." Nick dug into the pocket of his Levi's and pulled out a fifty-dollar bill. He handed it to the astonished bellhop. "Better yet, tell him I've checked out."

The kid looked at the money, looked at Nick, and then back down at the fifty. A smile slowly spread across his face until it was ear to ear. "Yes, sir, Mr. Fortune."

Nick watched him leave, all the while wondering how long it had been since fifty lousy bucks could turn his whole world around.

Silky material drifted across the stool next to him.

Damn, he'd forgotten about the blonde.

"I knew it. I just knew you were Nick Fortune."

He tipped his head to the side and sent her an apologetic smile, not feeling sorry in the least. "Sorry."

"Oh, no need to apologize." She settled herself more comfortably on the high stool, looking as if she planned on taking up permanent residence. "I can only imagine how annoying it must be to have strangers come up to you all the time."

The bartender walked by and collected Nick's empty.

The blonde waved him to wait and then turned to Nick. "Can I buy you another?"

"No thanks."

Ignoring him, she turned back to the bartender. "Bring Mr. Fortune—Nick"—she angled her head his way and tried what Nick could only imagine was her most seductive smile on him, which left him unmoved, before facing the bartender once again—"bring Nick another of whatever he's drinking. And I'll have a . . ." She stuck the tip of her bright red nail in the tip of her teeth and thought for a moment. "A piña colada." She batted her eyelashes. "Don't you just love those drinks with the little umbrellas in them?" She giggled and smiled and waited until the bartender left before continuing. "I'm Ashlie, by the way. That's Ashlie with an *ie*."

"Nice to meet you." Good manners died hard.

A heavy application of makeup at first made Ashlie appear older than she was. But up close, Nick realized she was barely old enough to be legal. She was dressed in a short, skintight, bright red dress with unbelievably high matching heels. He'd bet his last race winnings that Hope had never worn a dress quite that . . . small. One he could wad up into a ball and fit in the palm of his hand—with room left over for shoes.

At the thought of Hope, his mood soured once more.

"My brother is a huge fan," Ashlie continued. "He has the races on the TV all the time. I guess I got hooked after watching so many. And that's how I knew it was you." She leaned forward and picked a peanut out of the bowl in front of him. Her arm brushed purposefully against his. She smiled and popped the nut into her mouth, then slowly licked the salt off her fingertips. "You're even better looking in person."

Even if Nick had been inclined to take her up on her clear invitation—which he wasn't—one look at her blond hair would stop him dead in his tracks. After today, he'd had enough of blondes to last a lifetime.

Their drinks arrived. Nick grabbed a few bills out of his pocket and handed them over.

"That's awfully nice of you."

Nick hadn't been born yesterday. There had been a lot more *Ashlies* who had "bought" him drinks. "No problem."

"Darren, that's my brother. He'd have a cow if he knew I was here with you. Last year for Christmas, I helped him shop for Darren Jr., his son. My nephew," she clarified, as if Nick couldn't have figured that one out for himself. "We had to drive to five different stores until we found what he was looking for. D.J.—Darren Jr., that's what we call him—just had to have that racetrack. You know, the one with your picture on it? And your car in it?" She flashed him another smile before curving her bright red lips around the straw.

"The clerk at the last store told us they were selling out quicker than they could get them in," she continued after taking a sip. "I don't know who was more excited on Christmas morning, my brother or little D.J. I just love kids. Do you have any?" she asked, switching topics faster than she blinked her eyes.

"No," came the automatic answer. Then a picture flashed through his mind of Hope and two nearly grown children.

"I didn't think so. I mean a guy like you . . ."

Nick knew exactly what she meant by *a guy like him*.

"And since you were voted *People* Magazine's Hottest Bachelor earlier this year, I guess I can assume you're not married?"

Nick's "No" was crisp and curt. That was one answer he was still positive of.

Ashlie held up her left hand and waggled her ring finger. "Me either." She glanced around the lounge, her smile pure invitation when she turned it back on him. "This place is kind of dull. I know somewhere we could go that's nice and private."

Nick was just about to say no when he caught the look in her eyes. It was like a mirror into his own vacant soul. He shook off the thought, wondering where that had come from. He was just in a foul mood and it all centered on one person.

"I'm sorry"—he softened his refusal with a lie—"but I'm waiting for someone."

She forced a smile. "Oh. Sure. Maybe another time."

"Hello, Nick."

The soft voice came from behind. Slowly, Nick turned around.

Hope stood there looking both determined and nervous. She'd changed out of the shorts and T-shirt she'd been wearing earlier and now wore a long-sleeved, white cotton shirt and a pair of jeans. She'd left her hair down, the sides secured loosely at the back of her neck. Its thickness fought the confines of the clip and curls cascaded over her shoulders and down her back.

There was nothing fancy or designer about her outfit. Nothing to make her stand out or draw attention. But that didn't matter. She still stood out, still drew attention. And not just his, he noted as he saw other men turn and stare. That pissed him off for no good reason.

He was just about to tell her to leave; he'd said everything he'd had to say earlier today, and the only thing that mattered was tomorrow when he was going to see his kids. But as he continued to look at her, he couldn't help but notice a deep-seated weariness that seemed to pull at her—push her down as if the weight of it were far too heavy for her delicate shoulders. Unwillingly, he felt his anger weaken, then caught himself. Hope was the last person who deserved sympathy.

Hope looked over to Ashlie. "Am I interrupting?"

There was a sharp edge to her voice. Nick would have laughed if there'd been anything humorous in their situation. *She* was angry. Rich. If she wanted to see *real* anger—give him about two seconds.

Glancing between him and Hope, Ashlie obviously felt three was a crowd. She stood and grabbed her purse. "Don't mind me, I was just leaving." But before she did, she scribbled something on a small white napkin and pushed it into Nick's hand. "If you should change your mind."

Hope watched the young woman's disappearing back for a few moments before facing Nick once more. "Sorry if I ruined your plans for the evening."

She didn't sound sorry in the least.

He started to ask how she'd located where he was staying and then stopped. This town was the size of a dime. Everything about it reminded him of the place he'd grown up—the place he'd spent the first nineteen years of his life fighting like hell to get out of. Small towns with small minds. Where when your father was the local drunk, you were branded right along with him.

"Why are you here, Hope?"

"Isn't it obvious?"

"What's obvious is that unless you've brought my kids to see me"—he made a show of looking around even though he knew Joshua and Susan weren't with her—"I have nothing to say to you. I said everything I had to say earlier. Tomorrow, bright and early, I'll be on your doorstep and my kids had better be there."

"That's where you're wrong, Nick. There's a lot we need to talk about." Hope's voice held a strength he'd never before heard.

Good. She'd need it by the time he was through with her.

Nick turned back around, ending a conversation he had no intention of having.

"You can't pretend I'm not here," she said after a slight pause.

With every part of him, he wanted to ignore her. But even back when they were just kids, Nick had found that all but impossible. "Why not? You've been doing a damn fine job of pretending I don't exist for the last sixteen years."

"Nick—"

Her voice was cut short and against his better judgment, he found himself looking to see why.

Her gaze was no longer on him but focused on a point across the counter. Nick turned to see what had captured her attention.

Hovering nearby, intent on soaking up their every word, stood the bartender. He didn't even have the manners to turn away when Nick stabbed him with a stare. Instead, he shrugged and kept on staring as if this were the most excitement the bar had seen in years.

Knowing the size of the town, it probably was.

Nick would be damned if he was someone's sideshow. Besides, now that he thought about it, there were a few things he wanted to say to her that were better said tonight, away from Joshua and Susan's earshot. He stood. "Fine, let's talk."

He didn't bother to see if she followed as he made his way to the back of the room, across the deserted dance floor. He found a table in the corner and pulled out two chairs. He was about to take his seat when he realized it didn't matter where they sat in the bar, there was never going to be enough privacy for what he had to say. Not only did they now have the bartender's full attention but just about everyone else's as well.

Obviously Hope had come to the same conclusion. "Maybe we could go somewhere else?"

Nick didn't know much about this small town, but he was sure it wasn't any different than the one he'd been born into or the others he'd sailed through. Everything but the bars closed with the setting sun. He thought about the few possibilities left and, zeroing in on the only one that made sense, he offered, "We could talk in my room."

IN my room.

The speech Hope had carefully rehearsed since leaving the hospital flew out of her head. She felt herself grow flustered—her heart sped up and her palms started to sweat. She took a step back and then another, smacked into a nearby chair. It skittered a short distance across the wooden floor. Even with the jukebox playing and the din from the other patrons, the noise seemed overly loud.

"N-no . . . I . . . d-don't . . . th-think . . ." She stammered and stuttered before clamping her mouth shut.

"Grow up, Hope. The suggestion wasn't a come-on."

Mortification flushed her cheeks. She felt as young and naïve as he accused her of being. She was an adult. A mother. No longer a love-struck teenage girl who'd willingly and eagerly done anything he'd asked. So why was it that he could still unnerve her?

She squared her shoulders. "I know that."

She drew in a breath and regained control of her emotions, or as much as she could. She glanced around the lounge—

more to avoid Nick's gaze than anything else. Several pairs of eyes—and ears—were still focused on them. Staying here wasn't an option. Going up to Nick's room wasn't even a consideration. The first had no privacy and the second, *too* much. She thought quickly. "Take a walk with me?"

For a moment, it didn't seem as if Nick would respond. Then, "Lead on," was all he said.

They left through the hotel's main entrance and made their way down Main Street. With each step they took, she felt his nearness. It was as if there were only so much oxygen in the air, and a man like Nick was granted more than his fair share. It had always been that way. Even when they were teenagers.

Even though it was the height of tourist season, downtown was deserted. Businesses had locked up hours ago, flipped their *OPEN* signs to *CLOSED* before heading home for the evening. Victorian-inspired streetlamps, more for decoration than practicality, lined the walkway. But even in the weak light, Hope easily found her way along the familiar path.

When Dana had asked earlier what it was like seeing *The Nick Fortune*, Hope had shrugged off the question. Now she could think of little else. This Nick Fortune—the man walking next to her—was not the boy she remembered. This Nick was everything she'd believed and also feared he'd become: a success, for sure, but also a man driven by ambition, fueled by a single-minded determination that left no room for anyone or anything else. He radiated a power and a control she was sure many found seductive and intriguing—like the woman in the bar. But not Hope. She'd lived with a father who thought only of himself, and it had led to the ruination of their family when he'd left and never come back. He'd left, and a few years later, so had Nick.

Men left. It was the only truth Claire had ever given Hope.

Yes, Nick would leave again. Walk away without a backward glance. But this time, Hope would be prepared. Earlier today he might have said he wanted to see Joshua and Susan, but she knew better. He'd never be the type of father her children deserved. Not only did she know the boy he'd been, but the whole world knew the man he'd become. Against her better judgment she hadn't been able to stop herself over the years from reading everything she could find about him. Watching each television interview, every news clip. This Nick was the same as the Nick she'd known. A man with a mind solely on his career and being the best of the best. A man poised on the brink of being immortalized as the only driver to capture eight Sprint Cup championships. The last thing he'd want was a couple of kids, but that suited Hope just fine. There was only one thing she needed from him, and the moment he was tested, he could walk away again. They didn't need Nick. The three of them had been doing just fine on their own.

"Any idea where we're headed?" Nick's voice broke into her thoughts.

She glanced around, got her bearings.

At the far end of Main Street, across the road, lay the opening to the boardwalk. It had been built decades ago; the thick planks looped along the inlet of water the town had been named for. Softened by time and the sea, the walkway appeared almost silver in the soft moonlight. Over the years, this boardwalk had become a place of solace for Hope and seeing it now, she realized it had been her unknown destination all along.

Hope inclined her head. "There."

They made their way across the street and as they were just about to step back up onto the opposite sidewalk, Nick's hand softly supported her arm. For the barest of moments his grip hovered against her elbow and then dropped away. A rush of cool air brushed across her arm and she shivered, not sure if it was from the air or the loss of his touch.

The weather-beaten boards creaked under their feet. The usually popular spot was deserted and the long, gently curving expanse of boardwalk stretched before them. As they walked along, she took a deep breath of the salt-tinged air, letting the magic of this soggy piece of the Pacific Northwest soothe her as it had all those years ago when she'd first arrived, scared and pregnant.

The boardwalk flared wide as they came upon a curve that overlooked the large bay. On a clear day you could see Mount Rainier in the distance. But tonight, it was only shadows and moonlight. In silent agreement, they stopped.

She stared out across the dark bay, not seeing the water at all. She knew what she had to say, but no matter how long or how hard she searched, she couldn't find an opening. The fabric of their history had so many loose threads, an end was all but impossible to locate. Then she realized the beginning was the only place to start.

"You know what I remember most about growing up?" She didn't wait for him to answer but plunged ahead, afraid if she stopped, she wouldn't have the courage to start again. "I remember long hot days down by the lake. I'd hurry through my chores and before Claire could think of any more, I'd race over to your house and we'd jump in your old Chevy pickup and drive like the wind. We'd spend hours lying on our backs, gazing at the clouds and swatting mosquitoes the size of hummingbirds. And we'd talk. For hours and hours. About nothing and about everything. About dreams and hopes and fears."

She rubbed her finger across the top board of the railing, felt its rough edges. Images of those long-ago days down at the lake crowded her mind. She could still feel the sun's rays prickling her bare skin and hear the laughter and shouts from other kids. Sometimes the memories felt as distant as the stars, and other times, times like now, they felt as close and bittersweet as Nick.

"But in all those times, I never realized those were *your* dreams, *your* plans. There wasn't room for anything or anyone else. Not me and especially not a child."

"You had no right to make that decision without me." His hard words cut through the soft night and into her.

For the first time since she'd started talking, she looked at him. In the moonlight, his eyes were as hard as stone. "And who was going to help me make that decision? You?" She gave a sarcastic laugh as anger and pain she'd thought long gone resurfaced. "How were you going to help when you couldn't even return my calls?"

"I called," he said flatly.

"In the beginning, yes."

"Don't blame this on me, Hope. We both know who's at fault here. You hid my children from me." Anger radiated from him, punctuated his every word.

She drew back, caught off guard by its potency. How dare he act like the injured party here. He'd abandoned *her*. Abandoned their children by not returning her calls, cancelling his phone, making it impossible for her to contact him. All the hurt and resentment she'd felt all those years ago pushed to the surface. She wanted nothing more than to lash out at him. To let him know how deeply his abandonment had hurt. But getting angry was not going to help. She needed his cooperation. Needed it desperately. And if continuing to keep her anger and hurt bottled up would help her gain that, she'd do it gladly. Joshua was who mattered now. Not her and definitely not the past. All that mattered right now was the very real and scary present.

"Nick, you don't understand—"

"I understand. I understand that for nearly sixteen years you've kept my children a secret from me and now you're trying to justify your lies. Well, I'm not buying what you're selling. It's obvious you believed they were better off without me in their lives." He raked his hand through his hair and stared out across the water. Moonlight glinted off the impossibly hard angle of his jaw. But just as quickly as he'd turned away, he turned back. "Tell me this, Hope. Why? Why after all this time did you call me now?"

There were so many ways to reply to that question but, in the end, she knew there was only one. "Joshua has leukemia and needs a bone marrow transplant. Our best chance for a match is with a family member. I need you to get tested."

Five

CANCER.

His son had cancer.

Oh God.

A hundred different emotions hit him at once. A hundred questions. How? Why? When? It wasn't until Hope started talking that he realized he'd asked his last question out loud.

"Joshua was diagnosed a little over six months ago. Acute lymphoblastic leukemia. We began treatment immediately and everything seemed to be going well. At the end of his treatments, Joshua was in remission and it was like being given the gift of him all over again. Life went back to normal. Doctor's appointments became almost routine, and then at one appointment the doctor told us . . . the doctor t-told us . . ."

The catch in Hope's voice snapped Nick out of his numbness. For the first time since she'd told him of Joshua's illness, he looked at her. Really looked at her. And what he saw tore him apart.

Her face had gone white and her lips trembled with barely-contained anguish. Tears streaked down her cheeks. And her eyes. God. The pain in them was a blow to his own soul.

"Everything was s-s-supposed to be o-okay," she said, and he could see how hard she was struggling for control. "Joshua was supposed to be fine. After his appointment we were going to a music store in the University District to try out the guitar he'd been saving for." Her words caught on her tears.

She looked impossibly young and vulnerable standing in front of him with her eyes full of fear and a world of pain stacked on her small shoulders.

He felt her heartache as clearly as he felt his own. Before he could stop himself, he reached up and wiped her tears away.

He couldn't shake the image of her standing in the doctor's office, happy and excited and thinking about the day ahead. Then, with just a few words from the doctor, their world had been ripped apart once more.

Everything was supposed to be okay.

Her words burned through him.

Joshua was supposed to be fine.

Emotion clogged his throat.

Her breaths came in ragged gasps that seemed to almost break her in two. She looked up at him, tears streaking down her face. "I-I d-d-don't know if I'll be s-s-strong enough for him again."

"Oh God, Hope." The years slipped away and once more they were teenagers with nothing or no one besides each other to shelter them from the stormy world. Without thinking, without remembering what had or had not been said during the last sixteen years, he gathered her in his arms. She stiffened but he didn't let go. He kept his arms around her, holding her, gently rocking her. A sob caught in her chest and a shudder swept through her, but still she held herself erect as if she'd only had herself to rely on for so long she was afraid to let anyone else in.

"Please," he whispered. "Lean on me. Let me help you."

"I can't."

Nick swallowed hard and tightened his embrace. "You don't have to shoulder this all by yourself. I'm here." He leaned forward and where his fingers had earlier traveled, drying her tears away, he kissed those same spots. Tentative at first, he brushed his lips across her cheek, the corner of her mouth, her bottom lip, trying to let his actions communicate the feelings he couldn't put into words. He pushed her hair away from her face, kissed the tears from the corners of her eyes.

"Hope," he breathed as he tilted his head back and looked into her eyes.

Her eyes echoed his own pain, his own need to reach out and find solace. At that moment it was as if they were the only two people in the world. When he bent down, she met him more than halfway. Their lips touched.

The blast of a nearby car horn had the effect of a bucket of cold water.

Hope jumped back. She touched a trembling finger to her mouth, her eyes full of confused bewilderment. "No . . ."

"Hope." Nick reached out for her.

She stepped back. "I . . . I'm sorry. That wasn't supposed to happen."

"Hope," he said again as he tried to close the distance between them, only to have her retreat once more.

"This wasn't why I came to see you." She stepped back again. "I only wanted . . . I only meant . . . Oh, hell." She released an uneven sigh. "I only wanted to talk. To tell you about Joshua."

A gentle wind battled with her long hair and blew it across her face. She tucked the loose strands behind her ear only to have to repeat the process seconds later. "You'll get tested? To see if you're a match?"

"Of course." Her doubt irritated him.

At his instant answer, her shoulders sagged. "Thank you."

Thank you?

Thank you?

Her gratitude burned a path straight to his gut. Was she really *thanking* him for helping his own *son*?

He clenched his jaw to keep from responding. Now wasn't the time to tell her what he thought of her thank-you.

She dug through her purse and pulled out a business card. With only a slight hesitation, she closed the gap between them and handed him the card. "This is the name and number of Joshua's doctor. Please call him. He will make the arrangements for your testing."

Nick took the card. "I'll call immediately."

"Thank you."

His jaw set again at hearing those two words he'd just now come to despise.

"Well, then." She took a few steps back. Her purse strap slipped off her shoulder; she readjusted it back on. "Dr. Parker will let me know the results so there's no need for you to call . . . What I mean to say is, since we won't need to see each other again, this is good-bye. And thank you, Nick. Thank you."

Nick barely heard what Hope was saying; he was too intent on the card in his hand. *Dr. Thomas Parker, Pediatric Oncologist.*

Doctor.

Oncologist.

Letters so small they should be rendered all but insignificant, but if anything, their diminutive size packed an even more devastating punch. Made the horror of what he'd learned this evening all that much more real and yet unbelievable at the same time. Nick looked back up, ready to try to explain it to Hope. But she was halfway down the boardwalk, hurrying away. And then he remembered what she'd said.

We won't need to see each other again.

This is good-bye.

"Go ahead and run," he said into the night, grabbing for his cell phone, ready to move heaven and earth to save his son. "But this is far from good-bye."

* * *

HOPE shut her front door and locked it. Closing her eyes, she sank against the smooth wood and drew in several deep breaths, trying to slow her racing heart.

She'd kissed him.

Kissed. Him.

She dropped her purse and keys onto the tiled entryway. The small thud and jingle echoed loudly in the too-quiet, too-dark, *too-empty* house.

Oh God, what had she done?

Suddenly, she wished she hadn't agreed to Susan spending another night at Chelsey's. Maybe if her daughter were here, distracting her, Hope would be able to shake the memory of what had happened. But she feared nothing could.

Her fingers brushed across her trembling lips. It was almost as if she could feel his hands on her again, wiping her tears away, supporting her in his strong embrace. She closed her eyes, tried not to remember . . . but heaven help her, how was she ever going to forget?

But she'd have to. This time she wasn't going to give him a second chance to break her heart, because her heart wasn't the only thing at stake here—so were her children's. And their well-being, their happiness, meant more to her than anything.

Nick had agreed to get tested. That was all that mattered. And if he was a match—God please please let him be!—she knew Nick would be in and out of their lives with as much impact as a television weatherman. There was no way he would stick around for any length of time.

Determined, she pushed away from the door and headed into the kitchen, flicking on the overhead light as she entered. She turned on the burner under the kettle and waited for the water to heat. Maybe a cup of tea would help.

The answering machine flashed red, indicating she had several messages, but she ignored them. No doubt they were creditors. She knew it wasn't the hospital; they'd call her cell

if she didn't answer the home phone. The creditors could wait
another day to hear from her. Instead, she picked up the phone
and dialed a number she knew by heart.

This call had become a nightly ritual between Hope and
the nurses on Joshua's floor. It didn't matter how many hours
she spent at the hospital, she still needed to make this one
last call before she went to bed. If it wasn't for her job or
Susan, Hope would have long ago taken up permanent residence alongside Josh, gladly sleeping on the floor if it meant
being able to stay close to him. But even if that had been
possible, Joshua didn't want that. He wanted life to remain as
normal as possible—as impossible a feat as that was. But for
his sake, Hope did her best. She'd do anything for her children, and if that meant smiling when she didn't feel like it
and rambling on about the most mundane of things, that was
what Hope would do. So to please Joshua she filled their hours
together with commonplace things, trying her hardest to coax
a smile from him. She told him about their neighbor's new
escape artist puppy who would wander over to their back door
and whine until he got a treat. And heaven help Hope if she
wasn't there to indulge him. The little terrier terror would dig
holes in her front yard until his tummy was satisfied. She
regaled Joshua with the latest antics of their postal carrier,
Mrs. Langstein. A lovely woman who, for the past decade,
ever since her husband had passed, had taken it upon herself
to play matchmaker. Time and time again, she'd purposefully
misdelivered the single people's mail on her route in hopes
of making a love connection. And then there was Mr. Baxter,
a retired aeronautical engineer who now filled his days with
gardening. He'd turned his front and back lawn into rows upon
rows of vegetable beds. Many nights, Hope (like all her neigh-
bors) would come home to find a generous bag of fresh-from-
the-garden vegetables on her front porch.

They were silly, seemingly unimportant things, but Hope
knew how much Josh liked hearing them, so before she arrived at the hospital, she made sure she was well versed on

any and all of the happenings from their little community in Tranquility Bay.

Retrieving a mug and teabag from the cupboard, she waited. On the second ring, Mary, an older woman with grown children and pictures of her half-dozen grandchildren prominently displayed at the nurses' station, answered.

"Hi, Mary. It's Hope."

"I was just thinking it was about time for your call. And before you ask, Joshua's fine. He hasn't woken up since you left."

"Thank goodness. This morning was tiring, but I know the visit with his friends did him good. Hopefully took his mind off tomorrow's treatments."

"Yes," Mary said with a familiar sympathy.

"Do you happen to know if Dr. Parker got back the test results?"

"I haven't seen them, but I'll double-check if you like."

"No, that's okay. He didn't think they'd be back until tomorrow anyway."

"You know what they say. No news is good news."

"Yeah," Hope said without conviction. Once, she'd believed in that. Now—now she knew the truth.

Melancholy threatened to settle above her like a dark cloud, and Hope quickly changed the subject, forcing it away. "So, how many more days till you leave?"

"Two and counting," Mary replied. "Hawaii. Can you believe it?" She gave a slight laugh. "Frank and I haven't gone on a trip since . . . well, since I don't know when." She laughed again. "I'd say we're due."

Hope smiled. "Overdue. If I don't see you in the morning, have a great time."

"I'll bring us all back a lei and a little of that magical white sand. We could all use a little magic. Now you get some rest. Your Joshua is in good hands."

"Thanks, Mary. For everything. Good night." Hope hung up the phone and leaned back against the counter. She knew Mary was right; she knew he was in good hands, but every minute she wasn't with him she felt torn. Worry gnawed at her and guilt burrowed in and refused to leave. Her son needed her, and she needed to be there with him. And then there was Susan . . .

A fresh wave of worry swept through her. She had two children, but with Joshua needing so much of her time and there being only so many hours in a day . . . There just wasn't enough of her to go around.

Lean on me.

Let me help.

Nick's words came back to her.

Right. Lean on him. He'd give her as much support as a cooked spaghetti noodle.

The kettle whistled. She was just about to pour the boiling water over her dry teabag when she stopped and then set the still-full kettle back on the burner. Tea wasn't what she needed.

But what did she need?

The answer eluded her.

She flipped off the kitchen light intent on heading to bed, where she was sure she'd spend another night tossing and turning. But as she was leaving the kitchen, the blinking light from the answering machine caught her attention once more. For all of two seconds, she was tempted to continue to ignore it.

She pressed the button marked Play.

Not surprising, the first two messages were from creditors. She'd tackle those later. The third call was from Ben.

"Hi, it's Ben. I know you're at the hospital but I didn't want to bother you on your cell—and we all know I can't text." She could hear the smile in his voice. "I just wanted you to know I was thinking of you and am here whenever you need me."

The machine clicked off.

For several long moments she stood in the darkened kitchen, staring at the answering machine. It was late but not too late to return Ben's call, but still she made no move to call him.

Unbidden, her thoughts returned to Nick and the kiss they'd shared—the kiss she'd actively participated in. A fresh wave of remorse hit her. How could she have let him kiss her? And worse, how could she have kissed him back?

He'd abandoned her, that was true. But that was in the past and she wasn't a teenager anymore. Passion didn't rule her heart and her actions. She was stronger. Some (Dana) would even say *jaded*. But that wasn't true. Now Hope knew what to value. Her children, always. And if and when the time was right, someone like Ben. Someone steady and thoughtful, patient and understanding. If she needed a shoulder to lean on (which she didn't) Ben would be there for her. And for Joshua and Susan. All she had to do was pick up the phone and he'd be there.

Nick came when you called, her traitorous heart reminded her.

Yes, but he'd leave again. Jetting off to one state or another. To this race or that. To that redhead or that brunette. He hadn't changed a bit in the last several years. His exploits were legendary and accessible to anyone with an Internet connection.

Hope didn't delude herself. Nick's kisses might set her on fire, but Ben's were like a warm, comfortable blanket. No highs and no lows. Ben would be home every night and not in a different time zone or country each week. She could grow old with him.

But could she love him?

Yes, of course she could. Ben was the man for her.

"WHERE have you been? I call, you don't answer. I leave messages, you ignore. Do you have any idea what I've been going through? I'll tell you what I've been going through. Hell, that's what. I've been dodging calls from the whole damn country."

Nick held the phone away from his ear and let his business manager rant and rave on the other end. After over ten years of working together, Nick could picture Ken stomping around his house, yelling into the phone and pulling at his already thinning hair. A short man in his early fifties, with a potbelly and the tendency to never wear matching socks, Ken Sterling was nothing to look at, but what he lacked in physical attributes, he more than made up for in off-the-charts intelligence. A former CIA man, Ken had worked behind the scenes, gathering information where others had failed. His financial genius had netted the government billions. But for all of his success, after more than two decades, Ken was ready for a change. So with his passion for racing and his Midas-like touch with money, he'd sought and carved out his ideal job. Over the course of the last ten years, Ken Sterling had more than quadrupled Nick's investments. But right now, Sterling's problems were far from the top of Nick's list of priorities.

Had it really been only less than an hour ago when Nick had learned the devastating truth about his son? It seemed as if a lifetime had passed since then.

The knowledge threatened to cripple him, but if there was one thing Nick had learned during his years of racing, it was that if you stopped moving, you were run over in the dust.

In the last three quarters of an hour he'd placed over a dozen calls, talked to the people he needed to talk to, and left messages when they weren't available. Sterling had been one of his last calls.

"Nick? Have you heard a word I said?"

Nick stopped his pacing. "No."

The distinct clink of ice being dropped into a glass and liquid being poured came across the line. "I hope you're listening now because we have problems. Let me recap. Pepsi is threatening to sue because you missed the shoot. Noble Oil—you remember them, don't you? Your sponsors? Well, they're climbing the walls—and me—because of Pepsi's threats. I've been playing patty-cake with the producers from the Diane Sawyer special, keeping them content until I could reach you and nail down a date for the interview. And Dale,"

Ken said, referring to Nick's crew chief, "Dale is convinced you've been kidnapped by the opposition. And I'm not even going to mention the race this weekend."

Business matters were the last thing on Nick's mind at the moment. "Patty-cake, Ken? I didn't know you had it in you."

"Make jokes. That's great."

Nick turned serious. "I told you before I have no intention of appearing on some television show."

"*Some* television show, he says." There was a pause and Ken took a drink. "Jesus, Mary, and Joseph, Nick. Do you have any idea how many gray hairs you give me? This isn't just some television show. It's Diane Sawyer, for crying out loud. Every other track jock would give their right nut for this opportunity. Hell, they'd even give their left nut, too, if needed. Think of the publicity. Noble wants this. Bad. And you should too."

"I said drop it."

"Fine, but tell me this. You're on the backstretch of racing. When it's over, what then?"

Nick didn't answer. He knew racing was a young man's sport, but, hell, he was only thirty-four, definitely not ready for a walker. And besides, he wasn't going anywhere until he clinched that eighth championship. There was no way he was going to give up before he'd conquered it all. He wasn't on the final lap of his career, far from it. Besides, he had plenty of other interests in his life—even if he couldn't remember them right at the moment.

Hope's image chose that second to come back to him, how she looked standing on the boardwalk, in the moonlight, with tears running down her cheeks.

"Nick, damn it, you're not listening again."

"I need a favor."

For the first time since the conversation had started, his business manager was silent. In all their years of working together, Nick had never asked for anything. It was obvious by Ken's continued silence that the statement had thrown him.

"Anything," Ken finally said with a sincerity and somberness that humbled Nick.

Hope flashed into memory again, but this time it wasn't her sad green eyes he saw reflected in the moonlight, or her lips he'd kissed. A kiss that had been so feather-light it shouldn't have had any impact on him at all but, in fact, the opposite was the truth. No, what he was remembering now was all her years of deceit. Of keeping his children from him. And there was the one horrifying thought that Nick tried to keep at bay but couldn't. What if now, when he'd just found out about his son and daughter, he lost one of them? That knowledge churned in his gut.

Nick wasn't going to listen to another word Hope had to say. He was done with her lies.

"I need you to do a background check on a woman named Hope Thompson. She's also used the last name Montgomery." Nick gave Ken all of the information he had—little as it was.

"Anything in particular you want me to look for?"

"Everything," was Nick's only answer. He didn't bother to tell Ken to keep his inquiries discreet. He didn't have to.

Ken gave a short laugh. "Why did I even ask? Or, can I ask?"

"It's personal."

"When did you develop anything personal that I don't know about?"

"As much as you'd like to think differently, you don't know everything."

"Not for lack of trying."

"More like prying."

Ken laughed. "How soon do you need the information?"

"Yesterday."

"Naturally. Now about—"

Nick cut him off. "Everything else has been taken care of."

"And the race on Sunday?"

"I haven't missed one yet."

"Not even when you had cracked your ribs or busted your

leg. Okay, I'll get back to you as soon as I have the information. And this time, answer my damn call."

No sooner had Nick disconnected the call than his cell rang.

"Nick, it's Mark Brandt. I know it's late but your message said to call the moment I got in."

Nick had never been so glad to hear from the team's private physician as he was at that moment. "Thanks for calling."

"No problem. I gathered from your message that it's a matter of some urgency."

"It is." Nick had always considered himself to be a man who could handle anything. But right now, what he needed to say nearly broke him. He cleared his throat and then said in a straight rush, before it truly did break him, "My son has leukemia and needs a bone marrow transplant. I need to get tested to see if I'm a match."

Silence. Then, "I'm sorry, Nick. I didn't even realize you had a son."

"No one does."

"I see."

"No, I'm sure you don't," Nick said honestly.

"You're right. I don't. But understanding isn't a prerequisite for helping. What can I do?"

"I need all the information I can get on acute lymphoblastic leukemia. As soon as possible. Also my son"—the word *son* still tripped awkwardly from his mouth—"my son, Joshua, is being treated by"—Nick glanced at the card Hope had given him—"Dr. Thomas Parker at Mount Rainier Children's Hospital. Find out everything you can about him and the hospital. I want Joshua being treated by the best and at the best."

"You got it. Anything else?"

"I'm near Seattle now and have put a call in to this Dr. Parker but because of the hour, I'm sure I won't hear back from him until the morning. I don't want to wait. I want this expedited."

"Let me make some calls."

Nick thought quickly. Fame had its benefits—like a highly skilled physician only a phone call away. But it also had its drawbacks. He wanted to spare his son the negative aspects for as long as he could. "To keep a lid on this, I'd rather you did the test."

"I understand completely. Is your plane in Seattle?" Dr. Brandt asked.

"Yes."

"I'll be waiting as soon as you get here. In less than twenty-four hours we'll know."

It was exactly the answer Nick had wanted.

In five minutes he was checked out of the hotel and on his way to the airport. But no matter how fast he drove or how quickly he moved, he couldn't shake Hope or their kiss from his mind.

Six

WHEN the doorbell rang at eight the next morning, Hope's already accelerated heart rate turboed into hyper speed.

He was here.

She took a deep breath.

He was really here.

Yesterday Nick had been so adamant about seeing Joshua and Susan, but then they'd actually talked, touching on what it really meant to have two children—Joshua's illness, the worry, the heartache . . . The Nick Hope remembered would have run from all that reality. There were too many things conspiring to tie him down to a small town far from the fame and adoration he so desperately craved. Part of her had been certain that after a night of thinking all that through, Nick would run as far and fast as he could. That he hadn't shocked her (and scared her) more than she'd like to admit.

She walked down the hallway, slowed her steps. She would not hurry to the door, to the man who had left her with only his broken promises.

Maybe he's changed.

Dana's words came back to her.

She reached for the doorknob, turned it.

But it wasn't Nick who stood on the other side.

"Dana," Hope said, sinking against the side of the door.

"Well, you don't have to look at me like I'm the Grinch who stole Christmas. Besides, I came bearing gifts." Dana held up her arms. In one hand was a white paper bag with the logo of their favorite bakery, located on Main Street. In her other hand was a cardboard drink carrier holding two steaming, insulated cups.

Hope eyed the white bag. "Blueberry?"

"Is there any other muffin worth eating?"

Hope smiled and swung the door wide.

Together they made their way into the kitchen. Dana set the bag and drinks on the round kitchen table and, with a familiarity from years of friendship and shared meals, they had plates, knives, and napkins on the table in moments. No sooner had they sat down when Dana said, "What's the occasion?"

Hope smiled. "You tell me. You're the one showing up on my doorstep with sugar and caffeine."

"The perfect combination, so true." Dana cut her muffin in half. "But what I was referring to was you. I know you work this morning at the grocery store, but this is the first time I've seen you put on makeup and curl your hair for the locals."

"Just needed a pick-me-up today." Hope averted her gaze and quickly took a sip of her tea. She winced as the hot liquid burned her mouth. "Mmmmmm, Earl Grey. My favorite." She fought to change the subject. Cautiously, she took another sip, keeping herself occupied so she wouldn't have to immediately answer Dana. Slowly, she lowered her cup and eyed her best friend. "Now it's your turn. What gives?"

"I have no idea what you're talking about," Dana lied horribly.

"Blueberry muffins. Earl Grey. With cream and sugar, I

might add. And an early-morning visit from my very best friend who hates early mornings. What's that saying? Beware of those bearing gifts?"

Dana laughed. "All right. I confess. But don't play the innocent with me. You know why I'm here. Or, more accurately, *who*."

Nick.

Before Hope could stop herself, her gaze went to the front door.

"So," Dana prompted. "Did you find him last night?"

"Yes."

"And?"

And I kissed him. Heaven help her, that was her first thought.

"Did you tell him about Joshua?"

At the sound of her son's name, Hope's thoughts were pulled right back where they belonged—right back to what was important. "Yes, and he agreed to get tested." Saying the words aloud brought her a new sense of relief. Nick had agreed. Soon, they would have that match for Joshua and then everything would be okay.

"Thank goodness," Dana said, echoing Hope's own thoughts. "I was so worried . . ."

A frown wrinkled Hope's forehead. "Worried? You, the eternal optimist?"

Dana smiled, took a bite, chewed, then swallowed. "Yeah, after I bumped into Mrs. Hingle at the bakery."

"Mrs. Hingle? Mrs. I-love-to-gossip Hingle?"

Dana wiped her fingers on her napkin. "The one and only. After she told me that Nick had left town, I was worried that you didn't get a chance to—"

"What?" Hope jerked forward. Her hand flung out and knocked her tea over. Hot liquid spilled across the table. She reached for the pile of napkins, grabbed a handful, and began to sop up the mess, but her mind was far from the task. "What did you say?"

"I said I was worried you didn't get a chance to speak to Nick. When you left the hospital, you weren't even sure where he was staying, so . . . Hope, are you okay? You look pale."

Without answering, Hope abandoned the soggy mound of napkins and went into the kitchen. She flung cupboard after cupboard open until she found what she was looking for. She pulled it from under a stack of cookbooks. The words *Tranquility Bay Telephone Directory* glared back at her. She could have Googled the number on her cell but knew that would take longer. Quickly, she flipped through the thin paper pages, tearing some in her haste. Her eyes scanned the pages, slowing when she hit upon the *T*s. She ran her forefinger down the page. In less than a minute, she'd found the number she needed and placed the call.

"Tranquility Inn," the receptionist answered on the fourth ring.

"Mr. Fortune's room, please," Hope said.

"Who?"

"Nick Fortune," Hope said slowly and clearly. "Could you please connect me to his room?"

"Oh. *Him*." The female voice perked up. "He checked out sometime last night."

Hope went completely still. "No, you must be mistaken. Please check again."

"I don't need to. It's not like we get many celebrities here."

"Are you sure?"

There was the distinct sound of gum being popped. "Yeah, I'm sure."

Nick was gone. Without a word. Just like that. Just like before.

"Ma'am? Are you still there? Did you need anything else?"

Hope must have mumbled an appropriate response because the receptionist was saying "Good-bye" just a moment before the line went dead.

"Hope?" Dana's soft voice came from behind her. "What is it? What's wrong?"

Hope couldn't move. "He left," was all she managed to say a few moments later.

Less than twelve hours after learning he was a father, Nick had fled.

FOR the next eight hours, Hope didn't stop long enough to catch her breath, let alone long enough to let her thoughts catch up with her.

Business at the grocery store had been booming. It was the height of the tourist season, after all, and combined with the gorgeous, bright, sunny day, it seemed as if everyone was out and about. Several friends and acquaintances had come up to Hope while she worked to wish her well and let her know that Joshua had been and would continue to be in their thoughts and prayers. Each heartfelt sentiment touched Hope more than they would ever know.

When she left work and it took her three tries to get her car started, she refused to let that get her down. And when she got home and collected the mail and saw that the bulk of it was bills—and more bills—again, she plunged ahead, fought for some of that optimism Dana seemed to come by so easily.

Once more she attempted to get in touch with her mother, and once more, failed. She also tried Nick. But the only number she had for him was his office, and it went to voice mail.

Silently she chided herself. How could she have forgotten to get his cell number? Or *all* his numbers, for that matter? Someone like Nick must have dozens of ways for people to get in touch with him. Next time she saw him she planned on rectifying her mistake immediately.

If she saw him.

How could he have just left without a word? But she knew how. It wasn't the first time he'd vanished on her. But it would be the last.

A quick glance at the clock told her she had a little over

half an hour before Susan was due home. Putting a pot of water on the cooktop to boil, Hope unloaded the bag of groceries she'd picked up after work. Chicken breasts. Lemons. Capers. Parsley. Linguine noodles and a few other essentials. All the ingredients she'd need to make Susan's favorite dinner: chicken piccata. Hope had also picked up a box of brownie mix—a favorite of Joshua's. Or they had been. These days he didn't feel like eating much, but still she tried. Even if it was junk food from a box. At this point she'd be happy to see him eat anything. While she and Susan ate dinner, she'd put the brownies in the oven so they'd be ready to take to the hospital.

Hope had just turned the browning chicken in the pan when she heard the front door open. Drying her hands on a towel, she walked out of the kitchen. "Hi, sweetie," she said when she spotted Susan closing the front door.

Susan turned. "Oh. Hey, Mom. I didn't think you'd be home."

"Of course I'm home. I told you I would be. We had plans to head in to the hospital together after I got off work. Remember?"

"Oh. Yeah. That." Susan dropped her backpack on the entryway tile and made her way into the living room. Flopping down on the couch, she grabbed the remote off the coffee table.

"I'm just finishing up dinner. Ten minutes, tops."

Susan flicked on the TV. "Thanks, but I'm not hungry."

"It's your favorite."

Her daughter didn't bother to look at her. "Thanks, but no thanks."

A frown marred Hope's brow. "Did you eat at Chelsey's?"

"No."

"Then you must be hungry. We'll eat and then—"

Susan shot her a glare. "I said I wasn't hungry. And I'm not going to the hospital." She turned back to the TV, began flipping through channels.

Hope stared at her daughter's profile, a feeling of helplessness overtaking her. Over the last few months a rigidness had settled along Susan's jawline, pulled at her usually bright and happy eyes. Her once-fashionista daughter who wouldn't dare leave her bedroom without looking like she'd stepped out of the pages of a high-end magazine now, more often than not, wore sweatpants and old T-shirts of Josh's no matter who she was with or where she went.

Determined to make some sort of headway with her daughter, Hope headed into the kitchen. She took the pan of chicken off the burner, turned off the heat, then returned to the living room. She stood next to the couch.

Susan refused to look at her, but Hope wasn't having any of it. "Lift," she said just like she'd said thousands of times before. With a roll of her eyes, Susan lifted her legs. Hope sat and with the gentle pressure of her hand, Susan lowered her legs until they were lying over Hope's lap.

Channels continued to click by.

Hope smoothed a hand over Susan's gray sweatpants. "Did you have a nice time at Chelsey's?"

"Yeah. Great."

Susan's tone told a different story.

"It's been a long time since Chelsey spent the night here. Why don't you invite her over the next time you girls are going to hang out? I could make whatever you wanted for dinner. Pop popcorn. You could get movies. Whatever you want. A fun girls' night."

Susan's thumb paused on the remote. "Chelsey's leaving."

"Well, not forever," Hope said, baffled by her daughter's fatalistic tone. "Chelsey's mom stopped by the store today. She told me about their upcoming trip to Disney World. They'll only be gone for two weeks. It's hardly—"

"But she promised . . ."

"Promised what?"

"Nothing. Never mind." Susan tossed the remote onto the coffee table. "I'm really tired. Night."

Before Hope could respond, Susan was off the couch and down the hall. Her bedroom door closed behind her with a finality that let Hope know there would be no reaching her tonight.

Half an hour later, Hope softly knocked on Susan's door before opening it. The room was dark, not a single light turned on, but early-evening shadows illuminated the window, the bed Susan lay on. She was facing away from the door. Away from Hope.

"I'm about to take off for the hospital. You sure you don't want to come with?"

Her daughter didn't answer.

"Susan?" Hope said, taking a step farther into the room.

"I'm sure, Mom. Night."

Hope hesitated. She understood Susan's reluctance. No one wanted to go to the hospital, especially not a teenager, but Hope hated leaving her daughter home alone and she hated knowing Joshua was in a hospital room by himself. "I know Josh would love to see you. Are you sure—"

Susan flopped over, scowled at Hope. "God, Mom. How many times do I have to tell you? I. Don't. Want. To. Go." She turned back over, pulling her comforter high up on her neck.

Hope let out a sigh. She walked over to her daughter and gave her a kiss on the top of her head. "Okay. You can stay home tonight, but I'll expect you to come with me tomorrow. I'll be back in a few hours. Call me on my cell if you need me. I left your dinner warming in the oven. I love you." She waited for a response but knew one wouldn't be coming. Giving her daughter a final kiss, Hope left the room, closing the door softly behind her.

At the hospital, Hope did her best to cheer up Joshua. But he was in as dark a mood as his sister. Hope tried to entice him into playing a game of cards, but he had no interest. She tried a couple of board games, but they fell even flatter. Even the pan of brownies was a complete and utter failure. The smell of them had upset his stomach so badly she'd hurried them out of the room and given them to one of the nurses to put in their break room. Hopefully they would enjoy them. In the end, Josh settled on a movie. Some action flick that had to do with some comic book hero. Josh had seemed about as interested in it as Hope had been.

Long after the credits rolled, Hope stayed by her son's side. Only when he was asleep and there was no way she could put it off any longer did she leave. But like always, she felt torn. Years ago she'd seen a movie starring Michael Keaton. The character he played had found a way to clone himself. The idea tantalized Hope. If there were multiples of her, she wouldn't feel as if she were always letting someone down. As if she were always failing. One of her could stay with Joshua full time as she longed to do. Another of her, with Susan. And another could work her job at the grocery store—maybe even picking up more hours to help with the ever-growing number of bills.

It was only later, during the darkest hours of the night, when she was lying in bed, that she found it impossible to keep her fears and worries at bay. Without the brightness of daylight to banish them, they broke through. Too many nights she muffled her sobs into her pillow, not wanting to wake Susan. Even as she clung to the belief that Joshua was going to be fine, that a donor would be found, and the doctors would cure him, there were nights where faith was hard to find.

And just when she'd thought she'd gotten through the day without traveling down that mental road so clearly marked *closed*, she thought of Nick. Of last night and how she'd let the moonlight trick her into seeing something in his eyes that wasn't there. She'd once again believed in his promises, let his words and soft touch melt through her defenses, reach a place deep inside her that she'd thought had long ago been permanently sealed off.

It was as if she'd learned nothing during the last sixteen years.

Then her anger at him boiled over to anger at herself.

Several times during the day she'd caught her reflection. Saw the extra care she'd taken with her makeup and hair. She'd gone through the effort for a man who so clearly didn't deserve it, but what really was at the crux of her fury was that she'd even thought to spend that time on her appearance. What did it matter how she looked when the real issues at stake here were weighing her down nearly to her breaking point?

And there was one other thing she couldn't stop thinking about.

Even with their history, even with their past and seeing his present in magazines and on television shows, why had she been so tempted last night to believe in him when he'd said, "Lean on me"?

The telephone rang. Hope jolted upright and grabbed for her cell that was never far from her reach. But it wasn't her cell. It was the home line. Panic spiked down her spine. Nothing good ever came from a late-night call.

She scrambled to the side of her bed and grabbed the cordless on her nightstand, worried the sound would wake Susan and even more worried about who was calling.

Please, not the hospital.

Please, not Joshua.

"H-hello?" Fear clawed at her throat, made talking all but impossible.

"I know it's late but this is the first chance I've had to call."

Nick.

It was Nick calling, not the hospital.

"I've just about wrapped up everything down here and should be back in Tranquility by tomorrow."

Hope had no idea where "down here" was, and she didn't ask. Didn't care. Only one thing about Nick concerned her. "I spoke with Dr. Parker and he said you haven't made an appointment."

"That's right."

Fury spiked her temperature. She gripped the phone tighter. "Why not?"

"I met with my own doctor today and am having him run the test."

It took her a moment to process what he was saying. "Your own doctor?"

"Yes. Mark Brandt."

She sagged back against her padded headboard, felt her anger leave as quickly as it had come. "That's why you left? To meet with your doctor?"

"The most important reason, yes."

She could no more stop the tears that flooded her eyes than she could control the emotion that wobbled her voice when she managed to whisper, "Thank you."

Nick didn't seem to notice. "As I was saying, I'll be back tomorrow. I'll have to leave again in the evening, but I want to see Joshua and Susan before I go."

Slowly his words began to penetrate her euphoric bubble. She sat up. *See them tomorrow. Leave again.*

Her past was stepping all over her present.

Leave again.

That one phrase played over and over in her mind. Nick had gotten tested, that was the most important thing, but her children's hearts were equally important. Being a parent wasn't something you tried out—like a new pair of shoes or, in Nick's case, like a new girlfriend. Right now he might believe he wanted a relationship with his son and daughter, but what he didn't understand was that when the newness wore off, when he got bored, or when something better came along, he would be gone. Just like before. And she wasn't about to let the pain of that type of abandonment touch her children. "I don't think that would be a good idea."

"What wouldn't be?"

"You seeing Joshua and Susan."

Two beats of dead silence. "What?"

"Please, Nick, try to understand. I don't think—"

"I don't give a damn what you think. I want to see my children. I *am* going to see them."

"Nick, being a father is a hundred percent commitment."

"Don't you think I know that?"

"Frankly, no."

A foul word burned the lines.

She searched her mind, struggled to find a way to make him understand. "Why didn't you call?"

"What?"

"Yesterday you made the same promise that you were going to be here, at my house, first thing in the morning to see your children and yet you never showed."

"I told you why."

"I know you left to get tested, and that means everything to me. But Nick, what if I had told Joshua and Susan you were coming and you didn't show? How do you think that would have made them feel?"

"Damn it, Hope, this isn't some game we're playing. These are my children."

"No," she said. "They're mine. Tell me something, do you own a home?"

"What does that have to do—"

"Please, just answer. Do you have a house?"

"Of course."

"How often are you there?"

There was a heartbeat of silence, and then another. The silence became telling and just when she thought he wasn't going to respond, he answered.

"About four weeks a year. But don't you dare try to tell me that how often I'm at some damn house has anything to do with my kids."

There was a finality in his voice; Hope knew whatever she said next, he wasn't going to listen. "Tomorrow Susan and I will be at the hospital by eleven. Why don't . . ." She stumbled, paused. In a couple of weeks, a month at the most, she knew Nick would change his mind and decide that being a father didn't fit into his life. And when he made that decision and walked away, the only way her children would go on unscathed would be because they wouldn't know that it was their father who was leaving them. An abandonment like that was something you never got over. A fact Hope knew firsthand. "You can meet us there, but on one condition."

"I'm listening."

She drew in a deep breath, knew that this was her final card to be played. She just hoped it was the right one. "For the time being, I don't want to tell Joshua and Susan who you are. They're dealing with a lot right now and I think it would be best if we waited. Upsetting them, especially upsetting Joshua, would not help his condition at all."

There was a long pause. "What are you proposing?"

His almost reasonable tone surprised her. "We'll tell them you're an old friend. One from my childhood."

Another pause. "When would we tell them the *whole* truth?"

"Oh, Nick, I don't know. Let's just play it one day at a time, all right? That's about as much as I can handle right now." Hope prayed that they'd never have to tell her children because, God help her, she didn't want them to hate her for her lie.

"I want what is best for Joshua and Susan, too. You know them better than anyone and if you think we should hold off on telling them, we will. But I'm not going to wait forever. When the time is right, if you don't tell them, I will. I'll see you tomorrow."

He hung up before Hope could say another word. She slumped back in her seat and clicked off the phone.

By some miracle he had agreed to her suggestion. That should have made her feel better, feel more prepared for what lay ahead tomorrow. But she knew she'd never be ready for what she was going to have to face in only a few hours.

Seven

TENTATIVE rays of morning sunlight crept through the open garage door. In the corner, a radio crackled out old rock-and-roll tunes. Humming along with Billy Joel as he sang about his Uptown Girl, Hope climbed onto the open front edge of the Wagoneer's hood.

When sleep had proven all but impossible last night, at the first sign of dawn, she'd gotten up and headed to the kitchen to make Susan her favorite breakfast of French toast and bacon, only to remember that she'd forgotten to pick up eggs yesterday. So she'd gotten dressed, written a quick note telling Susan she'd be back in a jiff from the store, then jumped into the Jeep only to find it wouldn't start.

It was a bad beginning to what Hope knew would already be a trying day.

Just last week she'd bought a new set of spark plugs and a few other items, knowing that the Jeep needed a tune-up. She just hadn't had the time to get around to doing it. Well, no time like the present. A few minutes later she was deep under the hood, hard at work trying to break the corroded spark plugs loose.

"Need any help?"

Hope jumped at the sound of her daughter's voice. She peeked out from under the hood. "Hey, sweetie. I thought you were going to sleep in."

Susan rubbed her eyes. "Yeah, well, the phone kept ringing."

With the radio playing, Hope hadn't heard the home line. If the call had been about Joshua, she knew they'd try her cell. Just to be sure, she fished her cell out of her pocket and glanced at the screen to see if she'd missed any calls. Thankfully, she hadn't. "I'm sorry it woke you."

Susan yawned loudly. "The call I answered was from Chels, so that's okay."

"What's Chelsey doing up so early?"

Susan shrugged and picked at a nail. "A group of kids are heading down to the lake and she was wondering if I wanted to go."

"Sounds like fun, but—"

"Yeah, I know. I told her I couldn't go because you're making me go to the hospital."

Part of Hope wanted to relent and let her daughter go to the lake with her friends. But over the last several weeks, Susan had come up with one reason after another to avoid visiting Josh. It had been nearly two weeks since Susan had last seen him. As much as Hope wanted to give her daughter the go-ahead to hang with her friends today, Hope knew she wouldn't. Joshua needed to see Susan as much as she needed to see him—whether she admitted it or not.

"I saw Maddy and her mom last night. When I told them you were coming in with me today, Maddy got really excited. She was hoping you'd bring her those books you'd told her about."

Maddy was a ten-year-old girl stricken with the same type of leukemia as Joshua. Over the last several weeks, Hope had gotten to know the little girl and her mother quite well. And despite their age difference, Joshua and Maddy had developed a strong bond as well. Cancer did that. Connected people—adults and children alike—where before no connection could have been found.

After Maddy had learned that Susan used to take horse riding lessons, the little girl hadn't stopped hounding Susan for every bit of horse knowledge she possessed whenever they saw each other. It was Maddy's dream to one day ride a horse. During one of their short visits, Susan had promised to bring Maddy several horse books from her own collection. Maddy had never forgotten, even though it seemed to Hope that Susan had.

Hope could have just as easily taken the books in herself, but she felt it was important for Susan to. Her daughter seemed to be pushing almost everyone away. Even now, Hope could feel Susan withdrawing.

Responding to her daughter's early question, Hope said, "I'd love some help." She motioned to the tall workbench in the corner and to the plastic bag on top. "Could you grab that bag from the auto parts store for me?"

For the next several minutes, they worked together. While Hope removed the old spark plugs, Susan took the new ones out of their small orange boxes and handed them over.

A warm breeze blew in. From next door, Mr. Udarbe's sprinkler system clicked on and the steady *ch-ch-ch* drifted in and blended with Neil Diamond's gravelly voice coming from the radio. A lawn mower rumbled to life.

As Hope twisted the last spark plug into place, she wondered how she had ever taken her peaceful, mundane existence for granted.

"I don't know why you don't sell this old beast, Mom. It's broken down more than it runs."

Hope angled around and sat on the front edge of the engine compartment. She wiped at her greasy fingers. "Sell Gertrude? But she's part of our family."

Susan rolled her eyes. "Jeez, Mom, nobody names their cars. It's . . . it's just weird."

Her daughter's expression was too serious, like it was most of the time lately. Wanting to put a smile back on Susan's face, Hope pretended to be shocked and leaned forward, covering the headlight closest to her with her hands. "Shhh, or she'll hear you."

A reluctant grin tugged at Susan. "Get a grip, Mom. The thing's a gas hog, it's always breaking down, you have to sit on a pillow to reach the steering wheel, and it only gets AM stations."

"You're right, but I'm attached to the old girl. We've been through a lot together."

"Yeah, right. And the Wright Brothers would insist on flying their first plane even if Boeing offered them a brand-new 747."

"Well, until Boeing comes knocking on our door and hands me the keys to a plane, I think I'll stick with Gertrude."

"747s don't use keys," a deep voice interjected.

Hope nearly tumbled off the Jeep at the sound. She turned so quickly, her head spun.

Standing in the garage's entrance was Nick.

Dressed in jeans and a black Henley shirt with the sleeves pushed partway up his forearm, Nick Fortune was the epitome of every woman's fantasy. It didn't take a genius to understand why he'd recently been voted *People*'s Hottest Bachelor and Sexiest Man Alive! As if one title weren't enough.

Lean on me.

She hated how her traitorous thoughts betrayed her. And hated too how instantly aware she became of how she looked in her stained mechanic's overalls and hair that she had hardly brushed before containing it in a ponytail.

Hope crawled down from the Jeep.

"I tried calling," Nick said, moving toward them. "But no one answered."

Susan, obviously feeling uncomfortable at being caught in

her pajamas, took a few steps toward Hope and tried to hide behind her mom.

It didn't work.

The moment Susan stepped out from the dark corners of the garage, Nick's eyes found her. He couldn't stop staring at her. "Hello," he finally said. Hope wondered if she was the only one who heard how clogged with emotion that single greeting was.

"Uh, h-hi."

Hope looked back and forth between the two. The moment wasn't lost on her. An uneasiness settled in the pit of her stomach, and her hands, tucked safely out of sight in her overalls, knotted into fists. She plastered a smile on her face. "Susan, this is Nick. An old friend." If her voice wavered on the last two words, she was certain she was the only one to notice.

Nick took a step forward. Over the years Hope had seen him in countless interviews and never once had he looked nervous. But now, he looked as tense and unsure of himself as one of her high school kids standing before the class for the first time, reciting Shakespeare. "It's a pleasure to finally meet you."

The irony of his words weren't lost on Hope.

Susan was just as jittery as Nick. "I . . . um. Yeah. Wow. You're Nick Fortune. I've seen your picture. Seen you on TV." She scuffed her slippered foot against the cement floor. "You know Mom?"

Why hadn't Hope thought of this? Of course Susan recognized Nick.

Susan glanced down, caught sight of her pajamas. Embarrassment burned her cheeks. "I gotta go." Without another word, she disappeared through the garage door that led into the kitchen.

Nick stood rooted to his spot, staring at the door Susan had disappeared through. "She has your eyes."

A stillness invaded Hope. "And my stubbornness."

"As I recall, it was your mother who had the stubborn streak."

At the mention of Claire, a tightening formed in the pit of Hope's stomach. What her mother had was a lot stronger than stubbornness.

"It's not just her eyes," Nick finally said, slowly turning to face her. He shoved his hands down the front pocket of his jeans, his thumbs out. "She has your hair, your nose, your small hands. And probably your same tiny feet, but I couldn't tell in those slippers." A ghost of a smile crossed his face. "She also sounds just like you, too."

"You only heard her say a couple of words."

"No, I didn't." His gaze was steadfast on hers.

He'd been listening to them. Standing outside her garage, watching them.

Nick let out a breath, as if he'd been holding it a long time, then ran a hand across his face. "I wasn't prepared, I mean, I'd seen her picture, but—" He looked directly at Hope again. "I can't get over how much she reminds me of you."

Hope didn't know what to say to that. If it had been someone else—*anyone* else—she would have told them of the time when she'd answered the phone and Susan's then-boyfriend, Kyle, had confused the two of them. By the time Hope could interject and clarify the mistake, they'd both been a little embarrassed. Now, it was something they joked about.

It was a small thing, a memory so insignificant only a family member would recall it. But even though those tiny moments by themselves didn't seem to amount to much, they added up and, slowly, year after year, became the thread that bound lives together. For some reason, Hope didn't want to share it with Nick.

Nick looked back to the door.

To anyone else, he appeared invincible standing there in her garage, his shoulders squared, his feet planted firmly on the ground. But Hope wasn't anyone else. Even with the passage of so many years, some things didn't change and some

things you didn't forget. Right now, the way Nick was standing so stiffly erect, as if he were impenetrable, was exactly
the same way he had looked when his father would come
stumbling into school, yelling at the top of his drunk lungs
for his *no-good-bastard-of-a-son to get his ass out here*. And
school hadn't been the only place it happened. It was one of
the reasons the locals had stopped hiring Nick. Not because
he wasn't the best worker they'd ever had, but because of his
father.

"She's nearly sixteen and you caught her in her pajamas,"
Hope explained, answering his unspoken question. "That's
why she ran off so quickly."

His relief was barely perceptible, an ever-so-slight loosening of his shoulders, a minuscule shift that eased some of the
tension from his body, but she saw it nonetheless. And seeing
it sparked her anger. Even after so many years she was still
attuned to his every nuance while he didn't know a thing
about her. "Why are you here, Nick? Have you heard anything?"

"No. It's still too soon."

Hope had known that, but she still had to ask the question.

"Dr. Brandt knows how to reach me when the results come
in. Now all there is to do is wait."

"I've never been good at waiting."

"Yeah, neither have I."

Hope's nerves were getting the best of her, tying her up in
knots. "You didn't answer my other question. Why are you
here?"

"I'd think that was obvious."

"What's obvious is that we were going to meet at the hospital."

"We landed early," was his only explanation. He walked
away from her and over to the opened hood. "I see you still
know how to work on cars."

She glared at him. Didn't he understand how just showing
up upset her whole balance? She wasn't ready—she wasn't

prepared. She needed to be on solid footing when confronted with Nick. Having him catch her off guard, under the hood of a car, in mechanic's overalls for crying out loud—quicksand. If he had done like they'd agreed and come to the hospital, she would be able to handle this better. But when had anyone been able to make Nick do something he didn't want to?

Not her.

He picked up one of the empty spark plug boxes, studied it for a moment, and then set it back down. "I don't think new spark plugs are going to be enough," he said as he continued his inspection of the engine.

"She just needs a little pick-me-up." *If only.*

Nick took a step back from under the hood, angled his head toward her, and grinned. There was nothing phony in his smile. It wasn't that fake "magazine grin" she'd seen on so many of his pictures but an honest-to-goodness, no-holds-barred, the-boy-from-Minnesota smile. A smile that had disrobed her of her good sense and a few other things too many times to count.

He resumed his inspection. With careful scrutiny, he scoured the Wagoneer's engine before turning his attention back to her. And then it seemed to her as if he gave her just as thorough a look over. "What this car needs is retirement."

When had he gotten so close? The solid expanse of his chest captured her entire view. She couldn't help but remember a time when it had been the most natural thing in the world for her to find solace and strength in his arms. When he'd held her so close that the only thing she heard was the beating of his heart.

Hope reached down and grabbed the empty auto store bag off the ground and began shoving part boxes into it. She needed to do something that moved her away from him. Why did her mind continually find a way to loop back around to their past?

Gathering the last piece of trash, she made her way over to the garbage can in the corner and stuffed the bag in on top. She turned and faced him and with the distance now between them, she could breathe again. "The only thing that concerns me about Gertrude is if she will get me back and forth to the hospital."

"Gertrude? Ah, Hopeful, don't tell me you're still naming your vehicles?"

Hopeful. Her heartbeat sped up and her palms turned clammy. How could just one word from him make her remember and feel so much?

"You know about Mom naming things?"

Susan's question startled them both. Neither had heard her return.

Hope turned to face her daughter and all but gasped in surprise. Her daughter looked beautiful. Instead of the baggy sweats and oversized T-shirts she'd adopted of late, today she wore her favorite pair of jeans, a teal shirt, and flip-flops. Last Christmas, when Susan had begged and pleaded for the designer jeans, Hope had balked at the hefty price tag. But from the moment her daughter had unwrapped them, Hope hadn't thought twice about the cost. The look of joy on her daughter's face had been worth every penny.

Like before, Nick couldn't seem to tear his gaze away from Susan. "I do."

"The Jeep's not the only thing she's named."

"Oh?"

"She names everything," Susan continued. "The lawn mower, the telephone, the broom, even the toaster. And if that weren't bad enough, she talks to them like they're real people. Take Henry, for example."

"Susan," Hope said, but there was no stopping her daughter.

"Henry?" Nick prodded Susan to continue.

"The vacuum."

He leaned against the fender of the Jeep, crossing his arms. "I hate to tell you this, Susan, but your mom's been naming things since before you were born."

"Really?"

Nick nodded. "My senior year I bought a pickup from an

old farmer. It had been sitting out in his field, rotting away, and he let me have it for a song. It didn't run, most of the body had rusted away, and I swear some animal had taken up residence inside. But there was something about that truck." A ghost of a smile found Nick. "I spent the next three months solid working on it. I scoured junkyards for replacement parts, spent every dime I'd ever saved on restoring it, and poured hours of hard work into it. I'll never forget the first time I took it out. Man . . ." His voice trailed off into the memory. "The first day I drove it to school, kids crowded around to see. Someone asked me where I had dug up the old Ford. I was just about to answer when your mom informed him that Lucy was a classic 1956 Chevrolet pickup."

Susan rolled her eyes and gave Hope one of those you-didn't-really looks before turning back to Nick. "I hope you set the record straight and told everyone that your truck wasn't named Lucy."

Nick grinned down at Susan and then to Hope, laughter reflected in his eyes. And in that instant, she was sixteen again and in love with the hottest, baddest boy in school.

"How could I? You mom had put in nearly as many hours working on her as I had."

"Mom?"

He nodded. "Where do you think she learned so much about cars?"

Susan looked at Hope and there was a new little glimmer of respect in her eyes. "Cool."

"Yeah," Nick said, and this time his attention was solely on Hope. "Cool."

Susan couldn't stop staring at Nick. She pulled at the ends of her ponytail that hung over her shoulder. "I still can't believe you know my mom. I mean . . . Unbelievable. Chelsey's gonna flip when I tell her. Will I see you again? I mean . . . Mom and I have to leave, but I guess maybe not if the car won't start. Mom?"

Nick shut the hood. "We could always take my car."

"You're coming?" Susan asked, excitement spiking her voice, brightening her eyes.

Hope wiped the palms of her hands against her overalls. "I asked Nick to join us. I thought Joshua would like the extra company."

For the first time Hope could remember, Susan smiled at the thought of going to the hospital.

"Cool," her daughter said again. "But I don't think Gertrude is going to start."

"She'll start," Hope said.

"Susan has a point. Like I was saying, we could take my car."

Hope followed his gaze out the garage door and to the flashy red sports car that was built for two. "And where do you propose we all sit? On the hood?"

Nick's hand rested on the hood of the Jeep. "A quick call to the rental agency and I could have a new car here in less than fifteen minutes."

Hope shook her head. "No thanks. The Jeep will start. She always does."

"Are the keys in the ignition?" he asked Hope.

"Yes."

Nick spoke again to Susan, and Hope saw the effort it was taking him to keep his tone light. "Why don't you hop in and let's see what we've got."

Happily, Susan rounded the Jeep and climbed behind the wheel.

When her daughter was safely out of earshot, Hope said, "Just so we're clear, Susan and I will be going in my car. You can follow in yours."

"I didn't come here to upset you," he said. "Today is going to be hard enough. Why don't we call a truce?"

A truce.

With Nick.

The possibility of it set off all kinds of warning signals in her head. But it was also a lifeline she couldn't refuse.

For better or worse, he was here. *For a while.*

She stuck out her hand, felt the heat from his as he took hold. "Truce," she said.

"Truce," he repeated.

And, as if to seal the deal, the Jeep rumbled to life.

Eight

NICK hated hospitals. He hated the look of them, the smell of them, and even the taste. During the last fifteen years he'd been in and out of more emergency rooms than he cared to remember, but he had to admit that as far as hospitals went, Mount Rainier Children's was the most inviting one he'd ever seen.

An enormous architectural feat of glass and steel, the hospital encompassed what had to be at least a whole square block. Colorful signs punctuated the landscape, clearly directing vehicles and pedestrians alike. Flowers blossomed and overflowed from meticulously maintained beds. Near the main entrance a large fountain held center stage. In the middle of its pool, a man-made hippopotamus peered out. The fountain's gentle sprays cascaded over the amazingly lifelike metal structure, glistening its dark surface. The effect was surprisingly soothing. It was as if the whole purpose was to make a person forget, for just a moment, where they were. But, as the glass doors *whooshed* open and Nick followed Hope and Susan inside, there was nothing—not a flower, fountain, or fake hippo—that could make him forget.

The interior of the hospital was nothing like he thought it would be. Bright murals covered the walls. A fish tank larger than most cars dominated the entrance. And the people. He couldn't get over how many people there were or how fast they were all moving. And loud. Weren't hospitals supposed to be quiet?

A few people glanced in his direction and then did a double take as recognition flared in their eyes. Over the years Nick had grown accustomed to the notoriety he received. It wasn't something he sought or desired, but he'd learned early on it came with the game. He truly appreciated the fans and tried to give back to them for as much as they gave to the sport. But today wasn't about who he was or what he did. He gave a nod in greeting to those who waved and said a quick hi in passing but didn't stop. He couldn't even if he wanted to. Hope and Susan were quickly navigating their way to a large bank of elevators; Nick had to hustle to keep up.

"Over here," Susan said, motioning for Nick to join her in front of an elevator door toward the far end. He was about to ask her why they'd gone all the way down the hallway to this elevator when she explained, "The hospital is built on a hill, so not all the elevators go to every floor." She pointed to each elevator. "See how they're marked: Whale, Train, Balloon, Airplane."

For the first time, Nick noticed the different themes.

"You need to be careful you get on the right elevator. To see Josh, we need to take the Balloon elevators."

Nick was glad for Susan's easy chatter; it broke the silence. Hope had barely said two words to him since they'd left her house and arrived at the hospital. They'd ended up taking separate cars—like she'd wanted. And that had been just fine with him. Except for the part when Hope had insisted that Susan ride with her. He wanted time alone with his daughter— and with his son—to get to know them. One way or another he'd make sure that happened.

Before they'd left, Hope had run into the house and changed

into a long skirt and a pink pullover top. If she wore makeup, he couldn't tell, and in the short amount of time she'd been in and out of the house, she couldn't have spent any time styling her hair. Instead, she'd piled it on top of her head in some sort of messy bun.

For the last sixteen years Nick had been surrounded by women who knew exactly what to wear, how to walk and how to talk. Around the racetracks, gorgeous women were as plentiful as cotton candy at the fair. Their allure was all too apparent. But without even trying, Hope, with her hard fought for smile and tired eyes, captured his attention like none of those women could.

"The first few times we came, we got lost every time. Remember, Mom?"

"What, honey? Oh, yes, we did have a hard time finding our way around." Hope turned to Nick, a frown creasing her brow. "Joshua's chemotherapy treatment is scheduled for just after two today. Chemo is where—"

"I know what it is." Even if Nick hadn't spent the whole plane ride back reading and learning about leukemia, he still would have known.

"Afterward . . . after chemo, Josh doesn't usually feel well. It would be best if we just let him rest."

Nick had read about that too. "If that's your polite way of telling me to get lost, don't worry. I'll make myself scarce. He doesn't need me hanging around then."

Hope nodded, clearly relieved. "Thanks."

The elevator doors *pinged* seconds before they opened and the three of them, plus a handful of other people, got on. Nick was thankful no one on seemed to recognize him.

As the elevator began its ascent, Nick knew that the weightless sensation that settled in the pit of his stomach wasn't caused by the ride. In just a few moments, he was going to see his son.

Susan stood close to him. The small confines of the elevator, combined with the number of people, caused her to stand closer to him than he was sure she normally would. He tried not to make it obvious, but he couldn't keep his eyes off her. He wanted to capture and remember every nuance of her movements, every angle of her face. She couldn't be taller than five-six or five-seven, her mother's height, because the top of her head barely hit his shoulder. He couldn't help wondering how tall Joshua was. Was he as tall as his twin sister? Or taller? At Joshua's age, Nick had already been an inch or so over six feet. He thought back to the picture he'd taken from Hope's refrigerator.

The elevator gave a slight lurch and caused one of the people in front to accidentally knock into Susan. She stumbled, bumped lightly against him. Instinctively, he reached out and steadied her. She smiled up at him, thanked him for his help, and in that moment that same funny weightlessness hit him again.

"Joshua is going to be happy to see you," she said. "He won't believe it, though. A celebrity."

Celebrity.

Not a friend or their father but a stranger they'd only seen on TV or the Internet or in magazines. Not that Nick expected more, but still, it stung.

"I'm looking forward to meeting him," Nick said.

Arriving at their floor, Susan walked on ahead and Nick found himself next to Hope.

She created as much distance between them as possible without making it obvious and that should have suited him just fine. But somehow it didn't. There was nothing in this situation that fit. No road map to follow. He was doing his damnedest to figure it out as he went.

His eyes strayed to her hands, saw the way she continually wrung them when she thought no one was looking. Part of him wanted to take her hands in his, hold them tight, offer her comfort. But then another part—the part that remembered her deceit—wanted to quicken his steps and catch up to Susan.

Large double doors loomed before them, but instead of

passing through, they veered off into a smaller room. Inside were several sinks, stacks of gowns and other medical supplies, and soap and hand sanitizer.

Susan was already at one of the sinks scrubbing her hands with the precision of a surgeon.

Hope explained, "Anyone who enters the oncology department has to wash first. Every patient here has a weakened immune system, so we need to do our best to make sure we don't bring in extra germs."

Nick followed suit, but sometime between the soaping up and rinsing, it hit him. Like nothing else had. Reading about a disease was completely different than its ugly reality, and just behind those doors were very sick children. And his son was one of them.

They were halfway past a nurses' station when a nurse with hair as brown and sleek as a seal's skin stood up and called out for Hope.

Hope stopped and smiled at the young woman, and Nick wondered if anyone else noticed how much that smile seemed to take out of her. "Good morning, Katie."

"Morning. I thought we'd be seeing you shortly." Katie turned to Susan and said hello, too. But as she was talking to them, her eyes kept straying to Nick, and he knew it was only a matter of time before more people recognized him.

"Dr. Parker was in earlier and asked me to page him when you came in."

A look of utter desolation came over Hope. "Is it . . . is there something I need to know?"

"Oh, no." The nurse looked genuinely upset that what she'd said had caused Hope such anxiety. "I believe he only wanted to talk with you about a change in Joshua's treatment schedule. If you could wait here for a moment, I'll see about locating him."

The nurse returned to the desk and picked up the phone.

"Susan," Hope said. "Why don't you take the books to Maddy? I know she'd love to see you."

Susan hesitated.

"Please?" Hope said, holding out a bag. "It would mean a lot to her."

Reluctantly Susan took the books from her mom. She turned to leave, took a step, then stopped and turned back. "Do you want to come?" she asked Nick.

Nick wanted to stay with Hope, hear what the doctor had to say, but there was no way he could refuse his daughter's request. "You lead, I'll follow."

Susan seemed relieved.

"Who's Maddy?" Nick asked a few moments later as they passed a wall mural depicting penguins taking a ride in a hot-air balloon. It wasn't that he was overly curious about a girl he'd never met, because he was so focused on his own daughter and son right now, but he loved to listen to his daughter. To just hear her.

"She's a girl I met a while back. She's got what Josh has. She's ten and has only been able to go to school for three years—and those weren't even in a row. She's been sick a lot." Susan slowed, then turned down a hallway. She hesitated for a fraction, looking at Nick. "I used to think it would be cool to be sick and not have to go to school, but now, well . . . you know."

Nick studied his daughter's upturned face. In so many ways she was nearly full grown, and when he got those glimpses he felt such a sadness and an anger when he thought of all the time he'd missed. But right now, looking at her, he could still see how young she still was. "Yeah. I know."

They stopped at a door on the right. Susan was just about to knock when the door opened and a woman stepped out.

"Susan," the woman said, sounding surprised and tired.

"Hello, Mrs. Keene. I brought these for Maddy." Susan held up the bag of books.

"You are going to make her day. She's down at radiation right now. She'll be disappointed to have missed you."

Susan tried hard to hide it, but she seemed relieved at the news. "Tell her I said hi and I hope she likes the books."

Mrs. Keene took the bag from Susan. "I'll make sure and tell her. Maybe you can stop back by before you leave today?"

Susan stuffed her hands into the back pockets of her jeans. "Yeah. Maybe."

Mrs. Keene gave Susan an understanding smile. "No worries if it doesn't work out. But I did just buy Maddy a new set of markers and a drawing pad. They're on the chair by the window. Do you want to go in and leave her a note? I know she'd love that."

"Sure." Susan turned to Nick. "Back in a sec." She opened the door and made her way to the chair by the window.

"Is this your first time to the hospital?" Mrs. Keene asked.

Nick turned his attention away from his daughter. "Am I that obvious?"

"Only to a mother who's spent half her daughter's life in this place." A whisper of a smile creased her face. "Are you here to visit the children?"

"Children?"

"We get so many celebrities on this floor I'm getting pretty good at recognizing faces. Even football players and I've never watched a game!" She smiled. "You're the racecar driver, right? The guy on the cover of *People*?"

"I'm Nick."

"That's right!" She readjusted the books in her arms. "Nick Fortune. Sorry. Faces I'm great with, names not so much."

Susan reemerged. "I left the note on her pillow. She can't miss it."

"Thanks again, Susan. Maddy's going to be so happy. But why didn't you tell me you had a celebrity with you? My baby girl has had a few rough nights, so I'm operating on little to no sleep. I almost didn't make the connection."

"Nick's a friend of Mom's. He's here to see Josh."

"It's such a treat for the kids to get visitors, especially

famous ones," Mrs. Keene said to Nick. "Josh is a great kid. Tell him hi from room 419. He'll know who it's from. Oh, and Susan? Can you ask Josh if he'd add Maddy on his Snapchat? I think that's what it's called." She laughed, gave her head a small shake. "Technology and names. Not my strong suits."

Nick and Susan wove their way back down the hallways they'd come. Susan navigated the confusing maze with ease. As they walked along, Nick couldn't help but see inside some of the rooms. So many young kids.

"Here we are," Susan said.

With a start, Nick realized they were standing outside the door to his son's room. As Susan started to open the door, Nick frowned. He wanted nothing more than to be with both his daughter and his son, but he knew Hope would want him to wait. Not that he felt like he owed her this courtesy, but it wasn't for her. It was for Joshua. Nick didn't want to do anything to upset his son. "I think I'd better wait for your mom."

"You'd be waiting all day, then. Once Mom gets talking to the docs, she's gone." Susan rolled her eyes in that typical teenager fashion that never would go out of style. "You'd think she was the doctor the way she drills them with her list of questions. I'm surprised they don't turn and run when they see her coming."

Nick had a hard time matching the quiet girl he had known with the woman her daughter described. The Hope he'd known would not have had the courage to question doctors.

Susan's hand went for the door once more.

"Still, I should—" Before he could finish, she opened the door.

Susan seemed to hesitate for the briefest of moments before walking inside. Her delay had been so fleeting, Nick almost believed he'd imagined it.

"Hey, Josh," she said.

Nick wavered, and then he saw the young man lying on the hospital bed and there was no force great enough to keep him away.

Joshua pushed himself upright, then sat up in the bed. He grabbed the baseball cap from his bedside table and pulled it on over his thinning hair. He didn't say a word and his facial expression didn't change, but it seemed to Nick as if those two small acts took everything out of him.

Nick felt paralyzed, rooted to where he stood. The young man in the bed was so different from the young man in the picture. Nick knew from the date stamp in the bottom right-hand corner that the picture had been taken just over two years ago, but looking at his son now, he would have thought a decade or more had past. Joshua's appearance was so altered. His skin was so pale that he all but disappeared against the stark white pillowcase. The only color on his face was the dark circles under his eyes. And those eyes. Those blue, blue eyes. Nick knew them only too well. They were the same ones he saw every morning in the mirror.

Nick had been in more wrecks than he could remember, broken more bones than he could count. A handful of years back, he'd fractured his leg two days before a race. The doctors told him it had to be casted immediately, but Nick had refused. In a cast, he couldn't race. So for four hours behind a wheel, he'd endured excruciating pain as he pounded the track and pushed his body. He'd thought he'd known true pain. But now, looking down at his son, he realized he had been a naïve fool.

Afraid he'd be caught staring, Nick scanned the room as he fought to rein in his emotions. In so many ways the room was a typical hospital one: a narrow, adjustable bed; a tray on wheels; a chair in the corner; a window on the far wall. Machines surrounded the bed, beeping intermittently. A bag of fluid hung from a tall silver pole; its clear fluid *dripped, dripped, dripped*. But that was where the similarities ended. This room looked more like a teenager's bedroom than a hospital room.

Photos of happier times and posters (mostly of football) covered blank spaces on the walls. A row of get-well cards lined the windowsill. In the far corner, a bundle of balloons floated, their vibrant colors a welcome relief against the dull white walls. Stacked on a shelf near a small sink and mirror were several board games and a football. A pale blue afghan lay across the arm of a chair, as if it had been left on purpose, for nights Hope stayed late and needed something to help her stay warm. A small stack of books was on the stand next to Joshua's bed, along with an assortment of miscellaneous things: a box of Kleenex; a pad of paper; a couple of pens; a plastic cup with a straw; an opened roll of mints, its silver wrapper unfurled. Instead of hospital-issued bedding, a red and blue comforter covered Joshua. A robe hung from a door Nick thought probably led to the bathroom. Slippers were tucked underneath the bed.

A lump settled in Nick's throat. It was a room you *lived* in, not one you just stayed in for a few days. The realization nearly brought him to his knees.

Susan sat down in the chair by the head of the bed, tucking her legs underneath her. "Nick, this is Josh. Josh, Nick. He's a friend of Mom's."

Suddenly, it occurred to Nick that he should have brought something. A gift. A card. A game. *Something.* "H—" Nick cleared his throat, started again. "Hello, Joshua." Nick stood there with his empty, empty hands and felt like the outsider he was.

"Hey. I know you. You're a football player, right?"

"No." Nick shifted his weight and crossed his arms. Cleared his throat.

"Don't mind him," Susan said to Nick. "The drugs have scrambled his brain." To her brother, she said, "He's the race-car driver. You know. Nick Fortune."

"Oh. Wow. Cool." Joshua angled his head toward his sister. "He knows Mom?"

"Crazy, right?"

Joshua scratched his head, knocking his hat askew. Tugging on the bill, he pulled it back into place. "Where is she?"

"Mom? Waylaid by the white coats." Susan opened the drawer next to her and rifled through. "I stopped by Maddy's room. She wasn't there but her mom was. Said to tell you hi and when your phone gets fixed, add Maddy on Snapchat."

"That little pest," Josh said, but it was obvious by his tone he liked the young girl. "Just what I want. More visuals of this place. But yeah. For her."

"Denny texted again. Said he's gonna be in town on Friday and wants to stop by and see you."

"Tell him—"

"I'm not your secretary. You tell him."

"I can't, remember? My phone's broke."

"Yeah. Yeah. Mom needs to get it fixed, but you do have a phone by your bed." Susan made a motion toward the room phone. "Use it."

Joshua slouched in the bed. "I'm not using *that* phone. Text Den to stay away. I don't want to see him."

"He's one of your best friends. I don't know why you don't want to see him."

Josh shot Nick a look that clearly said he'd rather Nick wasn't privy to this conversation. "None of your damn business," Josh said to his sister.

"I told you—"

"Text him." Josh glared at his sister, then lowered his voice. "Or I'll tell Mom about you and Kyle. About that night you said you were at Chelsey's."

Susan slammed the drawer closed. The metal connected with a loud *clank*. She flounced back in her chair, a deck of cards in her hands. She opened the box, upended it, and waited for the cards to slide into her hand. With stiff, jerky motions, she began to shuffle. Several cards flew onto the floor. She grumbled, then picked them up. "Fine," she finally said to her brother.

Through the exchange, Nick had felt uncomfortable, but he didn't know what to do. Stay. Leave. Stay? He hadn't realized how long he'd been staring until Josh started to squirm under his scrutiny. Nick looked away. Once again he saw the signed poster of the Seattle Seahawks and remembered the autographed football next to the board games. He walked over to where it rested on the shelf, picked it up, examined it. "Nice. You must be a fan."

Josh shrugged. "Not really."

"I'm usually out of town, so I don't get to catch many games, but when the Vikings made it to the playoffs, I was there." Nick gave the ball a small toss, then put it back in its stand. "Your team's been doing great the last few years. Do you see many games?"

"A few."

Susan grunted. "He watches them all."

Nick hid his smile. He'd never had a brother or sister, and it was fun to watch these two interact. "I tried out for football my sophomore year. Couldn't play to save my life."

Joshua eyed him out of the corner of his eye. "Not at all?"

"Total washout. How about you? Do you play?"

Josh shrugged. "Some."

Susan gave another snort. "Josh has played *forever*. He's the quarterback on our high school team."

"Quarterback. Nice." Nick nodded in approval. "You must be good. Really good. Maybe I could watch one of your games this fall."

Josh averted his gaze, stared blankly out the window. "I don't play anymore."

The vacant look Nick had glimpsed in Joshua's eyes before he'd turned to look out the window tore at Nick. He'd seen that same look in fellow drivers after they'd received career-ending news. But that wasn't Joshua's situation. Nick knew he needed to do something—say something—to give Joshua hope. To wipe away that look of utter devastation that had entered his eyes. But what? What did Nick know about helping a teenage boy? Especially one who was dealing with all that Joshua was?

Feeling completely and utterly helpless and useless, Nick

stared at Joshua. Looked to Susan. He saw the cards in her hands and said the only thing he could think of: "Anyone interested in playing cards?"

"No," Josh said, still facing the window.

"He doesn't feel like it because we only play Go Fish. It's the only game Mom knows."

"I can't say Go Fish is one of my favorites either."

"What do you like?" Susan asked, unfolding her legs. She drew the wheeled table up close and began to shuffle once more. "Hearts?"

Definitely not. The heart was one area Nick didn't think he was very much of an expert on. He shook his head.

"Gin rummy?" she tried again.

"No. Don't know that one either."

"Crazy Eights?"

"No."

"Be Mean to Your Neighbor?"

"Never even heard of that one."

"How about Old Maid?"

Nick burst out laughing. "They actually have a game called that?"

"Yeah," Susan said, clearly exasperated with his lack of card knowledge. "How about canasta? All old people know how to play that."

"Old, huh?" He chuckled. "Definitely don't know that one."

Susan stopped shuffling and stared at him. "Well, what do you know how to play?"

"Poker."

Josh turned back around. "Poker?"

"Yeah. It's about the only card game I know, but not sure you two would be interested."

"You're not talking about poker where you play with matchsticks or pretzels or toothpicks, are you?"

Nick dug into his pocket and pulled out some change and a few small bills. "Sorry. This is all I got."

A smile broke out across Joshua's face. Leaning over, he

opened the same drawer Susan had been searching through earlier. When he sat back up—a bit winded, Nick noted—he held a small plastic container. He emptied it onto his comforter, and a jumble of change spilled out. "Mad money," he said. "Or, at least that's what Mom calls it. For a run on the vending machines if I feel like eating. Susan's got the whole place staked out."

She nodded, began dealing. "Second floor. Best selection."

Nick grinned and picked up the cards Susan shot his way. This was one game he was going to enjoy losing.

HOPE pushed through her son's hospital door to the sound of laughter. Honest-to-goodness laughter. It was so unexpected, she stopped in her tracks. In front of her was a picture she never thought she'd see: her children and Nick, together.

Seated on opposite sides of Joshua's bed, Susan and Nick were deep into a card game. Heaped in the center of Joshua's serving table sat a small mound of coins and a few dollar bills. Nick's elbows were braced on the tray, his cards fanned out before him. The fabric of his shirt stretched across his back, making him seem larger than life, a solid presence in this stark environment. Susan was in a nearly identical pose, hunched over her cards, staring at them intently. Her lips were pursed in deep concentration. She looked to Joshua, to the pile, then back to Josh again before centering her gaze on Nick. "Can he really do that?" she asked.

"Yes," came Nick's reply, a smile hovering. "But only if he doesn't get caught."

Josh threw his head back and laughed again, loud; his cheeks flushed. "Who me? Get caught? Never. Read 'em and weep. Full house. Kings over eights," he said as he laid down his cards, waited for the other two to fold, then scooped up the money.

"Cheat!" Susan cried.

"Only if you can prove it." Josh kept corralling his winnings.

"I don't have to. Nick knows how you did it. Don't you, Ni—" Susan broke off. "Mom!"

Three pairs of eyes focused on her at once, but only one set had the power to unbalance Hope's equilibrium. For several moments, she was captivated by Nick's stare. His gaze seemed to be probing, searching for something she didn't understand—or if she was completely honest with herself, something she didn't *want* to understand.

"Hey, honey. Hi, Josh." Hope walked to the end of the bed and gave Joshua's covered foot a squeeze. "How are you doing?"

"He's cleaning me out, that's how he's doing," Nick said, rising. His chair scraped against the linoleum.

Joshua's grin widened. "Yeah, I made all of . . ." He counted the money. "Three dollars and twenty-seven cents."

Nick chuckled and the sound of his deep, strong laughter resonated around her, in her.

"What took you so long?" Susan asked, gathering the cards.

"Dr. Parker was with a patient when the nurse paged him."

At the mention of his doctor's name, Joshua slumped back against his pillow, the sparkle fading from his eyes. "What did he want?"

It was like a blow to the stomach, so deep did Hope feel his despair. "They've upped your chemotherapy to noon."

As if on cue a nurse came through the door. She nodded a quick hello to all of them before centering her attention on Joshua. "Hello, Josh," she said in a cheerful voice. "Ready?"

As the nurse busied herself, Hope turned to Nick to see him already gathering his coat and preparing to leave.

"That's my cue," Nick said. He held out his hand and after only a moment's hesitation, Josh reached out and shook. "It was great to meet you, Josh." Nick's voice grew deep with emotion and Hope wondered if anyone else detected it, but as she glanced around, she realized she was the only one.

"I'll expect a rematch. And soon," Nick said, and Hope knew how much it must be costing him to keep his tone light.

"You got it."

As Nick turned to leave, he paused, his gaze on Hope. "Could I talk with you outside for a moment?"

"Sure," she answered, then said to Susan and Josh, "I'll be back in just a minute."

Hope followed him out into the hallway.

The minute the door closed Nick said, "Was that really all the doctor had to say?"

Hope nodded. "Yes. I'm sorry. I should have thought . . ."

A weight seemed to leave him. "Thank God."

"Nick—"

"I know what you're going to say. But I couldn't wait to see him—"

"Thank you." Hope didn't know who was more surprised, Nick or herself. Too many times she'd walked into that room and found her son lying on his bed, staring off into nothing, looking as if he couldn't wait to leave this world. But today . . . today had been different. And all because of this man standing next to her. "To hear Josh laughing when I walked through those doors, well . . ." How did she explain to someone what their lives had been like since Josh went back into the hospital?

"I would like to come back later this afternoon, after Joshua's chemotherapy," Nick said.

"After chemo is rough. A lot of the time he's nauseous and tired. He'll sleep for several hours. Some days he sleeps for the rest of the day."

"No problem. If he's not awake or feeling up to it, I'll make myself scarce until he feels better. And one more thing. I'd like to be included in all future consults regarding Joshua's treatments."

Hope drew in a deep breath. From now on, until Nick decided fatherhood wasn't for him, he was going to be a real presence in her children's lives. She realized too that when she visited the hospital, there was a chance she'd run into him.

"I have a few things I need to do in the city," Nick said.

"Oh?"

He shrugged on his coat, shoved his hands in the front pockets. "I thought maybe Susan would like to come along."

Hope felt a surge of panic. She didn't want Susan to leave with Nick, spend time alone with him. What if he forgot their agreement, told Susan who he really was? But it was more than that. Already, her children were forming an attachment to this man who would eventually leave. "No. I don't think that'll work. I have to leave by four thirty for work."

Nick glanced at his watch. "No problem. I can have her back in time."

"No."

Nick stared at her long and hard. "Why don't we ask her and see what she'd like to do?"

Hope knew what her daughter's answer would be and, less than two minutes later, as she watched Nick and Susan walk down the corridor together, she felt a fissure penetrate her family's foundation.

Nine

AFTERNOON traffic packed the downtown streets as Nick and Susan left the hospital. Cars honked, buses screeched, and frustrated pedestrians who couldn't cross the busy streets cursed the passing vehicles—but Nick barely noticed.

He'd just spent the morning with his children. *His children.* The enormity of that realization washed over him.

He thought back on the morning, the time he'd spent with Joshua and Susan: their farce of a card game that had turned into one big cheat fest, and the laughter they'd all shared. Gazing down, Nick looked at the young woman walking next to him. Remembered her kindness to that little girl named Maddy, and to her own brother, and Nick felt his heart swell with pride. Not that he'd had anything to do with the upbringing of this remarkable young woman. Hope had done this—Hope, who had barely been old enough to drive the last time he'd seen her—had somehow blossomed into an amazing mother. The home she'd created for her children. The sterile, normally depressing hospital room she'd turned into a teenager sanctuary for her son—or as close to one as possible. And Nick knew it wasn't by example. Claire Montgomery was one of the coldest women Nick had ever met. At the thought of Claire, Nick wondered if Hope had heard back on Claire's test results. He made a mental note to ask her next time he saw her.

"So," Susan said as they paused by the sidewalk's edge, "where are we going?"

A taxi rounded the corner, and as it approached, Nick stepped out onto the street and hailed it. When the yellow car slowed and then stopped, he opened the back door for his daughter. So many thoughts rushed through his mind at once, and all of them centered on the girl before him.

For the first time since his impulsive request to take Susan with him, he felt unsure. He knew next to nothing about teenagers—teenage girls in particular—but he was willing to do anything, learn anything, to become a part of his children's lives.

As Susan scooted across the black vinyl seat, Nick sat down next to her and shut the door. At her continued questioning look, he said the one word that had never failed him where a female was concerned. "Shopping. We're going shopping."

A large smile dawned across her face, and her answering "Cool" was enough to make Nick smile too.

HANGING up her smock, Hope flicked off the last of the lights and carefully made her way to the employees' rear-door exit. The grocery store was tomb-silent as she gathered her coat and purse and locked the door on the way out. She was beyond tired tonight. Working the night shift left little time for sleep—not that sleep came easily these days—but the more night shifts she could pick up, the more time it afforded her to spend with Josh during the day. And the extra money it provided during the summer months was invaluable.

The lot was deserted except for her Wagoneer. An ethereal glow from the parking lot lights made Hope's old Jeep look even more tired and worn. Both of them were in need of a major overhaul. Easing behind the steering wheel, she inserted the key and turned.

Nothing.

Nada.

Zip.

Not even a little cough.

Or a sputter.

She took the key back out and stared at it—as if that would somehow make a difference—then reinserted it.

Still nothing.

Twice in one day. That had to be some kind of record.

She dropped her forehead onto the cool curve of the wheel.

After what seemed like an eternity but in reality was no more than a few moments, she opened the door and got out. Moping about her broken-down car wasn't going to change the facts; besides, home was less than five miles away. She could walk.

Grabbing her purse off the bench seat and slamming the door shut, she set off.

She knew she could go back into the store and call Dana for a ride, but Hope also knew she wasn't fit company for anyone tonight. Besides, the walk would do her good. And Susan would be asleep at this late hour and wouldn't worry if Hope got home later than normal.

Her tired feet carried her out of the parking lot and down the street. It wasn't until several minutes later when she reached Gustofson Street that her steps slowed and she began to notice her surroundings. The warm night breeze coming off the nearby bay. The rhythmic sound of the water as it brushed across the shore and then swept back out, only to return moments later.

As the street stretched out in front of her and the continued sounds of the nearby water began to work their magic, Hope tried to figure out just why she was in such a foul mood. But she knew.

Nick.

And all those gifts.

A new laptop. The newest Xbox gaming system with over two dozen different games. A bag full of the latest movie releases. Some type of hovercraft or drone thingie that lit Josh up like a Christmas tree. But the gift that really captured Joshua's attention was the new phone. The latest and greatest iPhone with all the bells and whistles that Hope knew cost as much as a mortgage payment. She knew because she'd been trying her hardest to save the money to buy Josh one.

Nick had given Joshua the next best thing to a ticket out of the hospital—not only the means to communicate with the outside world on her son's terms, but also things to make the hours and days he had to spend stuck inside a hospital room pass with a little more enjoyment.

In her mind, she saw again Nick and Susan entering Joshua's room, their arms so full of gifts that a nurse had to open the door for them. Joshua's look of shocked disbelief when Susan had set gift after expensive gift in his lap. And Susan's excited chattering as she showed her brother not only what Nick had purchased for Josh, but what he'd gotten for her.

Tears stung her eyes. She couldn't believe she was—

Jealous.

The word bit deep, took hold. She felt smaller for having the feeling.

Maybe not jealous, exactly. Sad. Upset. Angry at herself for not being able to give Josh everything he wanted. She was his mother. A mother should be able to provide everything for her child.

But he's their father, her inner voice reminded her.

She shoved it away. Anger felt better than sadness; she latched on to it with both hands.

She understood Nick's need to buy them things. She knew he was trying to make up for lost time. Lost years. But there had to be a balance. Someone needed to talk to him, make him understand that what he was doing was wrong. And the only person who could do that was Hope.

Soft, fat raindrops began to fall from the charcoal sky. She looked down the road. To her left lay Main Street. To her right, the way out of town. To the left, the hotel Nick was staying at. To her right, the way home.

Right or left.

Left or right.

In that instant, it seemed as if she'd been standing at this crossroad for the whole of her life. Damn their truce.

With renewed energy in her steps, she turned left.

NICK stood by the only window in his hotel room. Below him lay Main Street, already deserted even though it was just a few minutes after ten. A soft rain fell. The streetlamps that lined the sidewalks cast soft cones of light on the steepled rooflines of the storefronts, illuminating the intricate scrollwork on the buildings' trim. On the far side, hidden now by darkness, was the large bay. Tranquility: an apt name for such a motionless town. He went to open the window, suddenly craving the smell of fresh air.

The window wouldn't budge. It was sealed shut.

Perfect.

He turned away in disgust and sat down in one of the room's two chairs: a hard, brown thing that had undoubtedly been all the rage in the seventies. Now it just looked as neglected as the rest of the furnishings.

Nick picked up the remote and hit the On button. The TV flicked to life. As he surfed the channels he wondered not for the first time what he was doing in this throwback town and not in Seattle, staying at some five-star hotel.

An *I Dream of Jeannie* rerun came on. With a grimace, he clicked to the next channel. A blonde manipulating a man into doing what she wanted. No thanks. He had enough of that reality.

He continued to cruise the channels, finally settling on late-night news. Not that he was interested in watching, but anything was preferable to the silence because in that quiet, he heard too much.

A newscaster with dark hair and blue eyes was speaking. Nick didn't hear a word the young man was saying; instead, Nick was remembering another young man with black hair and piercing blue eyes.

Joshua.

Nick hated this lie he was perpetuating. He wanted to tell the kids his real relationship to them, but after seeing Josh, Nick now understood Hope's concerns.

Today had flown by, his time with Joshua and Susan all too brief. But there would be tomorrow and tomorrows after that. Which meant he would be seeing a lot more of Hope, too.

His feelings on that were raveled. He was mad as hell at her for not telling him about the twins, and that wasn't going to change. But he also knew that against the odds, she'd made a true home for his children. One that far surpassed the houses either of them had grown up in. He thought again of Susan's kindness, quick smile, and quirky sense of humor. He saw Joshua's steely determination to remain stronger than his disease. And how he found laughter in a card game even surrounded by such a stark reality. Grudgingly, Nick had to admit those traits weren't ones his children were born with— they'd learned them from their mother.

But admiring the woman Hope had become and getting involved with her again were two completely different things. And he meant to keep them separate and apart.

Nick shook his head, flicked off the TV, and grabbed his phone. He was tired of the direction his thoughts were taking and wanted a clearer distraction. He punched in his crew chief's number. Dale answered on the second ring.

"Hello?" came the sleep-muffled voice.

"How's the track?"

There was a loud groan. "What time is it?"

"Late," Nick said, for once not caring about being inconsiderate.

"Just a sec." There was a rustle of blankets, the sound of running water, as if Dale needed to splash some on his face to wake up. "Okay," his crew chief said after only a few moments. "What was that? Oh, yeah, the track. It rained like a son of a bitch earlier this week and even if we don't see another raindrop, I'm still not liking the looks of turn two. I don't think she's gonna completely dry out."

"What's the forecast?"

"Forty percent chance of showers tomorrow but clear for qualifiers on Saturday. The weekend looks mostly clear, except there's a new system due to hit late Sunday afternoon."

"What time on Saturday?" Nick didn't need to elaborate. Dale knew he was asking about what time Nick was scheduled to run his qualifying rounds—the test runs that would determine Nick's track position come Sunday.

"One thirty. But I'd like to get in a couple of runs before that. I've been working on that tranny, making those adjustments we'd talked about. I'd like to take her out and see how she goes before the qualifiers."

Images of Susan and Joshua snapped into focus. For the first time since Nick had entered the NASCAR circuit, the upcoming race wasn't capturing his full attention. That knowledge floored him.

"I'll see you tomorrow afternoon," Nick said.

"Afternoon? Are you crazy? You need to be here first thing in the morning. I've reserved the track. That tranny—"

"Afternoon," was all Nick said before ending the call.

He stared at his phone, tempted once more to call Mark about his test results. But Nick shrugged off the idea. He'd already talked to him twice today and gotten assurances that Brandt would call the moment he knew anything.

Nick grabbed his coat, shrugged it on, and put his phone in the coat's pocket. He made for the door intent on getting something to eat. Halfway there, he stopped. Earlier tonight he'd spied a reporter snooping around, asking questions, and, Nick was pretty sure, snapping a few photos. News of his arrival would spread like a brush fire in this small town. But that didn't mean he had to fan the fire.

He ran through his options. Which weren't many, considering he was staying in a hotel without room service. Then Nick remembered the young boy who'd brought him the phone message the other night. He'd seen that same kid down in the lobby earlier tonight. Nick picked up the hotel phone and called down to the front desk.

Ten minutes later, with a hundred-dollar bill tucked securely in his pocket, the bellboy was heading back down with assurances to Nick that he knew exactly where to find a steak dinner.

Nick had only just resettled into the stiff chair when a knock sounded at the door. With a shake of his head, he got up, wondering what the kid had forgotten.

He opened the door. Only it wasn't the bellboy on the other side. It was Hope.

And in that instant, Nick knew exactly why he hadn't stayed at a hotel in Seattle. He'd come back to Tranquility for just this possibility.

SELF-RIGHTEOUS indignation had propelled Hope all the way down Main Street, through the rain and through the inn's front doors. Resentment continued to fuel her as she waited for Sally (an acquaintance she knew through the kids' school) to tell her Nick's room number, which she did with hardly a pause and not a question. A definite perk of small-town living! Hope's outrage carried her up to the second floor, bolstering her right until the moment her hand connected with the door of room 210. And then that momentous energy slid away as quickly as it had come.

Thoughts of fleeing tempted her, but before she could act on them, Nick was there, looking as irresistible as Hope remembered. She thought about how she must look: *exhausted* and *old* were the two words that came to mind. Dressed in her work outfit of black polyester slacks and red polo shirt with the store's logo imprinted on the left breast pocket, she felt dowdy. And that wasn't even taking into account her hair. The sudden rain shower had pulled it from its confines and left it loose and curly and dripping wet.

"Hello."

"H-hi." Thoughts of retreat were center stage once again. What had possessed her to come here? "It's late. I shouldn't have come. We can talk tomorrow—"

Nick stepped back and pushed his door open further. "Come in."

"It's late."

"You already mentioned that."

"We can talk tomorrow."

"You already said that too. Now why don't you say what you really came here to say? But preferably not standing in the hallway."

The open door loomed before her, and suddenly standing out in the hallway seemed childish. She was thirty-two years old, for crying out loud. An adult. A mother. Not a starstruck teenager unable to hold on to a single thought when the hottest bad boy in school spared her a look.

So why was her heart thundering and her palms sweating?

Hope eased through the door and made her way into the room. The only other time she'd been in one of the inn's rooms was several years ago during Thanksgiving. Dana's parents had come for the holiday and Hope had agreed to pick them up on the way out to Dana's apartment. But it looked to Hope that the décor hadn't been altered a bit since then.

"You can stand if you want, but I do have an extra chair."

Startled, Hope looked up. Taking a deep breath, she closed the door and moved to the seat across from Nick.

"Can I get you anything? Something to drink?"

"No. Thank you, I'm fine." She teetered on the edge of her chair.

"You're out late."

A drop of water fell from her hair and plopped onto her nose. She brushed it away only to have another droplet fall. "I was passing by and thought I'd take the chance of stopping to see if you were awake." Water trickled down her back and she fought the urge to squirm.

Nick got up and walked into the bathroom only to reappear a moment later carrying a white towel. He passed it to her. "Wasn't there parking nearby?"

"You could say that." Hope patted her face and then made a feeble attempt at drying her hair. Ever since she'd entered the room, she'd avoided directly looking at him, but now she lifted her gaze and met his. And instantly wished she hadn't.

Reclined in the chair with one ankle propped on the other and his hands casually folded across his flat stomach, he was the epitome of relaxed sex appeal. Expensive, exclusive, out-of-her-reach sex appeal; no matter how hard she fought against it, a part of her would always be attracted to this man to whom she'd given her young and yet-unbroken heart. But just as there were similarities between the man before her and the boy she'd known, there was also just as many differences. And it was to those differences Hope clung, using them to insulate her against the past. Against the memories that had been coming more and more frequently.

"I called the hospital less than an hour ago," Nick said, surprising Hope. It felt like an invasion of her family's privacy, having him check in at the hospital. That was her job. "Joshua was doing fine, and I can't imagine Susan getting into too much trouble since this afternoon, so if it's not about the kids . . ."

It was all the opening Hope needed. "Actually, it is about the twins. More specifically, the gifts you bought for them."

"I see."

No, he didn't. And somehow, she was going to have to make sure he did. "You can't go around buying Josh and Susan thousands of dollars' worth of gifts."

"Why not?"

Why not? "Because . . . because it isn't right, that's why. What are they supposed to think when a stranger shows up with more presents in one day than they'll see in a year? *Five years?*"

The moment she'd said "stranger," Hope knew she'd made a mistake. Nick's body tensed. He uncrossed his legs and sat up. His blue eyes that had only held laughter and love all those years ago were now sharp with condemnation. "Not a stranger by choice."

"You can't buy their affection, Nick."

"Maybe I went a little overboard today, but I've got a lot of years to make up for."

Hope let out a deep breath. The white towel lay like a misshapen ball in her lap. Smoothing it, she folded it, unfolded it, and then refolded it. "I know you're angry with me, but I can't help wondering if this isn't your way of getting back at me."

"Don't flatter yourself. This has nothing to do with you."

His words stung. Just as he had intended.

The ringing of Nick's cell phone stalled any further conversation.

Hope got up, glad for the interruption. She'd come and said what she wanted to say and now couldn't wait to get away. "I'm sure you'll want to get that," she said as she gathered her purse and coat.

Nick rose. "Wait. I'll get rid of whoever it is. We still have things we need to talk about."

"We can talk tomor—"

Nick held up his hand, silently asking her to wait as he glanced down at the number calling. Recognizing the number, he gave Hope a look she couldn't identify until she heard him say, "Dr. Brandt. Hello."

The strength went out of her limbs and she sank back into her chair.

Please, God. Please.

She studied Nick's face, heard him say, "Yes. I see. Are you positive?"

His expression gave nothing away and yet she knew. A wail started down deep, deep inside her, and when Nick ended the call and turned to her, she knew what he was going to say before he even did.

"I'm sorry."

"Noooo."

"I'm sorry," he said again, moving closer.

Through her watery vision she saw his deep regret, his torment, but she couldn't concentrate on that, so great was her fear.

"I'm not a match."

"No." She shook her head. "No. No. No. Dr. Brandt is wrong. He's wrong." She felt herself slipping, sliding down the front of the chair and landing on the ground. "He's wrong. We'll do the test again. You'll see. You are a match. Oh, God." Her voice caught on a sob and she felt sick. She looked at him, felt as if she were breaking into a million pieces. "You *are* a match. Don't you understand? You have to be."

HOPE'S words tore through Nick, leaving him raw and exposed. He had been so sure—so confident—that he'd be a match. But he wasn't, and the knowledge devastated him.

"What am I going to do now?" Hope was saying, her voice strained with pain and reed thin. "What am I going to do?"

"You're going to stay strong for Joshua."

"Strong." Hope said the word almost as if it were foreign. "I've never been strong." Tears streamed down her face. "All I ever wanted was to be the best mother I could, but . . . I must have done something wrong."

"You didn't."

"I failed him. It's my fault he's so sick."

Nick used the pad of his thumb to wipe her tears away. "It's not your fault."

"Why couldn't it be me?" Her cries became harder, her shoulders shaking uncontrollably. "It *should* be me!"

For the first time in his life, Nick wished he'd been born into a huge family. Where droves of people genetically linked to Joshua could get tested. "What about your mother?"

"Claire? The woman who won't even say her grandchildren's names, let alone see them? To make sure she gets tested, I'll have to personally go and drag her to the clinic."

Nick felt a surge of anger toward anyone who could be so callous to the suffering of a child. But when that child was your grandson . . .

"What else can I do?" Hope's question was muffled in heartache.

Nick thought about the numerous calls he'd made. How he'd had Joshua's records faxed worldwide to the most elite, highly sought-after pediatric oncologists. And, according to what Dr. Brandt had told Nick earlier today, those specialists had concurred. Mount Rainier Children's Hospital and Dr. Parker were doing everything humanly possible to save Joshua. There was nothing more they could do.

Nick looked down at Hope. She seemed so small and fragile sitting on the floor. So alone.

In a move as natural as breathing, Nick sank down next to her, tucked her head in the crook of his shoulder, and gathered her tight. He ran his hand up and down her back murmuring words, trying to offer comfort. He brushed her hair off her forehead and tucked the damp curls behind her ears. For the longest time, she sat stiffly in his embrace, refusing the comfort he offered, until finally, with a soft, anguished cry, she sank into him. His arms tightened protectively around her, rocking her gently. For the longest time, they sat there on the carpet, surrounded by their pain and grief, as they tried to find the strength they would need for the road ahead.

Long after Nick thought Hope had fallen asleep, she looked at him, her eyes brimming with so much sorrow it broke his heart.

"I w-was s-s-so sure you'd be a match." Her voice stuttered over the tears.

"Ssshhh," he murmured, kissing her forehead, her eyes, the bridge of her nose.

"I was so sure . . ."

Her sorrow was more than Nick could bear; he offered her comfort the only way he could.

Hope's soft lips parted under Nick's. He felt the momentary hesitation, the slight questioning, and then the sweet acceptance. Cradling the back of her neck in his hand, he deepened the pressure.

Desire flooded him. "Ah, Hope."

He angled his head, gently turning hers to better meet his.

She untangled her arms from beneath his and looped them around his neck, pulling him closer. His body pressed into hers, and she flattened against him.

"Nick." Her plea was like a long-forgotten caress.

A knock sounded at the door.

He ignored it. But they didn't go away.

Knock.

Knock.

"Nick." She shook his shoulder, obviously able to come to her senses a hell of a lot quicker than he was. "Nick, someone's at the door."

"They'll go away," he murmured against her mouth. "They must have the wrong room."

Knock. Knock. Knock.

Nick rested his head against the soft curve of Hope's shoulder. "I'm going to kill whoever it is."

"Mr. Fortune? Mr. Fortune, sir. I have your dinner," came the door-muffled voice.

Nick all but growled in frustration. Rising, he went to the door and flung it open.

The young bellhop jumped back in scared surprise. "Uh . . . h-hello, Mr. F-fortune. H-here's your dinner and change."

"Keep it." He grabbed another bill from his pocket—he had no idea of the denomination and frankly didn't care—and shoved the money at the bellboy, then slammed the door closed.

Turning, he faced Hope.

She was standing, her hair a gorgeous tousle of curls. Her coat on, her purse over her shoulder.

"Stay."

"I can't." She scooted to the door, had it opened in an instant, and was out in the hallway in a flash.

In less than ten strides Nick had caught up with her by the elevator. "Why can't you stay?"

"I just can't, that's why. And please don't ask me anymore."

The elevator doors pinged open.

Nick had always been a man who tackled an issue head-on, but one look at Hope's ruined face and he let the matter drop. For the moment. "I'll walk you to your car, then."

Hope looked startled. "No. That's okay."

Ignoring her, he stepped into the elevator with her.

They rode down in silence and walked through the small, softly lit lobby without talking. It wasn't until they were outside, standing under the awning, that Nick spoke. "Which way?" He glanced up and down the street but couldn't see her car.

"Oh. Um. I parked around the corner."

"You lead, I'll follow."

Hope hesitated. She glanced first to the right, then the left, then finally at him. "Look, Nick, I'm perfectly capable of walking myself home."

"Don't you mean driving?"

She let out a deep breath. "No, I mean walking. My car's back at the grocery store. It wouldn't start."

"Christ." Nick swore with more animosity than he was feeling, but it felt good to vent some of the frustration that had been building since the knock on his door. "Why do you insist on driving in that piece of sh—"

"I don't need this. Good night, Nick." Hope spun on her heel and headed down the street. Her strides were quick and sure, her shoes slapping against the wet pavement.

"Hope. Wait."

She kept right on walking.

Muttering a curse, Nick dug his car keys out of the front pocket of his jeans and dashed across the street to his rental. In less than forty-five seconds he'd caught up with her.

"Get in."

She didn't even spare him a glance.

"Hope, for God's sake. It's pouring. Get in."

Nick slammed the car into park and jumped out. He came around the front of the car and stepped in front of her. "In. Now."

She stared at him, undoubtedly deciding whether to call his bluff.

God, he wanted her to open her mouth and defy him because he knew exactly how he would shut her up.

"I—" Hope began, but when Nick took a step toward her, she must have seen something in his eyes because, without another word, she turned to the car and climbed in the passenger side.

The ride to her house was as short and silent as their trip down in the elevator.

Nick pulled into her driveway. He got out and headed around to her side of the car. But before he was even halfway there, she was out and running up the pathway that led to her front door. It closed behind her with a solid thud.

THE house was dark and silent as Hope closed the door. She didn't bother to take off her coat, or kick her shoes off, or turn on a light. Instead, with steely determination she marched over to the phone and picked it up, not caring that it was nearly midnight. She punched in the long-distance number and waited for Claire Montgomery to answer.

Ten

NICK stood in the darkened room and looked down on his sleeping son. Wind rattled the hospital room's single window, and the rhythmic *ping-ping-plunk* of the rain against the glass blended with the soft *hiss* and *swoosh* of the medical equipment surrounding Joshua. A sole night light, positioned above the bed, cast a yellow-gray pallor across Joshua's features. Even in the faint light Nick couldn't help but notice Joshua's drawn cheeks, the dark smudges under his eyes, and the ever-present pain that pulled at his features.

You're not a match.

Even now, several hours later, Dr. Brandt's words continued to haunt Nick. He wasn't a match. Two days ago he hadn't known he had a son and now, now he'd learned that not only was he a father, but he was a father who couldn't save his dying child.

A fresh wave of despair washed over Nick along with a sense of bitterness toward the woman who had denied him so much. But alongside that resentment mushroomed a sense of admiration. He saw again the pride in her eyes whenever she looked at her children, the fierce determination that steeled her words as she fought to save their son, and the absolute anguish that overtook her when they learned Nick was not a match.

Joshua stirred in his sleep, and Nick stiffened. A slight frown flitted across Josh's features as he tried to find comfort in a bed that offered none. Trying to roll over onto his stomach, he stopped halfway as tubes and IVs hindered his progress. Finally, after a few more twists and shifts, he perched himself partway on his side, facing Nick, and settled. Soon, a soft snore escaped.

Nick's hand slowly unclenched from the cold bedrail. He hadn't even realized he'd grabbed it when Josh had started to stir.

A lock of thinning hair had fallen across Joshua's face, and Nick stretched his arm out, ready to brush the hair away. Only before he did, he stopped, holding his hand in midair as indecision crept through him. What right did he have?

Nearly sixteen years ago he'd been denied everything when Hope had cut him out. He wasn't a member of this family. If Joshua woke and found Nick in his room, how would Nick explain his being there?

His children were nearly sixteen years old. And then another question haunted him. If by some miracle Joshua and Susan wanted him in their lives, what type of father could he hope to be?

Slowly, Nick withdrew his arm and it fell back to his side, hanging there all but useless.

He clenched his hand into a fist as frustration built. He should have rights, damn it. He should be able to come into his son's room at any time of the day or night and know he would be welcomed. Accepted. He should have been in Joshua and Susan's life from the beginning. And he should be able to find a way to save his son. He *would* find a way.

* * *

"OKAY, I've brought the suitcase; now are you going to tell me what this is all about?" Dana walked into Hope's bedroom and plopped the case on the bed.

Hope didn't turn around. She didn't dare. Instead, she reached into her open dresser drawer and pulled out a neatly folded stack of pants and threw them onto the bed. Shutting the bottom drawer, she moved on to the middle drawer. Two stacks of tops followed the pants. Using her hip, she slammed that drawer shut, then yanked open the top one, only to pull so hard it came off its track and fell to the floor. "Damn it." She left it where it lay and scooped up a pile of underwear and a handful of folded socks. She dropped them by the other piles on the bed.

"Hope." Dana put her hand on Hope's arm. "Honey, what's going on?"

Hope turned away quickly, dislodging Dana's hand. She knew she was being rude, but she couldn't help it. If she looked into her friend's eyes and saw the worry and concern she heard in Dana's voice, it would be Hope's undoing. And she was too close to the edge now.

Unzipping the suitcase, she tossed in clothes.

Dana's hand stalled her once more. "Please, won't you tell me what's going on?"

Hope wrapped her arms around her stomach. She felt a well of grief so large it nearly buckled her. "You can stay here, with Susan, right?"

"Yes, of course I can. Just like I told you earlier this morning on the phone. I'll stay for as long as you need me to, and I'll go and see Josh."

"Thank you. I know Susan's fifteen and can stay by herself, but lately . . . lately she hasn't been the same."

Dana sat on the bed. "Honey, lately none of you have been the same. How could you be? How can any of us be? But right now, it's *you* I'm worried about." Dana eyed the heap of clothes on the bed. "That's an awful lot of clothes for what you said would be a quick trip. Long or short trip, I'm here no matter how long you need me to be. But I know you. You wouldn't be leaving unless it was incredibly important. Will you tell me where you're going?"

Hope followed her friend's gaze and realized she'd all but emptied her dresser. She began to haphazardly shove almost all of her clothes back. "A day. Or two. I don't know."

Dana stayed Hope's frantic "unpacking" with a gentle touch of her hand. "Tell me what's going on."

Tears pooled in Hope's eyes, threatening to spill over. She swallowed hard. She felt as fragile as a china doll and knew she was barely holding on to her sanity as it was. If she started explaining to Dana, she would lose what little control she still had.

Concentrating on the task at hand, she flicked through the hangers, searching for her black coat. Where was the damn thing? And why in the hell did she have all these clothes? She didn't wear half of them. She searched deeper, farther back, until her hand came into contact with the feel of soft leather. Relieved, she pulled her coat out from the far back. As the garment came into the light, a pain erupted into her chest.

"Oh, God," she gasped, unable to catch her breath. Tears ran unheeded down her face. "Oh, God."

"Hope?"

Dana's voice came to her, but it sounded so far away, muted, as if it came from inside a tunnel. Hope tried to focus on it, to grasp onto something else besides what was in front of her. But no matter how hard she tried, there was no looking away. Through her watery vision, Joshua's red-and-white letterman's jacket swam before her eyes.

She leaned forward, tried to stem her grief, but that only made it worse. She was so close to his jacket she could smell the leather; the scent made her think of pep rallies, Friday night lights, *of Joshua*. "Oh, God."

"Honey, it's okay. It's only Joshua's jacket."

"He's not a match. God help us, Dana, he's not a match."

"Who? Who's not a match?"

Hope could barely get the word out. "Nick."

"Oh, honey." Dana gathered Hope in her arms and held her tight. Her embrace was strong and Hope found herself letting Dana support her, letting Dana be the strong one for just this once.

"I was so sure. So positive that calling Nick would be the answer. And now, now that I have, he's back in my life and the twins', and I—" Hope willed her tears to go away. She'd spent too many hours last night crying. Now, she needed to get busy. Keep moving. Be strong. Find a way to save Joshua.

She pulled out of Dana's hug.

She rehung the jacket and went into the bathroom. Gathering her toothbrush, toothpaste, deodorant, and hairbrush, she looked around the countertop and knew she was forgetting something but couldn't think of what it was and really didn't care. She walked back into the bedroom.

Dana stood by the bed, her eyes red with tears. The suitcase lay open on the bed in front of her; Hope's messy piles of clothes had been refolded and organized and repacked.

Dana wiped her eyes. "Are you going to tell me where you're headed?"

"To Minnesota. To Claire's to make sure she gets tested. I'm not taking no for an answer."

Shock registered on Dana's face. "You can't go alone. I'm coming with you."

"No." Now it was Hope's turn to lay a comforting hand on Dana's arm. "I need you here. Joshua and Susan need you here."

"But—"

"There's no other way."

"But why do you have to go? I mean, what if she's been tested and you just haven't heard?"

"She hasn't been. I called Joshua's doctor this morning and asked. Not only had he not heard anything but he'd double-checked with the doctor Claire was supposed to see.

They haven't heard from Claire. She has no intentions of getting tested. I know it." Just the thought of her mother's blatant uncaring was enough to make Hope feel sick all over again.

"But why go there? Why not call her on the phone and insist she get tested?"

"I've called." Hope thought of last night, of the numerous phone calls she'd made during all those dark hours. "But she's not answering. I'm sure she's screening to avoid talking to me. If I don't get there, Claire Montgomery will never see if she can save my son." Hope's voice caught on the last words.

"She can't really—"

"Yes, she can. She's not like your family, Dana. When there's a tragedy you band together. Claire wouldn't even begin to understand something like that."

Hope wiped her eyes. Tears and heartache weren't going to cure her son. Only a bone marrow transplant would, and time was running out. Hope could feel it as only a mother could. A relative was their best chance at a match. She knew what she had to do. She would fly to Minnesota and drag her mother to the doctor's office if that was what it took to get Claire to do the right thing.

"How are you going to get there?" Dana asked.

"I'm going to fly."

"You're scared to death of planes. Never mind that you've never been on one. I remember the year you saved to take the kids to Disneyland and you spent half your vacation driving because you couldn't step on a plane."

"I'll just have to get over it. I can't drive to Minnesota. I don't have that kind of time. And even if I did, Gertrude is in the shop. I need to do this *now*, Dana."

A soft look of understanding passed over her friend. "Yes, of course you do. But I know you can't afford this. All of your money goes to Joshua. I wish—"

"I know." Hope squeezed her friend's hand in gratitude. Dana didn't have the extra cash any more than Hope did.

Hope had tried booking a ticket early this morning when

it was clear that Claire refused to pick up her phone, but she'd been denied. Her credit cards were maxed. It was then that she knew she had only one option.

"So if neither of us has the money . . . how are you going to afford the ticket?"

Hope drew in a fortifying breath. She'd been awake all night just thinking . . . and dialing . . . and thinking, and calling her mother's number time and time again. After three hours and still no answer from her mother, Hope knew she needed to take a different approach. But when she couldn't book a ticket no matter how hard she'd tried and pleaded, the one idea that had been persistently pushing itself to the forefront of her mind, insisting on being heard, wouldn't be ignored a moment longer.

"I'm going to ask Nick for a loan." Hope was surprised at how normal it sounded; as if she'd said nothing more ordinary than *I'm going to the grocery store.* But she knew there was going to be nothing easy about the asking. Asking anyone for help had never been one of her strong suits, and asking the man who had abandoned her would be damn near impossible. But for her children, she would do anything.

"You're what?!"

The doorbell rang.

"That'll be the cab I called."

"Wait a minute. You can't tell me something like that and then leave. And a cab? Why? I can drive you to wherever it is you're going."

"No, I need you here."

The doorbell rang again.

From the top of her dresser, Hope grabbed the piece of paper. "Here." She handed it to Dana. "I've jotted down Claire's number and address just in case you need it. I don't know yet where I'll be staying"—definitely not with her mother—"but I'll call tonight and let you know. And"—she paused—"you should know that I haven't told the twins where I'm going or who I plan on seeing. If Claire refuses—"

"You don't want them to get hurt. I understand. What do I say if the kids ask about Nick?"

"They won't. Nick and I agreed that for now they'd only know him as an old friend of mine."

Shock widened Dana's eyes. "I'm surprised he agreed."

"To tell you the truth, I was too. Thankful but surprised."

The doorbell rang again.

"Don't worry. Claire isn't going to refuse you."

"You're right, she's not." Not if there was any way humanly possible for Hope to prevent it. "Susan's still sleeping. I tried waking her to explain I have to go and see someone about Josh but I don't want him to know that yet. For now, all I'm telling him is that I'm not feeling well. I told her I'd explain everything later. She mumbled an okay but I'm not sure she even heard. She can always reach me on my cell. I called Josh and explained I can't come to the hospital for a day or two."

Hope hated lying to her children, but she really didn't see any other alternative. Josh had accepted her explanation without question, knowing that anyone with an illness, even the slightest of colds, was forbidden in the oncology department. There was no way anyone wanted to compromise a sick child's already weakened immune system. Hope had been relieved when Susan had been too tired to ask too many questions. Hope knew it was a temporary reprieve, but she'd take it. Right now, all she could focus on was getting to Claire.

The doorbell rang again, louder. As if the person pushing the bell was growing impatient.

Hope glanced to the half-packed suitcase.

"Go," Dana said, shooing her out of the room. "Answer the door. I'll finish here."

Hope grabbed her purse from the bed and made her way down the hallway. She opened the front door, expecting to see the taxi driver. Only it wasn't the driver on the other side.

"Nick."

"We need to talk."

Eleven

NICK didn't waste time with pleasantries but stepped into the narrow entryway only to come up short.

The stunned, surprised look on Hope's face slipped away to be replaced with a look of—*relief*? Right. Nick would have laughed at his own gullibility if their situation weren't so dire. Relief was not an emotion Hope felt whenever he was near.

From the moment he'd shown up in Hope's yard, she'd been doing everything in her power to distance him as much as possible from her life. From his children's life. Without a doubt, this morning would be no different.

But he was done with Hope's barriers. She didn't want him in her life, she'd made that abundantly clear, but she wasn't going to keep him separated from his kids. Nick never again wanted to feel like he did last night standing by Joshua— removed, isolated. A stranger to his children. He was their father.

Before Nick could say anything more, a tall woman with red hair hurried around the corner of the hallway, a black suit-case thumping against her side. Catching sight of Hope and then Nick standing in the entryway, she came to an abrupt halt and let out a soft *oomph*. It was obvious by the redhead's expression that catching sight of Nick had thrown her off balance.

Hope didn't lose a beat. "Thank you," she said to the other woman, taking the suitcase.

The other woman momentarily forgotten, Nick looked pointedly to the suitcase. "Going somewhere?"

"Yes."

"Your trip is going to have to wait. What I have to say is important."

"Actually, I was on my way to see you."

If Hope had said, *They made a mistake and you are a match*, Nick wouldn't have been more surprised.

"Why don't we go out on the front porch and talk," Hope said, taking a step forward, her suitcase brushing against his thigh.

Separating. Distancing. She didn't even want him in the house. Nick stayed right where he was. "Why don't we talk in the living room?"

"Nick, be reasonable. It's not even six in the morning."

He glanced at his watch before he could stop himself. Was it really that early? He rubbed a hand across his eyes, across his jaw. He almost felt bad about showing up so early. *Almost.*

"Susan's still asleep," Hope was saying, "and I don't want our voices to wake her; besides . . ."

He waited, then prompted when it became clear she wasn't going to continue, "Besides?"

Hope hesitated, readjusting the suitcase's handle in her grasp. "I'm waiting for a cab," she finally said. "If I'm outside I can see when it pulls in."

Nick would have laid money that that wasn't what she'd originally been going to say, but he let it go. He had other things—bigger things—on his mind. Like figuring out a way to save his son. Wasting time arguing about where they talked was pointless. "Fine." He stepped to the side and opened the door. "Lead on."

It was then, when Hope went to walk by, that he remembered the woman standing behind Hope. It was clear Hope had no intention of introducing them.

Nick shifted, partially blocking Hope's exit and angled his head toward the tall woman behind her. "Are you going to introduce us?"

No. The word all but hovered in the air between them. Nick didn't need to be a clairvoyant to hear what Hope wanted to, but didn't, say.

The same frustration that had consumed him last night in Joshua's room overtook him once again. This was a small thing, Hope's reluctance to introduce him to someone she knew. But in his mind, it grew. Final straw and all that. It was time she realized he was here to stay.

He waited, not moving, looking first to Hope, then to the other woman, then back to Hope. It didn't take her long to get the none-too-subtle hint.

"Nick, this is Dana. Dana, this is Nick."

He held out his hand. "Hello, Dana."

Dana's hand felt cool in his. "So you're Hope's Nick." She grasped his hand tighter, almost giving it a squeeze.

Hope all but pushed him out the door.

She walked down off the small covered entryway porch, down the cement path, not stopping until she reached her driveway. There she set her suitcase down and then turned and faced him.

"Like I said earlier, I was on my way to see you."

"You weren't going to call first?" Nick knew the moment he said the teasing statement, it was a mistake. Not only did Hope not get his reference to the question she'd asked him the last two times he'd shown up at her house, but his attempt at putting some life back into her sad, bleak eyes backfired. A dark shadow came over her, obliterating what little color had been in her cheeks.

"What I have to ask is too important to say over the phone."

Apprehension tightened Nick's neck. He wasn't sure what

Hope was going to say, and truthfully, he wasn't sure he wanted to hear. "Hope, there's something I need to say—"

"No." She cut him off, then softened. "Please. Time is running out." Nick could see how much it cost her to say those words. "Joshua needs a transplant and the odds of finding a match through the marrow donor program are slim. Our best chance is with—"

"Claire."

They said the name simultaneously, and in that moment Nick knew Hope had been up all night just like he had, wondering and worrying and planning and praying.

"Yes." Hope nodded. "Claire hasn't bothered to get tested. I know. I've checked. I have to fly to Minnesota and force her to if she won't do it on her own."

"Fine."

"I need to borrow money."

"Fine."

Shock or surprise or a combination of both widened her eyes. "Fine? Just like that, no questions asked?"

"No questions asked."

"Don't you want to know how much I need?"

"No."

"It's for airfare," Hope explained. "And I want you to know, I'm not the kind of person who goes around asking for handouts. Needing financial help. I'm not irresponsible. It's just . . . It's just with Josh . . ." She shook her head, brushed the hair off her forehead. "Never mind. That's nothing for you to worry about. But I want you to know, I'll pay you back. Every cent. With interest."

"Christ, Hope. I'm not worried about getting paid back."

"Well, I am."

"I have enough money—"

"Either you agree to let me pay you back or I'll find a different way." Resoluteness strengthened her spine and sparked a fire in her green eyes. Nick found the combination intoxicating.

A car pulled into the driveway and they both turned. A yellow cab stopped behind Nick's rental. The driver shifted into park and lowered his window. "You call for a cab?"

"Yes," Hope called out. "I'll be with you in a moment."

"Okay." The window went back up as the driver waited.

Hope turned back to Nick. "I meant what I said. Every cent."

"I don't give a damn about the money."

"I do," she said quietly. "A lot."

It was clear that talking about money made Hope uncomfortable. For now, he let it go.

She picked up her suitcase. "Do you want to follow me to a bank, or—?"

"To the bank?"

"Yes. To get the money. Then I'll have the cab take me to the airport."

Suddenly, it hit him. She planned on making this trip without him.

Like hell.

"Wait a second," he told her before walking over to the cab. The driver lowered the window once more. "Change of plans," Nick said, reaching for his wallet. He pulled out a couple of bills and handed them through. "We won't be needing you after all."

The overweight man folded the money and tucked it in his shirt pocket. "It's your dime, Mac." He was gone before Nick could blink.

"Hey, wait." Hope came running up beside him. "Wait. Stop," she yelled at the disappearing taillights. She turned on Nick, anger in her voice. "Just what in the hell do you think you're doing? I needed that cab."

"No, you don't."

"Damn it, Nick."

He went back to where they were standing, grabbed Hope's suitcase, and deposited it in the trunk of the SUV. Definitely a car that could seat more than two. "We are going to see Claire."

"*We?*"

He opened the passenger door for her. "Yes, we."

THEY were on a plane. Together.

That fact alone should have been enough of a shock. But it wasn't. They weren't on just any plane, any flight to Minneapolis. They were on Nick's plane. *Nick's jet.*

He. Owned. A. Plane.

No wonder he didn't care about the money she'd asked to borrow.

She'd known he was wealthy, but this . . . She glanced around. This was like nothing Hope had seen before. Or imagined. Luxury, convenience, extravagance, and pure comfort were stylishly contained in the curved walls.

Hope stood just inside the rounded doorway and all but gasped in amazement.

Creamy white leather chairs were artfully positioned around the spacious interior. A dark wood—mahogany perhaps—created a sleek wainscot around the lower half. In its highly polished sheen, the dimmed overhead lights shimmered.

Nick walked up beside her and gently took her elbow, guiding her farther in. He motioned to the dozen or so oversized chairs. "Make yourself comfortable. Do you want anything? Coffee, tea?"

Or me popped into her head before she could stop it.

"Or something to eat?" Nick finished.

Pink stained her cheeks and Hope quickly reached down for her purse, pretending to search for something just so she could hide her heated face. "Um. No thanks."

"If you change your mind, the kitchenette is over there."

Hope peeked up and caught the general direction.

"And there's a phone on your left. Feel free to use it."

"Thank you," she said again.

"I need to talk to the pilot, so I'll be up front. Give me a holler if you need anything."

It wasn't until Nick disappeared toward the front of the plane that Hope drew her first easy breath.

We are going to Claire's.

We.

Never in a million years had Hope thought she'd be able to convince Nick to go with her. Not that she'd even entertained the idea of asking him. What would be the need? But to have Nick not only want to go with her, but insist upon it, left her shocked and speechless.

She chose a seat by the window and sank down into the soft leather. Fears and worries came at her at once, but she pushed them aside. She forced herself not to dwell on the negatives. On the fact that none of them—not her, Susan, Dana, or Nick—was a match.

Hope remembered clearly the day she and Susan had gone in to get tested. From the moment they'd had their blood drawn, Hope's emotions had run the gamut. For years, Hope had shied away from religion. From prayer. She'd seen the darker side of worship through her mother; it had soured Hope to believing in a higher power. But from the moment the doctor had told them Joshua was sick, Hope had done everything in her power to make him well. And that included prayer. Hours on her knees, pleading for her son's health. So while they waited for their test results, Hope had prayed and begged like never before. She prayed for Joshua's instant healing. Prayed she was a match. Prayed she could save her son. But her prayers about the results of Susan's test were jumbled. While great advances had been made in the extraction of bone marrow, there were still risks involved with the procedure. How could a mother desire to put one of her children at risk to save her other child? But then, how could she not?

Despair threatened to drown her. Hope fought to refocus on the positives. She *was* on a plane. She *was* on her way to Minnesota. She *was* going to see Claire today.

But she was with Nick.

Not a positive. No matter how hard Hope fought it and no matter how many years passed, the pain of his abandonment would not go away. She could still feel the cold rain soaking through her thin white dress, chilling her to the bone, as she'd stood on the courthouse steps, waiting, shivering, wishing, hoping, praying for a boy who never showed.

In three months, Hopeful, I'll be back. I promise. Three months to the date. Wait for me at the courthouse. I'll be the guy wearing the smile and holding the rings.

Even now, she was surprised how much pain the memory still caused. Not only because he'd never shown. But because she had been foolish enough to still believe he'd show even after he'd stopped calling her and disconnected his phone. How foolish could she have been? How blind and naïve. How stupid!

She'd waited and waited and waited, huddled under an eave that offered no real protection, still believing Nick would come. It wasn't until the thunder and lightning had started that she'd been forced home. It was as if she could hear that thunder all over again . . .

Hope jumped, startled. It wasn't her memory's thunder but the plane's engines preparing for takeoff.

With a tight grip, she clutched the armrest and squeezed her eyes shut. Over and over she told herself there was nothing to worry about. Absolutely nothing at all. People flew all the time. It was safer than driving a car—or so she'd heard.

She took several deep breaths and began to repeat to herself, *For Joshua. You can do anything for Joshua.*

The plane lurched forward. She dug her nails into the armrest, felt herself break out into a cold sweat.

Images of downed planes from the evening news flashed

before her eyes. All at once the impossibility of it hit her—
how could this great big tub of tin barrel down a strip of
ground and then propel itself into the sky?

She sucked in several more breaths and struggled to concentrate on anything else. She made a list in her mind of
things she needed to do. She'd call the hospital as soon as
they got in the air and she could loosen her grip, and she'd
try her mother again, too.

The plane picked up speed. Jostled and bumped. Hope felt
like a toy being tossed around in a child's backpack.

She kept her eyes closed, tried to relax her grip on the
armrests but couldn't. She would get through this, just like
she would get through a day with Nick. Just because he had
insisted on coming along didn't mean that he would be bur-
rowing his way any deeper into their family. For the here and
now he wanted to be a part of Joshua and Susan's lives, of
that Hope had no doubt. But what she did doubt was his ability to stick around. In a month or two or six, he'd be gone.
The only way to protect her heart and her children's was to
keep Nick at a distance.

They would fly to Minnesota and talk with Claire and then,
since they were using his plane and pilot and didn't have to
rely on a commercial flight and schedule, they could fly back
tonight. Short and sweet.

In less than twenty-four hours she'd be back home, back
to her children and her life. And she would have made sure
Claire had been tested. That was all that mattered. Not Nick,
not their past. Saving Joshua was her number one priority.

It took Hope a moment to realize that the plane had leveled
out. Carefully, she opened one eye and then the other. A beautiful blue sky dotted with fluffy cotton-ball-like clouds
stretched out before her as far as the eye could see. She made
sure to keep her gaze up, knowing that looking down was a
bad, bad idea. But just keeping her eyes open seemed to take
a Herculean effort, and she realized that lack of sleep from
the night before was catching up with her. She saw Nick make

his way back toward her. She recognized the look on his face. He wanted to talk. And there was a lot they needed to iron out. But the thought of delving into those deep, murky waters right now, when she was already wrung out and exhausted and worried beyond belief, was more than she could handle. What energy she did still have she needed to focus toward getting her mother's agreement to be tested. She let her heavy eyelids close. Pretending to sleep was better than having a conversation about things she didn't want—or wasn't ready— to discuss.

Twelve

NICK pulled into her mother's driveway. In a rental car he had procured without the slightest hesitation or question. Just like the airplane, he made everything seem so seamless.

He parked the car and cut the engine. Without the noise from the motor or the music from the stereo, the absolute silence in the vehicle became telling. But Hope didn't feel like breaking it. Couldn't, even if she wanted to. All she could do was stare straight ahead, straight out the windshield, and straight at a vision she'd thought she'd never have to endure again.

Directly in front of her, looking as unapproachable as she remembered, stood the three-story domain that had been her home—no, she shook her head. Not her home. It had been her . . . she searched her mind, trying to find the right word to describe what role this house had played in her life, but no matter how hard or how long she thought, the only thing that came to mind was *place of residence*. It was a cold description. Nearly as cold and unfeeling as the woman who lived in it.

Little had changed about her mother's house during the sixteen years Hope had been gone. The house was still painted a sterile white and the trim was still blue, but now, on closer inspection, the trim color was a lighter shade than the harsh, overpowering cobalt it had been all those years ago. The short driveway had been paved and white window boxes had been added, but her mother's pride and joy—her rose garden—was exactly the same. Row upon row of meticulously tended blooms filled the perimeter of Claire Montgomery's front yard.

A shuffling sound came from the driver's seat.

Nick. She been so caught up in her memories that she'd all but forgotten he was in the car next to her. That fact alone—that she could forget he was right next to her—told her just how much her upcoming reunion with her mother affected her.

Sunlight glinted through the window and cast his profile into sharp relief. Sometime during the drive from the airport to Claire's house, he'd shed his coat. His arms were tanned from the sun and toned from hard work. His body filled the interior of the rental car, but instead of feeling intimidated by his size, Hope found herself gathering strength from it. He looked so strong, so solid sitting next to her. For the first time since they'd left her house she realized how thankful she was that he was here with her. She had no problem facing her mother alone, but knowing Nick would be next to her brought her no small sense of relief.

Briefly, she wondered what he was thinking. What he was feeling. He was back in a town he hadn't been able to leave fast enough. Back to face a woman who'd told him every chance she got that he'd never be anything more than the son of the town drunk.

Nick angled in his seat. "Ready?"

She was here. She was at her mother's house. And she was ready. More than ready to do whatever it took to help her son. "Absolutely," she said, and opened the car door.

The porch boards squeaked as they made their way to the front door. With detached observance Hope noted there was no welcome mat positioned in front of the door, no pot of cheerful flowers to beckon visitors, no sign of greeting at all. Obviously Claire was as anxious for visitors now as she had been when Hope still lived here.

She rang the doorbell.

A dozen different greetings flitted through her mind as she waited. Part of her wanted to yell *Surprise!* the moment her mother opened the door and watch as the shocked expression took hold of her face. Another part of her didn't want to say anything until Claire made the first move. But the largest part of her wanted to just say, *Hello. Get your coat, I'm taking you to the doctor's.*

A moment passed, and then another. Hope waited a few more seconds and then pressed the doorbell again, harder. Knowing her mother, she'd be fixated in front of the television totally immersed by whatever religious program was being broadcast and wouldn't hear the bell.

Hope tipped her head and strained to hear inside the house, to hear the television, to hear those telltale footsteps come toward the door. But only silence greeted her. She laid on the doorbell again.

Nick took a step back and peered into the large front window. But Hope knew he wouldn't be able to see a thing; her mother always kept the curtains closed tight, just like she kept her heart.

"I'm going to check the garage and see if her car's gone," he said, straightening.

"You don't need to. It'll be here," Hope said, more to herself than anything else. She watched as Nick headed back down the pathway toward the garage. Her mother's car would be there, of that Hope had no doubt. It was Friday. After her father had walked out on them, Claire left the house only twice a week. On Wednesday afternoons and Sunday mornings. Wednesday was the weekly church luncheon and Sunday . . . Sunday was for church.

Her mother's routine had never wavered in the years Hope

had lived at home. Every Sunday, at precisely 9:45 a.m., decked out in hat and gloves with daughter in tow, Claire got behind the wheel of her blue Lincoln and drove straight to the Lutheran church on Fourth and Main. She parked in the same spot, sat in the same row, in the same pew, in the same spot, with precisely five minutes to spare before the ten a.m. service. After church she'd retrace her exact route home (unless there was a committee meeting organized by the good women of the church and they needed to stay an extra hour or two) and only deviate long enough to stop at the Piggly Wiggly, where she bought exactly one week's worth of groceries. No more, no less. Wednesdays held to almost an identical schedule, except no daughter and instead of sitting in the sanctuary, the women met in the church hall. There were no spontaneous trips or shopping sprees or a night at the movies. No part-time job (an inheritance from her parents had seen to that) or volunteer work. Claire Montgomery refused to deviate from her self-imposed schedule, even if it meant not seeing her only child perform in the high school production of *Romeo and Juliet*. Claire Montgomery was a woman you could set your watch by. And a woman who still wanted nothing to do with her only child.

This time Hope ignored the doorbell and pounded on the door. "Open up, Claire. I know you're in there." She pounded once again, just to make sure her mother heard, and just because it felt damn good. "Open up," she shouted again.

"Her car's gone." Nick was back beside her.

"Someone probably borrowed it." Hope pounded on the door again.

"You know as well as I do that she'd be the last person to let someone borrow her car."

Hope ignored Nick and beat against the front door again. Her mother had to be home. She had to be. They couldn't have come all this way for nothing.

"Hope." Nick placed his hand on her arm, gently stilling its movement. "She's not home."

"She has to be."

"We can come back later—"

"She's home. She just doesn't want to see me." Hope shook off his hand and left the front porch, making her way around to the back of the house. If her mother thought she could hide in the house and wait for Hope to leave, she had another think coming.

As she made her way around the side of the house, she stopped and peered into the windows. But just as she remembered, curtains blocked each window, making it impossible for her to see inside. She reached the back door and without even knocking first, she tried the knob. Locked tight. A sinking sensation settled in the pit of her stomach. Maybe Nick was right. Maybe her mother wasn't home.

No, she *had* to be.

Images of Joshua floated through Hope's mind and a fresh surge of anger poured through her. Damn her mother if she thought for one moment she could ignore her grandson.

Hope banged her hand against the fiberglass door. And then she did it again. And again. And again until she lost count. Her fist began to throb but she ignored the pain. She was going to get into that house and see her mother. Nothing was going to stop her.

"Open up, Claire. Open up," Hope yelled. She slammed her fist against the door again, but even as she did, the sinking feeling in the pit of her stomach came back.

"Hope," Nick said quietly from behind her. She hadn't even realized he was there. "Hope—"

"Don't. Don't you dare tell me she's not home."

"I wasn't going to."

"I'm going to get in."

"I know."

"Don't you dare try to stop me."

"I won't."

That brought her up short. "Then what were you going to say?"

Nick's wide stance didn't change, but Hope felt a subtle shift in him nonetheless. "If she's in there, she's not going to answer the door."

"Tell me something I don't know." Hope dropped her forehead to the cold door, her balled fist quiet by her head. It throbbed with pain. The rush of adrenaline that had fueled her only moments ago was gone. "I have to see her," she said, her breath fanning against the door. "I have to."

"Don't you think I know that?"

The hard edge in Nick's voice penetrated Hope. She lifted her head and looked at him.

"He's my son too, Hope. But banging on a door Claire's never going to answer is getting us nowhere. I think we should . . . Never mind. Just follow me." Nick turned and left.

Hope hesitated. She didn't like Nick's highhandedness, but she'd run out of her own options. Plus, right or wrong, there was a kind of comfort to be found in his strength, the conviction with which he spoke. Like he had all the answers. He was a presence she couldn't ignore even if she wanted to. And right now, she wasn't sure she wanted to. Besides, getting to Claire was all that mattered.

Hope found Nick at the back of the house, looking up to the second floor, looking up to her old bedroom window. At her approach he glanced down and to her. "We have a few options."

"Which are?"

"I can get in through a door."

"They're locked."

He gave her a look. "Do you really think a locked door can stop me?"

No. A locked door would have no chance against Nick.

Nick reached down and picked up a large rock lying by his feet. "I can smash a window to get in. Or . . ."

Hope wasn't opposed to a little property destruction if it meant getting her to Claire. But she'd save it as a last resort. "Or?"

Nick looked at the old drainpipe attached to the side of the house. He grabbed hold and took several hard tugs on it, and then looked back to Hope. "It's not as sturdy as it used to be but I think it'll still hold."

She didn't even have to ask him what he meant. She knew. When they'd been teenagers and being together had been the only thing that mattered, this drainpipe had been Hope's train ride to freedom. And she'd bought more tickets than she could remember. But Nick wasn't asking her to climb, he was already making his way.

"Wait," she yelled, and rushed forward to tug on the back of his shirt, halting his progress. She had been the one to shimmy up and down the thing when they were younger. Didn't he think she could do it now? But more importantly, she weighed less than Nick and that drainpipe didn't look too sturdy.

"What?" Nick turned around.

"What do you think you're doing?"

"What does it look like?" Nick grabbed hold once more, and hefted himself up. A creak sounded from the pipe.

"You're too heavy."

"I can make—"

Before he could even finish his sentence, the pipe creaked in protest again.

"Move." She stepped around him and placed herself between him and the pipe. "I'm going up."

"Hope, you could get hurt. This was a foolish idea. Come on. Let's just wait. She's not—"

"If you say she's not home, I'm going to pull this pipe from the house and bash you over the head with it. And besides, the idea wasn't so foolish when you were going to be the one to climb up."

Not waiting for his response, she grabbed hold with both hands and began to hoist herself up.

Nick's arm circled around her waist, pulled her back. He turned her around in his arms. Gently he lifted her chin until they were face to face. She found herself forgetting all about the pipe, all about Claire, as her gaze rose and met his blue, blue eyes. Compassion and a gentle understanding softened his features.

"I know how important this is to you. To *us*," he said. "But getting hurt will not help. Let's wait."

"I can't." Her voice was whisper soft. "I just can't." She broke out of his embrace and went to tackle the pipe. She knew he was right, or at least partly so. But she also knew she couldn't give up now, not when she was this close. She wasn't even sure she could still climb the thing. But she was going to try.

Lodging her foot between the house and the pipe, exactly like she had done all those years ago, she began the process of hoisting herself up all over again.

Before she even cleared the ground, Nick was there. Helping her. His hands on her back, supporting her, lifting her. She looked to him.

A wry grin creased his mouth. "If you're going to do this, you're going to do it with my help."

"Thanks." She positioned her foot and grabbed the drainpipe. It was cool in her grip. As she wrapped her hands around the pipe, her fingers brushed against the house's rough siding. With a little bounce, she began the process of pulling herself up. One step. Two. Three. With each inch gained, confidence returned. She could do this. But as quickly as she had the thought, her shoe began to slip. She dug in deeper. Grabbed tighter. But for naught. She gave a cry as she began to fall, knowing she was going to hit the ground.

But she didn't.

Nick was there.

He caught her easily, his arms wrapping around her, holding her tight. His embrace felt so good, so right. *Too good. Too right.*

She wiggled to free herself, but oddly, the more she tried to free herself, the tighter his hold became. It was almost as if he didn't want to release her. But that couldn't be right. His grip was firm but comfortingly so. In his arms she felt safer and more secure than she could ever remember feeling. As if the two of them together could conquer any problem life threw their way. But those type of thoughts were not the type of thoughts Hope should be having. Maybe she hadn't been born strong like Nick, but she had learned how to be strong the moment her babies had been placed in her arms. And she would continue to be strong for her, for them, and on her own.

"Let me go." Her words were spoken softly, half demanding, half pleading.

"Hope."

It took every bit of strength she had to hold his gaze. "Please."

His arms tightened even more protectively around her before slowly—oh, so slowly—loosening ever so slightly.

Still in his arms, she began to slide downward. Down the long, solid length of his body. He kept her close to him. Her soft breasts pressed firmly against his muscled chest, her less than firm stomach molded against his granite abs. And as her descent continued, she felt the hard ridge of his Levis' waistband, his muscled thighs.

Time seemed to slow. Stop. Each breath became more labored than the last, each slide, each rub, more sensual than the one before. It was torture to feel him like this. She wanted it to stop. She wanted it to go on forever. After too long (too soon? she still couldn't decide), her feet landed on the grass.

Nick's arms dropped away from her sides. Their loss was felt more keenly than she'd ever dare to admit.

"Sorry," she mumbled, readjusting her shirt back down, smoothing it into place. She refused to look up at him again, knowing how much strength it had taken her to do so just moments before. And also knowing her eyes might reveal too much.

"For?"

"Falling on you."

"I'm not."

She couldn't help herself; she looked up, caught the grin that curved the corner of his mouth. She felt the impact of that smile low in her belly and if she'd been back on that drainpipe, she would've slipped right back off. "I'm a little out of practice."

"I hope so," he said as his smile spread across his whole face. Without saying anything further, Nick bent at the waist and cupped his hands together.

She took a deep breath, shook off the thoughts and feelings he caused her to have whenever he was near, and got back to the business at hand. She placed her foot in his cupped hands. She found a foothold and once again lodged her toe in. Her hands wrapped around the pipe and she struggled to pull herself up. She lifted her other foot and wedged it in. Using hands to pull and feet to push, she shimmied up a couple of inches. "I think I've got it," she managed to pant. When had she gotten so out of shape?

His hands landed squarely on her butt and he gave her a push.

Oh God. Warmth from his hands permeated her backside. Spread to places it had no right to go. "No, really, Nick, I think I've got it."

In response, he gave her another supporting shove, holding most of her weight.

Heat seeped up her backside and tingled through her spine. Why couldn't he just let her fumble through this on her own? And why did he—oh, God, another thought hit her. *He* was *supporting* her. Why hadn't she laid off the stress-induced binge-eating of Cheetos?

"Nick, you can let go. I've got it."

He ignored her. "Here." His hand wrapped around her ankle and he gently positioned her foot farther up the pipe.

Unable to do anything else, she jammed her foot into the narrow gap between the house and the pipe and tried to lever herself up. Before she'd even budged, Nick was there, or, more accurately, his hand was on her backside helping her again.

"I've got it," she said again, sounding like a broken record. But damn it anyway, when was he going to get the hint? Okay, enough with trying to be polite. She looked down to him and all but groaned in misery when she saw that she was only a couple of feet from the ground. "Nick."

He looked up. "What?"

"Let. Go." She made a point of looking directly to where his hand was and then to him. Surely, *surely*, he'd get the hint this time.

Another one of those bone-melting sexy grins spread across his face as comprehension dawned. And in that instant she realized her blunder. The rat! He knew exactly what he was doing.

"Let go of what?" he asked a little too innocently, the pressure from his hand increasing ever so slightly on her backside.

Clamping her mouth shut, Hope dug deep, found new strength, and pulled.

Inch by inch she wedged herself farther up the pipe. Nick's hands fell away as she climbed beyond his reach and even though she refused to look down—somewhere between teenage years and carpool mom, heights had started to bother her—she could feel Nick's gaze watching her every move. She paused, drew in a deep breath, and looked up to her bedroom window, certain she'd climbed the distance of Mount Everest, only to realize her window was still several feet away.

She slid her hand up the cool pipe, along the back, near the house, and searched for a gap. Just when she didn't think she'd find one, her fingertips slipped into place and she grabbed hold. Not for the first time did she wonder just what in the world she was doing up here. But then an image of Josh would flash before her, and that was all it took. As she lifted her foot a creaking sound came from nearby. Hope looked around, startled.

"Hope," Nick yelled from the ground. "Get down."

"No," she said through her tightly held breath. "I got it. I got it."

"Get down *now*," Nick all but shouted up at her. "That pipe is going to give."

"No, no. It's okay." But to prove her wrong the thing wiggled and came away from the house. She looked back to her window, felt tantalized by its nearness. She toyed with the idea of continuing on. She was *so* close. But even as she did, the pipe swayed again.

"Hope!" This time Nick did yell. Loudly. "Get the hell down!"

It galled her to have to give in. She hated to give up. She looked up to the window and hesitated.

"Hope!"

She let out a deep, deflated breath. "I'm coming." She began to make her way down, but obviously she'd tempted fate a little too long. Before she'd even moved an inch, the pipe broke free from the house. Hope fell right along with it.

For a terrifying moment she felt herself plunging through the air. She was going to land in a heap, in her mother's backyard, undoubtedly with a broken bone or two. Oh God, what would Josh and Susan do?

She flung her arms wide, windmilled through the air, tried desperately to find something to grab hold of. But only air filled her grip. A sickening dread filled her as the ground rushed closer. She was falling. And falling hard.

But the crash to earth never materialized. Before she connected with the hard ground, Nick caught her.

A loud grunt rushed out of him as the full force of her weight landed on him.

"Goddammit, Hope. I knew I shouldn't have let you climb that." He didn't even wait until she was out of his arms to start yelling at her. As a matter of fact, he didn't even let her out of his arms. "Goddammit," he said again. "Don't you ever do anything that stupid again. Do you hear me?"

The whole neighborhood could hear him. She opened her mouth to speak, but he didn't give her the chance. His grip wrapped around her once more.

"Just what in the hell were you thinking?"

"I—"

"You nearly killed me, scaring me like that!"

"You don't need to shout!"

"I'll shout if I damn well want to shout!" His voice rose even higher, which she would have thought impossible only a moment before.

"What were you thinking?" He repeated his earlier question.

Hope didn't think he wanted an answer, but she was going to give him one anyway. "I was thinking about my son. And helping him." She was getting as worked up as he was. Who did he think he was? Yelling at her like that.

Nick's arms tightened around her as he shifted her in his arms until her eyes were mere inches from his. He gave her a hard look, but somehow, she didn't feel threatened by it. If anything, oh God, if anything, all she felt was desire.

The fight drained out of him. "*Our* son, Hopeful. Joshua is *our* son."

She looked into his eyes and felt herself . . . falling. But not down. She was falling back under the spell of Nick Fortune. And she didn't want to do anything to stop it.

"HELLOOOOO?" A voice called from the side of the house, and Nick and Hope broke apart with a jerk. An older woman with tight white curls, wearing an outdated housedress and apron, rounded the corner of the house. "Helllllloooo," she called out again.

Hurriedly Hope brushed the wrinkles out of her clothes and smoothed her hair into some semblance of order.

"Hello," Hope said, wondering who this woman was and

what she was doing at her mother's. The Claire Hope remembered never had visitors.

"Well, land alive, I thought I heard someone over here. And then when I saw the car in the driveway, well . . ." The woman walked closer and Hope caught a whiff of vanilla.

"I'm Mrs.—" The elderly woman broke off as she caught her first good glimpse of Hope. "Oh, my. It's little Hope Marie. Goodness. It's been a fair stretch but I'd recognize you anywhere."

Hope was still a little unsteady, but it wasn't from her fall. She tried to smile but felt it wobble as she remembered the look in Nick's eyes and the feel of his arms around her. "Mrs. Roseburg. It's nice to see you again." Mrs. Roseburg had been her mother's neighbor for as long as Hope could remember.

"This is a surprise. Claire never mentioned one word about you coming."

"A surprise, for Cl—my mom, too," Hope said with a smile. "I—we," she clarified, gesturing to Nick, "were in the area and thought we'd stop by." The words rang hollow even to Hope, but really, there was nothing to be gained by delving into the truth.

Mrs. Roseburg seemed to notice Nick for the first time. Scrunching up her eyes, as if that somehow made her vision clearer, she zeroed in on him and gave him the full once-over. Hope knew the instant she recognized him.

"Aren't you Jack Fortune's boy?"

Hope had nearly forgotten how this town had treated the son of the town drunk. She almost had, but obviously the town hadn't.

"Yes, ma'am," Nick said, and while his voice gave nothing away to Mrs. Roseburg, Hope heard the underlying tension.

"Hmmm. Thought so. Heard your dad passed a few years back. Sorry to hear," Mrs. Roseburg said as an afterthought.

"I wasn't." Nick didn't mince his words.

Mrs. Roseburg pursed her lips. "Don't s'pose you were.

Pair of hell raisers, you were. Pure and simple. Did this town more harm than good. Carrying on, drinking. Fighting. And Lord a'mighty. The way you would tear through this town in anything with four wheels! Hard to believe you didn't kill yourself or"—she shot a look at Hope—"anyone else. Don't think they ever rebuilt that tavern you plowed into with your daddy's truck." She reached into the large front pocket of her apron and withdrew an embroidered handkerchief. "Not that a tavern did anyone any good."

"They rebuilt it." Nick's voice didn't carry a hint of emotion.

Mrs. Roseburg wiped her nose before tucking her handkerchief back into her apron pocket. "You haven't been back since you left. I would've heard if you had been. So how do you know they rebuilt it?"

"I know."

The definiteness in Nick's voice told Hope all she needed to know. Somehow he had played a major role in making that happen. Undoubtedly financed its complete rebuild, if not pounded some of the boards himself.

Mrs. Roseburg harrumphed. "Well, your daddy's with our Savior now. Maybe He—"

"My father was an alcoholic and a mean son of a bitch who didn't give a damn about anything or anyone. Where he's at there isn't any salvation."

The elderly woman drew back. "I see you haven't changed. Still as blasphemous as your father." She abruptly turned from Nick and spoke only to Hope. "Your mother's not home."

Hope had been staring at Nick. Something about the way his jaw had hardened and his posture had stiffened told her that Mrs. Roseburg's words affected him more than he wanted to let on. Hope felt the need to reach out and comfort him, but just as quickly as the thought came, she shook it off. Comfort him about what? He was rich and successful. A celebrity. Surely his bruises from childhood had long ago faded. And then Mrs. Roseburg's words penetrated.

Hope whipped back around and faced her mother's neighbor. "She's gone? My mother's not home?"

"Left yesterday. Won't be home until tomorrow."

"I can't believe she wasn't home." Hope said for the fifth time from the passenger seat.

Nick chose not to answer, just like he had the other four times. Come to think of it, he hadn't said a word since he'd shoved his cell phone number into the old woman's hand, told her to call the minute Claire returned, and then all but dragged Hope away from that place.

Aren't you Jack Fortune's boy?

Nick's grip tightened on the steering wheel, turning his knuckles white. Jack Fortune's boy. No matter where he went or what he achieved, some people would never see him as anything but the son of the town drunk. Not that his teenage exploits had improved their perception. The opposite, in fact.

When Nick was ten and his mother had died, he'd tried to be perfect. Perfect son. Perfect student. He didn't want to cause his father any more grief. But no matter how hard Nick tried in school and at home, nothing made a difference. By the time he was fourteen and his father had all but abandoned him, except when he needed a whipping post or another bottle, or a ride home from the bar he'd gotten kicked out of after they'd confiscated his keys, Nick was through being good. He erupted with as much force and fanfare as a volcano. If the town was going to paint him with the same black brush they used for his father, by God, Nick was going to make sure they applied a heavy coat on him. From that day forward, he set out to earn every one of the disapproving looks the townspeople had been throwing his way for years.

Nick's gaze slid to Hope. He felt his grip loosen. Only she had seen him differently. Glimpsed something in him he'd never seen himself. But what that had been, Nick had never figured out. Probably because it hadn't existed. *Didn't* exist.

Ever since Hope had landed in his arms he'd been having fantasies he was better off not having. Oh, who was he kidding? Those fantasies had started almost from the first moment he'd seen her again.

They came to an intersection. Nick eased up on the gas. Almost two decades had passed since he'd driven these roads, but he knew them as well as he knew his way around a racetrack. He looked right and then left, then back to the right. After a moment, he flicked on the signal and headed right. Into town.

"Where are we going?" Obviously believing he wasn't going to answer that question either, she immediately followed with, "Do I need to repeat that question too?"

He eased down on the gas, got the car back up to speed. "We need to find a hotel and then grab something to eat."

"Hotel?" The hitch in her voice didn't go unnoticed.

He turned at the next intersection. "Where did you think we'd spend the night? Surely not at your mother's."

"No, but I just thought . . . I mean . . ."

"You thought what?" Her expression was hidden from him as she stared out the passenger window.

Hope expelled a long breath. "You don't need to do this. You don't have to stay. Claire's my problem and I'm sure there's somewhere else you should be. Just drop me in town. You can take the rental car to the airport. I'll get another car and after I see Claire, I can catch a commercial flight home."

There *was* somewhere else Nick should be. Somewhere where a lot of people were expecting him—counting on him. He'd never let down his crew before; the complete opposite, in fact. But even as he entertained the idea that he should leave, fly out to the race, he knew he wasn't going anywhere.

"You have it all worked out, I see." Anger simmered through him.

Her gaze was still fixated out the window, studiously avoiding him. Well, what he had to say was too important for her to ignore.

He pulled the car off the road and onto the shoulder, then shoved it into park. The car lurched forward, then settled. Startled, she faced him.

"Joshua is my son too," he said with a simple finality. "Whether you like it or not, I'm staying. We're getting a hotel room for the night and then we're going to get something to eat."

"Oh, God." Fear flared across her features.

"Not the usual response when I invite a lady out to dinner."

For a brief moment her look of distress was replaced by one of annoyance before returning to one of worry. Obviously she didn't like his reference to other women.

"No," she said, shaking her head, then repeated herself more forcibly. "No, that's not it. Today is Friday. Tomorrow Saturday."

"Your point being?"

She pursed her lips and sent him an exasperated look. "The doctor's office is open today. A weekday. Even if my mother returns tomorrow, that's Saturday. The office will be closed and won't reopen until Monday. I can't be away from the kids that long. I can't—"

"Whenever Claire returns, weekend or weekday, middle of the day or middle of the night, the doctor will see us."

"But how?"

"Having a face and name people recognize can be a real pain in the ass but there are times it can be a benefit, too. You don't need to worry; the doctor will see us whenever I call."

The tension around her eyes lessened and she sank against the seat. "Thank you. I don't know what else to say but thank you."

Nick felt his temper rise once more. "Stop thanking me."

Hope didn't seem to hear him. "But really, what I said earlier still goes. You don't need to stay. Who knows when Claire will return. Like I said, you can leave and I'll—"

Nick shoved the car back into drive and burned rubber as he pulled back out onto the road, effectively shutting her up.

She was never going to accept that he was Susan and Joshua's father. That being here was just as important to him as it was to her. Well too damn bad.

But as they got closer to town he couldn't help but wonder if maybe he should have taken the easy way out. Maybe he should leave. And then maybe, maybe he would stop thinking about the long night ahead. With just the two of them. In a hotel.

Thirteen

HOPE stared down at the unopened suitcase on the hotel bed, unsure of how it had even gotten here. Unsure of how *she'd* gotten here. Before she'd even had time to react to Nick's assertion that he was staying until they saw Claire, he'd found a hotel, checked them in, and then ushered her to this room with a parting statement that he'd be back in an hour to take her to dinner. Hope didn't know what she found most infuriating—Claire not being home, Nick's highhandedness in believing she'd do whatever he said, or the fact that she'd been worried he'd get only one room and not two.

She looked around her room—her single room. Obviously that was one worry she didn't need to have.

This afternoon when she'd fallen into his arms and felt the breath go out of her—not from the fall, but from being so near to him—she'd thought he'd been as affected as she'd been. But that in a nutshell summed up their whole existence all those years ago. When she'd been so young, too young, and so much in love. More in love with him that he'd ever been with her. Once again she silently cursed herself, wondering when her weakness for Nick Fortune would ever go away.

She slumped down onto the bed, reached for her phone, and saw she'd missed two calls from Ben. She felt guilty; she hadn't returned his call from the other night. But there was more to her sense of guilt, and that she didn't want to examine too closely. They'd only been on a dozen dates or so and Hope wouldn't even call all of them dates. Half of them had been just to grab coffee. Ben had never even met the twins. But still she felt like she had been disloyal. Before she could think twice, she called his number.

"I was hoping I'd hear from you," Ben said after answering. "How's Joshua?"

"He's good. The same. I'm sorry I haven't called you back sooner. Life has been . . ."

"I get it," he said. "I mean, I don't have children so I can't understand everything you're going through, but I can try."

Hope scraped her hair away from her face, let it fall down her back. "You really are a great guy," she said in all sincerity.

"Why do I feel a *but* coming on?"

Hope didn't say anything for several moments. Was there a *but*? She hadn't thought so when she'd called him, but now . . . She looked to the room's far wall, to the door that connected her room to Nick's. "Life has become complicated," she said, trying to find her way through a conversation she hadn't planned on having.

"Would this have something to do with the twins' father?"

Hope sucked in a breath. "How—Why would you ask that?"

Ben gave a short chuckle but it held no mirth. "I might not be the sharpest tack in the pack, but the minute you told me you were contacting him, I worried something like this might happen."

"Nothing has happened," Hope said quickly. "Nothing will happen. It's not that. It's just that my life right now is . . ."

"Complicated," he said, parroting her word. He let out a

long sigh. "Hope, if I thought I had a snowball's chance, I'd put up a hell of a fight for you."

"Ben, it's not like that."

"Take care, Hope. And know that I'm pulling for Joshua. For all of you."

What was happening? How had a simple phone call turned into this?

"Ben, wait."

"Good-bye, Hope."

The line went dead.

She stared at the phone, still not exactly sure what had happened. She had no thoughts of breaking up with Ben when she'd called him, but she hadn't been the one to break up. He had. Shouldn't she feel devastated or sad and not relieved? It had been a struggle to find the time to see him. Every time he asked her out, she had felt guilty having to turn him down once again. But dating Ben—dating anyone—right now was not something she desired. She should have been honest with him weeks ago. Why hadn't she been? Because he was a great guy and she hadn't wanted to hurt his feelings.

There was only one thing to do after breaking up with your kinda-not-exactly boyfriend.

Dana answered on the second ring. "Hello?"

"Hey you."

"Hey you." Dana's voice spiked in pleased recognition as she repeated their standard greeting.

"I spoke with Josh earlier and he said you had stopped by. Thank you. I hate the thought of him being in that room all day with only doctors and nurses for company."

"You don't have to thank me. You know that."

"I know, but thanks anyway." Hope brushed the hair off her forehead. "And Susan? She didn't answer her cell when I called."

"She and Chelsey headed to the mall this afternoon."

Had it really only been this morning that Hope had left? In those few hours, she felt as if she'd lived a week. Today had been a roller coaster of emotion. Worry over Joshua. Her mother. Ben. Nick.

Nick.

How had their lives become so intertwined in such a short amount of time? But it wasn't a short amount of time. Whether Nick was a physical presence or merely a memory, he had always been a part of her.

"I'm glad the girls are having fun," Hope told Dana. "And you? Everything okay at home?"

"Everything's fine. Stop worrying."

"As if."

They both laughed softly but without any real humor.

"Did you remember to feed Fonz?"

"You're asking about a turtle? Something's going on. Spill."

Hope expelled a deep breath. She never could hide anything from Dana.

Hope was spending the night in a town she didn't want to be in, near a man she was afraid she was once again falling for. But those were the last things Hope wanted to talk about, so instead she said, "Ben broke up with me."

"Good."

"Good? That's all you have to say? You who've been none too silent on your feelings toward him?"

"He wasn't right for you and you know it. You never even introduced him to the kids, and don't tell me it was because Josh is sick—you started dating Ben a couple months before. And I won't even talk about the lack of spark between you two. You were like brother and sister. You need someone with heat. Someone with passion. Someone with *speed*!"

Speed. Didn't take a genius to see where Dana's mind was headed. "Knock it off. I'm here to see my mother. The woman who can't leave her house except for God and groceries has decided to take a trip and is gone until tomorrow."

Dana was silent for a moment. "I'm so sorry. I know how anxious you are to talk to her. How important it is."

"Yeah."

"What are you going to do?"

"Stay until I see her. As long as you're okay and can manage another day."

"Don't worry about anything on this end. I've got it covered. I'm even remembering to charge my phone."

Hope smiled. "But are you remembering to keep it with you?"

"Yes!" Dana said with mock indignation. Then she said, "So let's talk about what you're avoiding and what I'm dying to know. Where are you sleeping tonight, and, more importantly, who's staying with you?"

Leave it to Dana to cut to the chase.

"I'm staying at Ten Lakes Motel," Hope said, answering the easier of the two questions.

"And?" Dana asked with just a little too much enthusiasm.

Hope twirled a loose thread on the hotel comforter around her finger. "And nothing."

"And nothing, my big toe. Don't think you can fly out of here with *that man* and not fill me in."

Hope knew it was pointless to try to evade Dana's questions. "Yes, Nick's staying here." She pulled the thread, tugging at it until it broke.

"One room or two?"

"Two," she said quickly, then added, "as if that was ever a question."

"I can hope, can't I? If I was trapped overnight. In. A. Hotel. With *Nick Fortune*—"

"Stop saying his name like that."

"Like what? Like he's a god? Um. He kinda is. Have you looked at him? *H. O. T.* Hot! The man has action figures modeled after him, for crying out loud. Tell me the rooms are connecting, at least."

Hope looked toward the interior door that led to Nick's room. "Not adjoining," she lied, and then added to the fib. "He's not even on the same floor. There's a . . . a convention in town and the place is all but booked solid."

"Hmmm." Dana didn't sound convinced. "You know you can't avoid him forever. He is Joshua's father."

Like she could forget. "I'm not avoiding him."

"If I know you, you're going to sit in that hotel room *by yourself*, without eating or sleeping, until you're able to see Claire tomorrow."

"I'll sleep."

Another lie, but this time they both knew it.

"What about dinner? You have to eat."

"Actually"—Hope plucked at another loose string—"I'm going to dinner with Nick." Why had she gone and said that? There was no way she was going to have dinner with Nick. No way at all.

"Well, good for you. You two need to talk. Now listen, before you go out, look in your suitcase. I packed a couple of extra things just in case something like this came up. And before you yell at me, remember, a man is more amiable when staring across the table at a beautiful woman dressed in a killer little black number."

Hope caught her reflection in the mirror on the opposite wall. "You're my best friend, so you have to be blind not only to my faults but my physical appearance. And God bless you for that. But only you think I'm beautiful."

Dana scoffed. "You forget I saw the way he looked at you this morning. That man wants to eat you up. So I say hand him a spoon and have fun! You deserve—and need—it." Dana hung up before Hope could utter a word.

Minutes ticked past but Hope didn't move. Instead, she stared at the end of her bed, at her still-unopened suitcase.

"THERE'S somethin' wrong with my hearing 'cause I know you just didn't say what I think you said."

Nick leaned back in the chair and stared out the window. The sun, still hot and bright even this late in the afternoon, glimmered off a small lake, one of the surrounding ten from which the hotel took its name. "There's nothing wrong with your hearing. I won't be there."

"I'm in the damn Twilight Zone if you're really telling me you're not racing on Sunday." Dale's exasperated exhalation came across the phone. "What the hell is going on?" Dale asked, clearly confused. "Everything we've worked our asses off for is about to materialize and you're gonna throw it away. This isn't just another race. This is—ah, hell—if I have to tell you what this is, you aren't the Nick Fortune I know. That man has never missed a race. Not when he had pneumonia, not when his leg was broken, and sure as hell not when he just 'won't be there.' That man raced. Because racin' is your life."

Your life.

Those words hung in the air, weighed it down. A week ago, Nick would have instantly agreed, but now? Now . . . it seemed impossible that in one week so much could have changed. "Something came up."

"Something came up. Why didn't you say so?"

"Sarcasm doesn't become you."

"Pissing away what we worked so hard for doesn't become *you*."

"It's one race, Dale, not the whole damn season." But even as Nick said it, he couldn't believe his decision either. He felt the words almost like a blow to his midsection. "Tell the crew I'll see them next week."

"One race, huh?" Dale didn't say anything else for the longest time and then let out a long sigh. "This is me, Nick. Tell me what's going on."

Nick's gaze flashed to the door connecting his room with Hope's. For the last half hour, ever since he'd left Hope at her room, he'd found himself looking at it more and more. He knew it was crazy. Knew he shouldn't be here with her. But as hard as he'd tried to work out the details, figure out how he could be in two places at once, he knew it was an impossibility. And then the image of his son in that hospital bed would flash in his mind and Nick knew he wasn't going anywhere. Right now, there was nowhere else he wanted to be. And while confronting Claire was of the utmost importance for his son, Nick knew that wasn't the only reason he didn't want to leave.

"Nick?"

He didn't take his eyes off the door. He wasn't leaving, but he also wasn't ready to explain to Dale why not. "Something important, that's all."

"More important than racin'? There's nothin' more important than racin'. Hell, you were the one who taught me that."

"Tell the crew I'll see them next week." He ended the call. And even though it was late and he knew Evelyn wouldn't be in the office, he called and left a message on the machine. Something had been on his mind since his conversation with Maddy's mom. "It's Nick. Let's look at my schedule, see what tracks are near children's hospitals. If the hospital thinks a visit from someone like me would help, let's make it happen." He was about to hit End, but paused, then added, "Even if the hospitals aren't nearby. I still want to visit. Also, next time I'm in the office, I want to discuss where to allocate my charitable donations. Thanks."

TWENTY minutes later Nick was showered and dressed and standing in the hallway in front of Hope's door. He hesitated before knocking, feeling as nervous as a pimply-faced teenager on his first date. When he'd left Hope earlier, she hadn't been thrilled about his suggestion to go to dinner. Maybe *suggestion* wasn't the right word. But if he hadn't insisted, he knew her well enough to know there was no way she'd agree. She'd been cold and distant to him ever since he'd shown up at her house, and she didn't show signs of softening.

Well, maybe there'd been a few.

Thoughts of the kiss they'd shared pressed to the forefront

of his mind. That, and remembering the feel of her in his arms from earlier today had him thinking things he knew he was better off not thinking. She'd made it clear she didn't want him in her life—or his children's lives—but if she thought he was going to walk away, she was mistaken. And this dinner was his opportunity to enlighten her on exactly how serious he was.

He was surprised when Hope answered on his first knock. As if she'd been waiting.

He was just about to say hello when he caught sight of her and felt the words dissolve in his throat. She took his breath away, literally.

Nick had been around a lot of beautiful women. Women who knew how to use their charms, their looks, their bodies, to entice and attract. He'd taken a dip in the pool but on his terms. Always. He'd never found it impossible to walk away. But as he stood facing Hope, the one woman he didn't know if he could ever forgive, he knew he'd met his match. Because forgiving her was a completely different thing than being able to forget her.

She wore a black dress that was tame in comparison to so many others he'd seen, though on Hope, it was anything but. The soft material clung in all the right places, emphasizing her waist and hugging her breasts. The dress was short, stopping midthigh and giving way to her long, tanned, *bare* legs.

Pink toenails peeked out from narrow straps that seemed too delicate to hold her high heels in place. The shoes made her already dainty feet seem even more delicate, and her legs—

Hell, he'd better stop thinking about her legs or they weren't going anywhere tonight.

Her dress didn't have a plunging neckline, or an up-to-there hem, and for a moment Nick wondered why he was so entranced. But then he caught a look at her face and he knew. She'd swept her hair up into some type of knot at the back of her head with a few soft curls escaping. With her hair pulled back, her high cheekbones were more prominent and so were her large eyes. Those mesmerizing green eyes that used to keep him tossing and turning on his teenage bed late at night. Her beauty was classical—timeless—and too damn alluring.

Nick cleared his throat, tore his eyes off her legs, and tried his greeting again. "Hello."

"Hi."

"You ready?"

She nodded. "I just need to grab my purse."

They left the hotel in silence and Nick directed her to the rental car. As he opened her door and waited for her to get in, he wondered at her thoughts. He knew she'd be thinking about Joshua, and Susan, and Claire—just as he was. But as he caught a glimpse of her bare thigh as she slid into the car, he couldn't help but wonder if she was also thinking about him as much as he'd been thinking about her.

Shutting her door, Nick rounded the car and slid behind the wheel.

Hope sat as far right in her seat as she could get, her hand gripping the door handle.

A smile found its way to his mouth as he checked the traffic before easing onto the road. "You know, some people think I'm a pretty good driver."

She turned to look at him. "What?"

"Every time we're in a vehicle together and I'm driving, you hang on for all you're worth."

She let go of the door handle so quickly it was almost as if it stung her. "I do not."

He grinned. "Yes, you do."

She wrapped both hands around the purse on her lap as if afraid she'd go for the door handle once more. "If I do, it's only because I've seen you drive."

Nick's grin grew. He'd been a hellion when they were teenagers. Driving as fast and as far as a few bucks' worth of gas would take them. "Give me a little credit. I'm a little smarter behind a wheel than when I was a teenager."

She looked out the passenger window for several moments and then turned back to face him. "No, I meant I've seen you drive. On TV."

"Which race?"

"Um. The one with the oval track."

He laughed.

"Actually, I've watched a few races. Two. Three. Ten. Twenty." Her smile was soft and tentative and alluring as hell. "Too many to count."

An inexplicable emotion filled Nick. She'd watched him race. He didn't know why that surprised him, but then again, maybe he did. She seemed to want nothing to do with him, so then why would she have watched him race? "What did you think?"

"That my first instinct to hold on tight was the right one."

Nick laughed out loud. Slowing, he flicked on his signal and turned the car onto the freeway on-ramp.

She settled in her seat and Nick was pleased to see she wasn't still hugging the door.

They drove for several moments in silence. As he caught sight of the passing landscape, he realized he'd forgotten how beautiful this part of the country was. Wildflowers bloomed along the side of the road, seeming to frame the green trees with their color. Every once in a while, where the trees thinned, a lake shimmered in the setting sun.

"Where are we going?" Hope asked.

"There's a restaurant in St. Paul that I thought we'd try."

"Oh. I thought . . . I mean, I just figured we'd find a restaurant in Banning."

"I don't think many things have changed in Banning since we left. And if I remember right, Bubba's Burgers was about the highest culinary experience to be had."

"You mean you didn't feel like eating at a greasy spoon?"

He shook his head. "But if it was ice cream we were after—"

"Aunt Patsy's Parlour," they both said in unison.

"Now that was some ice cream," Nick said.

"Remember her strawberry banana shakes? And how every month she'd feature a new homemade flavor?"

"I think I tried every one."

"No, you *bought* every one but then would give it to me," she said. "Definitely not what my figure needed."

Nick took his eyes off the road and gave her body a thorough once-over. "Your figure is still perfect."

She fiddled with the strap of her purse. "I hope you don't think I was fishing for a compliment."

"Have you ever? Besides, fact is fact."

She shifted her position, ran her hands along the handle of her purse once more. "And here I thought racecar drivers had perfect vision. You need to get your eyes checked."

"And you, Hopeful"—he shot her a look—"need to look into a mirror a little more often."

She cleared her throat, looked down at her lap, out the window, anywhere but at him. "So, tell me again where we're headed?"

Nick smiled. She wasn't immune. "You're too beautiful for Banning. I want to show you off."

TOO beautiful.

Hope felt herself reeling from Nick's unexpected compliment. She'd never been beautiful, let alone *too beautiful*. But to hear him say it, to see the look on his face as he said it, as if he believed it wholeheartedly. Truth was, she wondered if she was so stunned because it had been so close to her own thoughts about him.

She cast another furtive glance his way. While many other things could be said about Nick, there was one undeniable truth: He was the most handsome man she'd ever seen. Hot, as Dana had so correctly said. It didn't matter if he was in Levi's and a T-shirt, in his racing gear, or dressed more formally as he was tonight in a black suit and a crisp white shirt that only seemed to emphasize his tanned skin and black hair.

Though she wouldn't have believed it initially, Hope was actually thankful Dana had thought to pack her black dress.

After hanging up the phone, it had taken Hope less than five minutes to decide to wear the dress. Dana had been right—you could catch more flies with sugar than you could with vinegar—or however that old adage went. And Hope knew she'd need every advantage she could get tonight, because Dana had been right about another point too: She and Nick needed to talk.

Their lives could never mesh. What type of dad did he think he would be? Certainly not one who would be around. Thanks to the Internet, she'd done a little research of her own this last week, and what she'd learned had only confirmed her suspicions. The NASCAR circuit didn't allow for personal time. And Hope knew firsthand how devastating it was to be the child of a parent who couldn't—or wouldn't—make time for you. To love a parent so much that you started blaming yourself when they never had time for you. She was determined not to let that happen to her children.

At the thought of Susan and Joshua, guilt settled like a boulder in her stomach. She shouldn't be here, dressed up and going out to dinner when her son was sick and thousands of miles away. She should tell Nick to turn the car around—to head back to the hotel. They could talk in the lobby or on a park bench. Or—

"Don't."

She shifted on the smooth leather seat until she faced him. "Don't what?"

"Feel guilty. You need to eat."

Surprise hit her. "How did you know what I was thinking?"

Nick pulled alongside the curb and parked. "You forget I know you. And besides, we're here."

Hope glanced out the window and drew in a sharp breath. She knew this place, or, more accurately, knew of it.

La Petite Grenouille was an exclusive, highly renowned French restaurant that catered to the elite. Located in the beautifully maintained historic district, the restaurant had been written and raved about more than Minnesota's beloved baseball team.

As teenagers Hope and her friends had joked when it came time to plan where they were going out to dinner before a big high school dance. They'd all laugh and repeat *La Petite Grenouille* in terrible French accents, but even then they'd known how out of their league this place had been. Dinners at La Petite cost about the same as one of their parents' paychecks. And even if they could afford the staggering price—which of course they couldn't—they knew reservations would be impossible. Even calling months in advance didn't guarantee a table. You also needed the right name to go with that reservation.

Before Hope could open her door, a uniformed valet was beside the car, assisting her. The first thing she noticed was the soft classical music that seemed to come from the sky; the second thing was the people.

A large crowd of expensively dressed patrons hovered around the front entrance. A waiter attired in classical black wove through the restless crowd, offering petite hors d'oeuvres and tall, fluted glasses of champagne. As Hope watched she could see the impatience of the parties waiting, saw the women fan themselves and then fan themselves a little harder when their escort returned only to tell them their wait would be a little longer still. It didn't take a rocket scientist to realize that the crystal glasses being passed around were not only to cool heated bodies, but also to cool heated tempers.

Someone bumped into her and she felt herself pushed to the side. Nick reached her, took her elbow, steadied her. Her sense of nervousness grew. She didn't belong at a restaurant such as this. And, looking at the man standing next to her, the man everyone was beginning to recognize—she didn't belong with him either. The more seconds that ticked by, the more she felt like Alice after her fall down into Wonderland.

Nick gently steered her toward the entrance.

Large antique urns flanked the wide double doors that looked to have been crafted around the time of the first crusade. A profusion of well-tended flowers and lush greenery cascaded over the ornate containers and trailed down their sides. Striped awnings hung over the leaded-glass windows.

The more she saw, the more out of place she felt. Not realizing what she was doing, she took a step backward and then another. She didn't belong in a place like this. She wasn't a La Petite Grenouille type of diner, she was hamburgers and fries and floats at places like Aunt Patsy's Parlour. She was drive-through stands and all-you-can-eat buffets where the kids were free on Tuesday nights. She was . . .

Nick let go of her elbow and slipped his arm around her waist. Expertly he maneuvered them through the crowd. The buzz of voices grew in volume as more people recognized Nick.

Hope's sense of surrealness mushroomed. But never once did Nick's arm leave her. He continued to guide her forward, through the crowd and the large wooden doors.

The minute they stepped inside the restaurant, a waft of mouthwatering smells hit her. Her treacherous stomach growled, reminding her she hadn't eaten all day. Instinctively she placed a hand on her stomach, as if that could somehow stop its rumblings, and silently told herself it had better stop; from the look of the crowd it was going to be a long, long wait.

As Nick made his way to the hostess, Hope couldn't help but compare herself to the immaculately dressed and coiffed twenty-something standing behind the tall, slim lectern. Even wearing the dress Dana had packed and spending more than her normal two minutes on her hair and makeup, she felt outshined by the beautiful young woman who worked here. If she hadn't already felt out of place, she certainly now would have.

"*Bonjour,*" the hostess said to Nick.

"Hello. A table for two."

She barely glanced up from the seating chart. "Two, *monsieur*?"

"Yes."

"That'll be . . ." She consulted her chart. "We will have a table ready in approximately two hours." Her voice held a note of boredom, as if telling patrons there was an extensive wait was the norm rather than the exception.

Hope was about to suggest they find another restaurant. While the restaurant and all its ambience were beginning to wrap her in their magic, not to mention the delicious smells coming from the kitchen, the last thing she wanted was to spend two hours waiting for a table. Two more hours with Nick, surrounded by strangers, having to make small talk when what she needed to tell him could only be said with privacy. But not too much privacy, she quickly amended. A blush spread across her cheeks as she remembered this afternoon and the feel of his arms around her. Even when they'd been in the car, she'd felt her attraction to him so strongly, she'd sat as far to her right as possible. "Nick, why don't we—"

"Monsieur. Monsieur Fortune." A short, round man handsomely attired in a tuxedo hustled toward them from the interior of the restaurant, a huge smile creasing his plump face.

The hostess glanced up sharply. Caught her first true glimpse of Nick and drew in a quick breath. It was clear she'd just now realized who he was.

"Monsieur Fortune, this is a pleasure. A pleasure indeed." The tuxedoed man held out his hand. "Allow me to introduce myself. I am Monsieur Deschanel and am honored you have come to my humble restaurant. Please, follow me."

Nick shook the man's hand and then once more placed his hand on the small of Hope's back, guiding her forward. As they followed the owner through the restaurant, it dawned on Hope that there would be no waiting, no cooling their heels outside. No pacing and wondering how much longer until their table was ready.

Having a face and name people recognize can be a real

*pain in the ass but there are times it can be a benefit, too.
You don't need to worry; the doctor will see us whenever I
call.*

A sense of surrealness stole over Hope—not only because
of the preferential treatment they were receiving tonight but,
more importantly, because of how it would help Joshua. But
as the pressure and warmth from Nick's hand continued to
penetrate her dress's thin material, his nearness claimed all
of her attention.

Whispers of conversation reached Hope.

Isn't that?

No. It can't be . . .

It is!

The racecar driver . . .

Nick Fortune!

Nick took it all in stride. The whispers, the stares, the VIP
treatment.

"Please forgive my niece," Monsieur Deschanel was saying. "We are blessed with many friends tonight. But for so
distinguished a guest, we do not make wait. Always, I have
special table."

He continued on, leading them back into the restaurant,
which seemed to go on forever. Hope would have never
guessed it was so large. They passed a set of double doors
where loud music and even louder voices could be heard. The
owner must have seen her questioning gaze.

"A wedding reception," he explained. "So much joy. So
much happiness, yes?"

Hope's glance lingered for a moment longer than was necessary on the closed doors. Then she forced a smile and a
happy tone when she replied, "Yes." But she must have failed
on one or both accounts, as Nick shot her a look she couldn't
quite decipher.

They came to a small alcove. Tucked into its own private
nook, with curved stone walls and a large picture window
providing a spectacular view of the water, the table was, in

one word, perfect. A pressed white cloth, a shallow crystal vase with half a dozen perfect pink roses, and a chandelier nestled high in the rafters only added to its already alluring appeal. With its intimacy, the noise of the other patrons had all but vanished, and in its place was the soft strains of the classical music she had first heard when they'd arrived.

"I hope this is to your liking." The owner smiled at Hope as he pulled out her chair.

"It's perfect," she said, taking her seat. "Thank you."

"Private, yes?" the owner said with a knowing smile as he shook out the elaborately folded napkin and placed it across her lap.

A blush spread across her cheeks and she fussed with her napkin.

In a matter of moments Nick was seated across from her, menus were produced, water poured, and a bottle of champagne (compliments of Monsieur Deschanel) appeared. When the owner went to pour the champagne, Nick politely motioned he'd do it himself.

"Very good, *monsieur*. Enjoy your dinner."

"You can come out from behind your menu now," Nick said after the waiter had gone.

"I wasn't hiding," she fibbed.

"I know you, remember?" he said, smiling, repeating the words he'd said earlier in the car. And just like before, those words found a hollow inside her that she hadn't even realized she possessed and began to fill the void.

Nick lifted the bottle from the chilled silver bucket. He filled the crystal flutes to a perfect three-quarters full, letting the bubbles bloom to the rim.

"Something tells me you've done that a time or two."

Nick set the expensive-looking black bottle back in its holder. "Done what?"

"Poured champagne. You do it with such . . . precision," she said, shrugging, giving him a tentative smile.

He picked up his glass and tilted it toward her. "Here's to finally being able to take you to La Petite Grenouille."

Her glass arrested halfway toward his. "You wanted to come here?"

"I *wanted* to be *able* to bring *you* here." He clinked their flutes, took a drink.

His words flustered her. "You did?"

"Don't tell me you didn't know."

She stared at the bubbles fizzing up from the bottom of her glass, unsure of what to say. She wanted this evening to stay impersonal. She wanted to keep Nick at arm's length while she reasoned with him about the children. She wanted not to be affected by how he looked, what he said, but she worried that a battle she was still preparing for had already been fought and lost.

"I never realized. I mean"—she looked at him—"when all of us kids at school used to talk about this place, you never said a word."

He gave a halfhearted shrug. "What was I supposed to do? Let my best girl know I couldn't afford to take her out to dinner?"

"You did take me out to dinner. A lot of times."

He took another drink, then set his glass on the table. "I'd hardly call hamburgers or pizza dinner."

"And ice cream. Don't forget that," she teased, but then felt the smile ebb from her lips when she realized Nick was completely serious. "I definitely wasn't a *best girl* if you thought I expected this." Her voice was low and completely honest as she made a small, sweeping gesture with her hand to indicate the restaurant. And then, for reasons she didn't fully understand, she felt compelled to explain further. "It was never about *where* we went. Surely you must have known that. It was about *who* I went with."

"I wanted to give you . . ."

"La Petite Grenouille?"

"The world," he said simply.

Hope's breath caught. She tried to think of something to say but couldn't. Couldn't form a word or a thought.

Thankfully, the waiter arrived and saved her from having to respond.

"I'd be honored to share tonight's specials," the waiter was saying. But Hope wasn't listening.

I wanted to give you the world.

She stared down at the menu—which thankfully was not only in French but English as well. She tried to concentrate but the words blurred together and instead of being able to decide what to eat, all she could think about was what Nick had said.

She forced herself to focus. As she read down the list of entrées she realized two things at once: Each of them was mouthwateringly tempting, and they each sounded like they cost more than she made in a week. She looked for the prices, determined to order the least expensive item. But no matter how hard she looked, there wasn't a price to be found anywhere on the menu.

After a few moments Hope realized it had grown quiet. She peeked up and saw that both Nick and the waiter were looking at her expectedly.

"Has the *mademoiselle* decided?"

No! She racked her brain, trying to figure out a way to tactfully ask how much something cost, only to realize that there wasn't one. She looked to the menu once more and the first thing she saw was the word *chicken*.

Chicken. Perfect. She bought chicken every week at the grocery store. And usually it was on sale. She was just about to say she'd have the chicken when she noticed that there were five different chicken entrées on the menu.

The special. She'd heard Nick and the waiter talking about the special. And a special meant they got a good buy on something, right? So the price would be less. She closed her menu and turned to the waiter, a relieved smile on her face. "I'll have the special."

"Ah, excellent choice, *mademoiselle*. And may I recommend the steamed asparagus and—"

"Hope?"

She looked to Nick. "Yes?"

"Have you ever wondered what the English translation of *La Petite Grenouille* is?"

What a weird question to be asking her now. "No."

A wry grin settled on Nick's face. "Maybe you should ask our waiter."

Obviously Nick knew what it meant, but for some reason he wasn't saying. She turned to the waiter and before she could ask, he informed her. "Ah, La Petite Grenouille. The little frog."

"How charming."

"Not so charming when that's their special," Nick said. "And they're not so little."

"You mean?"

"Yep. Frog legs."

Hope's gaze shot back to the waiter. "Cancel that special order."

Nick laughed.

"It's not funny," she said, looking at her menu once more. "Now I'm going to have to find something else, and I'm really sorry but I just can't seem to make up my mind."

"Allow me?" Nick said.

She looked at him. He sat so relaxed, so confident in these posh surroundings that undid her. It made her realize once again what different paths their lives had taken. "Please."

For the next several minutes—more time than she allotted to planning her weekly food menu—Nick and the waiter perfected their dinner order. She listened as Nick ordered with a skill and sophistication she found mind-boggling because it was so foreign from the Nick she remembered and sexy as all get-out. Where had he learned to pronounce French words? Or what side dishes best accompanied the lamb he ordered for two? Or how to choose a wine?

"I just realized something," she said as the waiter walked away.

"What?" Nick asked.

"You've said a couple of times that you know me."

"I do."

"While that may be true, I don't know you. Not anymore. You live your life in the fast lane; I'd be uncomfortable if I weren't in carpool. You travel more in one week than I have in my whole life. You've experienced things, gone places, met people, I can't even begin to imagine. Just who are you, Nick Fortune?" she asked in a light tone, but he took her question to heart. Pondered it for a few moments and then replied.

"I'm the same guy you knew, only in a faster car."

She wanted to toss back a witty rejoinder, try to keep the conversation in the present, stop it from traveling down a path that led to their past. But then she realized that wasn't what she wanted after all. For so long, longer than was prudent or wise, she'd wondered about Nick's life. Now was her chance to appease that curiosity. "What was it like?"

"What was what like?"

"Your life in NASCAR." She smoothed the napkin on her lap, tried to hide how much she wanted to know. It shouldn't matter—not with all the years between then and now. But it did. It did to her. "For over a year, we dreamed about it. Talked about it. Planned how it would all work out." She smiled softly. "Obviously it worked out exactly as you thought it would."

"Not exactly."

Her hand stilled on her lap. "How so?"

Nick slid his silverware to the side, rested his forearms on the table. "I thought I was so good."

"You were. You *are*."

He smiled. "You always did have more faith in me than anyone else."

She tried to ignore the feeling his words stirred in her.

"I was a cocky kid with guts and raw talent, but that and a buck will get you a bag of popcorn. Took me two months to even get a job anywhere near a track. You know what that job was?" He didn't pause. "I sold hot dogs from a cart." He shook his head, grimaced. "To this day the smell of them still makes me nauseous. But they kept me fed and working near the tracks. Eventually I talked my way into a different job."

"Driving," she said with certainty.

"No. Like I said, things didn't play out like we thought they would." He intertwined his fingers, pressed his thumbs together. "My next job was running errands for a driver. It took me another year and a half after that to convince anyone to let me behind a wheel." He chuckled, gave his head a soft shake. "Actually, I never did convince anyone."

"What do you mean?"

"I stole a car. Well, not exactly stole. Borrowed. I was so mad and frustrated by then. Thought I knew everything there was to know about racing but no one would give me a chance. So when Tony—that was the driver I was working for—got out of his car one day, I hopped in. I knew one of two things was going to happen. Either I was going to get my ass thrown in jail or I was going to impress the hell out of them. Thankfully it was the latter. But it still took me several more months to get backing. An owner who believed in me enough to let me behind the wheel of one of his racecars." Nick's gaze refocused, intensified. "It was over two years after I left Banning that I got my first race."

She was stunned. "Two years?"

"Closer to two and a half." He was quiet for several moments. "And then life still wasn't as I'd thought it would be. The hours were grueling, harder than anything I could have imagined. Weeks went by where I couldn't remember my own name let alone if I'd slept in the last three days or eaten. But I kept my head down, busted my butt, and absorbed every bit of knowledge I could. Eventually, I found a better car, better sponsors. Won some races. My overnight success only took years." He looked down to his hands. "Years. So many so that—"

She didn't know why, but she had to stop him. Couldn't hear what he was about to say. "Your success is beyond impressive, Nick."

He was looking at her hard, as if trying to reason something out in his mind. As if coming to a conclusion, he leaned back in his chair. "Now that I've bored you with my life, I want to hear about you. Your life."

"Now *that* would be a boring conversation."

"I beg to differ."

She reached for her champagne, took a sip and then another. "My life has been ordinary, but I wouldn't change it for anything. So now let's talk about something else. Anything else."

"Anything?"

His suggestive tone electrified her nerves, and suddenly she wasn't thinking about the past but the very real present. Slips from drainpipes. Bodies pressed tightly together. And a hotel room with a connecting door. "It's a lovely evening. What a beautiful view of the sunset—"

"Nice try. No dice. If you won't tell me about you, tell me about Joshua and Susan."

Her relief was so great that he'd turned his attention away from her, she said, "What do you want to know?"

"Everything."

She gave a nervous laugh. "That could take quite a while."

"I'm not going anywhere."

Nick's voice was strong and sure, and Hope couldn't help but think that his words went deeper than face value.

Fourteen

DURING the next two hours Nick listened as Hope talked. At first she'd started slow and hesitant, almost as if she were carefully guarding her words. But sometime between their salads and main course, she had begun to relax. Maybe it was the questions he asked one right after the other about Joshua and Susan, maybe it was the candlelight and music, or maybe it was the three glasses of wine he'd poured for her when her glass was close to empty. Glasses he knew she didn't even realize she was drinking. But whatever it was, he didn't question it. Instead he relished the sound of her voice and the insight she provided about his children.

He heard about their school days and passions. How Joshua excelled in math and music and sports. How Susan was a science whiz and loved soccer and drawing. He learned that Joshua's first Little League hit was a home run and how Susan fell off the stage during a ballet recital when she was seven, but she'd handled it with such style that the audience ended up clapping and cheering. He learned about their grades and their friends. Some of the trips they'd taken and the pets they'd had and Fonz, Joshua's pet turtle. He learned more about Hope's Aunt Peg and the more he learned, the deeper his gratitude went to the woman who had treated Hope like her own daughter and his children like her own grandchildren. And while he enjoyed listening to it all, he couldn't help but feel regret for the years he'd missed.

"You mean Susan likes snakes but is deathly afraid of flies?"

"Yes," Hope said with a smile as she cut a small piece of lamb. "But I have a sneaking suspicion Dana is to blame for that."

"How so?"

She took a bite, chewed, swallowed. "Remember that old cult classic *The Fly*?"

"Who doesn't?"

"The twins certainly do," she said with a smile in her voice. "When they were little and Dana was babysitting while I worked late, the little munchkins snuck out of bed and watched without her knowing. We found them huddled behind the couch later that evening and ever since then, Susan hasn't seen a housefly quite the same way."

Nick laughed. "Poor thing. But what about Josh? How does he feel about flies?"

"Loves to catch them and torment his sister." She shook her head and smiled. "Those two and their antics have given me more than one gray hair."

"I don't see any."

"Candlelight is always a girl's best friend."

He couldn't help but think she looked good in any light. "How were they as babies?"

"What do you mean?"

Nick took a drink of wine. "Were they healthy?"

"Very," she said almost wistfully. Then she seemed to shake herself, refocus. "Except for when they went through a bout of colic. I didn't think I'd survive. One night, when I'd just about reached my limit, I bundled them up and headed to the one place that had brought me comfort when I'd first moved in with Aunt Peg. The boardwalk."

She looked at Nick and in that moment he knew they were both thinking of only a few days ago, when they'd been on that boardwalk and he'd learned of Joshua's illness.

She toyed with the stem of her wineglass. "I don't know how many hours I spent pushing them in their stroller up and down that boardwalk. But somehow it worked. The stroller, the night air, the water, all of it soothed them into a peaceful sleep. To this day, it's still one of our favorite spots. I can't tell you how many times I've gone searching for the kids when they missed curfew and I'd find them there, hanging out with their friends."

Her gaze clouded with the mention of happier times. Nick felt her pain and in an attempt to erase the sorrow from her eyes, he asked quickly, "Who was born first? Joshua or Susan?"

"Susan."

"I would have put money down Joshua had been born first." Nick flashed her a grin. "Now you know why I don't bet. How much did they weigh when they were born?"

"Now you're really making me think." She took a drink, set her wineglass back down. Unconsciously her hand paused on the base of the glass, trailed her fingers up and down the stem. "Joshua was just under four pounds. Three pounds, six ounces. And Susan was nearly two pounds heavier."

"Heavier?" Nick was surprised.

"Yes, but don't tell her you know. She'd rather no one knew that bit of trivia."

Nick chuckled. "When did they first walk?"

"Goodness, let's see. Susan took her first step right after she turned one."

"And Joshua?"

"He was walking at nine months. He wouldn't stay down."

"Nine months? Isn't that early?"

"A little, but Josh has always wanted to be ahead of the pack. Take his driver's learner's permit, for instance."

The waiter came, asked if they were finished, and when they both said yes, he cleared their dinner plates, leaving a dessert menu. Nick set it aside, impatient for the waiter to leave. He wanted to hear more. The moment the waiter left, Nick prodded her to continue. "What about his permit?"

Hope leaned back, running her fingers up and down the delicate stem of her wineglass. "Josh had made a countdown on my calendar until the day he and Susan could get their permits."

She smiled at her memory and Nick found himself smiling along with her. "When I got home from work that day the lawn had been mowed, the living room vacuumed, and the kitchen cleaned."

Nick nodded, now understanding. "Oh, I get it. Susan and Joshua had cleaned up the house so you would take them to get their permits."

Hope's grin widened. "Partially true. Joshua had done everything because he wanted to be ahead of Susan in the DMV line so he could make sure and tell everyone he had his permit before her."

Nick laughed with her. After their laughter had died away, he studied her face in the soft light. Some of the tension had left her, eased the lines around her eyes. He knew they'd been there for hours, but he wasn't in any hurry to leave. "When did they lose their teeth?"

Hope laughed loudly. "I'm going to need to consult the baby bibles for that one."

"Baby bibles?"

"Their baby books."

Baby books. Books that would show him all of the things he'd missed over the years. "Can I see them?"

The question seemed to catch her off guard. Her fingers stilled on the stem of her glass and her gaze wavered. "If you want to."

"For that, I'm going to buy you dessert."

"You can't be serious," Hope said with a small laugh. "I couldn't eat another bite."

"Dinner isn't dinner without dessert."

"Spoken like a man who doesn't have to worry about his waistline."

"M-M-Mr. Fortune?" A young man, no more than seventeen, hovered near the edge of their table. "M-Mr. Fortune. I watch you every Sunday. You're the best."

Nick set the dessert menu down. "Thank you."

"C-could I have your autograph?" He shoved a paper and pen at Nick.

Nick took the pen and paper. "Of course. What's your name, son?"

"Robert. Robert Murphy, sir. But everyone just calls me Robby."

"Well, Robby Murphy, it's a true pleasure to meet you." With an efficiency born from signing thousands of autographs, Nick jotted a quick note and signed his name. He then handed the paper and pen back to the young man and shook his hand.

"Hope to see you at the track soon," Nick said.

"Yeah. You bet. Dad and I are hoping to see ya at Indianapolis."

"Great track. Should be a good one. If you do make it, check at Will Call. I'll leave a pit pass for you and your father."

"Really? Wow. Thanks, man! Thanks a bunch!" Robby couldn't keep the huge grin off his face. "But hey, what are you doing here? What about qualifiers? You're going to be at Bristol, right?"

At the mention of the race he was going to miss, Nick felt tonight's ambience start to wane. "Not this week."

"Ah, bummer, man. Race won't be the same without you. But next week. You're gonna get 'em next week, right, man? Number eight! Eighth championship, here we come! Well, thanks again."

"I forget sometimes," Hope said after the young man had left, "how famous you are."

"Fame, for lack of a better word, is fleeting. Right now, some people recognize me because I'm still racing."

"And winning," she said with a smile.

"From your lips to the racing gods' ears."

She laughed softly. "What did he mean, 'qualifiers'?"

"A driver runs a couple of laps a day or two before a race," Nick explained simply. "His fastest lap determines his starting position. The fastest driver starts up front."

"What is Bristol and why did he think you were going to be there?"

Nick pushed his wineglass away. "Bristol is the speedway where Sunday's race is being held."

"And if you don't run the qualifiers?"

"You don't race."

"No exception?"

Nick shifted in his seat. Looked for the waiter so he could pay the bill and leave. He didn't feel like dessert now. "No."

"So you're missing the race?"

Nick retrieved his wallet, pulled out several large bills, and tossed them on the table. He pushed his chair back and started to rise, but Hope's hand on the sleeve of his jacket halted him.

"Nick?"

"I'm here. That's all that matters."

Her green eyes implored him. "Why? Why are you missing the race? Is it because of me?"

Yes. But instead of saying that truth, he said another one. "I'm here for my son."

THE roads were quiet as they made their way back to the hotel. But not nearly as quiet as the two people in the car.

A bright half moon shimmered off the lake and kept the night sky from complete darkness. Hope wasn't paying attention to where Nick was driving; all of her thoughts—her whole being—were still back at the restaurant and on what she'd learned.

Nick had chosen his children over racing.

Never in a million years had Hope believed that would be true. Everything in their past pointed to him being a leaver: a man who, like her father, wouldn't stick around. But ever since he'd learned about the children and Joshua's illness, Nick had been there.

But would he continue to be?

That was the question that still troubled her.

Nick slowed the car and turned into a parking spot. Hope came alert, looked around at her surroundings expecting to see the hotel. But, instead, she saw they were on the main street in Banning. She looked questioningly to Nick.

"I owe you dessert."

"I thought you'd given up on that idea."

Without saying anything more, he got out of the car and came around to her side and opened her door. It was then that she realized where they were.

"Aunt Patsy's Parlour," she said a little breathlessly. "I can't believe it's still here."

"I saw it when we were looking for a hotel."

"You don't think . . ."

"That Patsy Pollchuck is still alive and running it?"

"She was as old as Medusa when we were kids."

"Yeah, she was. Come on. Let's go in and find out." He stepped around her and they walked side by side toward the entrance. At the same moment Nick tried the door, she noticed the sign in the window.

CLOSED.

"Christ, this town is as dead as that one you're living in."

A frown settled between her brows. "What is that supposed to mean?"

Nick shoved his hands in his pockets. "Forget it."

"I don't think I should."

"I said forget it. It's not important."

"I think it is."

"Don't psychoanalyze me, Hope. I'm not the one who chose to go and live in a town exactly like the one we swore we couldn't wait to get out of."

Hope wrapped her arms around her stomach and took a step back from him. "I didn't have a choice."

"You had options."

"Name one."

"Me."

"You?" She choked on a bitter laugh. "That's a joke. If you were my option, where were you when I was seventeen and pregnant and getting kicked out of the only house I'd ever known?"

"You should have told me."

"I tried."

"Not hard enough."

Anger hit her, fueled her. "Don't you dare blame this on me. I did try. Many times. But you stopped calling. Stopped returning my calls. And then when your cell was disconnected, I got the hint. No, that's not quite true. I went on believing because I was that foolish, that naïve. Even after you made it abundantly clear you wanted nothing more to do with me, I still believed."

It was as if she were back standing on those courthouse steps, freezing cold, desperate for a glimpse of him. The memory cut like a knife. She wrapped her arms around her waist, trying to hold herself together. "While I might not have gotten the hint immediately, I finally did. So while you were chasing your dream, I found mine. Joshua and Susan. Through them I discovered the true meaning of love and commitment. So just leave, Nick. Leave like you did before and like you'll do again. *We*"—she stressed the word—"don't need you."

He clenched his jaw. "That's a damn lie."

"What is? That the moment you crossed the state line you forgot every promise you ever made to me?"

"I did call."

"Don't lie to me." She could hear the pain in her voice, pain and heartache she'd thought she'd long gotten over. "Don't lie," she said again, quieter. "Not now. Not when it doesn't matter." But it did. Even after all this time, she still felt the pain of his abandonment.

"I've never lied to you, Hope. And I'm not lying to you now. You were as glad to see the last of Jack Fortune's son as the rest of the town."

"What are you talking about?" She stepped closer to him. "What does your father have to do with this? You knew I didn't care who your father was."

"Forget it."

She was getting sick of that response. "How can you say that? If you only knew how I waited by the phone. Are you going to tell me you didn't get any of my messages?"

"No," he said. "I got them."

"Then why didn't you call? Why did you have your phone turned off?"

"It wasn't turned off by choice. Surely you must have known that."

She shivered but not from cold. "How could I know anything? You'd stopped talking to me."

"What was I supposed to say?"

"We'd made plans, Nick."

He swore, plowed a hand through his hair. "I was selling hot dogs and sneaking into unlocked cars to sleep at night. I was barely able to take care of myself; there was no way I could have provided for you. I was humiliated, Hope, and could no more admit my failure to you than I could to myself."

A hundred different memories rushed through her mind. "You should have told me."

"I convinced myself I wouldn't have to. That my big break was right around the corner. I was young and arrogant and had told anyone who'd listen what a big success I was going to be. Everyone in this town had laughed except you. You were the only one who believed. And I did call," he said, staring down at her. "But your mother made it abundantly clear that you had moved on with your life and wanted nothing more to do with the son of the town drunk."

"No. That's not possible. My mother would have told me you called. My mother—oh, God. She couldn't . . . she wouldn't . . ."

Nick took a step toward Hope. "Wouldn't she?"

The enormity of what Nick was saying hit her. She'd stood on those courthouse steps, waiting, and all the while Nick had never planned to show because her mother had told him Hope no longer wanted him in her life. Her pain was so great she felt it as acutely as a blow. "I didn't know. I never knew you talked to Claire."

"God damn that woman." The fury in Nick's voice was tangible. "*God damn her*," he said again. "I always knew she was a vindictive witch. When I see her tomorrow . . ."

He didn't finish his sentence, didn't need to. She could tell by the look in his eyes exactly what he was feeling. But then she thought more about what he was saying. And, more specifically, what he *wasn't* saying. "You knew what my mother was like, Nick. If you believed her, it was because you wanted to."

He didn't have a response.

THE moment Nick pulled up to the hotel, Hope jumped out of the car. She didn't wait to see if he followed her inside. She slammed her door shut and hurried into the brightly lit lobby. For several long minutes, long after she'd disappeared through the door, he sat in the near-darkness, thought about parking the car, and then knew there was no way he could go into that hotel—into his room—and stare at those four walls.

He jammed the car into gear and stepped heavy on the gas. The tires squealed as he pulled out of the parking lot.

He had no idea where he was going, or what he was looking for. The only time he'd found solace was behind a wheel.

Surprisingly, the roads were as familiar to him tonight as they had been back when he'd lived here. There were a few new additions, some modifications, but on the whole, life in Banning hadn't changed. He steered the car to a long, lonely stretch of two-lane highway that led out around the lake. The beam from his headlights was the only illumination on the dark road. He pressed harder on the accelerator, then harder still.

The old pavement swerved and curved. Long ago this stretch of bruised asphalt had been nicknamed Suicide Curves; over the years it had taken a number of lives. A new guardrail had been installed on the left to keep cars from missing a turn and plunging into the ice-cold lake. But Nick didn't have a problem. This road was as familiar to him as the thoughts that plagued him.

Coming around a sharp, ninety-degree bend, Nick slowed. There, on his right, nearly overgrown by brush and partially hidden by tree limbs, was a narrow dirt road.

The driveway was more holes than road. Nick kept the car to a crawl as he maneuvered around the potholes, slowing and swerving to avoid the worst of them. Several times the car bottomed out as it scraped against the dirt. Nick felt as if he were driving an obstacle course. Minutes later, he made it to the end of the road. Ahead of him was a small clearing.

Nick slowed. Stopped. Shifting into park, he rolled down his window and cut the engine. Without the noise from the motor, night sounds crept in. A breeze brushed through the tall grass, rustled through the leaves on the trees. An owl hooted. And then hooted again. He didn't bother to get out but left the headlights on.

Spotlighted in the white glow was a ramshackle cabin that looked as if a strong wind could blow it over. At one time the house had been painted white, but now the siding was bare and weathered with only patches that hinted at its former color. Even in the faint light from the headlights, he could spot the rot in much of the wood. The porch listed to the right and a portion of the roof had caved. Knee-high grass went all the way up to the foundation of the house. The windows were boarded up and there wasn't a path or flower bed in sight. The house was obviously abandoned.

But even when Nick had lived here with his father, it hadn't looked much different.

After Nick had started to earn a decent living on the circuit, he'd contacted his old man, offered to buy or build him a new house. But Jack Fortune hadn't wanted anything from his son. Not his money or his time and definitely not his presence. The last time Nick had spoken to his father, his dad had told him he'd rather be dead than hear from Nick again. Nick had obliged and never called again.

He tried not to think about the other call he'd never made again either.

Why had he come out here?

Disgusted with the view, Nick flicked off the headlights. But even with the lights turned off, the vision of his father's house wasn't erased from his mind. The house Nick had purchased early is his career so his father could live out his remaining days without a mortgage.

Nick had wanted out of this place so badly he'd been willing to do anything. Even trust a woman who he knew he shouldn't.

If you believed her, it was because you wanted to.

Hope had been right, at least partially so. Claire had offered him a pass. A way to save face from having to admit how completely he'd failed. When she had told him that Hope had moved on, he'd believed her. Not only because a part of him wanted to, but because it was what he'd expected all along. Besides, he had nothing to offer Hope. Less than nothing. And as the months turned into a year and then two, it looked like he never would. Even when he'd started to win, to make a name for himself, it still wasn't enough. Hope deserved more. As the years passed and his fame grew, a part of him believed she'd finally reach out, try to contact him.

But she never had. He'd briefly searched for her—for Hope Montgomery—but to no avail. Not that he'd looked all that hard, he was ashamed to admit. Now, he knew why he hadn't been able to locate her. But back then, it had been further proof that she wanted nothing to do with him, and that rejection had fueled him with a renewed fervor. For a driver who was already laser-focused to the point of obsession, Nick pushed himself and his crew even harder. And the harder he pushed, the more records he broke and races he won. He was going to make damn sure when people heard his name, success was what came to mind. Not his past or his father.

But as Nick stared out the windshield into the dark night, he couldn't help but wonder if in sacrificing everything to become a legend, he hadn't lost more than he'd gained.

HOPE stepped out of the shower and wrapped herself in the thick white towel. She took another towel from the stack and twisted it around her wet hair, turban style. When she'd gotten back to her room, the first thing she'd done was call the hospital and check on Josh. The nurse, someone Hope hadn't yet met, told her Josh was fine and sleeping. Hope had then called Susan's cell but once again, her daughter hadn't picked up. Hope left a brief message ending with *I love you*. She thought about checking in with Dana again but decided against it. There was no way Hope was up to a Dana inquisition. Hope's thoughts were too jumbled, too erratic. So, instead, she'd done the next best thing; she'd taken a shower. For the last thirty minutes she'd stayed under the hot, hot cascading water just thinking and wondering.

What Nick had said couldn't be true. He couldn't have called her all those years ago, could he? She knew her mother could be difficult at times—all right, all the time—but Claire wouldn't withhold something that important, would she?

Doubt and uncertainty filled Hope. If what Nick was saying was true, her mother had ruined whatever chances Joshua and Susan had at a real life with their father. Whatever chance Hope and Nick would have had.

But no, that wasn't entirely true.

She picked up the small bottle of lotion the hotel provided and knocked some onto her palm. With quick, almost angry strokes, she rubbed it into her heated skin. If Nick had truly wanted to get hold of her, he would have. When Nick Fortune wanted something badly enough, he found a way to make it happen. And obviously he hadn't wanted Hope enough. He wanted racing, just like he did now.

She'd seen the look in his eyes when that young kid had come up for his autograph asking about this weekend's race. She'd seen Nick's disappointment that he wasn't going to be there; instead he was stuck in a town he hated, with a woman he'd forgotten as easily as most people forgot the brand of toothpaste they used.

But what about what he'd said to her? With dawning realization, she knew that she had played a part in this too. Yes, she'd been young and scared, but maybe she should have tried harder. But even as her mind said the words, she shook them off. It had been his phone that had been shut off. He was the one who hadn't shown at the courthouse. He knew money or the lack thereof hadn't meant anything to her. He just hadn't wanted her. It was that clear. And he definitely hadn't wanted a child—let alone two.

She stood and unwound the towel from her head, angry at herself. Dwelling on the past was of so little importance right now. What mattered was her son and getting her mother tested.

Hope used the towel to dry her hair as best she could and then plugged in the hotel hair dryer and finished the job. She thought about braiding her hair or pulling it up into a ponytail but dismissed the idea. She was only going to put on her pj's and climb into bed with some late-night TV, so really, what was the point? Besides, it seemed like too much of an effort right now.

Barefoot, she padded across the carpeted room and unzipped her small suitcase.

She hadn't packed pajamas. The realization hit even before she had the suitcase open. For reasons beyond her, she'd packed enough clothes for a week but not pajamas.

She rifled through her clothes, looking for something she could use as a nightgown. Neatly folded in a soft pink pile at the bottom was the cashmere sweat suit Dana had bought her last Christmas. A luxurious and over-the-top gift Hope had loved even as she'd chided Dana for spending too much. But now Hope's only thought was: *Bless you.* At least one of them had the presence of mind to pack something Hope could sleep in.

She put it on, finding comfort in its softness. In a matter of moments she had the bathroom picked up, the lights dimmed low, and the TV on. She knew sleep would be fleeting at best tonight, as it had been for the last several months. Not only would her normal worries and fears keep her awake, but so would thoughts of Nick, and what she'd learned. And thoughts about tomorrow. About Claire.

She was just about to crawl into bed when a knock sounded on her door. She glanced at the bedside table. Nearly eleven. Fear landed in her stomach along with a familiar thought: Good news never arrived in the dark of night.

Rushing to the door, she fumbled with the locks. "Yes? Who is it?"

"It's Nick. Can I come in?"

Fifteen

"NICK?" Hope fought with the deadbolt. "What is it? Did you hear from Mrs. Roseburg?" She finally managed to wrench the door open.

Nick stood on the other side, two small cartons of gourmet ice cream in his hands. He held them up. "I owed you dessert."

"I thought something was wrong. I thought—"

Genuine concern came over his face. "I didn't mean to scare you."

Relief filled her and without even questioning her actions, she opened the door wide, inviting him in. She knew it wasn't the wisest move she'd ever made, but when had she ever done anything wise around Nick?

He stepped past her and into the room. His presence filled the small space. That always seemed to happen with him. It wasn't just that he was tall or broad and muscular. It was the little details that made the bigger impact. The way he looked a person straight in the eye and spoke with authority. He walked with a confidence she'd never seen in anyone else. He seemed one hundred percent comfortable in his body. A hint of his cologne—something that reminded Hope of the sea and the outdoors—drifted in with him.

He'd changed since dinner. A worn pair of Levi's hung low on his solid hips and a gray pullover stretched across his broad shoulders. She tried to keep her eyes off him, tried to concentrate on something—anything—but what her mind chose to focus on was something she'd been trying to forget: *I did call.*

And he was here, with her, and missing his race.

Nick walked over to the small table in the far corner and set the ice cream down along with two spoons and a handful of napkins. He looked around the room, paced over to the window. He brushed the curtain aside, gazed out for just a second, then drew his hand away and let the curtain fall closed once more. He turned back around and headed to the table. He toyed with one of the spoons he'd just placed there, then let it fall back onto the table.

He seemed preoccupied, as if something heavy was weighing on his mind and he couldn't decide if he wanted to go or stay. He picked up one of the cartons and turned to face her.

She wasn't sure if it was the poor light in the room or what, but his blue eyes were darker than usual and unreadable.

"Did you want some ice cream?" he asked.

"No," she said softly.

He looked back to the carton in his hand. "Yeah, neither did I. But I wanted to see you."

"You don't need to bring dessert to see me."

"Then what do I need to bring?"

His question sent a rush of heat through her and rocked her off her axis. A hundred different answers passed through her, some of them simple and some sinful.

"What do I need to bring?" he asked again but this time his voice was weighted.

"Nothing." Her voice was whisper soft.

"Come on." His voice was equally low but not soft. "A woman always knows what she wants."

I want you. Her heart betrayed her. She shook her head, not wanting to answer because she didn't trust her own words not to betray her.

Nick walked over to her, ran his hands up on the outside her arms. Even through the soft material, she could feel his touch, his warmth. Goose bumps pebbled her skin.

I called.

"I know what you should ask for."

"What?" The question was out before she could stop it.

"This." He cupped her cheeks in his warm hands, pulled her even closer.

She knew she should act rationally, probably offer up a protest. But he was too close and too handsome and she wanted him too desperately, so that when he leaned down, and settled his mouth over hers, he effectively cut off any protests she might have had.

The two kisses they'd shared earlier this week had been slow and lingering. This kiss reached the boiling point within seconds.

For so many months, Hope had done her best to keep her feelings at bay. If she let herself feel, that meant she had to feel all her emotions. Including her fear. And opening herself up to that was too scary a thought to contemplate. But in Nick's arms, with him pressed fully against her, holding her as close to him as he could, remaining numb was an impossibility. For the first time in months, she let go. She returned his kiss with equal intensity. As she deepened the kiss, she felt the hard length of him and was surprised when that knowledge didn't frighten but excited the hell out of her. Knowing that just their kiss had done that to him, she felt bold and just a little bit wanton and completely out of character. But that didn't stop her.

She reached beneath his shirt, slid her hands slowly up his stomach. Beneath her touch, his hard muscles bunched and his hand tightened on her upper arm. Pure feminine satisfaction shot through her. Her hands continued their exploration, up his chest, across.

"Ah, Hopeful, you don't know what you do to me." His rough voice tingled through her. He cupped the curve of her bottom with one hand, lifted her off the ground. With the new closeness, his mouth pressed deeper into hers.

The whole world seemed to fade away and it was only the two of them.

She tugged at his shirt, pulled it off. With his bare, broad chest in front of her, she did what she'd wanted to do ever since she'd first seen him on her lawn. Wrapping her arms around him, she hugged him close and laid her head against his chest, listening to the sound of his heart.

He leaned down and pressed a kiss against the top of her head. Then he gently tipped her chin up and pressed a kiss against her lips. His blue, blue eyes were passion-filled and she wondered if hers looked the same. He tugged at the bottom of her top, pulled it over her head, and tossed it aside. The moment her bare skin came into contact with his, a wanting so powerful swept through her.

Nick pushed at her shoulders, separated them. Cool air rushed across her, puckering her already aroused nipples.

He ran his hands down the outside of her thighs, effectively slipping off her pants. Soon she was standing naked in front of him. He pulled her back to him, devouring her in a hot, greedy kiss. His jeans bit into her and there was something deliciously wild about being completely naked while he was still partly clothed.

She reached for the waistband of his jeans, tugged him close. She worked at the buttons on his fly. Her hand grazed his flat stomach and he sucked in a quick breath. Feeling bold and wanted, she looked up at him at the exact same moment she took a cue from him and slipped her hand down the front of his jeans.

"Oh, God, Hopeful, I hope you know what you're doing."

She caressed the length of him. "I have no idea."

"Here, then. Let me show you."

And he did.

He did things with his hands and mouth that sent her clear over the edge.

He pressed his body against hers, forced her against the wall. At any other time she would have thought the weight of him would have been too much, but now . . . now it felt so right. He reached forward, grasped her thigh, and wrapped it around his waist. He ground his hips against her, pushing for and reaching a spot that sent shock waves through her body. His mouth found hers again and again. Deep, hot, sexy kisses. Kisses meant to entice and arouse and they did. He took her arms, lifted them above her head. He trailed kisses along her forehead, her cheek, her mouth. He nuzzled her ear, gently pushed her head to the side as he rained kisses down her neck. He continued his downward quest until his mouth hovered near her nipple. He blew hot breath against her, watched her nipple pucker even more. And just when she didn't think she could endure the sweet torture a moment longer, he took her in his warm mouth and sucked. Hard. Long. And so deep she felt it to her core. And just when she thought she'd come undone, he began the process all over on her other breast. Over and over he whispered things, erotic words and evocative images that she knew at any other time would have embarrassed her straight down to her toes. But right now, nothing had ever felt so right.

He growled low in his throat. "God, how I want you. How I've always wanted you."

His words sent a spiral of pure desire through her.

She unwrapped her leg from around him, surprising him by freeing her hands and pushing him a short distance away. But his surprise quickly turned to desire when she tugged and pulled at his jeans until they were on the ground next to her scattered clothes. "Not as much as I want you."

"Wanna bet?"

He was big and fully aroused, and Hope felt a pull deep inside her at the sight of him. She reached out, intent on taking control once more, but he wasn't having any of that.

He swung her up in his arms.

Surprise had her eyes going wide, questioning him.

"We're going to do this right."

"I thought we were."

His chest rumbled with laughter, bumped against her warm skin. She loved the feel of him against her.

"Do you realize"—the bed dipped as he carefully set her down—"that we've never made love in a bed?" His voice was husky.

She reached over to turn the light off, but his hand stalled her.

"Leave it on."

"But—"

"I want to see you." He turned the knob on the base twice, dimming the light. "That's all the concession I'm going to make." The look on his face promised her it would be more than worth it.

He began to kiss each finger, her palm, up her arm. Desire coiled and tightened in her stomach and all she could think about was him. This moment.

"I can't think straight when I'm around you."

Hope thought that was the nicest compliment she'd ever received.

He pinned her hands above her head once more, held them there with one hand, while the other skimmed across her skin, seeking and exploring, pressing against the inside of her thighs until she opened to him.

"God, you are so beautiful." His voice was strained.

She tensed, waiting for the touch she wanted so much. And then his hand was there, between her thighs, sliding over her, stroking her.

He leaned closer, his mouth only inches from hers. He settled himself over her, his warm chest pressed against her tender breasts. And then she felt him. When she didn't think she'd be able to take this sweet torture another moment, he was there. And the torture she desired above anything began all over again.

He was helping her to become someone she didn't know but someone she so desperately wanted to be. When he thrust inside her, she wrapped her arms around him, pulled his head down to her. She closed her eyes, luxuriated in the feel of him. Rock-solid muscles weighted her down but at the same time set her free. She rose up to meet him, joined with him.

He was looking at her, his gaze so intense, so filled with male hunger she felt herself sinking. And flying. Nothing else mattered. It was as if the whole world, and all of its problems, had slipped away and it was only her and him. And when she was lying next to him, her body pressed against his body, nothing had ever felt so right.

HOURS later, Nick rolled onto his back, careful not to wake Hope. After the night they'd had, he figured she'd need her sleep.

Ever since he'd started racing, sleep had been elusive the last couple of nights before a race. Thoughts of the race, strategies and game plans, were uppermost on his mind. But tonight it wasn't racing that kept him awake.

The room was a mess. Clothes were strewn everywhere. The painting—a nondescript landscape—that had been hanging earlier was now propped against the wall, its hook broken. The comforter was pushed off onto the floor, right next to the pile of damp towels from their earlier shower. Looking at those towels had him remembering what they'd done under the water, and that had him wishing Hope were awake and reaching for him like she'd done before. Last night had been incredible. More than incredible.

But that was where the problem lay. Last night hadn't been with just anybody, it had been with Hope. Life had just gotten a whole lot more complicated.

His phone vibrated, alerting him to a text message. It was from his business manager. Nick ignored the first part of the text—obviously Ken had just learned Nick wouldn't be at qualifiers or Sunday's race and was pissed as hell. The second part of the text drew his attention.

Full report on Hope Montgomery Thompson complete. Awaiting instruction.

Nick turned and looked down at Hope. Moonlight streamed through the window, bathing her in its soft glow. Blond hair spilled across the pillow in a sexy rumpled mass. He felt a stab of desire as he remembered just how her hair had gotten to be such a tangled mess. And he remembered a lot of other things too. Like the feel of her, the way she'd moaned his name when he was deep inside her, and how she was the only one who could make him lose complete control.

In sleep, she looked . . . peaceful. And younger. Gone were the worry lines that creased the corners of her green eyes, drew her mouth down and erased her smile.

He felt a familiar ache for all she'd endured, but he also felt a stab of admiration. She *had* endured a lot—more than most people could ever imagine—but instead of crumbling under its oppressive weight she'd risen above it, become stronger.

For years he'd thought he'd forgotten her, but now he knew what a farce that had been. He knew that last night was going to change everything between them. And while they knew a lot about each other from their past, there was a lot to discover about the people they'd become during their years apart. But those discoveries were going to be a hell of a lot of fun and nothing he wanted to learn from the pages of a report or especially from someone else.

Without thinking twice, Nick typed out a text to Ken: Burn it, then hit Send.

He set his phone back on the nightstand, then rolled over

and faced Hope. Her dark eyelashes fanned out against her pale skin. Her lips were puffy and more red than normal. Nick had no trouble understanding why. He knew he shouldn't reach for her, knew he should let her sleep, but even knowing all that, it didn't stop him. All he wanted was to find his way home again in her arms.

Leaning forward, he kissed her, slowly. Her eyes fluttered open and she stirred awake. She was looking at him like she never wanted him to leave, and before he lost himself once more in the magic of her, he said the two words that he'd meant to say earlier, when he first arrived.

"I'm sorry. I'm sorry I believed her."

Sixteen

SOMETHING woke her. Hope fought against the intrusion. A dream, a wonderful dream, floated just beyond her grasp and she knew if she could fall back into that peaceful sleep she could recapture it. *Peaceful sleep.* Two words she hadn't put together in a long time. She'd slept, she'd actually slept. A smile curved her mouth and she stretched languorously under the covers only to realize that her body wasn't as peaceful as she was. Muscles she didn't even know she had protested at the early-morning workout. She squinted her eyes, tried to block out the morning sun.

The phone rang—again. With a start, she realized that was what had woken her. Still more than half asleep, she fumbled around on the nightstand. Her hand bumped into the phone, knocked it off its base. Grasping and finding the cord, she pulled it toward her and held the phone to her ear. But the ringing didn't stop. Confused, it took her a moment to realize it wasn't the hotel phone ringing. Before she could wonder where else the noise would be coming from, the bathroom door opened, and out walked Nick.

Steam billowed behind him and it was obvious by the towel slung low on his hips and the one he was using to dry his hair that he'd had a shower. "Mornin'."

Surprise hit her almost the same moment embarrassment did. For some reason, she'd thought she'd wake up alone. She tugged the covers tighter. "Good morning." Her voice was thick with sleep and memories.

He walked over to his jacket, which was slung across one of the hotel chairs. Reaching into the pocket, he pulled out his cell. "Hello?"

His deep blue eyes were still on her as he talked, and the burning desire she saw in them made her feel wanted. Loved.

Her mind came to a sudden halt. Where had that come from? *Loved* was definitely not a word she'd use in the same context as Nick. What they'd shared last night was amazing. But no matter how wonderful it had been, it had been a mistake. Nick didn't love her and she wasn't going to make the same mistakes she'd made when she was younger. She wasn't going to fall in love with a man who couldn't love her back. Last night had been . . . a momentary lapse. A release. What mattered now was Joshua and getting him well and getting her family put back together again.

She turned away from the look in his eyes, fussed with the covers, brushed the wrinkles away. She needed to get to the bathroom, where she could close the door behind her, shut out the rest of the world—shut out Nick—and think. Sort her feelings. She looked around, tried to find something she could slip on because even though he'd already seen everything, he'd only seen it in the soft darkness of night. Bright morning light was a whole other story.

"Thank you for the call, Mrs. Roseburg."

Mrs. Roseburg. Hope's pulse sped up. Her mother's neighbor. That could only mean one thing.

"Your mom is back," was all he said.

* * *

LESS than thirty minutes later they were packed, dressed, in the car, and on their way. Hope pulled her sunglasses out of her purse and slipped them over the bridge of her nose. Even though it wasn't even nine, a hot morning sun was already making its presence known. But the sunglasses served another purpose, too. They weren't just keeping the light out, they were also keeping her feelings in. Too many times since the call, she caught Nick staring at her and she was afraid her eyes revealed too much. Not only about last night but about today. She was going to see her mother for the first time in sixteen years and ask her for a favor. The irony of that would have made her laugh if the situation weren't so dire. Ask Claire—a woman who had never done a kind act in her life. A deep-seated uneasiness blossomed into a full-grown panic as the miles between the hotel and her mother's house shrank.

Nick turned the car off the main road and onto her mother's street. His jaw was rigid and his knuckles all but white as he gripped the steering wheel. Obviously she wasn't the only one affected by the thought of seeing Claire.

He pulled into the driveway and parked.

"She's here." He motioned toward the front of the garage where a Lincoln Town Car was parked.

Hope drew in a deep breath. She wasn't worried that her mother would refuse to help Joshua; that she knew was inevitable. What was tying her stomach in knots right now was the inevitable confrontation to come. Because with or without her mother's consent, Hope was taking Claire to the doctor's office today.

Nick went to open his door, and without thinking, Hope placed her hand on his arm, stalling his motion.

He turned and looked at her.

"Thank you," she said simply. "For being here. For making the arrangements with the doctor. For everything."

"I don't know how glad you'll be in a few minutes."

"Why do you say that?"

Nick let go of the door handle and sat back. "Your mother lied. To you. To me. To our children. When I think about—"

"Don't." She heard the tremble in her voice, fought hard to stop it. She couldn't think about the *what ifs* or the *what could have beens* because if she did, if she allowed herself to go down that path, she'd lose sight of what was important. *Who* was important. And it wasn't her, and it wasn't Nick. "Believe me, we're going to have it out one day, but right now, I can only focus on Joshua and what he needs. Let me talk to her. Please."

"Afraid of what I might say?"

"No . . . Yes." She tried to smile, but really, there was nothing to smile about. "I need to be the one to do this."

Several moments passed in silence and then, without saying another word, he exited the car, came around to her side, and opened her door.

As they walked up the path that led to the front door, Hope knew Nick would respect her request that today be only about Joshua. But one quick look at Nick, and Hope also realized that at some point—and in the not-too-distant future—Claire Montgomery was going to have to face her past lies.

They reached the front door. Claire answered on the first knock.

For a moment Hope couldn't say anything. Her mother looked smaller, somehow, even though that didn't make sense. Older, obviously. Her hair was still dyed the same light auburn it had always been, and she was still dressed as if the pastor or God himself was going to come calling at any moment, but there were changes, too. Subtle things, small differences. A few more lines, a few more wrinkles. A stoop to a person's carriage that hadn't been there before. Changes that happen slowly, week by week, month by month, that didn't add up to much unless you weren't around to see them. Then, years later, taken as a whole, the difference was startling.

"Hello, Claire."

Her mother's expression didn't alter, and if Hope hadn't seen the almost imperceptible tightening of her clasped hands, she would have thought her mother was unaffected by her daughter's return. "This is a surprise."

"May we come in?"

"We?"

Hope moved to the side, giving Claire an unobstructed view of the man standing next to her.

Claire's face tightened. "You," she said in disbelief.

"Claire."

Hope didn't know who was more surprised. Always before it had been *Mrs. Montgomery.* But that had been when they were teenagers, and the tall, strong man standing next to her wasn't a boy anymore.

Her mother made no move to invite them in, and Hope knew it was up to her to take the initiative. "I need to talk with you." She didn't wait for a response. Instead, she walked past her mother and into the house.

The house, in contrast to her mother, hadn't changed one bit. Sage-green carpet still covered the floor, the same nondescript wallpaper still hung in the foyer, and the floral living room sofa and two mauve chairs were in the exact spots they'd always been.

Hope sat in one of the chairs.

Nick chose the chair opposite Hope, which left her mother with the sofa. Somehow Hope found that appropriate. Her mother all by herself on that large, hard sofa.

"I'm here about Joshua," Hope said without preamble.

Her mother had to force herself to stop looking at Nick and focus on Hope. "I thought as much."

"He needs your help."

Claire balled her hands in her lap. "I don't see why you found it necessary to bring him along." She made a motion with her head in Nick's direction.

Nick leaned forward and Hope knew it was only a matter

of seconds before he let loose on Claire. Hope looked at him, tried to catch his eye, and when she finally did, she silently pleaded with him to let her handle this. "Nick is Joshua's father, a fact I don't have to remind you of. So yes, he needs to be here. But the truth of the matter is, Mother, neither of us should have to be here." Her voice had become a blade of steel.

"Nobody asked you to come," Claire said.

"No, you're right. Nobody asked me to come. You forced me to. I have a sick child at home. A child I didn't want to leave. Joshua needs that bone marrow transplant, and as much as I hate to admit this, and as much as you probably hate to hear it, right now you are his best hope for a match."

"I already told you, Hope, I don't see what I can—"

"Don't," Hope all but yelled. "Don't tell me you don't know what you can do. We both know what you can do. What you *will* do. We're going to the doctor's, where you'll get tested."

"It's the weekend. Doctors' offices aren't open today."

"I've taken care of that," Nick said.

Claire raised her chin a notch and looked down at Nick from the top of her nose. "I just bet you have. Just like you *took care* of things when Hope was no more than a child."

"Mother—"

Claire snapped her head in Hope's direction. "I've waited a lot of years to say my piece, and I'm going to say it."

"Please do." Nick's voice was deadly calm.

Claire was a kettle ready to boil. "You had no right to do what you did. No right at all."

"Just what exactly did I do?"

Claire gave a self-satisfied grunt. "Still only as smart as your old man, I see."

The muscle in Nick's jaw began to tick.

"You got my daughter pregnant, that's what you did. Got her pregnant and then skedaddled out of town without a word to anyone. She had her whole life ahead of her. Her whole life. And then you ruined it."

"I'll admit I made mistakes," Nick said.

"You bet you did," Claire answered.

"But the mistakes I've made have nothing to do with Hope or my children." He sat forward, locking his gaze on Claire. "Joshua and Susan are one of the few things I've done right. The biggest mistake I made was listening to you."

"You never listened to me. If you had, you would have stopped coming around here."

"I listened to you." Nick looked at Hope, and the regret she saw in his eyes was nearly her undoing. "The time when it mattered the most, I listened to you."

Claire's brows knitted. "What are you talking about?"

"I'm talking about the phone call. The call you never told Hope I made."

"If you think your calling—"

"No more lies, Mother."

Claire glared at both her and Nick.

Hope couldn't take any more. She knew Claire had a lot to answer for, but she also knew that right now the only thing she could deal with was getting Joshua well. "We are here because of Joshua. Let's not forget that. We need to go to the doctor's."

Nick looked at Hope. By the look in his eye she knew he still had a lot more to say to her mother, but he would wait for another time. He stood. "I'll go start the car."

"But I can't—" Claire began.

Hope got out of her chair, grabbed her coat and purse, and marched over to her mother. "You have two choices, Mother. Either you walk out of this house on your own two feet or I'll carry you out. What's it going to be?"

Without saying another word, Claire got her coat and followed Hope outside.

THE trip to the doctor's was almost anticlimactic. When they'd left her mother's house, Claire had tried to insist on following them in her own car, but Hope had squashed that idea. She wasn't taking any chances. She could see her mother getting "lost" on the way and then they'd never be able to find her.

Nick, true to his word, had had everything prearranged. In less than twenty minutes, they were seated in an office, facing Dr. Arnt, who was seated on the other side of the desk. The usual generic pleasantries had been exchanged when the doctor (a young man with bleached blond hair and a dark tan) had unlocked the office's double glass front doors and led them back to his office.

The office building was new and tastefully furnished, but other than that, Hope didn't notice much except that they were the only four people in the building. No other support staff were present. She wondered how many strings Nick had needed to pull—how much money he had spent—to make this appointment happen. And then she wasn't wondering any longer as the doctor continued speaking.

"As I was saying, due to the circumstances, we're proceeding differently than we normally would in a case such as this."

How fully Nick had explained their *circumstances* remained a mystery to Hope but by the doctor's approach, he was obviously aware that Claire was a less-than-enthusiastic participant.

"Normally, we would have a potential bone marrow donor complete a medical history questionnaire before we proceed with the initial testing. In many cases, that initial questionnaire can rule out potential donors, but as time is of the essence, we will be combining steps to expedite matters." The doctor withdrew a several-paged document from a folder and handed it across the table. When her mother didn't reach for it, Hope leaned forward and took the questionnaire, shooting a glance her mother's way.

Claire hadn't moved one inch since taking her seat. She sat on Hope's left, Nick on Hope's right. Her mother sat stiff and erect, her purse braced on her lap, her hands wrapped tightly around the short, hard curve of her purse's handle. She neither smiled nor frowned; if anything, her expression was one of resignation.

"Mrs. Montgomery," Dr. Arnt said, waiting until Claire looked him fully in the eyes. "It's not uncommon for potential donors to be apprehensive and to have questions. I am here to address whatever concerns you may have and to walk you through the next few steps in this process. A woman of your advanced age—"

"I'm fifty-eight," her mother snapped. It was the first bit of emotion she'd shown since leaving her house. "Hardly advanced."

The doctor smiled understandingly. "True, but medically speaking, you are at the upper limit for a bone marrow donor. A harvest is seldom performed on anyone older than sixty. But be assured your age does not automatically rule you out," the doctor quickly added. "If these initial tests come back showing you are a match, your health history and physical exam will be the determining factors as to whether the doctors can proceed. Normally, after I or another doctor had reviewed your history we'd start with a cheek swab for the initial donor screening process, but again, to facilitate faster results, I'll be doing not only a cheek swab today but drawing blood."

"Will it hurt?" her mother asked.

"Today's blood draw? No. No more than the normal poke you get at a doctor's visit."

"How soon will we know the results?" Nick's voice startled Hope. It was the first question he'd asked since they'd arrived, and she was so focused on the mission at hand, she'd almost forgotten he was there.

"With the weekend upon us, it will take an extra couple of days to learn the initial results. I would hope by Tuesday or Wednesday we would hear something."

"And then?" Hope asked, already knowing. She had researched extensively about Joshua's illness and bone marrow donation. But she asked the question because she knew her mother would not.

The doctor turned his sympathetic gaze to her. "If your mother is a match and in good health, the harvest process will proceed one of two ways. Either by extraction of peripheral blood stem cells, or PBSC, or by the method most people are more familiar with—extraction of the bone marrow. PBSC," the doctor said, looking not only to Hope but to her mother and Nick as well, concentrating mostly on Claire, "is a nonsurgical procedure. For a few days leading up to the donation, the donor"—he nodded at Claire—"will be given injections of filgrastin, a medication used to increase the blood-forming cells in the bloodstream. On the day of donation, a needle is placed in the donor's arm to remove their blood, which is then passed through a machine that separates out the blood-forming cells. The remaining blood is then returned to the donor through another needle in the other arm. Since this is a nonsurgical procedure, not only are the risks far less but so is the recovery time."

"And the other method of donation?" This time, the question came from Nick.

"Unlike PBSC, bone marrow harvesting is a surgical procedure and therefore carries with it greater risks. Especially for someone of Claire's age. The procedure consists of using needles to draw liquid marrow from the back of the donor's pelvic bone. While this procedure is performed in an operating room and the donor receives anesthesia, once that wears off, the donor's discomfort, level of pain, and recuperation time can vary greatly. Most donors are able to return to their regular life within a week, but that is not always the case."

"Who determines which method is used?"

"Joshua's doctors."

Hope barely heard this question Nick asked or the doctor's response.

Needles.

Extraction.

Harvest.

Pain.

A new terror gripped Hope as the doctor's words replayed in her mind. She knew all of this. Of course she did. She'd done enough research to earn her own PhD. But now, sitting in the doctor's office, next to her mother, Hope also kept hearing: *Will it hurt?*

If by a miracle Claire was a match for Joshua, how would her mother ever be convinced to go through the procedure when she was worried about the all-but-nonexistent pain she'd feel from today's simple blood draw?

The rest of the appointment passed in a blur. After Claire completed the medical questionnaire, the doctor swabbed her cheek, drew blood, and asked her several more times if she had any questions. Her mother's answer was the same each time: No. As they were leaving the office, the doctor pressed his business card into Claire's hand and also handed one to Hope, telling both of them to call at any time if a question should arise. The doctor didn't hand one to Nick; Hope was sure it was because Nick already had all of the doctor's contact information.

"Best of luck," Dr. Arnt said as he accompanied them to the front door. "I'll be in touch with Joshua's doctors but as I said, don't hesitate to call if I can be of further assistance."

Little was said during the return trip to Claire's house. Hope tried to talk to her mother, explain more about the procedures, the next steps, answer unasked questions her mother might have. They only time her mother seemed to be aware of Hope was when Hope handed Claire the large manila envelope she'd filled with brochures and literature on bone marrow transplants. Claire had taken the envelope and placed it on her lap, under her purse, without saying a word. After that, Hope found it easier to stop talking.

Now, as she and Claire made their way to the front door, Nick having stayed behind in the car, she struggled to find the right words. What did you say to someone who wanted nothing to do with you but could possibly save your son's life?

No words were adequate.

With keys in hand, her mother reached for the door. In moments she'd be gone, shut away once again from Hope, from the grandchildren she didn't want. Without another thought, Hope took hold of her mother's hand.

At the contact, Claire's eyes widened and she drew in a quick breath.

"Thank you," Hope said. "Thank you for what you did today."

Her mother looked down at their entwined hands. A look passed over her face and Hope could have sworn it was a look of longing. But then it was gone so quickly, leaving Hope questioning if she'd really seen it.

Claire pulled her hand free. "Ask him. Ask him *when* he called." Without another word she walked inside, closing the door behind her.

For several moments, Hope couldn't move. She looked down at her hand, remembered the feel of her mother's palm against hers, and she shivered as she realized that her son's future lay in her mother's cold, cold hands.

Seventeen

HOPE returned to the car, slid into the passenger seat, and slammed the door. She grabbed the seat belt and tugged. The seat belt stopped short. She tugged again.

"Are you okay?" Nick asked.

"Yes." She yanked again. Harder. "Why do you ask?"

"Because you're about to pull that seat belt from its bolt."

Hope closed her eyes, drew in a breath, then tried once more. The belt slid easily, clicked into place. "My mother . . ."

"Always knew exactly what to say to upset you."

Ask him. Ask him when he called.

Nick put the car in reverse and backed out of the driveway. "I knew I should have gone with you when you walked her to the door."

Hope felt the start of a headache bloom behind her right eye. "No. It was better you didn't. Wednesday," she murmured, rubbing her temple.

"Maybe Tuesday," Nick said, once again reading her mind with pinpoint accuracy. "Dr. Arnt said the results may be back as soon as then."

"Maybe," she said, but her voice held no conviction. She wouldn't allow herself to invest in the earlier date. Too many times during this journey of Joshua's they'd been disappointed by delayed test results.

Summer colors blurred past as Nick maneuvered through town and then to the interstate. She knew without asking that they were headed directly to the airport. After receiving the call from her mother's neighbor this morning, they'd thrown their things into their suitcases and stowed them in the trunk before checking out of the hotel. There was nothing to delay their departure. She was glad. It felt as if she'd been gone for weeks instead of hours.

"It'll be good to get home," Hope said. "But . . ."

He rested his hand on top of hers and gave it a gentle squeeze. "You hate to leave without knowing Claire's test results."

"Yes, but there's no way I'd be gone from the kids that long. But what if she leaves again and this time she doesn't return? What if she's a match—*when* she's a match," Hope said vehemently, instantly correcting herself, "and we can't locate her? The Claire I remember didn't leave on overnight trips, but she was gone when we got here. And I never thought to ask her where she'd been. Not that it mattered. And not that she'd probably even tell me, not with our history. You saw her reaction when the doctor explained the procedure. It could be painful. Her recovery time could be lengthy. She could leave and we wouldn't be able to find her."

Nick gave Hope's hand another squeeze. "If Claire is a match, there is nowhere she could hide that I wouldn't be able to locate her. You have my word."

Before he refocused on the road, Nick's steadfast gaze held hers. In his eyes she saw the absolute truth of his words.

"Now, are you going to tell me what she said to you when you walked her to the front door? It obviously upset you, whatever it was."

Ask him. Ask him when he called.

Hope stared down at his hand atop hers, felt the warmth of the connection. From the moment she had opened her front door yesterday morning and Nick had been on the other side, he'd done everything in his power to help her. And then some. Not only had he been with her every step of the way during these last two days, he'd also worked incredibly hard behind the scenes to make sure Claire got tested as quickly as possible and the results processed just as swiftly. He'd been strong and unfaltering when Hope needed it the most. In the beginning—when Josh had first been diagnosed—Hope had been better. Stronger. But the constant worry and stress over time took its toll. These last couple of days, Nick had been her strength. And Claire had seen that. She'd never liked Nick. Had tried everything in her power to break them up all those years ago. Her mother lived an unhappy life; the only thing that probably brought her any joy was to cause misery for others.

Ask him. Ask him when he called.

"Nothing," Hope said. "My mother said nothing that mattered."

HOPE woke with a start and glanced around. Sleep wrinkled the edges of her mind and she fought to clear her head.

"Good afternoon."

She followed the sound of the voice across the plane's narrow aisle and saw Nick. "Hi," she said, stifling a yawn. She sat up, untwining the afghan from around her legs.

"How's your headache?"

She brushed her hair off her face and gathered it in at the base of her neck. With her right hand still holding her hair, she used her left hand to remove the elastic band from her right wrist, twining her hair through. "Better, thanks."

"That was some nap."

"Was I asleep long?"

"Not long." His grin exposed his lie. "About four hours."

She paused, then finished securing her hair in a low pony. "I guess the PM in Excedrin PM really does its job."

"We should be landing in just a few minutes. If you look out the window you can see—"

"No thanks."

He chuckled, walked the short distance across the aisle, and sat down across from her. "We're going to have to cure you of this fear of flying."

He was so close she could see the beginnings of a five o'clock shadow. She felt his nearness all the way down into her bones. No, she felt his nearness all the way deep into her soul. And that was a hell of a lot scarier.

"Don't tell me I snore," she said, trying to sound casual and light, trying to cover how his proximity unnerved her.

"Okay."

Embarrassment fanned across her cheeks. "How loud?"

"You don't snore. I couldn't resist teasing you. Besides . . ." He paused, didn't say anything for several moments. "I can't be the only guy who could have told you that."

Suddenly last night was between them.

"Sorry," he said. "That question was out of line."

"Yes, it was." Not that she had any wild tales to tell. She'd all but lived the life of a cloistered nun.

"Last night was incredible," he said, leaning forward and taking her hands in his. "*You're* incredible. I know I'm not the only guy who realizes that. You must have men banging down your door, but I'm not about to lose you again, Hope. I'm prepared to fight a whole posse if need be. Claim you as my woman." He flashed her a grin.

Fireworks erupted in the pit of her stomach—from his words or his sexy-as-hell smile, she didn't know, but it didn't matter. "Posse? Claim? I think you've been watching too many Westerns."

"It'd be a hell of a lot easier if we were living in the Wild West. I could pull out my six-shooter and drive them off."

Could he really be saying what she thought he was saying?

"You wouldn't need a six-shooter. I haven't had what anyone would call an active social life. Even if dating had been a priority, the opportunities weren't there."

"Bullshit," Nick said. "I'm a man. The opportunities were there. You either ignored them or were too busy being the great mom you are to pursue them. Which," he said with that same sexy grin, "is just fine with me. And before you say anything, I get the double standard. While you've been raising our children, I've been . . ."

"Pursuing an *active* social life?" She couldn't stop the twinge of jealousy when she thought of all the women she'd seen Nick with over the years. Magazines, the Net, television shows.

"If I'd known we'd find each other again, Hopeful, I would have lived a completely different life. But I can't change the past. I can only promise you that from this moment on, I'm yours. I meant what I said: I never want to lose you again. Or Joshua or Susan."

Tears filled her eyes. "I don't want to lose you again either."

When he tugged her from her seat and into his arms, she went willingly. This time he wouldn't go away. This time he would be there for her, for *them*.

His kiss was full of promises and made her feel complete in a way she hadn't in a long time. She felt delirious at his touch, over what he was saying.

"Ah, Hopeful," he whispered near her ear. His breath was warm, his kisses even more so. "The season is nearly half over. I know my schedule is hectic, but I'll fly up to be with you and the kids as much as I can. And when Joshua is well, I want all three of you to join me."

A darkness tried to invade her euphoria. She pushed it away. But no matter how hard she tried, it refused to budge.

"Join you?" She couldn't understand, shook her head, tried to clear her thinking. "Join you where?"

"On the road." He pressed a swift kiss to her lips, hugged

her tightly. "Honey, that's where I am February through November. Traveling. Going from one state, one track, to the next."

"But I thought . . . I thought that now that we were going to be together, you'd stay here, with us."

Nick drew back, a frown creasing his forehead. "What are you saying, Hope?"

Without his touch, she suddenly felt cold. The few inches he'd created between them felt as wide and as vast as the sky around them. "You're not going to stop racing?" She'd asked it as a question but knew she needn't have bothered. She already knew the answer.

"Stop racing? Why would you think that?"

"But Joshua . . . and Susan."

"Are my children. And I don't plan to ever be out of their lives again."

"But you said . . ." She couldn't go on.

"That I want to be with you. All of you."

She felt as if she were in a daze. Nick wasn't giving up racing. Once again, he was choosing his career over her. Over the children. A career that not only would take him away from them nearly all of the time but could easily kill him.

What a fool she'd been to believe in a future together.

"What type of life are you offering them?" She didn't wait for a response. "Think about what you'd be putting the twins through every time you raced. Every time you got behind the wheel, they'd have to worry that you might not survive. Joshua and Susan have had a college-sized education on how precious and fragile life is. They don't need any more."

"I know how valuable life is."

"Do you?"

"Life is a risk, Hope."

"You're right, it is. But there are risks and then there are *risks*."

Tears burned the backs of her eyes. "I can't be a part of

your life if you continue to race. And neither can Joshua and Susan. I won't put them in that position."

"The choice isn't only yours," he said after a lengthy pause.

"Give up racing, Nick. For us. For all of us."

"No."

She drew in a breath, tried to steady herself. "Just like that?"

A tic started in his jaw. "Let's talk about 'just like that.' Just like that you made a decision sixteen years ago to lie not only to me but to my children."

"I did what I thought best."

"You did what was best for you."

"How can you say that?"

Nick's jaw tightened. "You might be willing to throw away what we have because of who I am, of what I do, but I'm not going to throw away my chance to be a father to my children."

"How can you do this to them?"

"How can *I* do this to them? How can *you* do this to them? They have a right to know who I am."

"They are my children—"

"They are our children. Mine and yours. No matter what you think of me, or of what I do for a living, that's a fact you will never be able to change."

Whatever else Nick was going to say was cut off by the ringing of his cell phone. With a growl at the interruption, he got up and grabbed it. He looked as if he was going to turn it off without answering it, but then Hope saw him glance at the number.

"Fortune," he snapped into the receiver.

Hope listened with only half an ear to what Nick was saying, her mind still reeling from their conversation. She didn't realize he was off the phone until he spoke to her.

"Something's come up and I need to leave right after we land. I'll arrange for a car to take you wherever you want to go. But, Hope"—he waited until their gazes collided—"don't think this conversation is over. When I get back, I'm telling Joshua and Susan who I am. I'm done lying."

Fear shot straight through her, stabbed at her heart and sent such excruciating pain throughout her body that she couldn't draw a breath.

And then the words she'd fought all day to forget came back to her. *Ask him. Ask him when he called.*

Through blurry eyes, she looked at him, asked, "When did you call me?"

"What?"

"Sixteen years ago, when you called and my mother answered. When?"

"I don't remember."

"Think!"

Nick shook his head. "I don't know. Ten months or so after I'd left."

Ten months.

"You never had any intention of meeting me, did you?"

"What are you talking about?"

"The plans we'd made. To meet on the courthouse steps."

"Hope, I told you. I wasn't even able to support myself."

"It rained that day." She really didn't know what else to say. And truly, there was nothing left to say.

WEARILY, Hope set her suitcase down in the hallway outside Joshua's room (she knew its appearance would cause him to ask questions she wasn't ready to answer) and eased the door open. His room was dark, illuminated solely by a single wall sconce dimmed as low as it could go. She paused in the doorway, let her eyes adjust. From the moment she'd exited the limo Nick had hired and entered the hospital, she'd been inundated by harsh, overly bright lights. As her vision adjusted to his room's darkness, she saw that Joshua was lying on his side, facing away from her. Careful not to disturb him in case he was asleep, she closed the door quietly, but the moment the latch clicked, he rolled over.

"Hey, Mom."

"Hey, baby," she said, making her way to his bed.

Even in a room with more shadows than light, she could see how pale he was. How exhaustion pulled at his features, pain clouded his eyes.

"Are you feeling better?" he asked, and it took her a moment to remember the lie she'd told to cover for her trip. Fresh guilt assaulted her.

"Yes," she said truthfully. "I am." No matter what else had happened during the last thirty-six hours, the test was being run to see if her mother was a match. That was all that mattered. "But more importantly, how are you feeling?"

He tried to smile, but she could see the effort it cost. "Fine, but I missed you."

She took his hand in hers, kissed the back of it. "I missed you too." Once his fingers had been callused by his constant guitar playing; now they were as smooth as a toddler's. "Anything exciting happen while I was away?"

"Yeah. The place went nuts. Some crazy in the kitchen decided to swap out the orange Jell-O to strawberry."

Hope smiled. "Wild times to be sure."

Josh shivered.

"Are you cold?" She grabbed the extra blanket from the bottom of his bed and went to cover him. But he'd scooted over. She smiled. "Well, now I know you missed me. I usually have to pester, beg, and bribe you to let me snuggle." She slipped off her shoes and as carefully as she could lay down next to him. Gently, she pulled him into her arms, settling his head in the crook of her shoulder. He'd lost so much weight. She tried not to dwell on that as she kissed the top of his head and rested her cheek against his forehead. He let out a sigh and tucked in deep. She ran her hand up and down his arm, lulling them both with the rhythmic action.

"You didn't eat your dinner," Hope said a few moments later. "Not even the wild new Jell-O flavor."

"Who ratted me out?" His voice was tired, but his exhaustion had nothing to do with physical exertion and everything to do with the constant internal battle he fought just to keep going.

"Everyone's concerned, honey, that's all."

"Yeah. I know."

Even with the door shut there was no way to block out the noise. Footsteps hurried past the door. Voices drifted in— some quiet, some loud. Equipment was pushed up and down the hallway, wheels squeaking. The intercom system clicked on and off, never seeming to rest. *Call holding on line one for Dr. Krajcher. Dr. Krajcher, line one. Dr. Somlyo holding on line three. Dr. Somlyo holding on line three.* And even if by some miracle they had been able to block all of that out, the machines surrounding the head of Joshua's bed, monitoring his vitals, wouldn't let them forget. *Drip. Beep. Whoosh. Drip. Beep. Whoosh.*

"You know what I was thinking about today?" Josh said.

"No, what?" Her hand kept stroking his arm. Down and up. Down and up.

"Your homemade pancakes."

"With chocolate chips and strawberries?"

"Are there any other kind? And don't forget the whipped cream."

"And whipped cream." She smiled against his forehead. "I could make you some and bring them in tomorrow."

"Nah. I don't want them in here. When I get—" His voice caught, broke.

Hope waited, but only silence stretched before them.

She tightened her grip around his shoulder. "The minute you get home, I'll make you the biggest stack of pancakes you've ever seen."

He let out a sigh that turned into a shudder. She snugged the comforter more firmly around him, enfolded him more securely in her arms.

"Thanks, Mom."

Tears welled in her eyes and she tilted her head back, willed them not to fall. "Anything for my boy."

"Do you have to leave soon?"

She blinked, surreptitiously wiped at her eyes. "No way are you getting rid of me that easily." When the town car had dropped her off, she'd thanked the young man and told him he didn't have to wait as she didn't know how long she'd be. But the driver had flatly refused to budge, telling her Mr. Fortune had left specific instructions for the car to wait however long he needed to. Even if that meant staying all night. Hope had tried to reason with the young man, telling him she could call a cab when she was ready to leave. At his look of affront at the mention of a cab, she'd said she could call him then instead of a cab. But no matter her arguments or suggestions, the driver wasn't leaving and he would be waiting for her whenever she was ready to be driven home.

"I guess I can put up with you a little while longer," Josh said. "Wanna watch a movie?"

"Only if it's not a slasher film." She reached for the remote that was connected to a long cord.

"Nuh-uh," Josh said, taking the remote from her. "You'll have us watching a chick flick if I let you choose." He turned on the TV.

"If I don't get a chick flick, you don't get a horror one."

"Deal," Josh said. "Besides, I save those for Susan."

They settled on one of the *Mission Impossible* movies. Hope could not have said which one it was except that Tom Cruise starred in it, but by the time the credits were rolling, Joshua was truly and fully asleep. Hating to leave, she gave him a final kiss, turned off the TV, and eased off the bed.

True to his word, the driver was waiting for her the moment she exited the hospital.

Catching sight of her, he jumped out of his car and hurried around, taking her suitcase from her. "I told you to let me keep that while you were inside."

"And I told you not to wait."

"He said you'd be stubborn," the chauffeur said as he stowed her suitcase in the trunk of the car.

Hope had no doubt who "he" was, and she was tempted to ask what else he had said about her. But self-preservation kept her quiet. The less she thought about—or talked about—Nick, the better.

Eighteen

DANA was fast asleep on the couch when Hope got home. The blanket Dana had pulled over herself had fallen to the ground and as Hope picked it up, intent on covering Dana, her friend woke.

"Hey," Dana said, rubbing the sleep from her eyes. "You're home."

"I'm sorry it's so late." Last time Hope had checked her phone it had been nearing midnight.

"No worries, I got your texts." Dana swung her feet over the side of the couch and sat up. "Besides, you know I'm here for whenever and however long you need me."

"You didn't have to sleep on the couch. I told you to sleep in my bed."

"I like your couch." She patted the spot next to her.

Hope sat down. "Good couch. Better friend." She gently bumped her shoulder against Dana's. "How's Susan?"

"Asleep. Went to bed around nine."

"Nine? Really?"

"Yeah," Dana said, yawning. "I thought that seemed kinda

early too. But the first few times I checked on her, she was on her laptop. And then the last time, she was zonked."

"Zonking out sounds pretty good," Hope said, resting her head on the back of the couch.

"I made pizza."

Hope cocked a brow in Dana's direction.

"Yes, from a box. But hey, the crust was self-rising, whatever that means. That's gotta count for something."

Hope smiled. "Yes, it does."

"Won't take but a minute to reheat."

"Thanks, but I'm not hungry."

It was Dana's turn to lift an eyebrow in Hope's direction. "It's late so I won't pester, but know I've got my eye on you. You get any skinnier and I'm going to have to force-feed you."

Hope snagged a throw pillow from the corner of the couch and hugged it to her stomach. "You already do."

"Obviously not enough. If I can't entice you with my fresh-from-the-box pizza, how about with wine? I brought over a nice bottle of pinot grigio. I'll share as long as you withhold the white-wine-with-meat argument. Though I don't think meat on pizza really counts. Anyway, you know pinot grigio is my one and only love."

"I won't say no to wine."

Dana popped up and was in and out of the kitchen in moments carrying two wineglasses. She handed one to Hope. "To getting Claire tested," Dana said, gently clinking their glasses.

Hope returned the toast. "To getting tested." She took a swallow and couldn't help the doubt that crept in. What if her mother wasn't a match for Joshua? What would they do then? The national donor registry hadn't come up with any compatible matches. Her mother *had* to be a match because if she wasn't, the alternative was unbearable.

Dana gave Hope an assessing look over the rim of her glass. "So, should we toast to anything else?"

"Like what?"

"Oh, I don't know. Like you getting laid."

Hope nearly spewed her wine. "I didn't say—"

"Exactly. It's what you *didn't* say that told me everything. You wanna tell me about it?"

"What do you think?"

"So no, you don't. But you might as well because we both know that in the end, I'll find a way to weasel it out of you."

Hope hugged the pillow tighter. "How could I have been so stupid?"

"You're the last person I'd ever think of as stupid."

"You don't know what I did," Hope said.

"I think I do. And about time. You know the saying—use it or lose it. I was afraid that by now you'd lost it, it'd been so long."

"Maybe I did."

Dana took another drink of her wine. "That blush that is turning your face fifty shades of red tells me differently."

Impossibly, Hope felt her face grow even hotter. "Joshua is sick. I have no right to . . ."

"To what? To be happy? To be human?" Dana ran her fingers up and down the stem of her wineglass. "I thought maybe Nick would be with you when you came home."

"He—" Tears pushed against the back of her eyes. "He left. Again." Hope shook her head. "How could I have brought him back into our lives?"

Dana scooted closer, put her arm around Hope. "You didn't have a choice."

"I had a choice about last night."

"Sometimes our hearts don't give us one."

Our hearts.

For the second time in her life, she'd fallen in love with Nick. How could she have made the same mistake twice in her life? And then she realized the error of her thinking. She hadn't made the same mistake twice because she'd never fallen *out of* love with Nick. But this time it wasn't only her heart that would end up broken.

I'm done lying.
I'm telling Joshua and Susan who I am.

"Hope, what's wrong?"

Hope looked up at Dana. There were so many ways she could answer Dana's question, so many things she could say. She could tell Dana that while she'd been dreaming of a lifetime of tomorrows with all of them together, Nick hadn't been able to leave quickly enough.

"What am I going to do? How I am going to protect them?"

NOT long after, Dana headed home. Hope tried to convince her to spend the night, it was so late after all, but Dana said her man (Oscar, her cat) and her DVR were summoning her.

"Call if you need anything," Dana said with a final kiss and hug as she got into her car. "Anytime about anything. I'm getting better about my cell, I promise." She paused, her keys in her hand. "Now *you* promise."

"I promise."

"To?" Dana prompted.

"To call," Hope said, closing the car door.

Dana started the car and rolled down her window. "All I have on tomorrow's schedule is cleaning, so I'm yours if you need me."

"Cleaning? As in clearing out your DVR?"

"You know me too well. I'm four episodes behind on *Game of Thrones.*"

"Ah, your second love. After pinot."

"My third," Dana said, releasing her emergency brake. "You know I was only kidding earlier. You're my one true love. Now get some sleep. Love you!"

The house seemed even quieter when Hope went back inside. She locked the door behind her, then took the wineglasses into the kitchen, gave them a quick wash, and set them in the rack to dry. Shutting off lights behind her, she made her way down the hall. She paused at Susan's door, her hand on the doorknob. She was about to quietly slip in to give her daughter a good-night kiss when she noticed the narrow strip of light under her daughter's door.

"Knock, knock," she said, opening the door.

Susan was lying on her bed, her phone next to her and a bottle of fingernail polish in her hand. A plate with a half-eaten piece of pizza and her laptop sat next to her.

Hope leaned against the doorjamb. "Hi, honey. I didn't think you were awake. It's so late."

Susan gave a halfhearted shrug. "I wasn't. I mean, I haven't been for long." She continued to paint her nail, not bothering to look up.

"Dana just left."

"Yeah, I heard the door."

Hope glanced around. Her daughter's room was usually a chaotic mess of clothes and books and papers and jewelry and everything else deemed vital to a teenager's life, but now, the room was almost painfully perfect. Everything had been picked up and put away. Even the beige carpet had been vac-uumed. The spotless room should have made Hope happy, but it didn't. It was just yet another reminder of all the changes in their lives lately. "You cleaned."

Susan kept her concentration focused on her nails as she tried to put polish on her right hand. "I tried."

"It looks great."

Another shrug.

"Did you and Chelsey have fun?"

"It was okay. We worked on some stuff."

"I'd love to know what."

Susan paused midstroke, the tiny nail brush in her hand. "And I'd love to know where you went."

"I told you—"

"Never mind." Susan's voice held an edge. "I know you won't tell me. You never tell me anything but expect me to tell you everything."

Hope leaned her head against the door and rubbed a hand

across her eyes. She was so tired and the last thing she wanted was to argue with Susan. But lately it seemed they couldn't be in the same room together without being at odds. Nothing Hope did anymore was right. Nothing she said was right. Before Joshua's illness, the three of them hardly argued. Oh, they had the occasional scuffle but none of the teenage tempers Hope had heard about from so many parents. Joshua and Susan were perfect children. A hard lump caught in Hope's throat as she remembered her last glimpse of Joshua's tired body before she'd left him tonight. *Nearly* perfect, her mind corrected.

For a fleeting moment, Hope entertained the thought of telling Susan where she'd been—who she'd seen. But as quickly as the thought came, it went. What if Claire wasn't a match? What if Hope told her children about their grandmother and then it turned out all to be for naught? There would be no way for Hope to protect her children's hearts from breaking from their grandmother's years of abandonment. Hope would be the worst possible mother to expose her kids to that type of heartache. "I'm trying to protect you," Hope said. "You and your brother."

"Well, stop."

"I can't. I'm your mom." Hope crossed the room, tapped Susan's outstretched legs. "Lift," she said, just like she'd said thousands of times before. For a long minute, Susan didn't move, but then she lifted her legs. Hope sat and Susan lowered her legs until they were lying over Hope's lap.

As Hope sat there, next to her daughter, she heard the faint strains of music coming from Susan's iPod. "That's a pretty song."

"Adele."

Hope rested her hand on Susan's leg. "I think I've heard of her."

Susan rolled her eyes. "You're old, Mom, but not that old."

Hope gave a short laugh. "I'll take the compliment."

"Shoot." Susan capped her nail polish and grabbed for her

remover. Uncorking the pungent-smelling stuff, she poured some on a cotton ball and began scrubbing away the polish she'd just put on. "Why can't my left hand work as good as my right?" She scrubbed harder with the cotton ball.

"Here." Hope held out her hand for the cotton ball. Taking it, she cradled Susan's hand in hers and then gently began removing the still-wet polish. When she was done, she reached across her daughter and took the small bottle of polish down from the nightstand. She gave it a shake before uncapping it. "But if you were ambidextrous, you wouldn't need me."

"Yes, I would," Susan said quietly.

Hope leaned forward and gave her daughter a kiss on her cheek. "I'm glad."

Stroke by stroke, she began to apply polish to her daughter's fingernails. With each brush, fire-engine red coated her daughter's delicate nails. "What's this color called?"

"Red Hot Mama."

Heat spread across Hope's cheeks. There was no reason for it; no reason at all. Except for the fact that the last time Hope had painted her toenails, Nick had noticed. His eyes had darkened and when he'd looked at her, she'd felt her stomach do a flip-flop. Smoldering, that was the only way she could describe his expression. Smoldering with passion. And for the first time she understood the phrase "just one look." That was all it took. And her toenails were painted a tame pink. She could only imagine what he'd think of her in Red Hot Mama.

But then she realized he'd never see them.

"You were with Nick, right?" Susan's question snapped Hope back into the present.

How had her daughter known, and how had she landed on the one person Hope didn't want to talk about? "Yes."

"It's too bad. What happened."

Hope felt her body go hot, then cold, then hot again. Dana couldn't . . . She wouldn't have . . . No. There's no way Dana would have told Susan about Nick. Her friend would never do that. "T-too bad about what?"

"I know you don't like the news, Mom, but you gotta stop living in a bubble." With her free hand, Susan slid her laptop closer, opened it. After a few quick strokes on the keypad, she rotated the laptop around until Hope could see.

FORTUNE'S MISFORTUNES, the Internet article screamed in big, bold type.

> Accident injures a member of racing phenomenon
> Nick Fortune's elite pit crew. Little is known except
> that during routine maintenance, a floor jack failed,
> crushing the man's hand . . .

Hope couldn't read any more. "Oh, no . . ."

"Yeah. Ouch." Susan took the nail polish from Hope and set it on her dresser.

"How did you find this out?" Hope asked.

"I Googled Nick," Susan said with a shrug. "I still can't believe he's a friend of yours. He's famous. Like really famous. He gave both Josh and me his private cell number. He said we could call or text anytime if it was okay with you."

An emphatic *no* was about to cross Hope's lips when Susan continued, "He's really great. I mean, Josh and I didn't think he was really serious about it and all, but after we texted, he texted both of us right back. We've been texting a lot. Pretty cool, huh?"

So much for her daughter or son asking.

Susan swiveled the laptop back around and looked at the screen again. "I wonder if that's why Nick's not racing this weekend."

The texting was forgotten as it all started to now make sense. The phone call Nick had received as they were preparing to land. The reason he had to leave. Hope knew this accident wasn't the reason Nick wasn't racing tomorrow, but all she said was, "Yeah, I wonder."

"Mom?"

Hope refocused. "Yes, honey?"

Susan fanned her hands, then blew on her nails. "Do you think . . . I mean . . ."

"What, sweetie?"

Susan glanced down at her nails. "I'm trying—I mean, I'm trying with Chelsey's help to do something for Josh."

With as much distance as Susan had been putting between her and her brother, the news surprised Hope. "That's really nice of you girls."

"But now Chels is leaving on vacation."

floor jack fails . . .

crushing hand . . .

"Wh-what, honey? What did you say?"

Susan slumped down on her bed. "Nothing. Never mind. I'm just worried about Josh."

"Me too."

"Night, Mom."

Hope stood, pulling the covers down and then over Susan. She leaned forward and kissed her daughter's forehead. "Night. Love you."

Nineteen

IT was just after one o'clock in the morning two days later when Nick entered the hospital. He made his way to the long bank of elevators around the corner. Within moments he was on the fourth floor. With a familiarity that surprised him, he walked to Joshua's room, making sure he scrubbed his hands with a new thoroughness before entering. Quietly, he opened the door. A small lamp near Joshua's bed was the only light in the room. Carefully, so as not to wake his son, Nick eased the door closed and walked over to Joshua. His baseball cap was off and Nick could see the uneven thinning pattern of his hair. A pain, sharp and persistent, pierced Nick's heart. He would give anything to be the one lying in that bed and not his son.

Nick knew showing up in the middle of the night wasn't the wisest course of action, but he didn't want to miss another moment. He'd hated how he'd had to leave Hope so abruptly and fly right out again. But he hadn't had a choice.

He took another step closer to the bed and then stopped short when a movement near the window drew his attention.

Curled up on the chair, Hope slept. For just a split second, Nick thought she was a vision he'd conjured up. Ever since he'd said good-bye to her at the airport, she'd been in his thoughts.

Her makeup (what little she did wear) had long ago worn off, and her blond wavy hair tumbled out of a haphazard ponytail and cascaded over her shoulders. Her jeans and long-sleeved T-shirt were wrinkled, as if she'd been here for quite some time. But nothing, not her rumpled clothes or the fear that clung to her, could detract from her beauty.

He knew she'd want him to wake her and let her know he was there, but she looked so tired and he knew how little sleep she'd been getting. There would be plenty of time for them to talk later today.

He readjusted her blanket, careful not to wake her. Then, as quietly as he could, he pulled up the only other chair in the room. Positioning it next to the bed, he sat down.

Nick didn't know how long he sat there. As the minutes crept by and became hours, he lost count of the times he got up to check on Joshua. A nurse—Linda—came in every so often. The routine was always the same; she'd smile at Nick and whisper, "How's our boy?" before going about the business of checking on him. Nick felt useless. He wanted to help, had asked her several times what he could do, but she'd just smile again and tell him that his being here was the best help he could give Joshua.

Some hours later, as faint rays of soft pink sunlight made their way into the room, Linda returned.

"I heard the cafeteria had fresh homemade cinnamon rolls this morning," she whispered to Nick as she checked on Josh. "You've been sitting here all night. Why don't you go down and try one? Our boy here doesn't usually wake up for another hour or so."

Nick didn't want to leave, but he had the sneaking suspicion he was in the nurse's way. He stood and stretched his cramped legs. Maybe a short walk would do him some good.

Also, with the little to no sleep he'd gotten during the last few days, a shot of hot, strong coffee sounded pretty good. He glanced back to Joshua and Hope.

"Don't worry," Linda said. "I'll call if he wakes up."

"Thanks," Nick said, glad he'd thought to give her his cell number earlier. "Can I bring you anything?"

"No, but thanks for asking."

With a final look at Joshua, he made his way down to the cafeteria.

Even at this early hour, with the sun barely up, the cafeteria was bustling with activity. He poured himself a cup of coffee from the self-serve section, then found his way to a small table near the back. A large picture window on his right overlooked a small enclosed outdoor seating area. Large rhododendrons and sweeping ferns softened the hard brick walls. He had almost finished his coffee when he felt someone next to him. He looked up.

"Hello, Nick."

"Hope," he said, and heard the surprise in his voice. Standing, he pulled out a chair for her across from him.

She sat down.

The little sleep she'd gotten had softened the edges of her fatigue. But Nick knew one night of rest wasn't what was going to make her feel better. What she needed—what *they* needed—was a miracle for their son.

"Can I get you something?" he asked, retaking his seat.

"No. I'm fine."

"How did you know I was here?" he asked.

"Linda." Hope had put on a sweater before coming down to the cafeteria, and now she pulled it tighter around her. Nick saw her shiver. With a quick "I'll be right back," he went to the food counter. It didn't take him long to make another purchase: two cups of coffee and at the last minute one of the huge, gooey cinnamon rolls the nurse had told him about. He left his coffee black but added a healthy dose of cream and a packet of sugar to Hope's. Within moments he was back at the table.

"You didn't have to do this," Hope said as Nick handed her the coffee and cinnamon roll.

"Humor me."

She wrapped her hands around the mug. "How did you know I preferred cream and sugar?"

Nick was mesmerized by her. He tried to remind himself of his resolve to keep his distance, but every time he looked at her, he knew he was lost. "Some things you don't forget."

She wouldn't quite meet his gaze as she blew on her coffee, cooling it slightly, before taking a sip. She set the cup back on the table but kept her hands wrapped around it. "Between you and Dana, I'm going to get fat."

Nick ran his gaze over her. For that brief moment, he let his guard down and let her see just how much he desired her. When her eyes widened in surprise and a soft gasp escaped her, he knew she could see just how much. "It wouldn't matter what you weighed. You would still take a man's breath away. *My* breath."

She opened her mouth, as if she were about to say something, then closed it only to open it again. She fidgeted with her cup, rocking the bottom back and forth on the Formica table. "A girl could lose her head around you."

"Would that be such a bad thing?"

Her cup stilled. "For me, yes. Besides, you wouldn't have said that if you saw me when I was pregnant. I was *huge*. Like whale big."

An image of her pregnant popped into his mind. Her belly swollen and rounded. Pure male pride filled him knowing that he had helped create two such amazing kids. "I would have liked to see you then." Emotion roughened his voice.

She fidgeted in her seat, obviously uncomfortable with the turn the conversation had taken. "The nurse told me you'd been here most of the night."

"Yes."

She looked up at him. "I heard about the accident."

"Figured you would."

"Do you know him well? The man that was injured?"

"Scottie? Yeah. He's like a brother to me."

"You guys are that close?"

"We're a family. The crew, me, everyone who works in the office and shops. All of us."

She looked up from beneath a fringe of thick, dark lashes. "I didn't realize. I'm sorry, Nick. Sorry your friend got hurt. Is he going to be okay?"

A beat of pause. "His hand is busted up pretty good, but hopefully after it heals and with therapy he'll regain some mobility."

Her shock was evident. "Some mobility? It's that bad?"

"Yes," Nick wished he could downplay the severity of the injury but he wasn't going to lie to Hope. "But don't worry, Scottie will be taken care of. Like I said, we're family. Hope, I—"

"Please. I need to say something."

Nick didn't know if it was fear at what she was going to say or guilt or regret on his part for his past actions, or a combination of all three, but he needed to speak. "If this is about what you said on the plane . . . About me not showing up to the courthouse, I'm sorry. More sorry than you'll ever know. I hoped when we talked at dinner, when I explained what my life had been like, you'd understand what I had been up against. I'm not saying that excuses what I did but maybe helps you understand the reason I didn't meet you as planned had nothing to do with you and everything to do with me. My failing."

It was several moments before Hope spoke. "What happened all those years ago shouldn't matter—doesn't in a lot of ways. How can it when Joshua is facing what he is? But it hurt, Nick. It hurt more than I can ever describe. I stood there for hours in the rain, never doubting for a moment that you'd show. Only when it was painfully obvious you weren't coming did I start to understand."

"I was a kid, Hope. A stupid, stubborn, embarrassed kid.

I'm sorry. Please believe me. But to be honest, I never truly believed you'd want to marry me. Especially when it looked like my life was going to turn out no better than my father's."

"How many times do I have to tell you, who your father was had no bearing on my feelings for you? What more could I have done back then to prove that to you?" Almost angrily, she swiped her hair off her face. Then as quickly as her frustration flared, it was gone. "Honestly, I don't want to talk about it anymore. It's over and done with. In the past."

He knew that wasn't true just as much as she did. But he knew that trying to explain further right now wouldn't get him anywhere. "I meant what I said on the plane, Hope. I never want to lose you again. Our son is sick and that is scary as hell and causes a lot of uncertainties but there is one thing I am certain of and that's us. You and me and Joshua and Susan. Together we can get through anything."

"Nick, please, don't. It can't work. *We* can't work."

He wanted to get out of his chair and go over to her. He wanted to take her in his arms and hold her tight. He wanted to whisper in her ear that everything would be okay. They would find a way to make this work. He wanted to tell her . . . ah, hell, he wanted to tell her things she didn't want to hear. She'd made that abundantly clear. But some things were worth fighting for. "Hope—"

"Are you still planning to continue racing?"

He had to lean forward to catch every word, she said them so quietly. Almost as if she were afraid of his answer. "Yes."

"Because of that championship?"

"What do you want me to say, Hope? That winning an eighth championship doesn't mean anything to me? That I should just throw away what I've worked my whole life for? No, it's not everything, but it means a hell of a lot."

"That's where we differ, Nick. The only thing that matters to me right now is getting Joshua well."

"And you think that's not important to me, too?" God, she could frustrate the hell out of him. He wanted to shake her until she understood. He wanted to kiss her senseless until she stopped being so damn stubborn. "Why does it have to be one or the other? Why can't I love and care for my children *and* be a driver?"

"Because children come first. I know what it's like to lose a father."

"I'm not going to walk away like your father did, Hope."

She didn't say anything for the longest time. And then she looked at him. "What if you had been the one who was injured?"

"Hope, I could be a plumber and go to work one day and have a bathtub fall on me. Life doesn't come with guarantees."

"But some jobs are riskier than others."

For several long moments, neither of them said anything.

It didn't matter what he said, she wasn't going to change her mind and neither was he. So, instead, he changed the subject. "Have you heard from Claire?"

She studied him for a moment, then shook her head. "No. But I didn't expect to. I spoke with Dr. Parker after we got back and told him about Claire getting tested. He said he was going to touch base with the doctor we saw in Minnesota and, hopefully, we should get the initial test results soon."

Nick nodded. He didn't bother to tell Hope that Dr. Parker had told him the same thing when he'd called. All they could do right now was wait.

She rubbed a hand across her forehead and let out a tired sigh. Nick wondered how long it had been since she'd had a full night's rest. "Do you spend a lot of your nights here?"

She gave a little shrug. "Susan's friend and her family are flying out this morning for a vacation. Susan wanted to spend last night with Chelsey before they take off. This hasn't been a very fun summer for her. For either of them," Hope said quietly.

"For any of you," Nick countered.

Hope gave him a wan smile. "I didn't want Josh to be alone."

In that one short sentence, he saw the depth of her love and the wealth of her pain. "Susan's coming to the hospital later, right?"

"Yes. Chelsey's family is going to drop her off on their way to the airport, but how did you know? Oh, wait. She told me you were texting."

"She assured me you said it was okay."

Hope wiped her hands on a napkin, then dried the ring the coffee cup had left on the table. "You know the teenage motto: don't ask if you don't think you'll like the answer."

"I take it that means Josh didn't ask either."

"No."

"You're not mad, are you?"

She looked across the table at him and realized she wasn't. The last few days the kids had seemed more animated, especially Josh, like he had a secret. And now Hope knew what it was. And if texting with Nick was going to bring brightness into Joshua's day—and Susan's—there was no way Hope could deny them that. "I'm not upset."

"This might make you mad. I meant what I said on the plane. I want them to know I'm their father. I'm going to tell them today and I'd like you there, too."

Hope's eyes widened, and then her shoulders slumped. As if she'd just conceded defeat in a battle. She looked down to the cup nestled between her hands and then back to him. "All right."

WITH each step that he took that brought him closer to Joshua's room, Nick's certainty that he was doing the right thing began to slip away. He glanced to his side. Hope walked beside him. Her agreement after all the arguing shocked him. He didn't know what had changed her mind, but he was glad for it. But maybe she had been right; maybe telling Joshua right now wasn't the best idea. But what if he waited? What if he waited too long and there never was a chance?

He *was* their father, his inner voice argued. And he didn't want to lie to them anymore. They deserved better. But what if they didn't want him?

The question tormented him.

They came to the outside of Joshua's door. Voices from inside drifted out into the hallway. Relief filled Nick. For the first time since leaving the cafeteria, he drew an easy breath. He was sure one of the voices he heard was Susan's. They were both here.

Joshua was awake and sitting up in bed, his baseball cap firmly in place. Sitting sideways on the bed next to him was Susan. Their faces were turned away from the door. On the bed between them was one of the new laptops Nick had purchased.

Nick started into the room. A calmness stole over him as he remembered his earlier visits and daily telephone calls. Each time, Joshua and Susan had been open and friendly. Why should today be any different? Yes, he knew that what he was about to tell them would come as a surprise, but hopefully they would see it as he did. A wonderful surprise.

As the door closed, the twins turned in unison. A smile began to form on Nick's face. They could make this work. They *would* make this work. He would be their father. A better father than he'd had.

Joshua was the first to catch sight of him. When he did, his face contorted with anger. "Get out!" he screamed. "Get the hell out!"

STUNNED, Hope couldn't move.

They knew. Somehow, they'd found out who Nick was. Fear sliced through her when she saw how upset Joshua was. She knew this would only distress him, and that was the last thing he needed. He had enough to deal with at the moment.

"How could you?" Joshua continued to yell. But now, his fury was directly solely at Hope. "How could you bring him here?"

She swallowed hard. All those years ago, when she'd been

so young and Nick hadn't been around, she made the hardest decision of her life. A decision she had believed was the best for all. But now, when she looked into her children's tormented eyes, doubt began to creep in.

She took a step closer, stretched out her hand. What she wanted to do was grab them up in her arms and hold them tight, tell them everything was going to be all right. But the looks on their faces halted that desire. "Josh, honey, let me explain."

"Explain what? That you know I'm going to die so you brought him here?"

That brought her up short. "You're not going to die."

"Yeah," Susan said, "that's exactly what Tommy's mom said before the Make-A-Wish Foundation sent them to Disney World."

Josh laughed bitterly. "A last *hurrah* for the dying kid."

Make-A-Wish? What were they talking about?

Oh God, she finally understood. They thought Nick was a celebrity sent by the Make-A-Wish Foundation.

She took another step closer to the bed. "No, you don't understand."

"No, Mom," Susan said, picking up the laptop. She all but shoved it into Hope's hands. On the screen was a sharp color image of Nick and his racecar, and then a smaller photo of Mount Rainier Children's Hospital with the headline: *Can Fortune make a dying child's wish come true?*

"You're the one who doesn't get it." Tears pooled in Susan's eyes. "We know. We know why you invited him here." She shot a furious glance toward Nick. "Josh doesn't need any do-gooder. He's not going to die. Now make him leave."

Hope glanced over her shoulder to Nick. She wanted to blame him, yell at him that this was all his fault, but when she saw him, pain and remorse knotted her stomach.

He stood motionless. His face blank of emotion. You would have thought him unmoved, unfeeling, until you looked into his eyes and saw a depth of pain that tore at her soul.

Nick must have felt her gaze on him because he looked down at her. "I'll leave," he said simply. "I didn't mean for this to happen."

He was leaving—without telling his children. She waited for the feeling of relief she knew would come. Because this was what she wanted. What she'd always wanted from the moment he'd come back into her life. She wanted him to leave, wanted him to drop his unrelenting persistence in demanding that his children know who he was.

So why wasn't she happy? Where was that sense of relief?

And then she realized how her own thoughts had betrayed her. *His children.* For the first time, when she'd thought of Nick and the twins, she'd thought of him as their father.

With a clarity she hadn't possessed before, she saw in her mind Nick with the twins and the undeniable love he had for them. How he'd dropped everything and flown her to see Claire. How he'd seamlessly arranged their whole trip, from the car they rented, to the hotel, to the doctor they saw. How he'd spent last night in Joshua's room. The texts he'd been exchanging with the kids, trying any way he could to get to know them. But most of all she saw the tortured look on her children's faces and knew what needed to be done.

Slowly, she reached out, laced her hand through Nick's. Even though she couldn't see his face, she felt his surprise. Together they walked over to the narrow bed.

"Joshua, Susan," she began. She felt her face wobble, her words stumble. She stilled herself, tried to make herself strong. "Nick isn't from the Make-A-Wish Foundation." She drew a deep breath and said the words she thought she never would. "Nick is your father."

Twenty

CAREFULLY, Hope closed Susan's bedroom door and crept down the hall. After an hour of tossing and turning, Susan had finally fallen into a fitful sleep. It was after ten, and Hope was bone-tired, but she knew sleep would once again be elusive.

She wandered around the house, straightening the pillows on the couch, picking up a book Susan had been reading the other day and putting it on the shelf where it belonged. There were a few dishes in the sink. It took her only moments to wash them and put them away. She looked around the kitchen, hoping to find something else to do. But her kitchen was as spotless as the rest of the house.

Months ago, before their lives had been pushed off course, Hope would have given anything for a clean house and a few hours of downtime. But now, all she wanted was her old, hectic life back. Where the house had always been in chaos, and laughter and smiles had been as common as a houseful of teenagers.

She went back into the living room, turning off the kitchen lights. With nothing else to do, she turned on the television, keeping the volume low, and flicked through the channels searching for something to watch. A *Seinfeld* rerun, the late news, a paid commercial advertisement for yet another exercise product. Disheartened, she clicked the TV back off.

She had a bubble bath half drawn before she realized that soaking in a hot tub wouldn't soothe what was bothering her. She slumped onto the edge of the tub.

Nick is your father.

She drew a shaky breath, let it out slowly. Even now, all these hours later, she saw the confused, shocked looks on Joshua's and Susan's faces. She'd tried to gather them in her arms and hold them tight, but their stiff bodies and tight expressions told her without any words that they didn't want her.

For the next hour, she talked and talked, trying to explain the choices she'd made and how she believed they had been the best for everyone. But the more she talked, the more withdrawn they became. It was one of the hardest conversations of her life. She'd told them she was sorry over and over, but how do you apologize for a mistake that great?

The whole time she talked, Susan and Joshua said nothing; it was as if they'd turned into breathing statues. Joshua refused to look at her; he kept his gaze glued to a far corner. And while Susan never once looked at Hope, she couldn't keep her eyes off Nick.

Hope had nearly made herself hoarse and her heart had been breaking. The only thing she'd ever wanted for her children was for them to be happy and healthy. And she'd failed them on both counts.

Sometime later, Nick had finally spoken.

I want to talk to Joshua and Susan alone.

It had been the last thing Hope had expected. He looked at her and quietly said *please*. She'd looked to the children, knowing that if they gave her even the slightest hint that they didn't want to be alone with him, she wasn't budging. No matter what. But just then, Joshua finally looked at her and told her that he wanted to talk to Nick. Susan silently nodded in agreement. Seeing the quiet resolve of her children, she reluctantly left the room and waited. Half an hour later, Nick left without saying good-bye. When she went back into Joshua's room, the twins told her they didn't want to talk about it anymore. She'd tried but knew she'd have to wait until they were ready to discuss it more.

For the whole of their lives, Hope had been the one in charge; the only parent in a world that demanded two. Now, whether she was ready for it or not (and, quite frankly, she knew she wasn't), someone else was going to be making decisions regarding her children. And not just someone, but Nick. The thought terrified her.

She had always put her children first. There was never any question of her doing anything else. But Nick . . .

She tilted her head, let it rest against the cool tile of the tub surround.

He didn't understand that. Didn't understand you couldn't have a family and a dangerous profession too. It wasn't fair to anyone, especially not to his children.

As the tub gurgled and the last of the water drained away, leaving only a foamy white cloud of bubbles, Hope faced a truth she'd been trying to avoid: it hadn't been fair of her to keep his identity a secret from them. She saw that now. Realized that she should have done everything in her power to find him and tell him about her pregnancy. In her desire to protect her children, she ended up hurting them more.

Slowly, she got up and made her way into her bedroom. She dug through her dresser, found an old pair of flannel pajamas, and slipped them on. She was just about to crawl into bed when the phone rang.

"Ms. Thompson? This is the hospital. Joshua's missing."

HOPE sat on the couch. It felt as if a lifetime had passed since the call, but in truth, it had only been mere minutes, just enough time for her to call Joshua's phone (a nurse had an-

swered immediately, telling Hope what she'd already sur-
mised: Joshua had left his phone in his hospital room). Hope's
second call was to the police and her third to Dana. The
police officer had told her they would send someone right
over. And Dana's phone had gone to voice mail. Belatedly,
Hope remembered Dana telling her she had plans tonight.
Her cell was probably in the bottom of her purse, out of earshot, or uncharged. In that moment, Hope felt more alone than
she ever had.

Hope glanced out the window, saw the darkened world.
Not even a sliver of moon softened the harsh blackness of the
night sky. A steady summer rain beat against the glass. She
shivered. How could they expect her to just sit here, warm
and dry, when her son was somewhere out there all by himself
in the wet and cold?

She got up, rushed down the hall to her bedroom, and
threw on some clothes. It wasn't until she had her coat and
purse in hand that reason returned. She couldn't leave Susan
alone. And she needed to speak with the police officer when
he arrived.

Oh, Joshua, honey, please come home.

"Mom?"

Hope looked behind her and saw Susan standing in the
hallway rubbing her eyes.

"Mom? What's going on?"

"It's Josh, honey. He's . . ." Hope paused, tried to think of
a way to soften her next words, but then realized that there
wasn't a way. "Josh has left the hospital."

"You mean he's run away?"

"Yes."

Susan didn't wait to hear any more. She spun around and
raced back to her room. Hope was about to go after her when
Susan's door smacked back open and she reemerged. In less
time than it usually took Susan to answer the phone, she'd
gotten dressed. She'd pulled on an old pair of jeans, her pajamas still sticking out the bottom, and a hoodie. She half

hopped, half ran down the hall, shoving first one and then her other foot into a pair of sneakers. "I'm coming with you," Susan said.

Hope walked over to her daughter and wrapped her arms around her. "I need to wait until the police come and I talk with them, and then we'll go."

Susan slowly nodded against Hope's shoulder. They stood there for several moments, as if neither one of them knew quite what to do. Finally, Hope steered them toward the couch, where they sat down to wait.

"It's my fault," Susan whispered against Hope's shoulder. "It's all my fault Joshua ran away."

"It's no one's fault." Hope hugged her daughter even tighter.

"Yes it is. I was the one who showed him the Make-A-Wish article."

Tears stung the backs of Hope's eyes. She didn't know who she was crying for, Susan or Joshua or both. "It isn't anyone's fault," she said again, willing her daughter to believe. "And we'll find him. Don't worry. We will find him."

"It isn't fair," Susan said.

"What isn't?"

"It should be me. I should be the sick one."

"Oh, Susan, why would you think that?"

"Because," her daughter sobbed, "it's true. Joshua's the perfect one. Perfect grades, perfect athlete, perfectly clean bedroom. And me . . . I'm the screw-up. I couldn't even keep my room clean."

"Oh, God, baby." Hope rocked her daughter back and forth. Why hadn't she seen what Susan was going through? Guilt tore at her.

Susan was openly crying now. "That's why I can't go to the hospital all the time. It's so hard to see the kids, kids like Maddy. But when I look at Josh . . . I can't look at him, knowing it should be me in there and not him. Knowing that he's in there because I can't save him. I'm his sister! His twin!"

Hope cupped her daughter's chin and tilted her face up

until they were eye to eye. She used the pad of her thumb to brush the tears away from her daughter's face. "Susan, I want you to listen to me. What has happened to Joshua is terrible. No one deserves this. Not him. And not you. I want you to stop blaming yourself for his illness."

"I'm so scared . . ." Susan's voice was as fragile as a moth's wing. "I'm scared Josh is going to die."

A pain, so sharp and intense Hope would have doubled over if she weren't sitting, pierced through her. "We're not going to let that happen. Joshua is going to get well."

"I'll keep my room clean and get better grades if only Joshua would come home."

Hope tried to swallow, but there was a lump in her throat. "How about this? When Josh comes home, you can go back to being a slob."

A watery smile curved Susan's lips. "And the grade thing?"

"Now that one—"

The doorbell rang.

Placing a kiss on top of Susan's silky hair, Hope gently detangled herself and answered the front door.

It was the police officer. He introduced himself as Officer Owen. Hope led him into the living room. Officer Owen was young. Really young. She began to worry.

Surely they wouldn't send someone so inexperienced. How long could he have been on the force? Didn't they know that Joshua was sick and needed to be found right away?

Her fear compounded, became like a ball rolling down a snowy hill. It grew and grew until pretty soon it was too big to get around.

Officer Owen must have sensed her concern. In a strong, confident voice, he assured her that all was being done to locate Joshua. Taking off his hat, he sat down and pulled out a small black notebook. His first question was if Joshua had a cell phone or not. After Hope explained how it was still at the hospital, the officer nodded his head and continued to ask questions about Josh: his age, height, weight. Where were his usual hangouts? Who were his friends? Did she have a current photo? His compassion, professionalism, and competence slowly began to melt some of her fears.

Fifteen minutes later, Officer Owen stood. "I think that's all I need for right now." He took the photo of Josh from her and made his way to the front door. "We'll be in touch as soon as we hear something. Leave your cell phone turned on and the home line free as much as possible. It's important that we are able to reach you, or if Joshua tries, he can get through."

"I want to go out and look for him," Hope said.

Officer Owen put his hat back on. "I wouldn't advise that, ma'am. Nine times out of ten, these kids return home after a couple of hours. We need you to be here if and when Joshua comes back. Or if he calls."

"But—"

"Trust me, ma'am," he said as he handed her a card with his name and phone number. "It's for the best. I promise, we are doing everything to locate your son. The best thing you can do is to wait here. Don't forget to let us know if you hear anything."

Hope watched his back retreat out the door and down the path toward the driveway. The wind kicked up, pushing the rain toward her. She shivered, wrapped her arms around her stomach, and prayed. And prayed and prayed and prayed.

She went back into the house and shut the door. Susan was waiting. Hope looked at her coat and then to the phone. For sixteen years she had taken care of her children all by herself, and her first instinct was to do that again tonight. But what if she did leave and Joshua called? Indecision sliced through her. She wanted to be out there, searching. But she knew she needed to be here, too, just in case. She needed to be two people.

Two people.

She wasn't in this alone anymore. Tonight hadn't been just about telling the twins Nick was their father, it had been about her finally accepting that he *was* their father. Why hadn't she called him already?

Frantically, she swiped through her list of contacts on her cell and called Nick.

"What are you doing?" Susan asked, coming up behind her.

"I'm calling your father."

"You're what?"

"You heard me." She turned and looked at her daughter, hoping she wasn't making a mistake. "I'm calling Nick. I need help."

"What about Dana?"

"She won't be home for hours yet."

"I can go look," Susan said softly.

Hope wrapped her free arm around her daughter. "I know you can, honey. But without a driver's license, you wouldn't get very far." She gave her daughter a reassuring smile and waited, tapping her foot as the phone rang once, twice, three times, then four. Hope put the phone on speaker so both of them could hear.

Nick finally answered. "Hello?"

At the sound of his voice, the bravado of strength she'd been clinging to since the hospital called abandoned her. Her voice wobbled and a lump formed in her throat. "Nick, it's Hope."

"What's wrong?"

"Is Joshua with you?"

"No. Of course not. Why—Hope, what's wrong?"

"He's run away from the hospital."

There was a slight delay and a noise crackled through the lines. His voice, sounding distant and scratchy, finally came through. "I'll be there as soon as I can." The line went dead.

Susan stayed by her side, and for several moments, they didn't move. The refrigerator hummed in the background and the clock that hung above the door leading out to the garage ticked away. After a while, Susan stepped back and gave Hope a questioning glance. "What was all that noise on his phone?"

"I think it was his plane."

"His plane?"

Hope nodded.

"And he's turning around and coming back?"

"Yeah," Hope said. "I think he is."

RAIN fell in fat, persistent drops, giving the sky a dark and dismal look. Nick flicked on the rental car's wipers and scowled out the window. Only in Washington would it rain in July.

He kept his eyes trained on the dark street and tried to remember if Joshua had had any warm clothes with him. But he didn't know. Hell, he didn't know most everything about his children.

He exited the airport and turned left. The miles flew past; he kept his foot pressed on the gas, not caring that he was speeding. The streets were deserted and with the free road, he flew.

Goddammit! This was his fault. He should never have pushed Hope to tell the kids who he was. He should have just played along, kept pretending he was only a friend. Even when they thought he was from the Make-A-Wish Foundation, he could have explained that away. No one had been more surprised than he was when Hope had told their children who he was.

He silently swore once more and pushed a hand through his hair. God, the look in Joshua's eyes had been enough to rip his heart out.

The miles sped past. In less time than he would have thought possible, he was nearing the small town of Tranquility. Streetlamps bordered the narrow road, their ethereal light filtering down into the damp, dreary night. For the first time he noticed the reader board at the grocery store. *Get Well Joshua!* And as he turned onto Hope's street, he noticed the balloons tied to the stop sign, with a large sign: WE ♥ U JOSH! Nick felt a lump in his throat. This little town—the town he'd so quickly and wrongly stamped with his own prejudices—

was full of heart for his son. The realization shamed Nick; he'd judged before knowing. A mistake he wouldn't make again.

Hope's house was lit up like the Fourth of July. Every outside light was on, and from the bright glow that came from each of the windows, it looked as if all of the interior lights were on as well. It was as if Hope were trying to light the way home for their son.

The car jerked to a stop and Nick barely took the time to kill the engine before he raced up to the front door. He took the porch steps two at a time and was just about to knock when the door was flung open.

"Nick," Hope said, her voice throaty as if she'd been crying. Her face was pale, and standing there she looked so alone, so small and fragile.

"Have you heard anything?" Nick asked, taking her in his arms.

She shook her head, her cheek brushing against his chest. "No. And the p-police . . ." She stumbled over the word, drew in a deep breath. "The police told me to stay here in case Joshua called or came home. But it's so hard to just wait."

"It's going to be okay," he said. "We'll find him."

As if she'd just realized where she was, she stepped out of his embrace. "Thank you for coming."

"Stop thanking me. He's my son, too."

She stared at him for several moments. Then, finally, she said, "Yes, he is."

She stepped back into the house and gestured for him to follow.

Warm air hit him and he once again thought of his son out there in the cold. Nick felt antsy. He didn't want to go into the house, he wanted to be out looking for Josh. He took one look at Hope's face and knew she felt exactly the same way.

Nick looked around. "Where's Susan?"

"My friend Dana showed up and she and Susan are out looking for Josh. The police are also looking, concentrating their efforts mainly in Seattle, near the hospital, but . . ."

"But what?"

"I don't think he's in Seattle. I think he'd come here. Come home. But he didn't, did he?" She looked up at him, huge pools of tears gathering in her eyes. "He didn't come h-home."

Staring into her heartbroken eyes, Nick felt so damn helpless. He gathered her in his arms.

For a moment she let herself be held. Then, sniffling, she pulled back. Put distance between them.

He dug the keys out of his pocket. "Here," he said, handing them to her. "Take my car and go look, you know it's what you want to do. I can stay here."

She stared down at the keys, weighed them in her hand. "I want to," she said softly as she looked up at him. "God, how I want to, but I should be the one who's here in case he calls or comes home."

"Then tell me where his friends live, where he likes to hang out."

"How would you find them? You don't know this town. Besides, Susan and Dana and the police are checking there."

"Hope, I go to a new city each week and manage to find my way around. Just tell me where he might be."

OVER three hours later, Nick's worry had grown tenfold. He'd gone to every place Hope had written down, questioned all of Joshua's friends and anyone else that Nick saw or woke up with his door pounding, but so far, nothing. Every fifteen minutes, he called Hope to check in, even though he knew his call was unnecessary. She'd call him if she heard any news. So far, nothing. No one had seen or heard from Joshua.

Once more, Nick made his way down Main Street. He'd covered this area already, but right now he was grasping at straws. Rolling down the window, he let off on the gas and let the car slow to a crawl. Through the opened window, he scanned the storefronts, alleys, and side roads, praying for a miracle. He called out Joshua's name and then listened, hoping to hear a reply. But all he heard was the gentle lapping of the water as it hit the nearby beach and then flowed back out into the bay.

Tranquility Inn came up on his right and he braked to a stop. Earlier he'd gone in and talked to the night staff. He'd gotten the same answer from them that he'd gotten from everyone else: no one had seen or heard from Joshua, but they were looking and praying.

At this late hour, the place looked deserted. There was no movement inside and the lights had been dimmed.

Nick eased his foot off the brake and let the car roll forward. Ahead, on his left, was the boardwalk. It was where he had been when he'd first learned of Joshua's leukemia. That conversation seemed like a lifetime ago.

Nick pulled into the small parking lot and cut the engine. The bay was so close he could smell the salt in the air and hear the shallow waves. He remembered Hope telling him about the time when the twins were young and had colic. How she'd bundled them up and put them in their stroller and brought them down to the head of the bay to stroll along the boardwalk. The walk and the water had soon soothed them into a peaceful sleep. It had become one of their favorite spots, she'd said.

One of our favorite spots.

With a sense of urgency, Nick got out of the car and made his way to the boardwalk. Water pushed against the solid beams and brushed against the underside. He wasn't even a quarter of the way down the walk when he saw him.

Huddled against the railing, Joshua stood, a dark shadow against the black night.

"Joshua," Nick called out.

Joshua turned toward him, his pale face bright in the darkness. "Go away."

"I can't do that."

"Get back in your car and drive away. Pretend you never saw me."

Nick walked closer, then stopped when Joshua took a step back. His son looked tired and in pain. His shoulders were rigid, and perspiration dotted his forehead and trickled down the side of his face. Nick wanted to rush forward and grab him, hold him, but he knew Joshua would only try to break free and run. Possibly hurt himself even further. "Everyone's worried about you, especially your mother. Why don't you come back with me? We can go and get your mom and then head to the hospital."

"The hospital." Joshua's voice was flat, emotionless. "I'm not going back there."

The rain had eased up. A light mist was all that was left.

"Then where are you going?"

Joshua stared out across the water, scuffing his foot across the boards. His shoes looked to be at least two sizes too big, as were the clothes he was wearing; Nick didn't want to even think about where his son had dug them up—more than likely, dug them *out* of.

"Anywhere but here. Some place where I won't cause so many problems," Josh said at last.

"Joshua," Nick said stiffly, emotion clogging his throat. "You don't cause problems."

"Yeah?" Josh spat the word at him. "What would you know? The only reason you're around now is because I'm gonna die."

"That's not true."

"Then where the hell have you been?"

"I'm here now," Nick said with conviction. "And I'm not going anywhere."

Joshua stared at him for several long moments. "One of the nurses let it slip that you were tested to see if you're a match, but you're not."

Nick swallowed hard. "No, I'm not. But that doesn't mean they won't find someone very soon who is."

Joshua's eyes narrowed. "Don't you lie to me, too. I see the truth every day in the nurses and Dr. P. They know my number's up. And Mom . . . jeez." He kicked hard at the bottom rail. "I don't want her to have to worry anymore."

What did he say to that? "Your mother will worry no matter what. It's her job."

Joshua's grip tightened on the weathered handrail. "Maybe . . . maybe it would be better if I just ended it now."

Nick felt as if he'd been punched in the gut. "Don't say that." He swallowed hard, knew he hadn't said the right thing, but what was the correct response? He didn't have any experience with this. With kids. He drew in a breath, thought about a dumb ad he'd done where the slogan was *Just Do It*. Because, right now, Nick was the only one here, the only one Josh had, and Nick had to just do something.

Slowly, he walked forward and placed his hand on his son's shoulder. Joshua was ice cold. Nick shrugged out of his jacket and placed it around Joshua's shoulders, holding it on him, trying to lock in as much heat as he could.

Josh bowed his head, blew out a shaky breath. "Do you know what happens in a couple of months?"

"No."

"It's my birthday. Last year, when I turned fifteen, all I wanted was to be sixteen. You know? Have a driver's license, hopefully get a car one day. Maybe then I could take Belinda out . . ."

"Belinda your girl?"

"Yeah. No. I mean she was. But now . . . My stuff is just too real to deal, ya know? She hooked up with my best friend, Denny. Well, he's not my best friend anymore."

"After a shit move like that, I'd sure as hell think not."

A small smile crept across Joshua's face, and then it was gone. "Life's just too hard."

When Nick had first started looking for his son, he'd naïvely thought finding Josh was going to be the tough part. Now, he saw how wrong he'd been. Inside, he was crying for all of the pain and heartache Joshua had gone through. He wanted to make it right; he wanted to take it away. He knew he could easily steer his son's weakened body to the car and force him back to the hospital. But that would be the easy way out, the quick fix.

Children come first.

He remembered Hope's words, understood them fully for the first time. He drew in a deep breath and tried to help his son make sense of this senseless disease. "Life is hard. And you've been dealt a hell of a hand, Josh. I don't know many men who could have coped as well as you have. If I could change places with you, I'd do it in an instant. I'd give anything to free you from this." He swallowed hard, tried to regain his composure. "But I can't. I don't know why this has had to happen to you, but it has and somehow you've got to find a little more strength to finish this battle. And while I don't know the *whys*, I can tell you this: it's during these times, when we think we can't go on, but we do, we find out just who we are and what we're made of. You are an amazing man, Joshua, with an amazing future."

"How would you know?"

Nothing in Nick's life compared to what his son was going through, but maybe there was something he could say that would help. "Eight years ago I crashed during a race. The doctors said I'd probably never walk again, let alone race. But I did. We Fortunes are stubborn that way—it takes more than a bad diagnosis to level us." He looked down at his son. "Not only was I back next season, I won the championship that year."

"I didn't mean it," Josh said.

"Didn't mean what?"

Josh kicked at a rock on the boardwalk and sent it sailing off into the water. "At the hospital. When I yelled at you. I didn't mean it. I was just mad."

The lump in Nick's throat doubled in size.

Joshua tilted his face toward Nick. "I'm . . . I'm glad you're here now."

"Yeah, I'm glad I'm here now too."

"Can I ask you something?"

"You can ask me anything."

Joshua tipped his ball cap back on his head and scratched. "My hair—or what's left of it—is driving me crazy. It itches, ya know? And Mom, every time more of it falls out, she gets all sad. I was wondering . . ."

"Yes?"

"Well, I was kinda hoping that you could shave my head." Joshua looked at him again, and his blue eyes that reminded Nick so much of his own were filled with uncertainty and a tentative hopefulness.

"Yeah," Nick said, so overcome with emotion he could barely form the words. "I can do that."

"Thanks."

They stood next to each other and gazed out at the water. The tide lapped at the beach and a few cars rolled by.

"Joshua?"

"Yeah?"

"Don't give up. Great moments are waiting for you."

"Was winning that championship your greatest moment?"

"No." This time the emotion broke free and trembled his words. "My greatest moment happened when I met you and your sister for the first time."

Twenty-one

IN the hallway outside, the hospital was stirring awake. Muted voices drifted through the closed door as night nurses prepared to leave and the day shift arrived. Every so often, a clang and a bang could be heard as custodians emptied the garbage cans. The steady drone of a floor cleaner moved down the hall. But inside Joshua's room, all was quiet.

Hope stared down at her sleeping son. One tear and then another trailed down her cheek. She'd thought she'd used up her store of tears, but she'd been wrong. She could hardly take her eyes off him, afraid that if she did, he'd disappear once more. Even now, so many hours after Nick had called to tell her that he'd found Joshua, the intense relief she'd felt was still with her.

After Nick's call, he'd driven Joshua back to the house. While Dana had stayed behind with a tired Susan, Nick had driven the three of them back to the hospital. The moment they pulled up to the emergency entrance, a whirlwind of activity had ensued. Joshua had been wheeled back to his room, where the doctor and nurses had examined him. They replaced his IV and catheter that he'd ripped out before he'd fled. He'd developed a low-grade fever that they believed was caused by an infection. They administered antibiotics at once. And through this, Joshua silently endured it all, even though it was clear to see he was exhausted and in pain.

Hope turned to the man standing next to her. "I know you don't like it when I say thank you, but thank you," she said in a throaty whisper. "Thank you for bringing our son back."

Nick reached down and engulfed her hand in his.

The dim light from the medical equipment surrounding Joshua's bed illuminated Nick. She could see the light stubble of a new beard roughening his strong jaw. He was wearing a worn pair of Levi's, a T-shirt, and his leather jacket. And even though she knew those were the same clothes he'd had on for nearly twenty-four hours, he looked unaffected and in total control. His cologne, subtle and masculine, had her remembering a night not so long ago when he'd also offered her comfort and compassion. But then, in the morning, when daylight had come, so had reality. It had been a harsh reminder that what Nick offered came with a timer.

She looked down to their entwined hands and felt her resolve start to weaken. But old fears were too hard to dispel. She couldn't afford to place her heart in Nick's hands again. She'd done that once already and it had taken her nearly a lifetime to get it back. But there was something she could do. Needed to do. Slowly, hesitantly, she turned to Nick. "I'm sorry." She said it again, just so she could be sure he heard her. "I'm sorry for not doing everything in my power to find you and tell you about the children. They have a right to know you."

"I'm sorry, too. And I meant what I said: I want us to try to be a family, Hope."

His words made her heart all thumpy and soft and had her wishing for a future she knew she could never have. "I know you'll be there for the kids. I see that now."

It was an evasive answer. She knew it and so did Nick. She

saw he wanted to say something, but the door into Joshua's room opened and Dr. Parker walked in.

"Ms. Thompson? Ah, and Mr. Fortune. Good, you're both here. Could you please follow me? There's something we need to discuss."

They followed Dr. Parker down the bright hall and into a small office. Once in, he shut the door behind them and then went around to the front of the desk and took his seat, gesturing for Hope and Nick to take the seats across from him.

Nick pulled out one of the chairs for Hope and waited until she had sat down before taking his seat next to her.

The doctor started right in. "I was going to wait until the results came back from the additional blood work I ordered, but after last night . . ." His voice trailed off and she knew what they were all thinking. Joshua was losing hope.

Dr. Parker leaned forward and placed his elbows on his desk. A broad smile crossed his face. "I believe we've found a donor."

Joy—undulating, unrestricted—poured through her. A donor! It was what they'd all been praying so hard for. Nothing could stop the feeling of pure happiness that bolted inside her. Nick's hand closed over hers and when she looked over at him, the same emotions she was feeling were reflected in his eyes. "Say it again," she asked the doctor, wanting to make sure this wasn't a dream. "Please, tell me again."

Dr. Parker smiled. "We've found a donor and she looks to be a perfect match."

A perfect match. It was a miracle!

Hope knew from earlier conversations with the doctors and from her own extensive research that in a bone marrow transplant a perfect match was one in which all six HLA antigens matched. It was too incredible for words.

"As you know," the doctor continued, "this is very good news. With a perfect match, Joshua's odds of developing GVHD have just been significantly reduced."

"GVHD?" Nick asked.

"Graft-versus-host disease. In cases where the donor is not a perfect six-antigen match, the recipient's odds increase for developing graft-versus-host, a disease where the transplanted marrow attacks the patient's organs."

"When will the transplant take place?" Hope asked the doctor.

"If everything goes as planned, in one week."

One week. She could hardly believe it.

"As you know," Dr. Parker continued, "there were a few minor complications from Joshua leaving the hospital. We'll need to get his infection under control and then begin conditioning."

Nick leaned forward in his chair but didn't let go of her hand. At first she'd thought he was offering her support, but when she looked over to him again, she thought maybe he needed her as much as she needed him at this moment. "That is where his chemotherapy and radiation treatments are increased, right?" Nick asked.

"Yes." The doctor nodded. "We need to eradicate all the remaining cancer cells in Joshua's body and make room in the bones for the new marrow. During this phase of treatment, your son's immune system will be even more fragile." He looked to both of them. "As with before, family and visitors will have to be extremely careful. We cannot risk someone coming in to see Joshua who is sick. Also, while we encourage family and visitors, we don't want Joshua to become overly tired."

Hope nodded. And then something Dr. Parker had said earlier hit her. "You called the donor 'she.'"

"Yes, the donor is Joshua's grandmother."

Shock was the only word that could describe what she was feeling. Her mother, the grandmother who couldn't even remember her grandchildren's names, was the only person who could save Joshua's life. "Has Claire—my mother—been told?"

"Yes," Dr. Parker said.

"And"—Hope was almost afraid to ask the question—"she's agreed to be the donor?"

"She has. I was told she was surprised when she learned she'd need to fly here as the surgical procedure will need to be performed at this hospital. But she was assured all her travel arrangements and related expenses would be taken care of."

"I can handle those," Nick said.

Hope looked at him. She should've been surprised by Nick's answer but wasn't. In the short time Nick had been back in her life, his generosity had known no bounds.

"All right," Dr. Parker said. "I'll put you in touch with the transplant coordinator in charge of Joshua's case. Please keep them up to date."

And then the full impact of everything Dr. Parker had said hit Hope. "Surgical procedure?"

"Yes," Dr. Parker said. "In Joshua's case, our best scenario for success is to surgically harvest the donor's bone marrow. Your mother's bone marrow. It's unfortunate, but we do not believe the nonsurgical PBSC method would be as effective."

Surgery. Hope's heart began to race. "And this has been explained to my mother?"

Dr. Parker leaned back, rolling a pen between his two open palms. "As I'm not the doctor in charge of her procedure, I can't say for certain, but I would imagine so."

I can't say for certain.

All the fears Hope had experienced while sitting in Dr. Arnt's office came rushing back. To give her grandson life, Claire Montgomery faced a daunting series of events. Would she do it? Would the grandmother who hadn't even wanted to meet her grandchildren place herself in harm's way for one of them?

The doctor stood, his smile still in place, completely unaware of Hope's inner turmoil. "Naturally I haven't said anything to Joshua. I thought you would like to be the ones to deliver the good news." And then he left.

Nick squeezed Hope's hand as he stood. "Come on, let's go tell our son the news."

"Nick, wait."

Concern darkened his features as he sat back down. "What's wrong?"

"I'm scared," Hope admitted. "You heard Dr. Parker. They are going to have to do the more invasive of the two methods. The riskier of the two. The more painful. The greater recovery time. How can I believe my mother would agree to that?"

Nick rubbed the lower half of his face. "I want to say there's absolutely no way Claire would say no, but we both know there is. I guess there's only one way to find out for sure."

It was the same conclusion Hope had drawn. She fished her cell out of her pocket and dialed quickly, desperate to know.

"Hello?" her mother answered.

"Hello, Mom. It's me, Hope."

"I was expecting your call."

"We just finished talking to Joshua's doctor. He explained you're a match." Hope took a breath, held it for a moment, and then asked, "Did they explain the procedure to you?"

"Yes. A lady called and explained everything in great detail."

Hope's heart felt as if it were pounding out of her chest. *Great detail.* "Mom." Hope closed her eyes, said a prayer, and asked the only question that mattered. "Will you do this for your grandson?"

There was a beat of silence. And then another. And then a third. "Yes," her mother finally said.

Hope sagged forward in utter relief. "Thank you. Thank you. I wish . . . I wish I had a better way of expressing just how very much this means, Mom, but words seem so inadequate. Thank you," Hope said again. "I'll call you in the next day or two with the travel details. Please don't worry about that. Everything"—Hope looked to Nick, and he nodded—"everything will be taken care of. And Mom. Thank you."

"I . . ." Her mom started to speak, then said, "I'll wait for your call."

"Bye, Mom."

"Good-bye, Hope."

This time when Nick stood and said, "Come on, let's go tell our son the news," Hope followed without hesitation.

FOR the longest time, Joshua didn't say anything after he heard the news. It was as if he were letting the information soak in, settle, find a solid perch where it was secured. Where nothing could knock it off and take it away.

Nick watched Joshua and felt his admiration for his son grow. As with everything else Nick had seen Joshua endure, he handled this new news with a maturity and grace that far exceeded his years. Nick looked to Hope and realized she had given their son those gifts.

"My grandmother?" he finally said.

"Yes, honey," Hope answered, tears pooling in her eyes, magnifying their green depths.

"I'll have to thank her," Josh said quietly.

Hope nodded her head again, as if speech were impossible at that moment. She was sitting up toward the top of the bed, on the edge, holding Joshua's hand. Every so often she'd reach out, brush her fingers against his cheek, run her hand up and down his arm, all without ever letting go. It was as if she couldn't let go. Like she needed to touch him every moment to reassure herself.

A little later, Dana and Susan arrived and with the addition of the two of them, the room took a festive turn.

The nurses, learning the news from Dr. Parker, had filtered in over the next few hours to wish Joshua well and tell him how excited they were for him.

The time passed quickly. When Joshua began to doze, the four of them made their way out of his room and down the hall.

Dana gave Hope a hug. "I'm so happy for you. For all of you," she said, looking not only to Hope and Susan but Nick as well.

Since Hope was planning on staying a while longer at the hospital, Susan asked if she could go home with Dana.

"Sure, go ahead," Hope told Susan.

Dana and Susan hadn't taken more than ten steps when Dana turned and asked Hope, "What about you? You'll need a ride because your car is still in the shop."

"I've got it covered," Nick said.

Hope looked at him, clearly surprised. That was okay. He needed her off her game for what he planned next.

Susan came back to where Hope and Nick were standing. The closer she came, the more tentative her steps became. "Bye, Nick," she said softly, and then, quickly, as if she feared she'd lose her nerve if she didn't do it right then, she gave Nick a hug and a huge smile.

Nick's arms closed around her. Nothing had ever felt so right. "Bye, Susan."

Still smiling, Susan rushed back down the hall, Dana following.

"Do you want to grab a Coke or something while Joshua's sleeping?" Nick asked.

"A Coke sounds great."

The small family lounge at the end of the corridor was deserted. The minute they stepped through the doorway, Hope began to rifle through her purse, pulling out her wallet and digging for quarters for the soda machine.

Nick already had out a handful of *mad money*, as Josh called it. Inserting the coins, he made the selections and hit the button. One can, then another *clunked* into the tray.

He turned, handed one to Hope.

"Here." She had several quarters in her hand.

"For God's sakes, Hope. It's just a can of pop. I've got it covered." He turned and sat down. She took a seat across from him.

She leaned back, closed her eyes, and let out a deep sigh. "My mother," was all she said, and it said it all.

"Yes." He shook his head, popped open his Coke, and took a drink.

"I know you don't like it but I'm going to say it again, thank you. For handling the travel arrangements."

"You're right. I don't. But you're welcome."

Hope's hair was down, not in its usual ponytail or twisty thing on top of her head. She ran her hands through it, fluffed it up, then brushed it away from her face. She tucked her legs under her and leaned back, studying him. In that moment, she looked more like Susan's sister than her mother. "It's weird," she said.

"What is?"

"You. Being here. Taking care of things that are normally my responsibility. Talking to the doctors, making arrangements." Her voice was low, almost reflective.

"Does it bother you?"

Her elbow was propped on the arm of the chair. She leaned to the side, letting her head rest in the palm of her hand. "Yes." She gave a soft smile. "And no. I meant what I said earlier. I am sorry. Joshua and Susan are your children too. It's just that I've been the only one to take care of things for so long." She fiddled with the top of her unopened pop. "For a long time I was so angry at you."

"Are you still angry?"

"I don't think so. Oh, I don't know. Right now all I can think about is Joshua."

Nick sat forward on the edge of his seat. He reached across the narrow room and clasped Hope's hand in his. "I think about Joshua all the time, too. But I also think about you and me. And I'm sorry, too. I've made a lot of mistakes that I'm not proud of."

"I wish . . ."

"What?" he asked.

A delicate smile brought her beautiful cheeks into clear focus. "Nothing." She said it as soft as a first kiss. She didn't say anything more for a long time, and then, "You're great with them, you know. Well, except for the expensive gifts you can't seem to stop buying them. I thought we had an agreement. Anything over twenty dollars we were going to discuss."

"It was a hundred."

"Ha. Ha. It was fifty."

"So you do remember."

She laughed. "Only when I want to."

Did she have any idea how she captivated him?

"And speaking of our agreement," he said. "Just remember it didn't include purchases I made for you." He opened her fingers, dropped a set of keys into her palm, then closed them. "I talked to the auto mechanic and it's just as I expected. Your car is beyond repair."

She weighed the keys in her hands. "On any other day, that news would hurt. Don't ask me why, but I love that old car." She looked up at him and smiled. "But after what the doctor told us and the gift Joshua is going to receive, nothing can dampen my mood."

She reached for her purse and was just about to drop the keys inside when she looked at them. "These aren't Gertrude's."

He wondered how long it was going to take her to notice. "I know."

She went to hand them back.

"No." He stopped her. "They're yours. Just not to the Wagoneer. There's a Lincoln Navigator in the parking lot for you. It's green. The same color as your eyes."

"Nick . . ." She tried again to hand him back the keys. "I can't accept this."

"The car's yours."

"No."

"Yes."

"No."

"Yes," he said again.

"No," she said, a lot more firmly. And then, "I can play the yes-no game all night. I've had nearly sixteen years of practice."

She had him there. He tried another approach. "You need a reliable way to get back and forth to the hospital."

"You buying the kids stuff is one thing; you buying me anything is another."

"Damn it, Hope, stop being so stubborn. You're the mother of my children and the most important person in Joshua's life. He needs you, and you need to be here with him. How do you expect to accomplish that without a car?"

"I'll ride the bus. I'll take a cab. I'll buy a new car."

They both knew how impractical the first two suggestions were and the impossibility of the last one.

"I don't have time to argue with you, Hope. I have to leave tonight. And don't even think of trying to resurrect Gertrude. I won't have you driving around in that death trap."

At the word *leave* her face changed. Once again, she'd closed herself off from him, taken that laughing, teasing, beautiful woman and hidden her.

"You're leaving."

"Yes. I missed one race, I can't afford to miss another. I thought you understood that."

"I think I finally and truly am understanding that." She untucked her legs and went to stand.

He laid a hand on her arm. "What does that mean?"

"Let it go. Please. It's been a long day." She gave a short, humorless laugh. "To say the least."

Nick wanted to push her for answers, but he also knew that right now wasn't the time. He opened his mouth, went to say okay, but heard himself say instead: "Come with me."

"Come with you? Where?"

"Anywhere. Everywhere. But for starters, how about to Sunday's race?"

"Nick. That's impossible."

"Nothing's impossible. The race is in California. I could have you there and back within a few hours. Don't answer. Not yet. Think about it, please. Think about giving us a chance. I don't want to miss out on another sixteen years."

He left the room before she could say anything more.

Twenty-two

"YOU missed the turn. This isn't the way to the hospital."

Dana flicked on her turn signal and merged into the right lane. I-5 was all but deserted on this early Sunday morning. The blush of a sunrise was only a hint on the horizon. "Hitch-hikers can't be choosy," Dana said, spearing Hope with a quick glance.

"I'm not a hitchhiker."

"No," Dana agreed. "But you are stubborn."

"Yes," Susan said, piping up from the backseat. "Very."

"Anyone who refuses to drive their beautiful new SUV relinquishes their right to dictate the course." Dana accelerated.

"I wasn't dictating, I was only pointing out you missed the turn. And you know why I won't drive it. It's—"

"Yes, yes, yes," Dana said with a tired sigh. "I know. *He shouldn't have. It's not right. It's too extravagant. I'm capable of buying my own car.* Yadda. Yadda. Yadda."

"You do listen to me! I knew there was a reason you're my best friend. But aren't you going a little fast?"

Dana pressed down a little harder on the gas. "No dictating course or speed."

"Bossy and stubborn." This from the backseat again. "And if you won't drive the Nav, I will. License in T minus fifty-eight days and counting."

Hope looked at her daughter. "You're not driving her, no one is." Hope swore she heard Dana mumble *We'll see*, but she chose to ignore her friend. "And 'the Nav'? Seriously?"

"Cool, huh? Josh and I picked out the name together. And the Nav is a he, not a she."

"Very cool name," Dana said, flipping her arm back toward Susan, palm up. "High five." She and Susan slapped hands and then finished with a fist bump.

Hope shifted in her seat. "Aren't you two a barrel of fun this morning."

Susan scooched forward until her head peeked through the middle of the front seats. "Mom, I love you but you've been a terror all week."

Hope frowned. "I have not."

Dana passed a large semi and then swerved back into the right lane. "Yes, you have."

Hope tugged on her seat belt, trying to loosen the restraint. All of a sudden she was feeling claustrophobic. "So let me get this straight. Not only am I stubborn and bossy but also a terror? Some besties you two are."

"And Josh," Susan said. "He agrees with us wholeheartedly."

"So now you've been discussing me?"

"Always," Dana and Susan said at the same time.

"Well, that's great." Hope rotated back forward and looked out the front window. She knew she'd been more on edge lately, but she definitely didn't think she'd been that bad. There was a lot going on in her life. Her son was in the hospital, for heaven's sake. It only made sense she'd be a little more tense than usual. But she knew that wasn't the only reason.

"We've all agreed," Dana said, getting in to the far right-hand lane. "What you need is a change of scenery."

"What would you call this?" Hope gestured to the outside. "Since you missed our exit, this is a change of scenery. Wait." She straightened. "Wait a minute. This is the exit for the airport." She swiveled in her seat, facing her friend and her daughter. "Just what is going on?"

"We've been talking." Dana slowed on the off-ramp.

"You, Susan, and Josh?"

"Me, Susan, Josh, and Nick."

Nick. The other reason she'd been so edgy. "What does he have to do with this?"

Dana stopped at the bottom of the off-ramp. Before turning left, she leveled Hope with a look. *The look.* "Everything."

Hope looked the other way. She was starting to get a bad feeling. "Okay. You've had your fun or whatever this is. Time to head to the hospital. Joshua is expecting me."

Susan's outstretched legs had replaced her head. They were stuck through the middle of the two front seats, her orange sneakers bouncing to a beat only she heard. "No, he's not," she said in a voice loud enough to guarantee Hope heard.

"Of course he is. I have been at the hospital every day—"

"Exactly," Dana and Susan said in unison.

"Exactly," Dana said again, quieter. "Every moment possible, you've been in that chair by Joshua's bed. It's taking a toll. Before the transplant this week and then Joshua's recovery following, you need a break. To get away for a few hours—"

"You're kidding, right? There is no way I'm going anywhere."

Dana handed Hope an airline ticket. "It's all arranged."

Hope refused to take the ticket. "What's all arranged?"

"You. Nick. His race today."

Nick's race! "This is preposterous. I'm not going anywhere except to the hospital."

"I told you," Susan said, withdrawing her legs and sticking her head back through the seats. "Josh, are you hearing this?"

"Josh? How can he hear this?"

Susan lifted her phone and wiggled it in front of Hope's eyesight. "Uh. Speakerphone, Mom."

"Hey, Mom," Josh said.

"Hi, honey. Don't worry, I'll be there soon."

"No." Josh's voice came through the speaker loud and clear. "I want you to go to the race today. All four of us do."

"Joshua, I'm not going to leave you alone in a hospital room and go to a race."

"Who said I'd be alone?"

"Yeah," Susan said. "What am I, chopped liver?"

"Pâté, sweetie. We're pâté." Dana pulled alongside the curb at departures, shifted her Honda into park, then faced Hope. "The brats and I have the whole day planned. You don't need to worry about a thing. Cafeteria raids. Wheelchair races. Binge-watching our favorite show—"

"*Game of Thrones*," the twins chorused, the pair of them always in sync.

"A completely inappropriate show for fifteen—"

The twins cut Hope off. "Almost sixteen."

"And puh-*leez*, Mom." This from Susan. "If you knew what kids our age watch."

"Yes, but I'm not their mother, I'm—"

"Going to save that argument for another day. Now here," Dana said, trying once again to force the airplane ticket into Hope's hand. "Nick wanted to send his plane, but I told him you would absolutely say no to going if he did that, but he wanted me to make sure and tell you his jet could have you back home in what would feel like minutes if need be."

Hope stared at the *first-class* ticket in her hand. "I am absolutely saying no."

"We like Nick," Josh and Susan said. "We like him a lot."

"And he likes you," Dana said. "He likes you a lot."

Hope leaned against the headrest. "I'm trapped in a Dr. Seuss book." She rolled her head to the side, looked at her best friend and daughter, then to the phone that connected her to her son, then to the ticket Dana still held. "Thank you. All of you. I understand what you're trying to do. And I appreciate it. But I'm not leaving."

"Mom?"

Hope leaned closer to Susan's phone. "Yeah, Josh?"

"You keep telling me I'm going to be okay."

"You are."

"I need you to do something for me."

"Anything. You know that."

"I need you to show me you believe I'm going to be okay. I need to *believe* that you *believe*, Mom. Please. It's only for a few hours. Besides, you've kinda been driving me nuts."

"Driving us all nuts," Susan added.

"Please," Josh said.

Hope wanted to argue, but something in his voice stopped her. But how could she leave him?

"Please," Josh said again. "Please, Mom, do this for me."

The tenor of his voice left her without any doubt that he really did need this from her. "Okay," she said, taking the ticket from Dana, still not believing what was happening. What she had just agreed to. "Okay."

"HAVING fun yet?" Nick asked as he came up alongside her. Dressed in his black-and-silver racing suit, with his sponsor's bright red-and-green logo emblazoned across his chest, he looked every inch the champion he was.

"It's incredible," Hope said, unable to keep the awe out of her voice and not wanting to. They stood in pit road, behind a thick, concrete barrier that came up to Hope's thighs. With so much activity going on around them, Hope could see the need for such a barrier that did its best to separate man from machines. The place was swarming. Racecars lined the opposite side of the wall, while on the side where Nick and Hope stood, pandemonium ensued. Literally hundreds—if not thousands—of people rushed around, and the race wasn't due to start for another hour. It took a lot more than the forty men behind the wheel turning left for three hours to orchestrate this show.

When she'd first arrived a little less than an hour ago, she'd tried to keep up with all the activity. She'd soon learned that was an effort in futility. From drivers, to crew chiefs, to pit crews, to officials, to sponsors, to reporters from all the different media outlets, the spacious area began to feel almost confining. And that was before you added in all of the family and friends. It was chaos in the making. But, surprisingly, chaos was far from present. While it was true there was a palatable excitement in the air, there was also a controlled purpose. The majority of the people present were skilled professionals performing technical jobs with a high level of proficiency and efficiency.

"I can't believe you're finally here," Nick said.

"Finally? I can't believe I *am* here. It's crazy. If I had more than two minutes to think, I would have never boarded the plane."

"Then our plan worked."

She looked up at him, shielding a hand over her eyes. Even though it wasn't even eleven, the sun had made its presence known. The thermometer had already hit eighty-two. As the day wore on, she knew temperatures in the midnineties were expected. "Just how long have you four been concocting this?"

"About two minutes after I asked you."

A warm wind blew her hair across her face; she brushed it away. "Waited that long, did you?"

He smiled and wrapped an arm around her shoulders.

Before Hope could respond, a photographer appeared out of nowhere and snapped at least a dozen pictures before moving on. All morning, whenever she and Nick were together, the same scene played out over and over. "Doesn't that bother you?" Hope asked.

"In the beginning, but not anymore. Does it bother you?"

"It's different. And that's how I feel before the pictures are printed or posted or whatever they do with them. I'm not sure how I feel about that."

Nick pulled back on her shoulder until she was looking up at him. "I know how I'll feel when pictures of you and me together hit the media. Proud. Happy. Happier than I've been in years. I never want to lose you again. I hope you know that by now."

"Nick, I . . . I'm here. I'm trying." And she was. Nick's choice of career still frightened her, but she couldn't deny her feelings for him. She owed both of them this chance.

"That's all I can ask." He brushed a kiss across her lips. "By the way, our son and daughter have told me if you text or call one more time, they're turning off their phones."

"Oh, they are, are they?" She laughed, then chewed on her bottom lip. "Have I really been that bad?"

"Hey, Nick!" A young man loped up to their side. Like Nick, he wore a racing suit but in a bright blue and orange.

"Jarrett," Nick said, extending his right hand. The men shook. Even in the crowd, with all the noise around them, Hope could hear the *click-click-click* of cameras.

"Well, damn," Jarrett said with a bright smile. "Knew it was too much to hope you'd also miss this race, old man."

"I figured you needed a handout so I bowed out of Bristol, but you're going to have to grow wings if you think you're taking today."

"Handout. Ha." The young man flashed Hope a smile so full of flirtation she knew he had to be a favorite among the ladies. "Leave it to the elderly to think the younger and *better-lookin'* need to be handed anything. We take what we want."

Nick chuckled. "You do, do you? How does Amber feel about that?"

Jarrett laughed loudly. "Leave my wife out of this. I'm Rick, by the way," he said to Hope. "Since he's so old and addle-minded, we'll forgive Nick for not introducing us sooner."

Hope was not immune to this young man's charm. "It's nice to meet you. I'm Hope Thompson."

"Well, Hope Thompson," Jarrett said. "The pleasure is all mine. About time Fortune brought a friend to watch him race. Let me know if Pop here needs to go to bed early; I'll introduce you to some drivers who like to have fun. Stay up past nine."

"Knock it off, playboy," Nick warned. "And the only late nights you're pulling these days have to do with diaper duty."

Jarrett laughed. "True enough. True enough. My son, Garrett," he explained for Hope's benefit, "is one and a half. A speed demon if ever there was one. Can't wait to get that boy behind a wheel!"

"Garrett Jarrett?" Hope asked.

"A hoot, right?" Jarrett laughed again. "Amber and I wanted a name nobody would forget from the first time it was announced through the loudspeakers."

"I think you succeeded," Nick droned with a half smile.

"Can't wait till that boy is old enough to drive." Jarrett continued to smile. "Hope, it was a true pleasure. Tell Nick to bring you around to the motor home after the race. Amber and I are gonna have a little get-together. Some of the other drivers and their wives are stopping by. We'll throw some steaks on the grill, you women can gab, and Nick here can polish my trophies." He cuffed Nick good-naturedly on the forearm. "No sulking after my win today, old man. I've eaten your dust too many times to count. Today's my day. I can feel it."

The men shook again, but before Jarrett headed off, a crash erupted behind them. Purely on reflex, Hope covered her ears as she whipped around in time to see half a dozen men scrambling around what looked to be a fallen engine. "That doesn't look good," she said, turning back to Nick.

"All part of racing," he said calmly as he steered them a short distance away, where it was a bit quieter and less hectic.

"Did I understand your friend correctly that his wife and son are at the race?"

A fan stopped by. Asked Nick for an autograph.

"Racing is a family affair," Nick said as he shook the middle-aged man's hand and signed his piece of paper.

"Good luck," the fan said in parting.

"Thanks," Nick said before turning back to Hope. He took up right where he'd left off. She'd seen him do it many times. Once at the restaurant and then too many times today to count. He appreciated the people who cheered him on; it showed in his interaction with them. "From February to November, a driver's life belongs to the circuit. You spend so much time on the road, a lot of the wives and their kids choose to travel with their husbands. After the race, I want to take you around, introduce you to some of the drivers and their wives. For all our competitiveness we're a pretty close-knit group."

"I'd like that." She hesitated, unsure of how exactly to ask the question that had been in the forefront of her mind ever since Jarrett had mentioned it. "Rick mentioned you've never had someone watch your race before."

"There's a whole stadium that watches."

She rolled her eyes. "You know what I mean. You've been photographed hundreds of times over with too many beautiful women to count."

"First," he said, taking a step closer, "I've never been with anyone more beautiful than you." Hope wanted to argue that point, but the sincerity in his voice and the desire in his eyes stopped her. "Second, don't believe every photo you've seen. Journalists just want a good story. But to answer your question, no. I've never had nor wanted anyone else by my side before a race."

A warm glow unfurled inside her at his admission. She leaned into him. "So, what was with all the old-man comments? You can't be much older than he is. He's what . . . twenty-four? Twenty-five?"

"Twenty-five."

"You say that like you're ancient."

"In the racing world it's thirty-four and out the door."

She gasped in surprise. "That can't be true."

"No. But close."

"He's awfully confident for someone so young."

"He's cocky, that's what he is." Nick reached for her hand and held it in his. A simple gesture that felt anything but. "But in the kid's case, he drives better than he boasts and that's saying something. The kid's got real talent." There was a grudging respect in Nick's voice.

"More talented than you?"

"Hell no."

Hope laughed. "Yeah, he's the cocky one."

Nick smiled down at her. "Around here if you're not confident, you're not fit to be behind the wheel. To do what we do, to drive at those speeds, you better believe you're a god for three hours on Sunday. But there's confidence and overconfidence, and some days that gifted young man forgets that. But hell, what do I know?" He ran a hand through his hair. "I'm an ancient thirty-five-year-old."

"Not until December twentieth."

He smiled, obviously surprised and pleased that she remembered his birthday. "You're right. Ancient thirty-*four*-year-old."

"So if it's thirty-four and out the door, does that mean . . ."

"What?"

The conversation had taken a serious turn, one she hadn't planned or wanted. Especially now, right before Nick's race. "Forget it. It's nothing."

"Hopeful, I *know* you. A fact you seem to forget often."

He did know her. Even with all the time and distance that had existed between them, he still knew her better than anyone else. But that didn't mean it was the right time for this conversation. "Let's talk about it after the race."

"After the race I plan on stripping you naked and keeping you in bed for as long as you'll let me. Plus, for the next few hours, you don't want me doing anything but driving. Especially not thinking about what you *didn't* say."

"Dirty pool, Mr. Fortune."

He gave her a wry grin. "Never said I played fair. I'm the guy who used our children and your best friend to get you down here."

"True." She worried on her bottom lip. "If it's thirty-four and out the door, does that mean you're thinking about retiring?"

It took him a few moments to answer. "No. I'm not. I want to keep racing for as long as I can, but I know that is causing problems between us. I want to find a way to make us work, Hope."

She turned in his arms, angling up to look at him. "I must want to, too. I'm here."

"I love you, Hopeful," he said simply. "I've loved you since I was eighteen years old. I haven't said anything before now because I didn't want to rush you."

Time slowed. The people, the noise, the confusion and commotion . . . all of it faded away until it was only the two of them.

"I love you," he said again.

They were the same three words he'd said to her long ago, when they'd been teenagers. Then, they'd meant everything to her. Now, they meant even more.

Tears pooled in her eyes. "You love me," she said, not quite believing it.

"I do," he said, brushing a tear from her cheek.

"I love you, too. But I'm still scared. I—"

He bent forward, kissed her softly and slowly.

She wrapped her arms around his neck, let the softness of his lips on hers, the warmth of their mingled breath, and the beauty of this newfound love infuse her.

"For now," he said, drawing back, "that's more than enough."

"Nick. Nick!"

A voice intruded.

"Here you are." Dale Penshaw, Nick's crew chief, half jogged, half walked to where they stood.

Hope thought maybe she should feel embarrassed being caught in Nick's embrace, especially since she'd met Dale only once before and that had been earlier today, but she didn't. Especially not when she felt Nick's arm tighten around her.

"I've been running all over looking for you," Dale said, bracing his hands on his hips, trying to catch his breath. "You forgetting we have a race to run? Come on. You need to get ready."

"Dale," Nick said, clapping the older man on his shoulder, giving it a squeeze. "I feel so good I think I could run five races today."

"Well, hot damn!" Dale grinned, smacking his hands together with all the excitement of a child. "Now there's the driver I haven't seen in a while. 'Bout time you found your way back. Hope," he said, turning to her, "I think I have you to thank. Come on, you two. We have a race to win!"

In less time than seemed humanly possible, they were back at the car and it was all hands on deck. Anticipation thickened the air. Nick's pit crew was a blur of color as they swarmed around Nick's car, checking, rechecking, and checking everything once more. Hope stood a short distance away: far enough to be out of the way but close enough to see all the action. Nick wanted to include her, but she waved him off with a smile. She didn't want his attention anywhere but on the job at hand. And just watching him was enough. She looked on as he oversaw each detail, discussed the car in depth with Dale and other members of the pit crew. He was a man who left nothing to chance. Nor did any member of his team. He was laser-focused and in complete control. The noise level kept rising, not only from Nick and his team but all the others around them. More than once Hope found herself covering her ears with her hands.

"Here," Dale said a short while later. He handed her a

headset. "Nick wanted to make sure you had these before the race starts. It's about to get loud."

"Thanks," she said, taking the headset. "But what do you mean *about to* get loud? It's already deafening."

He chuckled. "Honey, you haven't heard loud yet, but don't worry. These," he said, tapping a finger against the black ear protectors, "will keep most of the noise at bay. There's also a built-in radio. You'll be able to hear us during the race."

"Us?"

"The team. Me. Nick. The pit crew. The spotter. A handful of others."

On her trip down, Hope had used her phone, calling up Google, to learn all she could about Nick's world. She remembered reading that a spotter was a trained team member, usually positioned high above the track for the best vantage point, whose job it was to relay information to the driver and alert them of what was occurring on the track.

"So I'll be able to hear Nick during the race?"

"Absolutely," the older man said. "And me. Don't forget me." He chuckled again as he hustled away.

Nick walked over to her a few moments later, his helmet in his hand. "Good, Dale got you set up with a headset. I'll try to keep the dirty talk down so the crew doesn't get distracted."

She smiled at his teasing. "Keep your head in the race, mister. Though I don't know how you can think with all this noise."

Nick bent down and brushed his lips quickly against hers. "No worries. Besides, there's no time to think. Just act and react. If you pause to think, you're in trouble. Now give me a kiss."

"I just did."

"Yeah, but this one has to last for four hundred miles."

She wrapped her arms around his neck, pulled his head down to hers, and gave him a kiss that left him with no doubt as to how she felt.

"You've done it now," he said after they'd reluctantly separated. "You're my good-luck charm, I can feel it. I won't be able to start another race without you by my side and a kiss to send me off." He flashed her a final smile as he put on his helmet and made his way toward his car.

Her smile stayed firmly in place, but as he climbed in through the driver's-side window and settled into position, she couldn't help the worry that pleated her brow.

No time to think.

If you pause to think, you're in trouble.

"Come on." Dale was at her side, taking her elbow. "Let's find you a good seat, and here's a pair of binoculars. You'll need them too."

Before she knew it she was watching Nick take off from pit road. The cars roared past, stirring up dust and debris in their wake. On the track, they formed a line two cars wide. She could all but feel the drivers' impatience at the restrained pace, the unwelcomed control, like tigers straining against the leash, waiting to be set free. They wove back and forth, back and forth, warming their tires. Yet another fact she'd learned from her research. Just like she'd learned that their starting positions depended on their times achieved during the qualifying laps they'd run the day before. She remembered Nick mentioning something about that during their dinner. Nick hadn't won pole position—the coveted starting position given to the fastest time—but he'd earned a respectable third-place spot.

High in a tower overlooking the track, an official stood, the green flag in his hand.

She almost sent a text to the twins before remembering their *DO NOT TEXT* warning. The flag went up.

Anticipation built, swelling through the packed stadium. Engines revved. Thunder rose from the crowd. The loudspeaker crackled. She felt it building and building, sending a vibration through her. She couldn't sit still. She scooted to the edge of her seat. Then further forward still. She clutched

her hands over the headset that covered her ears but couldn't
have said why. The noise level was unbelievable, but instead
of being unbearable it was the beat to which everything
danced. It became the heartbeat of the race and the smell of
fuel, warm asphalt, and hot tires, its blood.

The green flag whipped down. The race was on! The drivers were off!

Thunder like nothing she'd heard before electrified the
crowd.

She jumped from her seat, grabbed the binoculars. She
focused on the front of the pack, searched for number five.
Nick's car. Everything was a blur. The cars moved at an
alarming pace, and it was all but impossible to find Nick. But
she could hear him. His voice and those of his teammates
erupted through the radio built into her headset. She tuned
out all the voices except for Nick's.

Car's good.

No longer loose.

Good adjustment on the rear. Tightened her up.

Back and forth the comments flew. Hope had no clue as to
what they meant, but that didn't matter. She spotted his car,
kept her binoculars focused, then all but growled in frustration
when he went across the backside of the track and she lost
sight of him. But soon he was back. Headed around the far
turn.

And on and on it went.

Minutes sped by as fast as the laps. She lost all sense of
time.

Cars roared onto pit road only to roar back out within mere
seconds. Each time Nick brought his car in, she watched in fascination as his crew worked at a furious pace of pure precision
changing tires, adding fuel, making adjustments, or doing all
three. The chatter across the headset was a shorthand, rapid-fire succession that everyone understood except her.

Sometime during the day a young man in a T-shirt with
Fortune Enterprises embroidered across the upper left side

in small black letters brought her an ice-cold bottle of water. She hadn't realized how hot the day had become or how thirsty she was. She thanked him before uncapping the bottle and taking a healthy drink.

Lap after lap after lap, cars thundered past. Chatter continued to fill her headset.

Watch eighteen! He's on your left. LEFT!

Oil on corner two. Stay high.

She's running hot. Keep an eye on the temp.

She, Hope quickly learned, meant Nick's car.

Two more times that same nice young man who'd brought her the bottle of water appeared to see if she needed anything. She always thanked him and said no. It had been hours since she'd last eaten, but even the tantalizing aroma of hamburgers on a nearby grill couldn't tear her away from the race. There was no way she was going to do anything as mundane as eat while Nick was racing.

Zoom. Zoom. Zoom. The cars sped past.

Then everything happened in slow motion.

The crowd jumped to their feet.

The announcer hollered through the loudspeaker: "Jarrett in the twenty-four car pushes into Mayer in the fifty-five."

Dale's voice blasted across her headset. *Contact, Nick! Contact on turn two! Go high! Go high! GO HIGH!*

The announcer: "Twenty-four is in trouble! Twenty-four is in trouble!"

Hope rose to her toes, straining to see through the crowd and the binoculars. Frantic to see what was happening. Desperate to see Nick.

"Jarrett into the middle of the pack and over! Jarrett has flipped!"

She didn't know who was talking. She didn't care. All she could focus on was the track. On the nightmare being played out before her.

Cars slammed into each other.

Flipped end over end.

Crashed into the concrete wall.

Metal screeched. Crumpled as easily as tinfoil.

Smoke billowed.

Parts flew.

Nick! Nick! Nick!

She hadn't realized she'd shouted his name until she heard his voice through the headset. *I made it.* His voice was solemn. *But it's bad.*

Bad still hung in the air when Hope heard the wail of an incoming ambulance.

SERENE paintings of landscapes and oceans hung on the wall. Large artistic pots held lush, vibrant foliage. Plush chairs were clustered in pods, some positioned toward flat-screen TVs. Magazines were fanned across tables. Water trickled over mosaic tile in a strategically placed wall fountain. It was an area designed to offer solace and comfort, but Hope found none. Hospitals offered her nothing but anxiety and fear.

Still holding her hand, Nick walked straight to the large U-shaped desk positioned in the center of the spacious entryway. A sign above read *Receptionist.*

At his approach, an elderly woman looked up and smiled. "Hello. How may I help you?"

"We're here to see two men that were brought in earlier. Jarrett and Mayer," Nick said, giving the receptionist the drivers' last names. "They should have been admitted a few hours ago."

Two. Two hours ago.

Hope still couldn't believe it. Even after the horrific accident that had sent Rick and the other man to the hospital, the race had continued with what had seemed only a fraction of a delay. Cars had been towed. Debris had been cleared and Nick had continued to race.

The receptionist clicked away at her computer. "Are you a relative?"

"No."

She halted, looked at Nick. "Not a relative of either of the men?"

"No," Nick answered again, chafing at the questions.

Compassion softened the older woman's features. "I'm sorry, but I'm unable to release any information unless you're a member of the family."

"But—"

"I truly am sorry."

Hope could see the inner battle Nick fought. Jaw clenched, stance rigid, he wanted answers but knew that questioning this woman further wouldn't give him any.

With determined strides, he led Hope to the large waiting room. He stopped next to the wall of floor-to-ceiling windows and, ignoring the many signs that asked for cell phones not to be used in the area, fished his from the inside pocket of his leather jacket. He let go of Hope's hand long enough to place a call.

"Dale, Nick. We're at the hospital but haven't learned a thing. They won't release—

"What?" There was a pause. "Shit!" His curse was explosive. "Yeah. All right. Yeah. I'll stay in touch." He ended the call as quickly as it had started.

He didn't move for several long moments, then turned and stared out the window, out into the blackness of the night. "Shit," he said again, his shoulders slumped. He rubbed a hand across his forehead. And then again. Slowly, he turned back around.

One look at his expression and Hope sank onto a nearby chair. "How bad?" she asked, though she feared she already knew.

"Dale had just received word. He was calling me as I was calling him. Mayer is going to be fine. A busted rib and a few scratches. Nothing serious."

"And Rick? How's Rick?"

"Jarrett," Nick started, then stopped. He sat down next to her, taking her hand gently in his. "The doctors did everything they could, but his injuries were catastrophic. Rick passed away a little over a half hour ago."

"Oh God." She tried to draw in a breath, couldn't. Her chest was frozen and then on fire. She gulped for air, found none. She clawed at her jacket, needed to get it off her. Needed to feel space. The room tilted, began to spin.

Nick knelt in front of her, holding her shoulders in his strong hands. He gave her a gentle shake. "Breathe, baby. Breathe."

Frantic, she sought his gaze. Gulped for air, once more.

"That's right. Breathe. Just breathe."

She focused on his eyes, the soft pressure of his hands, his strong, steady voice telling her to *breathe. Just breathe.*

"I'm s-s-so sorry, Nick. He was your f-friend. W-we just saw him. And his wife. And a b-b-b-baby . . ." On the last word, she lost it. Sobs racked her body, shook her so hard she would have fallen if Nick hadn't wrapped her in his arms and held her tight. He cradled her head in the palm of his hand, rested it in the crook of his shoulder. Tears poured out of her. "How could this happen?"

Nick took her literally. "From what Dale was able to find out, looks like Jarrett hit an oil slick that caused his car to bump into Mayer."

Bump. Such an innocent word. Bump hips. Bump noses. Bumper cars.

"Y-you said he was a g-good driver."

"He is." Nick cursed softly, raking a hand through his hair. "He was. What happened today was an accident that could have happened to anyone."

Happened to anyone . . .

"Ssshhh, Hope. It'll be okay. It'll be okay."

"N-n-ooo." She shook her head, unable to stem her tears. "No, it won't. What are they going to do?"

"Who, honey?" Nick asked softly, still holding her tight.

"Amber and their little Garrett Jarrett. What are they going to do now?"

Nick stroked her back, created a soothing rhythm. "Don't worry. We'll take care of them."

Hope drew back, sniffled, ran a hand under her nose. "What do you mean?"

"We're a family. I thought you understood that. Not in the sense that this hospital recognizes but a family in our own way. The racing community," he said, in case she needed extra clarification.

"I know, you've mentioned that before, but I still don't understand what you're saying."

Nick unfolded, stood, grabbed a small box of Kleenex off a nearby table, and handed it to Hope. She took it gratefully. "If they need it, Amber and Garrett will be well provided for. We take care of all the widows and their children."

Hope paused in blowing her nose. "All the widows? How many are there?"

The question caused Nick to pause. When he once again sat down next to her, she couldn't help but notice that now there was space between them. Had she created it or had he? "Racing involves risks."

"I know that. I *knew* that." She blotted her eyes, wiped her nose. "Or I think I did."

"I've never hidden that fact from you."

"No, but today shined a spotlight on something I did my best to look away from."

"What are you saying, Hope?"

She turned, angling herself until she was facing him. "What do you mean, exactly, by 'take care of them'?"

"We provide financial assistance to the widows who need it."

Financial assistance. Money. "Life is about more than money."

Nick drew back, crossing his arms across his chest. "Life is damn hard without it."

She'd shredded her Kleenex into a million pieces. "I won't

argue that fact. But all the money in the world can't bring him back. I think it's admirable what you and the others do, please don't get me wrong. But for all your support, Rick Jarrett's wife and his little boy are going to have to find a way to go on without him. I love you," she began.

"I love y—"

She held up a hand. "Please. Let me finish. I love you. But life is precious."

"Don't you think I know that?"

"Too precious to take unnecessary risks."

"Unnecessary meaning racing."

She set the box of Kleenex on an end table, then shoved the used ones into her pocket. "One day you're going about your life with your biggest worry being what to make for dinner. The next minute, you're sitting in a room with a doctor telling you your son has cancer. That's a risk you can't avoid. But this—" She waved her hand. "Racing? That's a risk you can."

"Hope," Nick said, reaching for her hands, taking them in his. "Don't do this. Don't walk away. I love you. I want to spend my life with you, with our children. And while this isn't the right time or the way I planned it or anywhere close to what you deserve . . ." He dropped down onto one knee, still clasping her hands in his. "I love you. More than I ever realized it was possible to love someone. Marry me. Marry me and let me spend the rest of my life showing you just how much I love you."

"Oh, Nick." Tears ran down her cheeks. "I . . . I . . ."

"Hopeful, I'm not that boy who left you on those courthouse steps. I'm not going to leave you ever again."

Slowly, she slipped her hands from his, but as her fingers slid from his warm grasp, she felt the detachment as keenly as if her skin were being torn from her. "But you might. That's my point. I tried, Nick. I really did. But I can't do this. I can't be with you only to worry that you might be taken away at any moment. I can't marry you, Nick. I'm sorry."

She could see how deeply she'd hurt him, but she was powerless to take away either of their pain.

"Life doesn't come with guarantees, Hope."

"No." She gathered her purse and stood. Stepped around him. "But it doesn't need to be lived on the edge either."

Twenty-three

AT nearly two hundred miles an hour Nick flew down the back stretch. Adrenaline pulsed through him as the car vibrated with speed and power. He let the roar of the engine and the hot, gas-tinged wind sink into his soul as instinct and pure raw talent took over. Behind the wheel, whether it was during a race, or like now, during a practice run, nothing broke his concentration.

Except today.

Never before had he had a problem shutting everything out and concentrating solely on driving. Just the opposite, in fact. During his years of racing, his tunnel vision and unwavering focus had become a source of admiration and good-natured (and some not so good) envy among the other drivers. It was what set him apart. What had helped to carve out the pinnacle he now found himself poised on. But today, it was as if he were a different man. And he knew the reason why.

Hope.

He knew he should shut her out of his mind, think instead of his son's upcoming transplant and the miracle of this second chance. But whenever he thought of Joshua or Susan, his thoughts wound back around to Hope.

We can't be a family if you race.

Nick slammed the gearshift down and stepped on the gas, turning sharply as the outside wall zeroed in.

Her words burned through him. She wanted him to become something he wasn't. *Someone* he wasn't. Racing was not just a part of him, it *was* him. And if she couldn't understand that, they had no future together.

So why did that thought leave him feeling tortured?

Rounding the final turn, he pushed heavy on the gas and flew past the finish line. He heard his crew chief in his headset, yelling his time. But for the first time since he'd started racing, he didn't care. And that scared the hell out of him. Because without racing, who was he?

But what if Hope was right? What if it was impossible to be both? A racecar driver and a father?

He came around to the far side of the track and slowed, then swung down pit road. Nearing his position, he braked. Immediately, his crew swarmed over the concrete barrier. Nick dropped the mesh window covering and climbed out.

"Thought you were gonna eat concrete on that last turn," Dale said as he walked over to Nick.

"Never," Nick said, grabbing a bottle of water from the nearby cooler and chugging down half of it.

"How'd she handle?"

For the first time in over a decade, Nick was caught off guard by the question. It was the same thing he'd been asked at least a thousand times before, but today, he didn't know how to respond. He took another drink and swished it around in his mouth, trying to wash away the grit and dryness and buy himself some time to formulate an answer. "She's good on the straightaway but loose in the turns." It was total bullshit and they both knew it.

Dale stuck his hands in the back pockets of his work overalls and kicked at a loose piece of asphalt.

"What?" Nick asked when Dale's silence became telling.

"Nothin'."

"Don't give me that. We've known each other too long."

Dale kicked at the pile. "My point exactly."

Dale was one of Nick's closest friends. Over a beer one night, Nick had told him about Joshua and Susan, and Josh's condition, but that was as far as Nick had gone. Hope was something Nick was going to have to figure out on his own.

"June wanted me to tell ya somethin'," Dale said.

"So now I not only got you yammering at me, I have your wife, too."

"She wants me to tell you she'd like to see you on Diane Sawyer."

"How did she know about that?" For months, the show's executive producers had been contacting anyone connected to Nick to see if they could help persuade him to do a one-hour special. The last thing Nick wanted was to sit in front of a camera and chitchat. He was a driver. Period. End of story.

Dale tilted back his cap, scratched his thick gray head, and then slid his cap back on, giving it a couple of rubs over the top of his head before finally settling it into place. "Those producers got our number somehow. They've been calling almost every day."

"I'm sorry."

Dale grinned. "You kidding? The wife's lovin' the attention. Gives her somethin' to tell her bridge group." Dale didn't say anything for a moment, then said, "I told her to stop answering their calls because I know you don't want to talk to them, but you know women."

"I used to think so."

"So, is that what this has been about?"

Nick recapped his water. "You mean my shitty driving and lack of concentration?"

"That's what I mean. I know your kid is dealing with a lot right now, and I also saw how your girl ran as fast as she could after that crash."

Your girl. But she wasn't his girl. She'd made that plain when she turned down his proposal. How could she throw away what they felt for each other? He loved her. She loved him, or so she'd said, but if she loved him how could she walk away? Obviously love wasn't enough. She wanted him to walk away from racing. Quit the one thing that made him great. He'd fought too damn hard to get out of that small town, to shake his father's shadow and make something of his life. And it was a great life—one he was damn proud of and one he wanted to share with her. Share with her and their children.

"That crash last Sunday was bad. As bad as they come." Dale ran a hand across his lower jaw. Looked Nick square in the eyes. "But I'm going to give it to you straight, Nick. Either get your head back in the game or get your car off the track. There's no middle road out there. You know that better than anyone."

Nick drained the last of his water and tossed the bottle into a nearby trash can. "Where's Bobby? Thought he had the track after us."

Dale eyed him. "Fine. You don't want to talk about it, we won't. I said my piece, but you keep driving like you've been these last few days and I'm yanking that engine out myself. See how far you get then. And to answer your question— Bobby cancelled his practice. His wife called it quits this past weekend. Said she couldn't take it anymore, especially after what happened to Jarrett."

Nick squinted into the sun. "I would've laid odds on those two making it."

"You and just about everybody else."

After Dale left, Nick unzipped the top half of his jumpsuit and straddled the short wall. All around him, his crew was busy reworking the car. A hydraulic jack clanked against the track as the car was hefted into the air. The quick staccato *whirr* of the cordless impact wrench cracked the air as bolts were zipped off and then snapped back on once the new tire was in place.

These men and the nearly fifty more who worked for Fortune Enterprises relied on him. Counted on him for their livelihood. But it was more than that, they were a family.

But Joshua and Susan were his family, too. His first family. And Hope . . .

She would never accept him into her life while he was still a racecar driver, but what type of man would he be if he walked away?

There were racers who were husbands and fathers. They made a family work. So could he. Why couldn't she see that? But no matter what happened between him and Hope, Nick was going to be a father to Joshua and Susan. The best father he knew how to be. He knew it might take time for a relationship to develop between the three of them, but he was a patient man, and he would wait a lifetime if that was what his children needed.

And then he remembered the calls they'd shared, the texts they'd exchanged, the tentative hug Susan had given him before she'd left, and he felt himself smile. Maybe it wouldn't take a lifetime.

RAIN had fallen all day. Persistent silver beads that no matter how quickly Hope's windshield wipers thumped back and forth, back and forth, still hampered her visibility. Red lights flashed in front of her and she slammed on her brakes. Traffic was a nightmare. Rush hour—never a good idea. Rush hour combined with a deluge—an even worse one. Even in Seattle, a city famous for the amount of rain it received, no one seemed to know how to navigate the wet roads.

Taillights flashed again. On the far right-hand shoulder, two cars were parked, their emergency flashers blinking. The bumper of one car and the hood of the other were smashed. Obviously an accident. *A bump.*

Images from that terrible day at the racetrack came flooding back, not that they were ever far away. And then another memory:

Marry me. Marry me and let me spend the rest of my life showing you just how much I love you.

She wrapped her fingers around the steering wheel and gripped as tightly as she could. It was almost as if she could still feel the pain of when she'd removed her hands from his . . . when she'd said no to marrying Nick.

She'd made the right decision. Absolutely. So why then did it hurt so much? And why did her heart insist on thinking about him day after day, night after night, when her son was what mattered?

She gave herself a mental shake, focused on the here and now. In less than fifteen minutes she was going to pick her mother up from the airport. Tonight was going to be challenging to say the least. And tomorrow emotional.

Hope still found it almost impossible to believe. Tomorrow Joshua would receive his transplant.

A myriad of emotions tumbled through her, not the least of which were fear and an excitement for the future she hadn't felt in a very long time. She tried to push the fear aside, tame it down to a reasonable concern, but it was hard. Her baby boy was about to undergo a major procedure and while the risk was great, the reward could be—*would be!*— exponentially greater. Joshua and his getting healthy was what mattered. That was what she needed to focus on.

Even on this dismal early evening, the airport was a hive of activity. Hope had to loop around three times before she found an open spot she could slip into. Well, *slip* wasn't exactly the right word. The Navigator was too big to easily slip in and out of normal-sized parking spaces.

Hope still couldn't believe she'd relented and started driving the SUV. But putting all things in perspective, figuring out a way to repay Nick was minor when compared to the necessity of a reliable vehicle and her son's health.

Hope scanned arrivals, looking for Claire. She knew her

mother's plane had landed. Through coordinating schedules with Nick's assistant, Hope had learned her mother had flatly refused to fly on Nick's plane. But no matter which plane brought her here, Hope could only be thankful her mother was coming. But where was she?

The minutes ticked by. *One. Two.*

Five.

Ten.

After nearly fifteen minutes, Hope ignored the *No Parking* signs, shut off the SUV, and clicked the locks as she walked into the baggage area. It only took her a moment to locate her mom.

While luggage thumped and thunked down the conveyor belt and people jockeyed for position to swipe their belongings as they glided past, Claire sat perched on a chair a distance away. She looked forlorn, seated by herself on one of the hard, black chairs that stretched the length of the room. Her wool coat (in the summer, really?) seemed too heavy for her diminutive frame—even if the weather had warranted its warmth. Her purse was perched on her lap, her hands wrapped around its hard, curved handle. A small blue suitcase was tucked in close to her leather shoes with their stubby heels.

"Mom," Hope said, reaching her. "Claire." Hope wanted to throw her arms around her mother, hug her tight for this miraculous gift she was giving their family. But she knew her embrace was unwanted and might even cause more friction.

Her mother looked drained as she stood and reached for her suitcase.

"No, let me." Hope picked it up. "I hope you had a nice flight."

"I've never believed there's such a thing as a good flight. Never cared for airplanes. Just isn't natural if you ask me."

Hope felt a twinge at how closely her mother's words echoed Hope's own thoughts about flying. "The car's right outside. I'm sorry if you had to wait. I thought you'd walk outside after you picked up your luggage. If you had let me get you a cell phone—at least for the trip—"

"As I explained to you and that woman that kept calling and calling, I do not care for those phones."

Hope knew her mother was referring to Nick's assistant. Apparently Claire believed one telephone call to coordinate travel arrangements more than sufficed.

Hope hit the button on the key fob that unlocked the doors as they approached the SUV. Surprisingly, she didn't see a ticket on her windshield. Maybe this weekend was going to go off more smoothly than she'd thought.

"A bit pretentious for a schoolteacher, I think," Claire said.

Maybe not.

Hope opened the passenger door and waited for her mother to get in before shutting it. She stowed the suitcase in the back, then took her place behind the wheel. As she pulled away from the curb, she wrestled with what to say. Finally, she just spoke from her heart.

"Thank you, Mom. The sacrifices you're making for Joshua—for our whole family—mean so very much. I know you're probably hungry and tired, but I thought we could swing by the hospital first so you can meet the twins. My friend Dana is there with them, too. She's looking forward to meeting you too. The cafeteria food isn't the best, but we could all eat dinner with Joshua, which would be nice. Or, if hospital food doesn't appeal to you," Hope joked, but her joke fell flat, "we could either go to whatever restaurant you like or I could cook you something at home."

"Home?" It was the first word her mother had spoken since getting in the car.

"Yes. I have Joshua's room all ready for you."

"I told that woman who kept calling I preferred a hotel. It's been arranged." Her mother unclasped her purse and removed a slip of paper. In perfect penmanship her mother had written down the name of the hotel and the telephone number.

"Yes, Evelyn had mentioned that, but I was hoping . . . I

mean, I thought . . ." Hope cracked her window, needing air, but when the noise and exhaust from rush hour floated through her window, she hit the button. Silently, the window glided up. "Never mind. Of course it's whatever you prefer. That hotel is close to the hospital, I know right where it is. We can check you in before or after we go to the hospital."

Her mother's hand tightened on the handle of her purse. "Please drop me at the hotel."

"Drop you? But dinner and the kids—" Hope broke off when she caught her mother's closed expression. "All right, Mom. I'll be back in the morning at six to pick you up. I'll be with you while you're getting admitted, but then I'll need to leave and be with Joshua. I'm sure you understand—"

"A car is being sent for me. There's no need for you to come."

Hope's mounting frustration only continued to climb. She and her mother had a strained relationship at best. But that didn't mean Hope wanted that to always be the case. What her mother was doing—the gift she was giving—was of such depth, there were no words, no expression of gratitude great enough. Hope's thoughts were still whirling as she pulled under the hotel's porte-cochere.

Before the SUV had even come to a full stop, her mother was reaching for the door handle.

"Mom." Hope reached out and gently rested her hand on the nubby sleeve of her mom's coat. Her mom paused, didn't move for the longest time, and then slowly looked over to Hope.

"I wish there were a way I could express how much what you're doing means. Maybe as a mom you can understand just how very much?"

Silence.

Hope plowed forward. She needed to say this. For both of them. "Since Joshua was first diagnosed, I've asked myself a million questions. Mostly 'Why.' Why him? Why not me? And if my baby boy had to have this—why wasn't I a match?

But now maybe I have an answer, or at least a partial one. I think by my not being a match—or Susan or Nick or anyone else—I think by it being you, we've been given a second chance. *I've* been given a chance. To say I'm sorry. Sorry for the years of silence, of pain and resentment. Sorry for things that have been said, and I'm especially sorry for the things that haven't been. Maybe because of this we will be able to find our way to a new beginning. I'd like that very much, and I'd love it if you got to know your grandchildren. I don't know why you never told me about your phone call with Nick, but I think you were trying to protect me. Now that I'm a mother, I can see that. We . . . withhold things from our children to spare them pain. But I now see how wrong I was to do that to my own children. I've made many mistakes with Josh and Susan, but no one ever tells you how hard being a parent can be. Especially not how hard being a single parent can be."

If Hope hadn't been looking closely she would have missed the barely perceptible widening of her mother's eyes.

"It is hard," Claire said. "Almost impossible raising a child on your own. Raising two on your own has to be . . . difficult."

It was the largest olive branch Hope had ever been handed, and she accepted it gladly, gratefully.

"Here, I have something for you." Hope reached into her purse and withdrew a letter and two pictures. "This is Joshua and Susan." The photos were candid shots Hope had taken of the kids only a few months before Josh's diagnosis. "And this is a letter from Joshua. He was worried when you saw him this afternoon he'd be asleep or not feeling well, so this was his backup." Hope smiled. "He's always been my planner, my thinking-ahead child. Maybe tomorrow or one day soon you'll be up to meeting them."

With more hesitation than reluctance (or that was what Hope chose to believe), her mother took the pictures and letter from Hope.

"Thank you," Hope said one last time, and before her mother

could stop her, she leaned across the seat and gave her mother a hug, letting her tears fall silently onto her mother's coat.

NEARLY twenty-four hours later, Hope sat by the head of Joshua's bed, in the same spot, in the same chair, she'd spent countless hours before. But tonight, instead of feeling only anxiety and despair, she felt something that was as foreign as it was welcomed: she felt happy. Optimistic. Hopeful.

Hopeful.

The nickname Nick had given to her all those years ago. As she held her son's hand and stroked his forehead with feather-light caresses, she finally understood the power behind that one word. Hopeful. Hope-filled. Yes, she was. She was hopeful, but she was no longer Nick's Hopeful. She couldn't be. Not when the only way she could be was if she was willing to live a life where she accepted that she could lose him at any moment. Living that life—one filled with constant fear—she could not do. She'd lived that way after her father had left. Then she'd lived that way again when Nick had left her alone on those courthouse steps. And then she'd experienced the biggest fear of all during these last several months right here next to this bed. She couldn't—wouldn't—live that way again.

Joshua let out a soft snore, then rolled his head to the side.

But Nick had been there for her today. For all of them. From the moment she, Susan, and Dana had walked through the hospital doors early this morning, Nick had been with them. He'd quietly and steadily offered Hope his support and strength when she needed it the most. And when the hours dragged and her worry blossomed, he'd let her lean on him, whispered words of comfort. And when worry weighted his shoulders and caused his brow to furrow, she took his hand in hers and returned what he'd given her. When Dr. Parker had finally appeared in the waiting room and told them that he was *pleased* and *cautiously optimistic* about today's transplant, it had been the most natural thing to fall into Nick's embrace after hugging Susan and Dana. And when he'd dropped a light kiss against her lips, she kissed him back. Today they weren't Nick and Hope, but Joshua's parents rejoicing in their son's bright new future.

"And my mother? Claire?" Hope asked the doctor. "How is she?" The only dark spot on the day had been her mother's insistence that Hope not spend whatever time with her that she could.

"I received a report from her doctor that all went well. Very well."

Hearing those words, Hope's joy was complete.

Hours later, after they'd all spent time with a groggy but happy Josh, Dana and Susan had headed home. Nick had stayed, sitting on the other side of Joshua's bed, holding vigil just as Hope had. She wasn't sure what time he'd taken off; she'd been too consumed with fussing over Joshua to notice.

Mary, the nurse, walked in. Her newly acquired tan looked good against her sunny yellow scrubs. "How's our boy?"

Hope smiled broadly. "Wonderful. Perfect. Sleeping."

"He'll probably sleep the whole night through," Mary said as she wrapped a blood pressure cuff around Josh's arm and then hit a button on the machine. The cuff filled with air, then began to tick down as it took the pressure reading.

"I can't believe he sleeps through that," Hope said in amazement.

"Good meds," Mary said, smiling. "And a peaceful mind for the first time in a long time. I bet Josh won't be the only one getting a good night's sleep tonight." She gave Hope a knowing look.

"He won't be. Especially since I won't need to leave tonight. My friend Dana is staying with Susan."

"I know how hard it has been for you not to stay with him every night. I'm glad you get to be here tonight. But you've been sitting in that chair for hours." Mary removed the cuff. "Why don't you go grab a bite to eat or a cup of coffee?"

"Oh, I don't know. I—"

"Go. Stretch your legs. I'll sit with Josh, fill him in on my trip to Hawaii. He's what my husband would call a captive audience." She laughed softly. "Go," she said again. "Shoo."

"All right. But only for a minute. I did want to check on my mom. Last time I looked in on her, she was still sleeping."

"You go along. We'll be here when you get back."

Hope brushed a kiss across Josh's forehead, sanitized her hands using the dispenser on the wall, and then slipped out of the room. She was closing the door, reaching for her cell in her back pocket, intent on calling Susan, when she barreled into someone. She would have fallen if strong arms hadn't held her up.

"Nick!" His arms felt so right around her and she felt bereft when, after she'd steadied, he released her. "I thought you'd left."

"I've been down the hall, in the waiting room. You and Josh had both dozed off so I stepped out for a bit. I didn't want to disturb you two, you both needed to sleep." He ran the pad of his thumb under her eye. "I was worried you were going to collapse when I saw you this morning, you look so tired."

Her skin came alive under his touch. "I'm stronger than I look."

He gave her a small half smile, tucking his hand into the front pocket of his jeans. "I know that. I know *you*, remember?"

"Nick, I . . ."

"You don't have to say anything. I know what you're thinking. You don't have to worry. Today isn't about you and me, it's about Josh. But, Hope, we are going to talk. Soon."

"I—"

"Am overwhelmed with the day, and rightly so. So I'm going to say good night to my son and then head out." He reached for the door handle to Joshua's room. "And Hope?"

"Yes?"

"While you're trying to make up your mind, remember

this." His arms snaked around her waist, swept her off her feet. She landed with a delicious thud against his chest. His mouth crushed against hers. This kiss was anything but comforting. It was hands and tongues and mouths and hot and sexy and carnal as hell. It was completely inappropriate for the hallway of a hospital and over all too soon.

He set her down just as quickly as he'd swept her up. Without another word, he walked into Joshua's room, shutting the door behind him.

Hope stood there dazed, her body still vibrating from his touch. She wanted him. Whatever else was true and not true— that was one fact she couldn't deny.

A nurse walked by and smiled at her, knocking Hope free from the spell Nick had cast around her. Knowing she was a chicken, she turned and hurried down the hall. The last thing she wanted was to still be standing rooted to that spot when Nick reemerged.

HOPE went to her mother's room only to find her still sleeping. As she turned to leave, her gaze landed on the small nightstand next to her mother's bed. In a place where her mother could easily see them were the pictures of Susan and Joshua and the letter he had written, the envelope unsealed.

Her mother had read it.

Hope found herself smiling as she made her way back to Joshua's room.

Twenty-four

TWO weeks later, Hope sat across from Dr. Parker.

"Joshua's prognosis is very good," the doctor said. "His body is accepting the new marrow with very few complications."

"Does that mean he can come home next Wednesday as planned?"

"As long as everything continues as it has been, I don't see any reason why not. Naturally, he'll need to come in fairly often for blood work and office visits, and he'll have to stay on the antirejection medications we've prescribed, but that can be managed at home."

Hope couldn't believe it. After everything they'd been through, Joshua was coming home. It was a miracle. She only wished her mother had stayed at the hospital long enough to meet her grandchildren, but she'd insisted on checking herself out as quickly as possible, refusing Hope's offer to pamper her while she recovered. But a nurse had confided in Hope that her mother had held up her discharge to double-check that she'd remembered to pack the twins' pictures and Joshua's letter. That was as much of a sign as Hope could wish for.

Hope got up from her chair and walked around to where Dr. Parker sat. He looked startled and surprised when she enveloped him in a hug. She didn't care if she was breaching a professional protocol. Nothing could dampen her joy. Joshua was coming home!

JOSHUA'S hospital room looked bare. Posters that had covered his wall had been taken down, rolled up, and tucked under his sister's arm for safekeeping. His iPad mini, laptop, gaming system, and a host of other things were also packed and ready to go. Hope couldn't believe how many games Josh had acquired and knew they were all courtesy of Nick—just like all the electronics that had made Josh's hours in here pass more easily. In Dana's arms was a box full of pictures, cards, and get-well letters.

"Now don't take this the wrong way, kiddo, but I don't want to see you around here again. Got it?" Mary bent down and gave Josh a hug. When she stood, her eyes were bright with unshed tears.

Josh laughed. "Got it."

Hope gave the nurse a hug, too. "Thank you. Thank you for everything."

"You're more than welcome. Now get out of here!"

Over and over this morning, Joshua and Hope had exchanged similar good-byes with so many wonderful people who had been such a vital part of Joshua's life during his stay at the hospital. Josh had also spent part of the morning talking to the friends he'd made, telling them good-bye, that he'd stay in touch and he knew they'd be out of here soon, too.

Josh had made a special visit to Maddy's room. He'd given the little girl a hug so big and loving, Hope couldn't hold back her tears. And when Josh ended his visit with promises to text and come visit when he could (and Snapchat, whatever that was), his grin had been so devastatingly charming, Hope knew she'd never see her son smile again and not think of Nick.

Even with a heart full of joy, there was sadness too. Hope couldn't help but ache for the children who would never walk out of here and the parents they'd leave behind.

"Hey, Josh. I'm Darryl," a young man said as he bustled in, pushing a wheelchair. "Are you ready to blow this joint?"

"More than ready. But I can walk, I don't need a wheelchair."

Her son was well enough to complain about a ride in a wheelchair. Could today get any better?

As much as Hope wanted to avoid him, Nick should be here to see this. Even though both Susan and Josh had told her that Nick planned to be here today, he wasn't.

She knew Nick texted and called regularly, and when he called the home phone, Hope found it hard to resist answering just to hear his voice. But she didn't. She'd only be torturing herself; there was nothing more they had to discuss unless it pertained to the kids. His calls to her cell went unanswered, and the only texts she replied to were ones specifically about the twins.

"And deny me my favorite part of the job?" Darryl lifted the foot pedals and Joshua sat down.

"Even when they're as heavy as me?" Josh joked.

"You're light as a feather," the young man quipped as he wheeled the chair out of the room. "Bet you'll be glad to see the last of this food. What's your favorite food?"

"Pancakes and tacos."

Susan made a face.

"I take it your sister isn't a fan," Darryl said, laughing.

"He dumps this horrible-smelling stuff on his tacos. It's gross." Susan made another face.

"Hot sauce doesn't smell," Josh said.

"Does too."

"Does not."

"Yes, it does."

"No, it doesn't."

"Do our children always fight like that?"

Hope batted the bundle of balloons out of her eyes. Nick. He was here. He'd made it. Her stomach did a little somersault, and she told herself it was only because she was happy for the children. She knew how much they wanted him to be here today. "Only when I'm very, very lucky."

"Hey, kiddo." He fist-bumped with Josh. Hugged Susan, said hi to Dana. Exchanged handshakes with Darryl.

"I didn't think you were going to make it," Hope said.

"Wouldn't miss it for the world." Nick reached for the box she was carrying and the balloons. "Here, let me carry that."

"I've got it."

Nick ignored her.

"Fine," Hope said, handing over the box. "But I can handle balloons."

Nick flashed her a half grin, then stacked Dana's box on top of Hope's.

As they passed through the lobby, Hope found it almost impossible to believe she no longer would be coming back here every day. Their lives would return to normal and her son would be at home where he belonged.

Hours later, when they were home and had enjoyed a lazy barbecue outside under the warm sun in their backyard, Hope found herself alone with Nick. She'd done her best to keep busy and keep them apart, but his measured glances had told her it would only be a matter of time.

"Done avoiding me yet?" he asked, coming into the kitchen.

Her hand paused, cling wrap half covering the bowl of potato salad. God, he smelled good and looked even better. "No."

He laughed. "I love your honesty. But I've given you your

time or your space or whatever the hell you girls call it, and it hasn't worked. By the way, remind me never again to take advice from our teenage daughter."

"I don't know. Time and space sounds like pretty sound advice to me."

"Of course you'd think that. You're a girl."

"Is that a bad thing?"

"Hell, no. Not normally. But in this instance, yeah. I should have followed my gut weeks ago and done what I'd originally planned."

"And what was that?"

"Kept you locked in a bedroom with me until you started thinking straight." Her tummy flip-flopped, formed a knot of desire.

"Ah, Hopeful. I've missed you."

"I've missed you, too."

"Thank God. I was beginning to worry you didn't like me."

"I like you too much and we both know it."

"Then stop running. You're letting fear navigate, and fear has never steered anyone down the right track."

She looked up at him and wanted to sink into him, let his arms wrap around her, let his kisses chase away her fear. But she knew the moment he stepped away—the moment he left again—all of her fears would be right back, magnified. "What Joshua went through . . . What our family went through was—"

"Hell," Nick said simply. "But Hope, Joshua is better now and that's what's important."

"But what if . . ." She couldn't finish the thought.

"You can't live your life worrying about the *what ifs*. Life dealt Joshua a shitty hand, but he doesn't want to dwell on that. He wants to put the past behind him and move forward." Nick paused. "That's what he wants for you, too."

"I'm a mom, I'll always worry."

Nick chuckled softly. "True enough. But there needs to be

a balance. Joshua and Susan want you to be happy, Hope. The kids are worried about you."

Hope straightened. "Worried? About me? But why?"

"They say you rarely smile. Or laugh. It's as if you're always waiting for the other shoe to drop."

Hope leaned her hip against the countertop, chewed on her bottom lip. "I never realized the kids had picked up on that."

"I think they know a lot more than you think."

"I *know* they know a lot more than I realize."

"Don't let fear win," Nick eventually said.

"I'm trying."

He tipped her chin. "I'm willing to give you time—"

"Time and space?" she asked, smiling at the words he'd used earlier.

"*Time*," he said again. "But just know, Hopeful, I'm not giving up." He brushed a quick kiss across her lips, then walked back outside.

As Hope watched him exchange a few words with Dana and then hug the kids good-bye, she couldn't help but feel a tug of disappointment that he hadn't kissed her like he had in the hallway at the hospital.

THE hot days of August gave way to the even hotter days of September. The first few weeks Joshua was home were the happiest and the most terrifying of Hope's life. Without the constant monitoring and supervision of the doctors and nurses, Hope felt frightened and inept. She worried constantly. What if Joshua developed an infection? Or jaundice? Started to reject? Or any one of the other many complications that could arise from the transplant? What if something went wrong and she didn't see it? She stayed home from work, hovering over him, undoubtedly driving him to distraction. She worried about him constantly and found sleep as elusive with him home as it had been when he was hospitalized. Some nights she'd wake in a cold sweat and rush to his room to assure herself he was okay. But as the weeks passed and Josh thrived, Hope began to relax little by little.

By the end of September their house had turned back into a home. Even though they still took precautions where germs were concerned, the house was once again filled with teenagers. Music played too loud. Voices raised too high. A mountain of dirty dishes. A messy house. *A well-loved home.* It was one of the best gifts Hope had ever received.

"So when are you going to stop being so stubborn?" Dana said a few nights later as they were watching some Adam Sandler movie the kids thought hilarious. Hope thought maybe the appeal would grow on her after a bottle (or two) of wine. Adam had been paused while Josh and Susan were in the kitchen making popcorn. Hope had made tacos but Josh hadn't even finished his first one. His appetite still lagged. Hope knew he didn't even want the popcorn but was helping his sister nonetheless.

Hope took a sip of her wine. "I'm not stubborn."

"You're the most stubborn person I know."

"Thanks."

Dana grinned. "It's as clear as the nose on my face that you're in love with that man."

Hope nearly choked on her wine. She hadn't been expecting that comment. She wanted to deny what Dana had said, but it was a truth she'd already admitted to herself and to Nick. She did love him. More now than when they'd been teenagers, as hard as that was for her to believe because she'd been so crazy in love with him then. But she was scared. She couldn't shake the crash from her memory, couldn't understand how she could commit to him when her life would be one of constant fear.

"I don't want to be like my mom," Hope said.

Dana's glass arrested halfway to her lips. "Um. You're not."

Hope smiled at Dana, loving her unwavering loyalty. "My mom has let anger and bitterness dictate her life. Am I doing the same thing with fear? I do love Nick. But every time I think I can get past his racing, I see that horrible crash."

Dana set her glass down on the coffee table. She took Hope's hand in hers. "First of all, you are not your mother. You never could be. But I think what you're really asking is, can you open yourself up to the possibility of pain? Of loss? And sweetie, that's a question only you can answer. But ask yourself this: what will you be missing if you don't?"

LATER that night, Hope bolted up in bed. Something had woken her. She flung off the covers and her robe was only half on when she left her room. She went straight across the hall to Joshua's room.

Empty.

She checked Susan's room, but her daughter was fast asleep. She then went to the bathroom. No Josh.

A noise down the hall drew her.

She headed to the kitchen and let out a sigh of relief when she saw him. He had the refrigerator door open and his head was poked inside.

"Hi, honey."

Joshua jerked back, bumped his head. Rubbing it, he turned and saw her. "Hey, Mom."

Hope glanced at the wall clock. Three thirty. "What are you doing up?"

Josh grabbed the jug of milk, shut the fridge door, and made his way over to the counter. "I'm kinda hungry."

Finally!

He got a glass from the cupboard.

"Would you like me to reheat some tacos?"

He wavered. "Nah. I'll just have the milk and go back to bed."

And then she knew. "How about some homemade pancakes?"

His eyes lit up for a brief moment, and then he said, "No. It's okay. It's the middle of the night."

"It has to be breakfast somewhere in the world."

Joshua laughed. "What can I do to help?"

"Not a thing," she said, laughing along with him and grabbing her apron out of the drawer. "You just sit and keep that appetite growing."

Within minutes, she'd found a bag of chocolate chips in the pantry along with the other dry ingredients she'd need. After a quick raid on the fridge for butter, milk, and eggs, she had the batter started and, in no time, pancakes sizzling. In the freezer she found frozen strawberries and started them heating in a saucepan on the stove.

In less than twenty minutes, she slid the large platter of pancakes onto the table in front of him.

His eyes bulged and he smiled at her. "I'm hungry, but not that hungry."

He'd eaten two pancakes and was on his third before he showed any signs of slowing. He closed his eyes and a sigh of pure pleasure escaped him. "Mmmmmm, I never thought I'd taste these again."

Hope sucked in her breath, felt the start of tears. "Oh, honey."

His pancake paused halfway to his mouth. "Sorry, I shouldn't have said that."

"No, it's okay. I want you to tell me how you feel. How you felt. In the hospital, you never wanted to talk about it."

"Yeah . . . well." He took another bite, chewed, swallowed.

"Tell me. Please."

He set down his fork, took a drink of milk, then wiped his mouth with the sleeve of his pajamas. "I don't want to hurt you anymore."

"Joshua, all you have ever done is bring me the greatest joy."

He looked down at his plate. "That's not true," he said in a quiet way that showed her just how much of a man he was. How much cancer had matured him—and how could it have not? "When I was sick, I was a burden to you, in a lot of ways.

I know I caused you all kinds of pain, but I didn't mean to. When I found out who Nick was and why you'd called him, I thought that was it. He wasn't a match and I was going to die. So I decided I'd run away, end it, so you didn't have to be hurt anymore."

"Oh, God, Josh." She was crying openly now.

"Don't cry, Mom. Everything's okay now."

She got up from the table and wrapped her arms around her son. Tears streamed unchecked down her face. "Yes, everything's okay now," she whispered.

Josh hugged her back. "Yeah, it is. And Nick helped me to see that."

"Nick?" His admission stunned her.

"It's what he said to me when I ran away."

Hope leaned back, perching on the seat next to Josh. "What did he tell you, honey?"

"I dunno. Stuff. He talked about living and dying and how life was hard. But I think what really hit me the most was when he told me how in order to really live, you have to take risks." Josh shrugged again. "So I did. I went back, and we found out Grandma was a match."

Hope was out of her seat again with him back in her arms, hugging him with a mother's ferocity she knew would never leave her.

"What's going on? Is something wrong?" Susan stood at the edge of the kitchen, rubbing her eyes.

Hope sniffled, then gestured for Susan to come closer. "Nothing's wrong," she said, pulling Susan into a hug along with her and Josh. "Nothing's wrong at all. Everything's perfect."

"Okay, Mom, you're getting weird," Susan said.

Hope laughed. "Mothers are allowed to be weird; it's in the book." Hope pulled Susan down on her lap, her daughter who was two inches taller than she was, but she'd always be her little girl.

"One day you're gonna have to show us this book," Josh said.

"Yeah. I want to see where it says 'Because I said so' is a valid answer."

Hope burst out laughing.

"Pancakes?" Susan asked. "And no one woke me?"

Josh shoved a huge bite into his mouth and grinned.

Susan went to the fridge. Opening it, she grabbed something and then came back to the table. She set a can of Reddi-wip next to Josh. "You can't have chocolate chip and strawberry pancakes without the whipped cream."

"No, you can't." Josh uncapped the can and squirted an impressively tall tower of whipped cream on his half-eaten pancakes. He then created an equally tall tower on top of the pancakes Susan had just piled on a plate for herself.

And just like that, it was like old times. Good times. The best of times. Susan and Joshua continued to eat. At one point, Josh got up and refilled his milk glass and told his sister to get her lazy butt up and get her own drink when she asked him to get her a glass, too.

With a smile, Hope listened to their bickering.

The words Nick had said to Joshua kept coming back to her. And the words he'd said to her. *Don't let fear win.*

For so long, she'd been afraid of risking her heart in case it got hurt again. She'd kept it protected, locked away except for where her children were concerned. But she was beginning to realize that wasn't a way to live. Loving meant risking. Risking your heart.

Yes, Nick still had a job that involved high risk, but he was right, life was unpredictable. You could do everything right and bad things could still happen. You only had to walk the halls of the pediatric oncology department to see that.

"Mom?" Susan said. "You look a little weird."

"Weirder than normal," Josh expanded around a mouthful of pancakes.

Hope took a breath and tried to slow her racing heart. She reached forward and held Joshua's hand in one of hers, and Susan's in the other. "Do you remember when we talked in the hospital? When you found out about Nick being your father?"

"Yeah," they both said.

She took another breath, gave their hands a squeeze. "I want to . . . No, I need to tell you again how sorry I am for not telling you about your father a long time ago. I thought I was doing the right thing. Protecting you. But now, now I realize how wrong I was. I'm sorry. So very, very sorry."

"Yeah, but Mom," Susan said, "you were like just a little older than me when you had us. I mean, wow." Susan looked to Josh, and he nodded in agreement.

"Even though I was young, I should have done things differently."

"Don't beat yourself up about it, okay?" Josh told her.

She squeezed their hands again. "Have I told you two lately how amazing you are?"

They grinned and Josh said, "Amazing enough to let me get a car?"

She laughed. "Let's talk about that later." She smiled at them again. "Now, I have something else I want to talk to you two about."

Susan and Joshua exchanged a grin.

"You don't have to tell us," Josh said.

"Yeah, we already know," Susan said.

"Know what?"

"That you . . . you know . . ."

"Like him," Susan finished. "Like Dad."

Hope smiled. "Amazing and smart kids. How would you feel if tomorrow"—she glanced at the clock—"I mean today, I fly down to see him? I'd take all of us, but—"

"I can't fly right now," Josh said matter-of-factly.

"Susan?" Hope turned to her daughter.

"Go," Susan said.

"I'll call Dana and—"

"Go," they said in unison, smiling.

"Really?"

"Yes," Susan said.

"Yeah," from Josh. "It's actually kinda . . ."

"Cool," his sister finished for him.

"Yeah. Cool," Josh said before taking another bite.

Twenty-five

HOW could it possibly take so long to get ready for a short trip?

After learning from the kids what track Nick would be at, she went online and booked the first available flight. With Nick paying off the balance of the hospital bill, her credit card had just enough room for the ticket price. The only problem was that the next flight to Indianapolis wasn't until tomorrow morning. She all but growled her frustration. She was tempted to pick up the phone and call him, but then she'd think about how it would feel to be in his arms, and him kissing her when she told him.

She packed and repacked her suitcase three times. She fretted over each item. She wanted to look her best when she saw him. She dug through her closet, found that little black dress she'd taken with her to Minnesota. She remembered the way Nick's eyes had raked her over from head to toe when she'd been wearing it. She didn't know if the opportunity would arise to wear it, but just in case, she packed it carefully hoping it wouldn't wrinkle.

Dana had agreed to stay over while she was gone. She knew the kids were old enough they didn't need anyone to watch them and Josh was doing great, but still Hope felt better knowing Dana would be there.

She heard a knock at the door and yelled for one of the kids to get it.

"Mo-*om*!" Susan yelled from the front of the house.

Hope wanted to roll her eyes like her teenagers. Couldn't they ever walk somewhere to talk to her instead of yell?

"What is it?" she asked her daughter when she reached the living room.

A man in a blue uniform was standing in her foyer. "Ms. Thompson?"

"Yes?"

He smiled. "I was under instructions to personally deliver this to you." He handed her an expensive-looking cream envelope. With a slight bow, he was gone, shutting the door behind him.

"What is it?" Josh asked from the couch.

"I don't know." Slowly, carefully, Hope slid her finger under the back flap and opened the envelope. She pulled out a thick piece of stationery. On the top was the embossed letter *F*.

Her heart began to pound against her chest and her breath came out in little short gasps.

Hopeful,

Please watch Channel 4 tonight at eight o'clock.

Nick.

She read the note again, and then again.

Her heart began to beat faster and faster still and she knew she needed to talk to him. Hear his voice. She didn't want to wait a moment more to tell him. She picked up her phone and tried calling but for the first time, he didn't answer. Or answer her texts.

"QUIET, I can't hear!"

"You be quiet!"

"You brats better both be quiet," Dana said. "Or I'll kick you out of the living room."

Dana's empty threat actually hushed the twins up. Hope would have smiled if she hadn't been so darn nervous. She glanced back to the clock. 7:56. One minute later than the last time she looked.

The four of them were in her living room, glued to the television set.

7:57.

7:58.

7:59.

Her stomach was in knots and her palms all sweaty. She'd tried to get hold of Nick all day, but he wasn't answering his phone. So she'd waited, knowing he'd call the children like he always did. But for the first time since meeting his son and daughter, he hadn't called. She was about out of her mind.

The commercial ended and the music announcing the start of the next program began.

"Good evening, and welcome." The music swelled and the image of Diane Sawyer came on the TV.

The picture on the television changed. Images of Nick flashed across the screen. They were pictures that captured his entire career, and as the images continued to play, Diane continued to talk.

"A little over a decade ago, a young man from Minnesota blasted onto the racing circuit and just as quickly into stock car racing history. NASCAR hasn't been the same since. As easily as a child's set of building blocks, long-standing records have toppled under his talent. Little did anyone realize that in just a few short years his name would be whispered in reverence alongside the likes of Waltrip, Petty, and the late Dale Earnhardt.

"I am, of course, talking about none other than last year's champion and the man positioned to take that coveted title once again this year, Nick Fortune."

The screenshot changed to a live image of Diane Sawyer seated in front of a fireplace and Nick seated across from her.

"Good evening and welcome, Mr. Fortune."

"Good evening."

"In an article earlier this year, *USA Today* is quoted as saying, 'Racing legend Nick Fortune has the potential of doing what athletes like Joe Namath, Babe Ruth, and Joe DiMaggio did, and that is to transcend the sport they're in.' What is your response to that?"

"I'm flattered. Very flattered. But I'm no Namath, Ruth, or DiMaggio. I'm just a guy who likes to race."

"Just a guy who likes to race?" Diane laughed. "Well, I think we should remind our audience just what *this guy* who likes to race has done." Another picture-perfect smile was flashed. "You're the youngest driver in history to win not only the Daytona 500 but also a Sprint Cup Championship. You've broken so many NASCAR records that it would take me five minutes just to list them. But I think the one record that has the whole NASCAR circuit—and just about the whole country—breathless with anticipation is that elusive eighth Sprint Cup Championship.

"With a Cup win this year, Nick, you will enter a sphere no one previously thought attainable. You will be the only man in history to have eight championships. What do you have to say about that?"

"Not bad for a skinny kid who just used to dream about watching a live race."

Diane laughed again. "Do you think the spectacular success has dulled your appetite?"

"Not in the least."

"What keeps you going? What keeps you motivated?"

"Quite simply, the best damn pit crew keeps me going."

"Let's talk about that crew for a moment. The Noble Warriors. I've heard rumors that nearly every other driving team has been after the Warriors' top man, your crew chief, Dale Penshaw. How much do you pay him?"

Nick gave a wry smile. "Hopefully enough."

Diane smiled. "Fair enough. Let's back up to an earlier question I had," she smoothly continued. "What does keep you motivated?"

Nick leaned back in his chair. "I'm not out there every Sunday trying to beat another driver, another car. I think that's true for most of the men on that track with me. We race because it's in our blood, it's what we have to do. In the past, what had motivated me was quite simply the next race. And the one after that. If I have a good race the week before, I want to get right back out there and build on that."

"What about that eighth title, Nick? How important is that to you?"

Nick paused and the camera panned onto him. His blue, blue gaze bore through the television screen. Hope felt as if he were looking directly at her. "If you had asked me that question a couple of months ago, I would have told you it meant everything. But now . . ."

"Now?" Diane prompted.

"Now there are only two titles that matter to me: husband and father. I plan on earning them both."

For what was undoubtedly the first time in her life, Diane Sawyer was speechless.

"Effective immediately I am retiring from NASCAR. My last race will be a benefit exhibition race supporting leukemia research."

"But why?" She finally found her voice.

That same sexy grin that sent Hope's stomach flip-flopping each time she saw it curved Nick's mouth. "Because, Diane, it has taken me nearly half my life to learn that love and family are more important than any title."

The interview continued, but Hope didn't hear it. She was smiling and laughing and crying so hard she couldn't stop. She knew Dana and the children were talking to her and to one another, but she didn't hear them either. All she could think about was Nick telling the world that she and their children were the most important things in his life.

A knock sounded at the door, and even though her face was a mess with tears, she answered it, not wanting to drag one of the kids or Dana away from the program. She wiped at her face, wondering who it could be.

She opened the door and the first thing she saw was a large bouquet of pink roses. The second was Nick.

Before she could say anything, he walked over to the kids, whispered something in their ears, and then after he got their enthusiastic nods, he came back over to her, got down on one knee, and held out a small velvet box.

Her tears started again and she couldn't make them stop. Especially when she looked into his eyes and saw the depth of his love.

"Say yes!" Susan and Josh yelled from behind her.

"No," Hope said, her eyes shining brightly.

Nick's brow rose. "No?"

"This time I want to ask the question, but first you need to promise me something."

"Anything."

"Don't stop racing. Not until it's what you want. I love you, Nick Fortune. All of you. Asking you to give up racing wasn't fair, I see that now."

A grin curved the side of his mouth. "Was there a question in there?"

Hope laughed and dropped down next to him, cradling his face in her hands. "I love you," she said again. "Marry me. Please. Marry me and make me the happiest woman on earth."

"Yes, Hopeful, I'll marry you."

The kids started to clap. Nick smiled at them right before he tossed the flowers aside and pulled Hope into his arms.

She fell against him, felt his arms encircle her waist before they tumbled to the ground, laughing and loving and kissing.

"Come on," Susan said, pulling Josh and Dana down with her. "Group hug!" They landed on top of Hope and Nick.

Nick let out an exaggerated groan, laughing.

Through a tangle of arms and hair and smiles, Hope's eyes found his. She reached up, kissed him with all of the love she felt. He kissed her back and she thought she might melt right there and then.

"God, how I love you."

"Not as much as I love you."

"You wanna bet?"

Hope shook her head, laughing. "But I meant what I said. Don't think that just because you love me, you're going to give up racing. We have an eighth championship to win."

"Are you sure?"

"Yes." Loving Nick meant loving all of him. Who he was and what he did. And in that love she found the ability to risk everything and gain even more.

Epilogue

NICK spun into the winner's circle, his tires smoking. A crowd surged forward, hands reaching through the window and clapping him on the back. A black baseball cap with his sponsor's signature silver logo landed in his lap. He took off his hot helmet and put the cap on.

He pulled himself out of the car window to shouts of congratulations and a roar of approval from the stands. The minute his feet hit the ground, it began to rain champagne.

His crew chief and the rest of the Noble Warriors were there—screaming and yelling and slapping his and each other's backs.

"You did it!" Penshaw yelled above the crowd. His grin was so wide and big, Nick was surprised it didn't split his face in two. "Number eight! Woo-hoo! It took us an extra year, but you did it! This is what you've waited your whole life for! You're a legend, my boy. A legend."

Nick smiled and laughed as his crew chief grabbed him into a tight hug, slapping him on the back, but all the while his eyes scanned the crowd.

Hundreds of people stampeded forward. Reached out, slapped Nick in congratulations or, if they couldn't reach him, just yelled.

The noise was full-volume high, the crowd so large it looked like one giant mass instead of individuals.

Finally, Nick spotted what he'd been looking for.

The crowd kept pushing him toward the winner's stand.

Nick good-naturedly pushed back, fighting to go the opposite way.

"Dad!" He heard Susan's yell. And then, less than a second later, came Joshua's. "Dad!"

Seeing Nick's destination, the crowd parted. He quickened his steps, broke into a run, and engulfed his children in his embrace, one in each arm.

"Oh, my, gawd, Dad. That was like the coolest ever," Susan said as she and Josh stepped back.

"The coolest," she said again. "I mean, on lap eighty-nine when you pulled back and used Bairenson to draft off of and then slingshot past. Man." Her eyes were bright. "Too cool."

The racing fever had hit his daughter. God help them all, Nick thought with a smile.

Joshua, on the other hand, had been hit by the fever of the track groupies. On more than one occasion, Nick had caught him standing around with his mouth all but hanging open.

But all Nick could do was smile. Joshua was the picture of health. He'd gained weight, his hair had grown back, and there was always a sparkle in his eye. Especially when he was watching the girls.

"Are you? Are you, Dad?"

He refocused on Susan. "Am I what?"

"Going to talk to Mom. About you teaching me how to race."

Nick laughed. "Like I'm brave enough to take on that debate." He looked around. "Where is your mom? She's never missed the end of a race before." Nick could picture her still trying to politely excuse her way through the crowd and up to them. He was just about to barrel forward and find her when Susan said, "About halfway through the race she got this really funny look on her face and said she had to leave."

Concern pummeled through Nick. For the last couple of weeks she hadn't been feeling well. And he knew why. She was pushing herself too hard. Once Joshua had fully recovered, she'd been on a mission. Organizing meetings, talking to doctors, the drivers, the other drivers' wives, and the top heads of NASCAR. Today, after countless hours of hard work, she had seen her dream become a reality. Over ten booths equipped with the necessary medical equipment had been set up around the racetrack's entrance. Spectators were invited to participate in a free and easy screening that would place them on the national bone marrow registry. Maybe, one day, because of these screenings, a life might be saved.

NASCAR's chairman and national commissioner had been the first two in line.

The event had been an even bigger success than they had hoped, and plans were already underway to host another screening at the next race. Both he and Hope were fighting to see that screenings would be available before each and every race.

But now, hearing that all this had made her unwell, Nick was going to turn a deaf ear to her protests and once and for all insist she hire an assistant.

Nick asked Susan and Joshua, "Do you know where she is?"

"Yeah," Josh said. "Back at the motor home."

To the utter horror of the racing commissioner and his sponsors, Nick surged back through the crowd and got into his car. He left as he'd arrived. Fast.

He was back at their "cottage," as Hope liked to call it, in minutes.

He pounded up the stairs, opened the door, and rushed inside.

It was empty.

He looked around the living area, walked down through the narrow hallway, and peeked into the bathroom. Empty, too.

And then he found her fast asleep in the back bedroom. He eased down onto the side of the bed. Her hair had fallen across her face and he gently brushed it away.

"Hey," she said, groggy from sleep, her eyes all soft and warm and so inviting Nick found himself losing himself in them, in her.

"Hey," he answered back softly.

"I must have fallen asleep."

"I guess so."

She smiled up at him. "I missed the end of the race, didn't I?"

"Yep."

"Some wife I am."

He leaned forward, gently kissed her. "Yeah, some wife." The way he said it had her smiling.

"I'm sorry," she said.

"Sorry for what?"

"For not being able to watch the whole race and, well, obviously, you lost or you wouldn't be here."

He just smiled and kissed her again.

"Nick," she said quietly after a moment's pause. "There's something wrong with my wedding ring."

He lifted her left hand, looked down. Three large, square-cut diamonds sparkled back from their platinum setting. "Looks okay to me."

"Yes, but there are only three diamonds."

"Right. One for each of you." When Nick had purchased the ring, the man at the jewelry store told him the three diamonds represented the past, present, and future. Nick didn't argue. But when he'd placed the band on Hope's finger, he told her what the diamonds meant to him. One for each of the joys Hope had brought into his life. One for her, one for Josh, and one for Susan.

Hope took his hand and placed it against the flat of her stomach. "Yes, I know. But now we're going to need four."

The impact of what she was saying hit him like a bolt. "Oh my God." He closed his eyes, tried to keep his emotions back, but knew he couldn't. He pulled her into his arms. "God, how I love you."

"Not as much as I love you," she teased back with her standard reply, but he heard the wobble in her voice. Knew she was feeling exactly what he was.

He tipped back, looked into her eyes. "Finally."

"Finally what?" she said through a watery smile.

"I'll get to see you fat."

She couldn't stop herself from laughing. "Yeah. Well, I'll finally get to see you change a diaper." She worried her bottom lip. "Nick, there is something you should know."

"What?"

"Pregnancy makes me crave certain foods."

"Like ice cream and pickles?"

"Well . . . no. When I was pregnant with the twins, there was one food I couldn't eat enough of."

"I'll buy out the store."

Hope smiled. "Sweet. But maybe you want to hear what that food was first."

"Doesn't matter. Whatever it is—"

"Hot dogs," she said.

He couldn't keep the horrified look off his face.

"Look on the bright side."

"Hot dogs don't have a bright side."

"My husband is an expert at cooking them."

His laughter bounced off the walls. He enfolded her back into his arms and wondered for the millionth time how he'd ever let her go.

A deafening noise permeated the motor home. The sound grew louder and louder the closer it came.

Hope scooted off the bed and walked out to the front. Nick

followed. She drew the curtain back and looked out the window and then gasped.

"Nick?" She looked at him questioningly. "Why are there hundreds of people outside our home?"

Home. Yes, it truly was. "I didn't lose."

She yelled and threw herself into his arms. "Oh, Nick. I'm so happy. This is what you've waited your whole life for."

"No," he said. "You, Joshua, Susan"—he placed his hand against her still-flat tummy—"and our new baby are what I've waited my whole life for. It just took me a little while to figure that out. But just don't think you're going to get a diamond every time I get you pregnant."

She laughed through her tears and was back in his arms. Nick laughed too because he knew damn well he'd give her anything she wanted.

Connect with Berkley Publishing Online!

For sneak peeks into the newest releases, news on all your favorite authors, book giveaways, and a central place to connect with fellow fans—

"Like" and follow Berkley Publishing!

facebook.com/BerkleyPub
twitter.com/BerkleyPub
instagram.com/BerkleyPub

Penguin
Random
House